Praise for *The Everlasting*

"*The Everlasting* explores large moral questions: How much do we owe to those we love? To ourselves? What does it mean to lead a good life? Can you do that without being religious? Smith's eloquent storytelling shows us glimpses of certain answers, sometimes serious but just as often comic. It's fitting that the latter tend to be provided by a fifth major character who interjects barbed commentary throughout: The Devil."

—*New York Times Book Review*

"*The Everlasting* takes place over the course of two millennia and follows the lives of four people pondering life's greatest question. It engages with history and humanity on a grand cosmic scale." —*Entertainment Weekly*

"Smith has accomplished a spectacular feat in harnessing the emotional thrust of a sweeping epic within the space of the average novel. *The Everlasting* spans two millennia with such strong assurance, the narrative never falters, even when it ascends to the eternal plane. . . . This novel is a wonder, building sensual prose toward a stirring inevitability." —*Shelf Awareness*

"A sparkling historical novel. Smith bounds through two thousand years of history, following four indelible characters as they grapple with questions of faith, freedom, and transgressive love. . . . Perhaps Smith's most appealing character is Satan, whose weary, ironic comments punctuate a narrative that shines with lyrical, translucent prose. A compelling, beautifully rendered tale of passion and pain." —*Kirkus Reviews*, starred review

"In this symphonic novel, Smith composes delicate variations on faith, love, and human transience in the eternal city. . . . The further Smith digs into Rome's layered past, the more captivating the story becomes. This is an ambitious novel whose characters must choose between sensual or spiritual love, gratification or self-abnegation, principled martyrdom or survival." —*Publishers Weekly*

"A rare book whose ambition is matched by its craft and emotional weight. . . . Combining the gravity of history with the tribulations of faith and the wit and wisdom of Satan himself. . . . An exquisite tapestry of history, religion, and heartbreak that's perfect for historical fiction and fabulism fans alike." —*BookPage*

"Smith ingeniously hooks these narratives together with a relic that morphs over time, so *The Everlasting* becomes a symphonic and timeless story." —*National Book Review*

"A lush, intellectually challenging, and sensuous pleasure. . . . Through the pen of Smith it is engrossing. The characters are deep and full, suspense builds across every page, and most importantly, we care about what happens to each of them."
                                                            —*Mississippi Clarion Ledger*

"Only Katy Simpson Smith could have written a novel of such elegance, emotional power, and grace. *The Everlasting*, a quadruple love story spanning two millennia, is no less than the story of love itself—its frustrations and thrills, its blunders and transcendent glories. Meraviglioso."
                                                            —Nathaniel Rich, author of *King Zeno*

"It is so very rare to find a writer whose blistering ambition when it comes to bringing history alive on the page is matched by an equal ability to build and break sentences in beautiful ways. Katy Simpson Smith is that writer, and *The Everlasting*—a bold and ingenious novel spanning multiple time periods and characters with the ease of David Mitchell's *Cloud Atlas*—is full of rich and brilliant ideas about Rome, home, free will, sin, sensation, and civilization. It's an incredible achievement." —Jonathan Lee, author of *High Dive*

"*The Everlasting* is, quite simply, a wonder: a mesmerizing quartet of stories rendered in lucid, accessible prose. This is a thrillingly modern narrative that, shifting effortlessly from voice to voice, feels like a good old-fashioned story, the story of a city, one of the world's oldest, wildest, sexiest (and, incidentally, my favorite on earth): Rome."
                                                            —Taiye Selasi, author of *Ghana Must Go*

"In *The Everlasting*, Katy Simpson Smith has magnificently reimagined what a historical novel might be, and what our near-now might look like if we could only properly see. A child, a princess, a monk, a father—each storyline feels charged, accurate, uncanny, and yet also touched by love. A distinctive and unostentatiously brilliant book."
                                       —Rivka Galchen, author of *Little Labors* and *Atmospheric Disturbances*

"In a rare display of lyrical erudition, Katy Simpson Smith's gorgeous novel lets us feel the depth and density of history by showing us how every life is both an echo of the past and a relic of the future."
                                                            —Hernan Diaz, author of *In the Distance*

"Following her wonderful and wonderfully ambitious *Free Men*, Katy Simpson Smith tops herself with *The Everlasting*, exploring the mysteries of faith displacing fear, grace given to the undeserving, and the eternal question of forgiveness. She is at the forefront of the best young American writers working today." —Mark Richard, author of *The Ice at the Bottom of the World*

THE EVERLASTING

ALSO BY KATY SIMPSON SMITH

The Story of Land and Sea

Free Men

THE

EVERLASTING

A NOVEL

KATY SIMPSON SMITH

HARPER PERENNIAL

NEW YORK • LONDON • TORONTO • SYDNEY • NEW DELHI • AUCKLAND

HARPER ⬤ PERENNIAL

A hardcover edition of this book was published in 2020 by
HarperCollins Publishers.

HarperCollins books may be purchased for educational, business,
or sales promotional use. For information, please email the Special
Markets Department at SPsales@harpercollins.com.

FIRST HARPER PERENNIAL EDITION PUBLISHED 2021.

Designed by Fritz Metsch

Library of Congress Cataloging-in-Publication
Data has been applied for.

ISBN 978-0-06-287367-5 (pbk.)

21 22 23 24 25 LSC 10 9 8 7 6 5 4 3 2 1

FOR THE BOYS

Go thou to Rome, —at once the Paradise,
The grave, the city, and the wilderness.

—PERCY BYSSHE SHELLEY, *Adonais*

CONTENTS

THE EVERLASTING

THE WILDERNESS

[2015]

IN A CORNER of a rented flat on one of the minor hills of Rome
drooped a pair of empty hip waders. Not empty. The mud caked on
their soles held microorganisms in suspension.

Tom broke off a piece of valley dirt to hold up to his screen.

"I don't see anything," his daughter said across nine time zones.

"Make a spyhole with your fingers."

Daphne curled her thumb and index finger into a whorl and
peered through the pin-sized gap. "Yes," she said. "Whales."

He left her to rescue the whistling kettle off the stove. When he'd
moved in a month ago, she made him give a laptop tour of the apartment; he carried her image like a baby in his hands through the half-
sized kitchen, the red tile room with low sofa and lower bed, the
expanse of the terrace, where she tried to scare the gulls with her
caw. As he poured the coffee, they shouted details of their day. She
saw him stumble on the way back, but he turned it into a Gene Kelly
tap step, and she made a face like, *Parents.* After he'd gone a week
without remembering to call, she'd stopped asking when she could
visit. Her father had limits. On her side of the internet, she held up a
macaroni portrait of her crush.

"He still wears Velcro shoes and doesn't know any jokes." She
pointed to the bow tie she'd glued on him, a *farfalla* painted black.

"But you said he's funny?"

Daphne tilted her head, her dreamy open bucktoothed mouth, right out of the frame. Tom pushed his computer to the left, as if he could somehow catch her in California.

"His *face* is funny." Her head came back, one finger tenderly in her nose. "It's like you and your bugs. I just want to look at him all the time. Is that how you know if—you know—if you like someone?"

"What does your mom say?"

"Not to be melomadratic."

Meloma dratic. The Latin name of an undiscovered bee.

The ostracods at the heart of his work were a kind of crustacean: as impertinent as his daughter, as pervasive, as fine. A research semester here, where the rubble was playground to man and shrimp alike, was a luxury. Pounding the door to his study, Daphne used to accuse him, in toddler terms, of misdirected love. (His wife had already laid down her arms.) But there on the slide was a mirror of the domestic. Gaiety and chaos and yes, cannibalism. He'd put his headphones on to dull the sound of tiny fists. Independence couldn't be learned too early.

Now out the open window a parakeet zipped by Venus.

"Do you think I'd look better with a bob?"

On the webcam, his daughter had grabbed her unruly hair into a bunch behind her neck and was examining herself in the corner of the screen. Lord help them, she was nine. When did a human first consider her own beauty? [When another human first denied it. Cf. Adam re: Eve. I, the snake, was the soother. Ask your questions; I, Satan, am the answerer.]

"You're already perfect," he said.

"*Dad.*" She collapsed on the breakfast table in a pile of pixels. "You don't know *anything*."

THOUGH HIS feet were still warm in the stream, a cold ring circled his ankles where the water met the air. The breeze scuffed along the surface, lifting the duckweed like shallow breaths. Tucked in their roots were several hundred ostracods, no bigger than mustard seeds, their innards hidden in shells that resembled two hands in prayer. To them, Tom's toes were monstrous fish, fat and half-drowned tubers. The water crowded with microscopic action, with bloomings and sex and feasts. What carnivorous frenzy was happening at the level of his soles, as aquatic protozoa met the rich and writhing landscape of his epidermis.

The only other humans in the Caffarella Valley were two old walkers passing each other on their circuits and a gang of Eritrean teenagers smoking in the bushes by the mill house, their laughs like woodlark song. In Tom's back pocket was the permit that allowed him to hop the nymphaeum's fence; it said nothing about bare feet. Sunsets often found him reconsidering his place in the ecosystem, but these were the mild crises of anyone who made a living triangulating data. Whatever form his ostracods took was designed by cycles of food and lack of food, cooling air and warming waters, fish with bigger bellies and men with tired feet. No matter how he measured, they would continue morphing, at glacial pace, long past the point when the last person who could interpret his scribbling had turned to dust. He put down his notebook and leaned back on the damp creekside grass, the thin green leaves folding around his bare neck, wrists. Man on photosynthesis on dirt. Under air, under ozone, under galaxy. His thoughts wafting out of his mind in sideways flares, invisible and evaporating. Some factorially larger scientist might peer down and take him for dead.

In the valley, no one spoke. No questions were asked, no answers expected. No one could be let down. *Shh*, he told his brain. *Shh*, he said to the figments of the undeveloped future. The invertebrate objects of his devotion couldn't even be seen. *You have to see it to believe it*, his daughter liked to say, picked up from a mattress commercial.

———

THEY FIRST met at noon. It was a Tuesday, sunny, and he was walking to loosen the hypotheses in his head. Given that ostracods thrive in agitated systems, in environments thick with pollutants, invasive species, human disturbance, are they adapting in the face of disadvantage or are they opportunists of collapse? Tom bumped into a teenager with oversized sunglasses. Do they overcome the stain of our presence or is human interference as natural to them as a flood? He leaned over to support his notebook with his thigh, licked his pen. Should we reexamine the "natural"? [Should you pull your miniature gaze from the puddles at your feet and collect data on your damage to women? Oh, pardon, are we not there yet?] A large explosive detonated a hundred feet to Tom's right; his vertebrae jolted back protectively. His body crumpled without the certainty of its spine.

She was in a crowd of several dozen smiling strangers when she turned from the overlook and, between two children clapping, saw him seated on the cobblestones. Later she told how she circled him, peripherally appraising. She said if she got as far as the truck selling soft drinks and plaster Colosseums and he hadn't moved, she'd call for help. The scene unfolded for her in quarter time: the long arc of stones, the smoke still hanging in the air, the man's brow bending from surprise to analysis, his jellied limbs now hardening, embarrassed at their own quick surrender, or was it a sacrifice, a fundamental defense of the core. When she reached the spinning postcard rack, he'd just managed to turn to the right, toward the once-sound. *Yes*, she thought, *investigate the disturbance*. His dark hair Italian, his open, dazed face decidedly not.

"*Va bene?*" she said.

He was aware of a shape appearing, a backlit envoy with some message about his fate. A black dress waving over two brown knees,

knees like citrus. The hair around her head as thick as the smoke. She reached out a hand.

"*Va bene*," he said, shaking his head, not a little humiliated. "*Non lo so*," he said. *I don't know.* But the hand was still there. So he took it.

She bought him a gelato because he had no money on him, and when he had a second to look around him, to take in more than just the smoke and the stones and her citrus knees, he said, "How'd I end up at the goddamn Janiculum?" Because if he had known where he was, the explosion that rattled his brain and sent him sprawling would've registered as a familiar daily occurrence: the cannon set off at noon.

THE JANICULUM girl asked what he did, and he said biology, streams and rivers, that sort of thing, and she said *But what exactly?* and he said looking for balance, water quality, how things interact, and she said *But what things?* and he said fairly small organisms and she said *Yes?* and he said, okay, ostracods. Crustaceans on a millimetric scale, you'd never even know you'd seen one. She said *Are they beautiful?* and he said they have the largest sperm, proportionally, of any animal, endless frail filaments that are four or six or ten times as long as the creature itself, great silk threads that dominate the rest of its anatomy—whips, just waiting.

Her eyes narrowed.

He didn't want to strike up an acquaintance; the point of Rome was an indulgent detachment. But his wife hadn't asked him a question about his work—about his job, yes, his day-to-day, but not his *work*—in years. They were, apparently, past that.

She said something about architecture school, or was it archaeology, and showed him the slivers of soil beneath her nails from Ostia, or was it Appia, but he was distracted by her patterns: the loops of accented speech, unplaceable, the twists of hair like chrysalises.

After the gelato, they didn't exchange numbers. She merely extended her hand again, this time to shake, and turned south toward the alley of trees that forked—right to Monteverde, left to Trastevere. She went left. He watched her slip through the disoriented stream of tourists, a fast snake. A last whirl of disco light from the sycamores caught the side of her face in sun.

Something was tilted in his head. He'd been on a walk, and there had been an explosion—not an explosion, a routine firing of a petite nineteenth-century cannon—and a fall, and then a woman and a scoop of *stracciatella* and a disappearance. An absence. He should find his way home again. He followed, imagining the mark of her footsteps under his, and took the right fork, toward Monteverde, and didn't consciously think that if she had appeared on the Janiculum once, she might appear again, but determined to direct his walks this way more often, because just look at that spin of light through the trees, just look at how late summer colored the hill.

His desk was under a window, the window opening out onto a terrace from which one could capture the intimacies of a half-dozen neighboring buildings. His eyes settled on the older man on the rooftop across the way. They weren't close; the stranger was two inches tall. For several days he'd been attending to his roses: he'd duck down, hands buried in a pot or trough, and pull back with some string in his hands, as if he were a mouse-sized tailor with a human-sized needle. But today the man had moved from the pots to the railing around the balcony, the string now obviously wire, the large movements alternating with time spent bent over a joint or a tangle, hands fiddling with something small. Tom returned to his computer, answered emails, followed a research link to a political website to a story about a pop star's collapse. When he looked up again, the wire had lifted off the rooftop entirely—it stretched out and up until it reached what appeared to be a makeshift satellite tower. The whole contraption was tethered to the man's terrace, was somehow bound to the very rosebushes that were being so assiduously tended, and Tom could in no way retrace the mechanics of its construction. First there were strings, the strings became wires, and now a tower had sprouted—almost floated—from the roof. What was once a garden was now an electrical sailing ship.

Sight was selective. One day you saw the woman who had been there all along. One afternoon the roses grew receivers. What changed? [The degree of your self-absorption. Have I told you about the summer when I—] The atmosphere, perhaps: the molecules that capriciously obscured random specks of vision; the photons fritzing as they passed through a pine canopy, or smog; humidity blurring the edges of a face until the brain registered it instead as a cloud. Recently his vision had been tricking him more often; objects in his periphery had a new habit of dancing. He blinked more often, and this seemed to help. He should ask a doctor about it—a cousin of his once had a tumor fattening on his optic nerve, and he claimed to have shrunk it by aiming his closed eyes directly at the sun for an hour a day—but who wanted to go to the doctor.

He went to sleep consciously thinking of anything but her; that consciousness kept him up. He calculated the likelihood of encountering her in the street (if a tourist crosses the Tiber twice every three days, and there are fifteen bridges between Prati and Testaccio . . .); he corrected himself and made a grocery list instead. The minutes crawled. He estimated the rate of decaying love (if neurogenesis speeds the degradation of memory, and he forced a dozen new experiences in the next twelve days—went parasailing, e.g., or learned how to cook octopus . . .); no—finish the NSF grant, order more tanks.

HE'D FOUND a postcard with a baby cherub puffing along through celestial blue, a cloud emerging from its rear end. "A *putto* pooting," he wrote his daughter.

The semester-long fellowship at the Università di Roma to study the effects of chemical pollution on aquatic crustacean populations had been a long shot. His wife had asked him not to apply; he'd said he wouldn't get it. They were in that uncomfortable limbo of loving while not-loving, which surely must happen to all happy couples who lived long enough. "Why are you both so polite?" Daphne once asked. The conversation they kept promising to have with each other was easily deferred. But now their daughter, that fierce bundle of nine years who had broken more dishes dancing through their kitchen than she'd ever voluntarily cleaned, was clamming up in school. Her teachers alerted them to a new self-consciousness. She stopped raising her hand; at recess, she restrained herself to the mildest games of four square; she tore her sandwich into bites beneath the lunch table before secreting them up to her mouth. To all the questions—*Are there problems at home? Is she being bullied? Spending too much time online?*—Tom and his wife said no, with *no* in fact meaning *we don't know.* "Boys," a friend of theirs had said. "She's just noticed boys."

His wife had been the one to ask him out, back when he was charmed by the idea of leaning against someone. She had a habit of swallowing her laughs, near-waist-length hair that she would cut when it began creepily wrapping around their newborn's limbs, and an inability to see Tom beyond what he chose to reveal, which could in no way be her fault, and yet somehow was. Ten years married, nine years daughtered, one well-timed semester apart. *Don't do anything I wouldn't do,* she'd said with a smile, which sounded to him ominous. He knew well what she wouldn't do, but his own capacity seemed like anybody's guess. The leaning, it occurred to him, was a trap. He inched away.

"Remember, you're a dinosaur," he wrote to Daphne. "A falcon, a shark, a hungry lion. You have claws and teeth and a roaring heart."

His worst failing as a father would be if she meekened into him. A moth. A snail.

THE MARBLE of the ancient nymphaeum was slick with moss. The wealthy used to picnic on its banks, and before that the water had been deemed sacred, undrinkable except by saints and virgins, and now it was just another pile of rocks in a city tumbled with them. No one passing knew Lord Byron once stood here, put the spring's "green wild margin" in a poem, rhymed its leaping rill with its summer birds. A caterpillar was lounging in the spot by the water where Tom usually sat. He found a dried leaf and scooped up the puff in a fumble of legs and prolegs. The surface of the pond was waxy and still. A quilt of sound: thrush, cricket, the flip of fish, dry lizard rustle, leaf, water, wind, some primal hum of soil, the *gnaw-gnaw* of soft-mouthed worms, the twist of protozoa.

A pheasant glided over him like a biplane coming in to land, its body swallowed by the glade of giant reeds. Here in the valley you couldn't read the past so easily. None of this motion and color existed five hundred years ago, before the oldest of the downy oaks. For continuity you'd have to pull back the soil to the four layers of tuff, the volcanic rock that held the valley and the springs in its palm. That was the substratum that dictated what would grow, what would come, and what would survive. Tom's ostracods were no more than months old, no less than five hundred million years old, and if people were so impressed by the span of human history caught in a single church in Rome, they should come marvel at his little monsters.

He took a few sample cups out of his backpack and began scooping the water along the pond's perimeter. He wore white rubber gloves; Romans weren't above knocking each other over the head with bottles and then tossing the shards in a nearby stream. If the water here was clean enough, there'd be sticklebacks, bug-eyed fish his Italian colleagues called *spinarello*. He'd heard of an ancient eel that lived in a Swedish well for 155 years. Sometimes he'd be tricked by a glowing white chicken bone some snacker had tossed, and once he found a plastic pony, magenta-maned, tangled in the *Equisetum*, common name horsetail.

One of his professors mentioned in a letter of reference that Tom tended to linger in the field. "I thought they should know what they were getting," he said. "I didn't make you sound distracted. Dedicated, more like. But in a peculiar kind of way."

"You used the word *poetic*."

He hadn't gotten that job.

But now he had been awarded four months in this verdant valley, a new set of species to learn, *Quercus ilex*, *Salix alba*. Corn buntings and serins, groves of butcher's broom, sloe, wild apple.

Four months needn't be the end of it. A shortage of aquatic biologists in central Italy worked in Tom's favor. He could prolong the project, drag out this gap, ease into expatriatism, and as he counted the things he'd have to live without he only got up to *Daphne*, *peanut butter*, and *a crushing accountability*.

He was wrist-deep in mud, his fingers grappling with the roots of a sedge, when a small child appeared at his side and chirped, "*L'acqua*."

"*Sì, sì*," he replied.

The child had dark hair clipped in a circle around its chin and stared at him with a stout, unblinking face. At four-ish years, its boyness or girlness was beside the point. It was wearing clogs, a half apron over a pair of shorts, and a T-shirt that said, in English, *I Am Grease Monkey!* It must have snuck in through a hole in the fencing. The child fell to the earth in a sudden heap and plunged its hands into the muck. Its tiny feet kicked behind, paddling on dry land.

Tom wasn't sure how the child's personal bacteria would affect the microorganisms that must now be fleeing the turbulence.

"*Nuotiamo!*" the child said. *We swim*.

He looked over his shoulder to see if a mother or uncle was near, but in this particular dip of the meadow, they were the only humans. He had just resolved to unveil his Stern Face, which needed no translation, when the child let out a sharp cry. It pulled a hand up from the water, and in its palm a diluted strand of pink wove into the clear water running off the skin. It looked slack-jawed at this violation of the body's wholeness, and then began to shriek. Tom dug into the side of the bank where the child had been splashing and felt a hard protrusion in the rootball of a club-rush; he wrestled out a short piece of bent metal.

"*Guarda*," he said, *look*, but the child was now on its feet, wailing at a distant figure who was trotting heavily toward them.

He wiped the mud away with his shirt and found the hook at the end that must have grazed the child's palm. The metal was scaly with corrosion, its silver marred with patches of orange rust. It had a tall stem—a proud capital J—and a sharp little barb on the upswing. About two inches long, all told. For a fishhook, it was rather Gothic.

The child was now in full flight, its pudgy legs kicking up lumps of clover. Tom waved an awkward hand as the caretaker flung herself onto her charge, swaddling its body against her chest, glaring across the field at the foreigner holding up a white rubber glove.

Tom put the fishhook in his pocket and reached for his collecting cup, now listing in the water. His eyes were creating diamonds from the light. A quick veil fell over his vision, in sync with a razor crossing his brain. He winced, and then saw the world again.

DAPHNE HAD made him promise to see the Important Sights, so he stayed in the city on Tuesdays, avoided parks and puddles of water to observe instead the buildings rising yeastily out of cobbled streets, frescoes depicting the gory and divine, a million men on mopeds. This too was an environment. Nuns suckered on chapels like remoras, Renaissance plaster wrapped around imperial columns like grapevine. What would Daphne most want to hear about? [Here's a softball! The scheme for my seduction of the species: knowledge, same as ever. Give that girl her ancestors, the warrior women: that palazzo you just passed with its faux-cave façade, its wildness in this urbanity? Plautilla Bricci, first female architect. Tell her not of the Gianicolo cannon, shot by men in drab, but of the cannon on top of Hadrian's tomb that Queen Christina of Sweden set off without aiming—what is aiming if not a form of misogyny?—blasting a hole in the Villa Medici, her belly laugh sending waves across the Tiber. Offer secrets. Tell her of your failed love; tell her of her unborn brother.]

At the Fontanone he found a seat between two lovers and a Chinese tour group and leaned toward the water, the clear and shadow-cut water. The spurting fountains pushed it toward him in panels, like quilt squares being continuously chopped and resized, matched up and shuffled on. Here they come; here they come again.

When the mustard Citroën slowed and honked, he had one hand half-dipped and was thinking that testing this fountain for ostracods wasn't the worst idea—the chloride the city pumped in would've prevented most algal growth, but his crustaceans were steely colonizers, able to withstand months of being cased in dry mud. A colleague once unwittingly carried four species home from an overseas research trip on his unwashed boots.

She cranked down the window and shouted at him. He grabbed his hand back.

"Need a ride?"

It was a scene from the movie in his head, the Technicolor version of a near-bachelor in Rome. It was so unlikely to be her, except he'd climbed enough steps to be near or at the Janiculum, and if she was some kind of nymph, her spirit tethered to an umbrella pine by the slumping statue of Garibaldi, then of course her range would include the Fontanone.

"Well?" Her voice like a trumpet, the silver kind played in clubs. He still couldn't place her—Haitian, or Barbadian, or Malagasy. He could ask, but he was still resisting attachment. Her skin absorbed the sun, sent it back in dark flames from her head.

He jumped up, wet-handed, and jogged to the Citroën.

"Where are you headed?" Her hair puffed around her face cumulously.

He should've replied *Wherever you're going*, but this wasn't, in fact, a film. "Oh, thataway," he said, waving his arm weakly.

"Get in."

He circled around the chattering car, keeping his body close to the yellow metal as mopeds zoomed past and a bearded man on a bicycle worked his legs up and down like an arthritic grape-stomper.

She weaved back into traffic as he fumbled for a seat belt. Not finding one, he held on to the door handle, watching the cannon overlook bend past on his right, a tight pack of tourists turning their heads toward him like an audience. "I met you there."

Her hands were at ten and two, thumbs tapping. Her hair buffeted her face in the gusts from the open window, and he wanted to reach over and pin it back, to pin her back, to throw something heavy on the brake and jerk the steering wheel so they'd roll to a stop under a stand of *Pinus pinea*, the smell of which through the open window would remind her of when she'd reached out a hand to salvage his dignity, and she would take his face in her hands and with lit eyes declare, "No, I met *you* there."

HE'D BEEN given space in a small laboratory in the basement of the Environmental Biology department, where he shuttled vials of

muddy water from the Caffarella Valley and sat on a metal stool
and alternated between the scanning electron microscope and the
high window that showed tree roots and human ankles. It felt like
a crypt with aquaria. He took his sandwich out to a concrete bench
beside the building's entrance, the world around him made of blond
brick and young people. They were future echoes of his daughter;
he studied them as if to pinpoint confidence, tie it to some trait he
could teach, some accessory. If he bought Daphne a black leather
jacket . . . A fritillary helixed from column to column, folding beneath drafts, flurrying when someone walked by.

A young man with a satchel across his back stopped and reached
a hand up to catch Tom's attention. The butterfly went glancing off.
He wanted directions. Tom pointed out the cafeteria with a series of
short words and gestures, his left hand trembling. He finished his
sandwich quickly, that soft Italian cheese that nearly liquefied the
lettuce, and waited for his blood sugar to equalize. He slid his hand
under his leg. *Trembling* was the wrong word. *Vibrating*, maybe.
Like his body was singing a song through closed lips.

Another young man emerged from the building and looked so
similar to the first—black jeans and a too-small collared shirt—that
Tom almost said, "*Non trova?*" But he didn't have a satchel, only a
sheet of paper.

"Water lab?" he asked.

Tom nodded, uncertain if he should be answering in the
affirmative.

"I am assigned," he said, and stuck his hand out. "Aldo. Tell me
the things you need."

Savelli, another basement researcher, had mentioned the department would be doling out assistants for the fall as the work-study kids
were shuffled around. Tom pulled his hand out from under his thigh; it
still felt as if each cell was sending up flags of electrical alarm.

"Orange juice?" he asked.

The boy shook his hand. "Nope. Anything else?"

"Nope."

"See you soon in underground," and the boy waved a farewell.

After lunch, Tom rinsed his beasts in distilled water, scrubbing the algae from their beards, and separated them. Some would live out the rest of their lives with no other nutrients; others would be assaulted with a volley of human-made chemicals and additives; and others would be given sweet green things on which to latch themselves and feed, babes at the teat. The tanks lined up beneath the window like a train of water waiting for its engine. Tom was too—what's the word? [craven]—to enjoy playing God. He preferred the secondary thrill of playing artist. In a petri dish atop a sheet of white paper, he arranged an island of duckweed and diatoms and eyedropped in two ostracods. To round out the tableau, he rested on one side the old fishhook he'd found, a pirate's anchor. He snapped a pic for Daphne. The little beans went circling, dizzy, like bumper cars, their segmented legs too filamentous to spot, the hinges on their valves silently creaking. He'd tried marking them—identification being the first step toward *identifying with*—but they were too bitty for the tinted pen, and the synthetic canthaxanthin he borrowed from the flamingo keeper at the zoo bled right through them. The pair motored to the tip of the submerged hook, fussed with the rust in hopes of something edible. He was a better father six thousand miles distant than he was in the flesh.

Another bolt crossed his vision, a quick frying of the eye. He grabbed the edge of the table and waited for it to pass. If he were still Catholic, he'd attribute the ramping symptoms to his own sins, but these days he had trouble determining what a sin was. He groped for a stool and sat, one hand against the side of his head, as if to hold his brain in. He'd been raised in a culture that valued autonomy over duty, self-actualization over kindness, and any therapist except a priest would tell him his emotional disloyalty was a vital expression of personal need that should be explored, even indulged. The modern condition.

During the Gulf War, they found ostracods in Kuwait covered with oil, with the heavy metal pollutants of war, still making their circuits: consuming, reproducing, aging. Tom wanted to know what soul stopped in that landscape to look for the smallest life-forms, and who would stop to look for him, and what they'd see.

"DO YOU miss me?" She had two fingers hooked in her lower lip, displaying her gums like a chimp.

"Not even a little." He pressed his nose to the camera at the top of his computer, so her screen was darkened by the forest of his nose hairs. "I hear you've been turning off your silly switch at school."

"It doesn't matter."

"It's different from last year, though, huh?"

She'd taken her phone out to the city she was building beneath the eucalyptus. There were four car washes and one high-rise. "I don't know," she said, propping the phone against the tree and beginning to deepen her moat with a screwdriver. He could only see her chin now, her thin shoulders.

"Your friends are still friendly?"

"Yeah. It's more, like, the boys. It's like they're playing some new game and didn't tell us the rules."

"Mom said you stopped wearing your favorite skirt." The one they had to wash twice a week, because asking her to put on something else was like asking her to avoid mud, or trees, or ditches.

"Girls wear skirts."

"Well—" His mind scrambled. He felt sharply his own absence from her developing consciousness in the years preceding this moment.

"I just want to be part of the secret."

"Oh," he said, "it's a very empty kind of secret. It's not that you're getting less fun to hang out with, it's that they're getting—I don't know, weird? It becomes harder to talk about stuff, feelings, that sort of thing. For boys."

"Why?" She'd grabbed the phone again and leaned forward, screwdriver aimed at him like a knife. "*Tell me the password*."

"Look, just treat everyone like they're a human, rather than a subspecies. Maybe when those turds grow up, they'll do the same."

"Is that what you do?"

"What I do?" What did he do? [You treat everyone like a crustacean.] He looked over at his open suitcase, the stacks of printed articles, the unmade bed.

"I got to go fill the moat with fruit punch. Believe me, Dad, I know I'm fun to hang out with."

THE MAN building the satellite tower had a guest. It was the plummy time of the evening, and Tom hadn't turned on the lamps or closed the shutters, so all that lit the dusk of the apartment was his laptop's cold glow and the wilting moon. The tinker pulled out a seat for the lady, lit the candles on the patio table. Tom could make out her head turning from left to right and imagined her speech: "*Ma, tutto é bello!*" The man tightened the knot in his tie. Their laughter reached Tom in a delayed wave, and he closed his computer. How easy to be a certain kind of man: a man who could identify a problem (lack of acceptable television reception, or lack of a giant astronautical sailing ship) and then choose to solve it, a man who had enough pride in his surroundings to bring a woman home, serve her wine and candlelight, assume that a closely knotted tie was a step closer to seduction.

Tom's last successful seduction had been at an academic conference in Minneapolis the year before he met his wife. He'd had an article out already that modeled a minor shift in the way scholars wrote about miniature organisms—even if anthropomorphism was a sin, it needed to be a sin broadly shared—and because the piece had been scorned for its "lyrical" tone (a stretch; he'd used a handful of adjectives outside the accepted set), he had earned some notoriety among grad students, who hungered for invisible dramas.

Her eyes sparked with recognition when he introduced himself at the hotel bar, and because she had a mess of brown hair piled in curls atop her head, he was flattered. He asked about her own research; she offered to buy him a drink. Two whiskeys in, they had gone upstairs because she claimed to have some graphs on the vitamin B consumption of phytoplankton, but had run into her dissertation advisor in that long shameful hallway where the staggered doors reminded Tom of a brothel. She shook Tom's hand and said loudly, "Thanks, I'll check out that journal!" and then cleaved to her advisor, retreating back to the elevators. He was stranded on a floor that wasn't his. An hour later, he heard a dainty rapping at his door. So perhaps she had seduced him.

But he'd enjoyed waking up with her body in the sheets. Her hair, no longer artfully tangled, looked disastrous, and there was a coin-sized dampness on the pillow beneath her mouth. He folded over her ear, so gentle, to glimpse the tiny bones there. What an organism. She twitched and snuffled. He slid out, took his clothes into the bathroom, and washed his face and armpits at the sink with the biscuit of soap and a silent stream of water.

He left a note on his pillow—*Do ostracods get cranky when they're hungry?* Downstairs, it occurred to him the note might be read as a flirtatious reference to shared breakfast plans. This he had not intended. He spent the rest of the day in stomach-locked terror lest he should run into her—there weren't huge numbers

of aquatic ecologists—but by sitting in on the least likely ses-
sions ("Advances in Coastal Hypoxia Modeling," "The Oligo-
trophic Levantine Sea: State, Challenges, and Management"), he
managed to elude her. He even left for the airport three hours
before his flight was scheduled—why? He'd found *her* attractive;
he'd done kind but exciting things to *her* body—and spotted her
at gate C10, flipping through an *Us Weekly*. She glanced up; he
jerked toward the men's bathroom.

Even with his wife, she'd been the one to rest her hand on his leg
when making a point, to stare into his eyes rather than answering a
question. That afternoon in the mustard Citroën he had wanted to
wrap his hands around the driver's neck, just to feel her pulse, and
what had he actually done? [The same thing God does when I send
Him my apologies, my ardency, a bouquet of bleeding souls begging
for salvation: nothing. You've managed to combine my errors with
His cowardice.]

As dark fell, the wavering points of light on the far-off patio
looked like a runway in fog. Tom had expected the woman to excuse herself before the wine was done, but no, the engineer had
gone downstairs for another bottle. He heard a thin strain of opera. The two were dancing. Slow, mostly in the hips, as if a wind
were twisting two bodies. Tom felt her skin vicariously. Her hands
positioned just so around his neck, the fingers hesitantly riffling at
his curls. Her breath, two breaths. Trying to align so their chests
moved together like a bellows. *O Lola, ch'ai di latti la cammisa* . . .
His leg finding its way between her feet, to the space there. Humans
were only halves.

He could call his wife now and spill out all his muddled thought.
Tell her he was afraid of looking in the mirror one day, surrounded
by the trappings of grown life, and seeing in his place a child. That
what he wanted was an unleashing, which is what a child wants. Tell

her his recoil from love was not incompatible with love. (He heard his own whine.)

He closed the shutters, turned on the lamp, retreated to the kitchen to set a pot of water on the stove. When it began to boil, he shut off the burner and watched the water slowly deflate. He poured it into his mug for tea, but the little left over he took to the sink and splashed across the back of his hand. *There* was the body! There it was.

THEY MET at the Ponte Garibaldi and leaned to the east to lap up the evening lights of the hospital on the Tiber's island. "If I'm struck by a moped," he said, "will you tell the ambulance to take me there?" This kind of talk presupposed a two-ness about them; the forming of such a unit was always an intimacy, but it felt good and warm to let the words summon the image: him in a tangled heap of limbs on the sidewalk, her kneeling over him, hands pressing his chest and face, telling the medic with authority what the remaining plans for his life would be.

"I don't think they take Americans," she said, walking on. A nutria paddled along the banks below them. "I'd have to stitch you myself. Yank out strands of my hair for thread. You'd look a bloody shambles after I'm done."

His wife had called him morbid.

The girl said the city wasn't meant to be seen but tasted, right down to the cat-piss grime on the Pasquino, where radicals had been pasting complaints for centuries. Her tongue on the stone wasn't what Tom meant by romanticism, but he let her guide him down the narrow streets of the Jewish Ghetto to the red-garlanded door of Sora Margherita, where they squeezed into seats next to a birthday party: the boy, his older sister, his parents, a half-dozen older relatives, none of whom paid attention to the guest of honor but argued about football while the child motored a small car along the edge of the table. The waiter brought them handwritten menus, and Tom tried to measure how long a silence would prompt him to talk of Daphne. Deflect one failing with another.

"Do you want to be more religious than you are?" she asked.

"Why would I?" If religion was loyalty, he wanted, just now, exactly the opposite.

"I mean, does being in Rome thrill you at all, in that particular way."

He took a larger sip of wine than he intended and let it swim around his teeth. Her face shone as if she'd never heard of a committee meeting, as if she lived in a grove, as if the inevitability of relational disappointment didn't apply. "You mean being around all these churches—"

The fried artichoke came out upside down on a plate, looking like someone had smashed it against the dish in a fit of pique. It wasn't technically in season, and Tom wondered what hydroponic fields these vegetables came from, and whether ostracods were thriving in the greenhouse runoff, and what the point was of studying something that was everywhere—or if everywhereness was the point. The artichoke was oily and sharp and made Tom's mouth squeeze.

"There's something in Corinthians," she said. "If there's a natural body, there's also a spiritual body."

"So you're religious."

She sucked on a leaf. "Heavens, no. I'm a moralist."

"That doesn't mean anything." The thought of a quarrel thrilled him; he and his wife couldn't even fight when falling apart.

The boy's car zoomed across the table at them and toppled her glass of wine. The women in the birthday party leapt to their feet, trading apologies with soft slaps to the boy's backside, and the Janiculum girl reassured them, and all the men just watched.

When the waiter had brought a new tablecloth and two plates of tangled *cacio e pepe* and the family had swept out of the restaurant, nearly leaving the boy, who'd found a safe spot under a bench, she leaned toward him, her teeth faintly pink, and said, "It means I get all the guilt with none of the reward."

THE TINGLING in his hands and the periods of dizziness, of head-aches that felt like a novice was taking core samples from one ear to the other, hadn't subsided. One night he stumbled on his way home from the grocery. A carton of tomato sauce flew into a bush, and two persimmons rolled rosily away. After a pause, the children across the street continued their game of tag, and Tom stood up to look for the gap in the sidewalk, or the rock, or the invisible trip wire of fishing line. His leg sent a humble message to his brain: *It was me. I just went.*

He collected the groceries he could see in the failing light and limped homeward, feeling betrayed. He spent the next few hours researching his symptoms, including the ones that were obviously unrelated (a raw tongue after consuming pineapple; double-jointed thumbs), and concluded that he had an inoperable brain tumor, or he had the rare but treatable Japanese Moyamoya disease, or he was suffering from medium levels of stress, like all healthy Americans. He knew that the mountains of North Carolina, where they'd taken Daphne for spring break, harbored *Ixodes scapularis*, the small-headed brown vector for Lyme. (In his wife's family, ticks were known as devil's buttons.)

After a night spent half-asleep, his subconscious caught in the traitorous networks of his arteries and nerve endings and colum-nar bone cells, he woke to an out-of-focus dawn, a breakfast of *fette biscottate* with apricot jam, and a nine a.m. phone call to the Aven-tino Medical Group, recommended for their multilingual staff.

Tourists are always imagining themselves mid-demise. They could squeeze him in at four. He packed a bag with collection cups and left the apartment, not wanting to ferment in his own suspicions. He picked his way down the ramps and stairs that led to the river plain, passing a feral budgerigar that was camouflaging itself as a piece of trash. In Trastevere, he wandered without direction, hunting small fountains. He hoped the moss-lined basins in front of churches and down back alleys would offer some comparative levels of manufactured chemicals. He scooped a cup from the shallow pool below the lion's head at the Fontana del Prigione, from the white marble palm of the Fontana di Ponte Sisto, from the ancient Fonte d'Olio outside the basilica, where he jostled through a clutch of guitarists to lean past the open shells. At the birth of Christ, it's said, oil sprang unsummoned from this spot. A fourth cup from the half barrel behind the mopeds at the Fontana della Botte, and then it was on to the east bank.

Only when he sat did his left leg begin to shake. Not perceptibly, he was sure, but with that particular internal jag that felt like an open current. Passing through the culinary circus of Campo de' Fiori, he'd picked up a slice of potato pizza and decamped to one of his favorite *fontane* along Via Giulia: a wide-eyed man with a slow dribble from his mouth. The water that now blended into his beard used to be wine, in the heyday of luxury fountain engineers. But when Tom sat on the curb beside him, the *mascherone* was just a surprised paleness in the moss. A wall lizard ran across the stone nose. The sun hit Tom uncomfortably, creating flares. A tangerine house looked fuzzy. A dog trotting by came in and out of focus, his legs expanding and contracting, as though a bubble had formed in the corner of Tom's eye. He balled up his trash, nestled it between collection cups in his bag, scooped from the tub beneath the dazed man's face, labeled it, marched onward.

He took a slow path through Rome's misshapen center, looping past the low bowl where ancient columns shivered in the heavy
traffic, snaking along the chain of people waiting to put their hands
in the mouth of Verità, climbing out of the miasma of exhaust and
myrrh into fresher air, mounting the hill of the Aventine. He entered
through five tall arches, and a woman named Mariateresa smiled at
him in a holy way and handed him a set of forms.

"My *codice fiscale*?" he asked, pointing at a line.

"Leave blank," she said.

The form asked about his symptoms. This was when he could decide he'd been exaggerating—malingering, even. So he sometimes felt
more tired than normal, or light-headed when he stood up fast; he was
nearing forty. The shakes could be too much caffeine, or not enough,
or sugar. The starry vision and headaches and occasional lurches of
memory were no more than him being overworked, as his wife always
warned. But because he was dutiful even in his mutiny, he listed all
of them, alongside their likely and innocent explanations. At least the
doctor would see that he knew the limits of his own limitations.

He turned in his homework, stared at the magazines without
picking them up, watched the receptionist field a series of calls. The
only other person in the waiting room was an old woman in a black
housedress, flesh-colored tights, and puffy black sneakers, the kind
worn by members of a dance team. She was resting her chin in one
hand; the other hand tapped a short cane against the carpet. The tapping was metronomic.

Mariateresa, with lifted brow and dimpled cheek, said, "*Signore?*"

He started up. The woman ceased her tap.

Dr. Tromba was his mother's age, sharp of face, with a swoop
of steely hair and a neat white jacket. She directed him to the vinyl
examining slab, and he sat like a schoolboy, hands in his lap. Her English had a slight French inflection, and he imagined young Tromba

misbehaving in a Swiss boarding school, harboring a crush on the pimpled son of a baron, envisioning herself as a modern dancer or a slalom champion, but never quite as a neurologist.

Her brow didn't furrow at his symptoms. She mentioned the tests she'd like to run, asked a few questions. No, he hadn't been urinating more than normal. No, he didn't have trouble swallowing. No, he didn't consider himself depressed, certainly not more than the average person. What did that mean? Oh, run-of-the-mill emotional complexity. He could at times feel worthless, because let's be frank, what can our worth be in a universe where our lives are brief polluting flashes in the cosmic pan? No, he wasn't attempting humor; he was attempting humility. He was a scientist. Ah, she saw now.

She asked him to stand, to walk, to touch various parts of his face; she looked in his ears, shined a light in his eyes, rapped his knees with a mallet. She pushed him gently to see how easy he was to knock over. She wrote up a menu: basic bloodwork and an MRI, with the option for others down the road, depending on what they found. He imagined the technicians as sixteenth-century explorers in lead vests, tunneling into the jungles of his nervous system.

"At this point, we're just ruling things out," she said.

"I've looked up some of this online," he said. "Of course."

Her placid face did not indicate her disapproval.

"Exhaustion, that's the easy one. Lyme is trickier, but manageable, right? What's the worst, is what I'm wondering. What am I crossing my fingers against." He despised the tone in his voice, the neediness.

"The very worst," she said, "is that you will die, without explanation, as soon as you stand up from that chair."

HE WAS not too far gone to ignore the fact that he'd concocted an image of the Janiculum girl that had very little to do with her reality.

In his version of her, the one magicked out of the loose filaments of his own desire, she was spontaneous to his methodical, open-hearted and fierce to his diffident, the whetstone that makes the iron blade sharper. Delusion, of course, is the carrier for love.

He admitted this to her—so much easier here, in the hot afternoon on the Piazza di Spagna, his confessor with a neon spoon in her mouth, than in the dark booths of his Catholic youth.

"It's chemical," she said, unconcerned. She dipped back into her gelato. "I thought you were a scientist."

When she reached to wipe the stroke of strawberry from his mouth, her slow thumb sent a dizziness into his bones. His wife had mechanically cleaned his face countless times, but like she was a mother, like he was a dog. Probably every beginning was like this; maybe none could be counted on to endure. Her hand smelled of violets and Parmesan.

To protect himself, he kept not asking who, in fact, she was.

The house where Keats died was cool and quiet, and they climbed the staircase like wading into water. From the window of the first landing he looked onto the hordes of shorts and sandals. Upstairs the rooms were small, book-lined. He studied the cases of relics—Milton's hair, a shard of Shelley's jaw—and the Janiculum girl disappeared into the far bedroom. He followed her. A narrow bed in a narrow room: a single fireplace, a window onto the Steps, a march of painted roses above. She had laid her cheek on the marble of the mantelpiece. He unconsciously brushed a strand of hair from her forehead.

"This sort of thing makes me unbearably sad." She lifted her head and rubbed a circle in the marble with her hand. The soft *R*s of her accent seemed designed for melancholy. "Severn would prepare Keats's dinner here. Bread or fish and milk. He was so hungry—constantly hungry."

"Why is it sadder when someone famous dies?"

"All the blood he spit up, and Severn just mopping up after him, writing letters, playing Haydn, buying fish." She moved to the window and pressed her nose against the glass.

"You like to touch things."

"It's the only sense that leaves a mark. To know that his nose, his cheek—"

"I doubt he went around leaning his face on every surface."

She turned back to him with disappointment. "Grief's fed by the imagination. I can most imagine what it was like to be my mother, so I was saddest when she died. I knew probably ninety percent of what it felt like to be my mother dying. I know Keats's mind a little less well, but well enough to put myself in that bed and want to tear out my heart because I knew all the blood coming out of me wasn't going to be put back in, and the woman I loved most in the world I'd never see again, and all my elegant thoughts would perish with me, and all I wanted was a roast beef sandwich but my friend kept leaving anchovies on the mantel like I was a goddamn cat." She touched the short post of the bed, just above the sign that prohibited it. "And most of the people who die every day I don't know at all, so."

HE IMAGINED the poisons of Rome bursting forth from cars and chemical plants and fabric factories, then settling like invisible ash on the city again, misting down onto the water, filtering onto the cilia and pseudopodia of mindless microorganisms. He ran his fountain samples through their battery of tests.

As he was heading out, stuffing papers in his satchel, he saw a commotion from the high window: Aldo and a young woman— Gabriella, according to his gleeful shouts—were tussling in the grass while undergraduates walked by unconcerned. She bit at his shoulder, and he flipped her on her side. They circled each other on hands and knees like children playing at beasts. Tom watched, his arms raised on the windowsill, for too long. When they had worn themselves out, Aldo sat by her prone form and patted a drumbeat on her calves. Tom felt a quick surge of yes, he could live here forever.

Dr. Tromba had given him an address for a clinic on Viale di Villa Massimo, north of the university, that had a better imaging department but a higher language barrier. He moved from point to point at the nurses' gestures and didn't question the nodes and cords that were being strapped to his skin. Perhaps this was the pleasure people felt at spas, abandoning their need to know. Only when they slid him into the tube did he begin to feel some tightening in his chest. Now he was aware of too much: that the magnets around him were organizing the water in his cells, and his coerced molecules were following orders. Gadolinium had been injected in his bloodstream and was banging on the doors of his brain. Somewhere in his body, abnormalities could be lighting up the technician's screen. Chemicals where they shouldn't be. Too much water; an absence of water. Absences of fat, of myelin. Of consciousness. What if he were a waterless soul, not a human at all but some spirit who was being sucked back out of the world again, punished for his lapses in judgment, those infidelities. What would the spots on his scan show? [My fingerprints.] A tumor in the shape of a heart. The plastic tube, too close, let out an electric *jang jang* that threatened to drive Tom mad.

They sent him home after the MRI; there was no one to pick him up. Back across the river, he climbed 256 steps from the flats of Trastevere to the plateau of his own neighborhood and up to the third-floor eyrie of his apartment, stopping to buy a cluster of greens and a wedge of fresh ricotta. The greens he stirred idly around an oiled skillet, and the ricotta he put on a plate, and with a single fork he moved between these elements of his supper, the sky beyond the open window gradually sagging, the terrace across the way empty of life, two parakeets crying from a phone tower.

"I DON'T understand what it is." Her eyes were red-rimmed, her hair still uncut and wild. She'd pulled her T-shirt up over her nose, a bandit with a taste for Metallica.

"It's Clinically Isolated Syndrome."

"A symptom?"

"Syndrome. That's the name of it."

Tom thought her face had frozen on the screen, her eyes focused a half inch below his in that disconcerting webcam way, but then she blinked. A beam of morning sunlight from the window was cutting across her bed, piled high with notebooks and stuffed horses and what looked like a raccoon skull, and when she leaned back, her forehead was illuminated. He'd asked his wife to hold off; she said she'd rather tell Daphne he was sick than wait till he was dead.

"What does it mean? Does it hurt?" She rubbed beneath her chin, her thumb and forefinger feeling under her ears.

In the box that showed what she saw, he was a dim face in a dusky room. Ten o'clock in California; her stomach would be filled with pancakes. With her sleepy eyes and the shaft of sun and her haloed head, his screen looked like an annunciation.

"I've had some sort of episode in which I've lost myelin."

"I don't know what that is."

"It's a combination of— It's like a buffer around the nerves. So the axons don't lose their electrical signals, like wrapping wires in plastic. It doesn't matter. CIS, that's what they call it, is when you have one of these episodes, and if you have more—"

"What?" She had leaned forward again, out of the sunbeam. How ugly, to hear these words crowd out of his mouth; he wanted her bright voice, her young complaints.

"That would be multiple sclerosis."

"Is that MS?" She'd covered her eyes now, so there was nothing left but hair.

They couldn't tell him when the initial episode had happened (*Have you recently been dizzy for twenty-four hours?*), and no, his daily brushes with pain weren't subsequent episodes; he'd know if the next one hit. It's just a matter of time, they said. Meaning not inevitability, which he first thought, but duration.

"It's one of those things that's so hard to really say for certain whether you have it, and this is just a first kind of foray down the path toward a place where they could make that diagnosis. CIS is dipping your toe in the water, that's it." What a failure of a father, incapable of matching a vocabulary to a situation. "If they don't see any brain lesions on the MRI, there's only a twenty percent chance of developing MS—which could take years, even if it does happen—so it's not something to be worried about." He waited for her to verify that his MRI hadn't shown any lesions (it *had* shown lesions, little mounds of snow in the darkness of his brain), but she was entirely still again. "Baby?"

The image had frozen. He closed his computer. A few minutes later, his phone rang.

"She just came crying at me," his wife said. "Apparently your face started jerking and she thought you were having an episode, but you weren't, it was just the— Do you want me to talk to her?"

That was the temptation. To let her do the work: the wooing, the loving, the mothering, the separating. She'd made all the decisions about what turned out to be the bulk of his life. So here he had fled, desperate to be free from the ease and risk of leaning. *Let me be a man alone*, he wanted to say, *and then I cannot fail.*

"Put her back on," he said. "I'm really sorry."

Murmurs, a sniff.

"It's going to take her some time," his wife said.

"What's the latest from the Fortress of Silence?"

"Principal says her grades are still up. She's just emotionally disconnecting. She pretended to be sick so she wouldn't have to do this skit in history class."

"You couldn't have made me do a skit at that age."

"This is *Daphne*. On the first day of fall she jumped on the kitchen table and sang her equinox song."

"So what, you think it's still about boys?"

"Have you talked to her about them?"

"*Them?* No, I haven't sat her down and explained the migration habits of things with penises."

"Well, none of this is making it easier."

He'd thought Daphne was fine. Daphne was his ally, a genetic branch from his own twisted tree. She didn't have *needs* the way his wife had *needs*—he didn't have needs. But his throat was hot and his brain was shrieking, the way kindling does before it breaks and burns away.

"I'm not asking you to come home, but—" His wife sounded briefly like their daughter. Small. "Can you come home?"

The images flamed in his head like his life was a field set fire to, and his memories were the mice flushed out. Their courtship, the submerged panic, the wedding, the good days, the days of exhaustion and doubt, the pregnancy too soon, the drifting and hoping that drifting was healthy, trying to find a therapist who agreed drifting was healthy, Rome and *her*, the sparks set off in his joints, his electric marrow, the aching center of him, her warm body, the body whose warmth could not be calculably greater than his wife's, and yet what was happening to the logic in him, it was melting, his whole rational life was on fire. Of course his brain was dissolving its own myelin.

"No," he said, and was certain of his villainy.

———

ON WEDNESDAY, he took a bus to St. Peter's Basilica and waited in a crowd of thousands until at the edge of the piazza a golf cart appeared, and the masses surged upward: mothers lifting their babies, *nonnos* craning, a construction worker next to Tom flashing his orange vest in the air. *Papa! Papa!* And the white ball of a man on the open cart waved back, his smile tender and permanent. Behind him, Tom heard the hiccup of muffled tears.

The pope took his place on the dais, settling into his chair like a collapsing soufflé. The cardinals flanking him bowed their heads in unison. The crowd shifted on its feet, wind through the grasses, but when the pope began to speak they quieted, leaned in. Tom put his hands to his neck. He wished to trick himself, temporarily, into belief.

In a statement that seemed to be about strong families—how to construct them, or perhaps prevent them from decay—the pope alternated between reading the prepared remarks and improvising when a thought struck him. The small white hand came up in a gesture of significance—the fingers clutched in an upturned beak—as he spoke of *la forza delle donne*. It wasn't so much that families were built on the backs of women, but that women were strong enough to put up with all the shit of any family, ancient or modern or whatever new devilry was headed their way. Understanding every tenth word, Tom felt their bite.

The wind was causing havoc as it braided through the columns of the piazza, and at several points the pope's dancing vestments blew across his face, muffling whatever instructions he had for the bastard men out there. A fallible pontiff, in the doctrinal age of infallibility, was somehow the most trustworthy. When he climbed back into his cart and motored away, one hand raised in perpetual blessing, the crowd cheered, crossed themselves, cheered louder. Religion, after all, was just a crowd aspiring.

SHE SPUN his wedding ring around his knuckle; it was caught by the eddy of his bone. He was trying to tell her about the throng, the *mass*, in both its meanings. How Francis was like a Beatle, how fervor has to center on something tangible, which made the Trinity all the more mystifying. Jesus, yes; God, all right; but what on earth was the Holy Ghost? [It was the love I sent to the Lord—a dove—that he regifted. It's the passion of futility; another name for parenthood.]

"What's she like?"

"Daphne?"

"No." She squeezed his finger.

He hadn't thought of the ring as a sign anymore. It was just a gold interruption between flesh and flesh. They were at a back table of a dark bar; she hadn't wanted to go anywhere. She looked tired—something about an exam, or an interview. He had a terror that leaving and being left were two inevitable sides of a coin.

"We met at a lake," he said. His wife had been wearing a hat the size of an umbrella, so her whole folded body was in shade. A wasp hovered at the plastic daisy on the brim. Tom had been staring—orange legs or yellow striped, he couldn't tell from that angle—and when she said *Don't be so obvious*, he pointed to the vespid. She hadn't screamed but simply removed the hat and frisbeed it into the lake, the wasp following the silk stamens.

"Did you have a church wedding?"

"She's patient," he said. "Though I wonder if I weren't someone she needed to be patient with, what else she could have been instead."

She let go of the ring, finished her espresso. "I always wanted to get married in a church. Stupid."

"It was a park, but we had a pastor."

"The grander the better. Give me Santa Maria sopra Minerva, right? You don't need to believe in God to want him to bless your bad decisions."

HE'D WASHED his hands and face of the sterile laboratory smell, had stared into the denuded refrigerator while thinking of something else, and had taken his satchel and a glass of wine to the terrace to watch the evening planes dodge the first stars. It was once again the purple time of day. He felt an absence, an unnerving quiet. His body was closing in on itself. His new tics, which had nothing to do with his sins, shamed him. He wanted to keep his body secret. This was one of the tenets of science, that knowledge unshared was hardly knowledge at all; perhaps a nervous system decaying without witnesses would never fully vanish.

He felt around for a pen beneath the crumple of articles and field notes in his bag but brushed instead against something small and rough. The fishhook. Looking like an old, old thing. He brushed it across his mouth, then ran his tongue over his lips. A faint taste of algae and rust. His father had been a history buff, collected bits of metal from the Civil War—one of the many reasons his wife didn't warm to holidays with his family—and always thought objects were older than they were. The hook, hand-forged but precise, could've survived from the Dark Ages. Or, why not, it could've dropped from the tackle box of Simon Peter himself, the first fisherman. Ready to make miracles, banish doubt.

Something sharp ripped in his chest, and he thought it was a second episode of demyelination, that the sclerosis was now multiple, but no, it was just longing in its cruelest, most unidentifiable state. He *wanted*, and it *hurt*.

He brought the hook down to his bare legs, rubbed the iron through the hairs there, idly dug the point into his skin, just a little, not enough to hurt, only enough to feel. He turned it on its edge, that uneven barb, the roughness against his own weak flesh, dragged it a little deeper, only to make a scratch. It felt good, like his loneliness was centered there, like the vast sheets of yearning could be blamed on a single thread, and it was here: this thin raw mark on his leg. Could he make himself bleed? [I know you're not listening, ye of little faith, but let me stop you here, or attempt. I understand the urge—hurt being thought the cure for hurt—but can I say it turns my stomach? We burn here, we singe and certainly we suffer, but it's the blood, God's red animal milk, that queases me. For the sake of creative copyright, leave the torture to my instruments. I've never done a thing as great as made a man, but were I your silent God, I'd sob to see my creations split themselves asunder.]

But he wanted to see the inside of his body, wanted to see if it was recognizable. He needed to find himself somewhere. He dug in. He nearly saw the pain, a thin, sharp flash, surprising. But just a scratch until he squeezed the sides of the wound together, and there: the red beads that puckered to the surface, already with a gloss on them, the reflection of what? The moon? Had his blood ever seen the moon? [There will come a night when you'll be struck by your unborn son's bicycle as, unbalanced and glee-shrieking, he crashes into your knees. It'll be a full moon, but that blood will be virtuous.] It felt like someone had plowed two hands into his flesh and was peeling it back, flipping it, was inverting him.

He wiped the fishhook on his shirt and dropped it in his satchel again. This must be how people on amphetamines felt. Just manifest the poison, go ahead and draw it out of the body, turn the vague clouds into real red blood, and move the fuck on. The clarity was intoxicating.

Put it to work.

He'd considered the effects of twenty-first-century pollutants on the growing patterns of his pond shrubs and tiny crustaceans, but he hadn't figured out how to separate this century of human interference from all the others. The valley had seen sheep herding, failed viticulture, picnicking nobles, armed conflict, lost baubles, fishermen in togas. There was no wilderness. Okay. Change the definition of pollution. Introduce symbiosis.

He reached back into the satchel for the pen, pricked his finger on the hook, *damn it*, grabbed some loose sheets of paper, and took them back inside, where he turned on the light in the kitchen, an exposed bulb that temporarily blinded him, and started to scribble. The list of compounds he wanted to test grew longer. The necessary experiment: determining if ostracods were not merely hardy survivalists but had evolved to prefer the bitter taste of civilization. If nature, like faith, was a human construction.

THE CLOSET-SIZED pasta shop on Via della Croce smelled like an old man had come in from the rain and begun crushing fresh tomatoes with his feet. They had been twenty minutes in line, on a rare cool day, and everyone was underdressed and hustling to squeeze in. Two middle-aged women behind them were in raptures.

"This is *exactly* how I imagined it," one said. She'd wrapped a blue scarf around her hair, hoping that someone would invite her on his Vespa.

Her companion was a little heavier, a little more sober. "One can hardly expect they'd have health codes. And no chairs?"

"That's how they eat here. The olive oil helps, you know how slim they are—or sturdy, that's the worst you can say. Just imagine."

Tom raised his eyebrows at his companion. She nodded sagely.

"And their clothes—oh, if they sat, they'd ruin them! Look at that one in the green. All those pleats." The Janiculum girl looked down at her swirling green skirt as the tourist continued. "That's the reason we can't be so stylish—we're always needing to sit down, for dinner, TV, you name it. And then things bunch around the waist, you know, and we want to unbutton, or just slouch around."

"Those little cafés have chairs," her companion said.

"Well, yes, for *tourists*, obviously. Where's the *romance* in sitting down? No, this is a city of action. You have to be standing up to fall in love."

At the counter they were shown two plastic tubs of pasta, a *tonnarelli* in that heady tomato sauce and a pesto *pachetti*; they both pointed at the red one and grabbed their cups for wine. The man doled out meals like he was performing a sacrament. Four euros each, and they crammed into an open space at the bar along the window, swirling their pasta around plastic forks on plastic plates, their lips turning gory shades of red.

"Do you want a bite of mine?" she asked. A nest of noodles, the same as his, dangled off her fork.

He opened his mouth.

"Yours is better," he said.

The woman with the optimistic scarf was guiding her companion out the door. "Plenty of fresh air outside," she said, "and we can watch the people."

"It's quite oily," the other said. She was eating as she walked, swayed by the promise of easy weight loss.

They disappeared behind a new crowd of customers.

"I'm grateful I'm here with you," she said.

"And not them?"

"And not them."

"I only wish we weren't standing up," he said. "It's hard on the heart."

She placed her fingers on his cheek, two in front of his ear and three behind, and lingered for an instant, the pressure from her smallest finger directing him toward her, that pinky caught in a curl, and he stood there, blank of mind, as she leaned up on her toes and asserted herself. Her mouth tasted like smoke—not cigarettes but campfires, like his mouth had gone camping in Wyoming. His first response was envy, that this person had untangled the knots of her life to such an extent that she could press her face on the face of a stranger without hesitation, as if she knew that each of her actions sprang from an innate wholeness and so was indisputable, as if love was a form of independence. His second response was a stabbing pain.

THE CITY

[1559]

AFTER THE TRUNKS from Florence had been put away and the footman had delivered the letter from her lover that she refused to open, Giulia listened at the door for the footstep of her husband—nothing—and then draped veils over the mirrors, took off her heavy skirts, and started in on the Battle for the New World, with the heathens on the verge of surrendering the high mount of Hispaniola. She thrust her umbrella into the rib cage of a writhing Indian; she spun around to lop off the head of a phantom approaching from behind. Blood spattered the silk upholstery. She grabbed the corpses by their ankles and swung them onto the bed to clear the field. A boy ran in front of her, his hands raised in a plea; she kicked open the window and hurled him by his hair into the street below. A man selling eels stared up at her.

On the island, not a soldier stirred. The lady knight Bradamante sheathed her lance and flipped a veil from one of the mirrors. Her eyes were dark and her hair was dark and her skin was darker than was considered pale. Inside her stomach an ant had taken hold. She held her side.

A knock on the door. "My lady, your husband requests your opinion."

"I have no husband," she shouted.

She squinted at her mirror self, who pantomimed. After resituating her breasts so she could look down upon their doughy tops like a shepherdess, and lacing herself loosely into both shirt and sleeves, she spotted her skirts still abandoned on the bed. Holy hell. She could take off her bodice and start over, or— She licked a few curls into place and left her room, yelling "Paola!" so her servant would know she was on the move.

On the staircase, a butler turned to look away.

At the head of the table, shelved between the platters and the porcelain, Bernardetto closed one eye. "My pet," he said, "half of you is missing."

She tossed the skirt of her underwear. "My legs are still invisible."

"And if the cardinal had been here?"

"I imagine all the ladies he's seen are without legs."

She sat down with a long neck and nodded to the servant holding the carving knife, an unknown Roman hired for the occasion and quivering. She waited until her plate had been filled to her satisfaction—all grease and herbs and jellies—and began to eat with a fast succession of tiny bites, as she'd been trained. "Like a rabbit, dear," her aunt had said. "No movement but in the lips."

"How many will be at the church tomorrow?" she asked. On the sideboard behind the table stood a towering cake made of stacked *savoiardi* and tiny marzipan fruits, and though she was already growing full from chicken, she would not leave the table without demanding a slice from that mountain of sweet. After her mother died, they'd sent her into the hills outside Florence to live with the nuns, who tried to convince her that apples were a great treat— she'd nearly starved herself in defiance until they returned her with a note explaining that her fixation on sugar was preventing her from a proper concentration on Christ.

"You won't be required to speak to any cardinals," her husband said. "They'd just ask when you last attended confession."

"They wouldn't." She snapped her fingers again and pointed at the cake, and the servant rushed toward it with a knife. "They'd ask about the money from the Pescara properties and whether we'd be interested in funding a monastery or two, or maybe a chapel made half of gold in Santa Maria dell'Orto, which is taking forever to be finished because they keep squeezing in more marble." The slice descended before her, and she smiled at it like a *putto* had flown down from the ceiling. The ant was ravenous.

"Must've been your blaspheming that did poor Ciccio in," he said.

Though her first husband—much older, now dead—had no use for banter, he'd taught her what he knew about the twisted paths of Florentine diplomacy. She'd been married to the new one four days and still wasn't sure what of him was useful. His lips opened and closed, fishlike, when he thought he was being clever.

"And what will do *you* in?" she asked. The cake was a wet, melty cloud. Some cook had left the *savoiardi* too long in the liqueur. She thought of sending a box of the miniature almondy apples to the Tuscan nuns with a note: *This is what a treat tastes like, you monsters.*

"The withholding of your beauty," he said.

The fork was still in her mouth. She never had to share a bed with Francesco, old Ciccio, because he had a mistress of thirty years who would nuzzle him just the way he liked—she once came upon them tangled in the yews, the half-toothless woman with a hand in his pants, her husband pressed against her neck like a child. For the second engagement, her cousin Cosimo swore to her innocence, and both families applauded. White as snow.

As a Medici, Giulia believed happiness was having to surrender nothing. She ran a finger across the smear of icing on her plate. "What's the latest with the pope, *il diavolo*?"

"May His Holiness live eternally," he said, cocking a head toward the servants.

"May His Holiness fast himself unto death," she said, "and be buried under a pile of outlawed books." She dropped her fork. "If you'd given me time to unpack, I might have found my skirts."

"You had them on in the carriage. Did you check there?"

"I don't recall anything in the carriage troubling them in the least."

He stood up and bowed to his lady. "You're a witch, and I'll send you back."

FIRST A letter to the duke, with all the appropriate details of travel (the poor meals, the night at the house of the minor noble, the first view of the ancient city, described as any traveler has ever described it, as a marble rug under which a child had hidden various lumpish toys), and then the letter to the duchess, with all the rest: the layer of dust on the horses, the fly in the carriage, the snores of Bernardetto, her clockwork courses still not coming, so she'd worn the linen rags for nothing. The way the handle of the door knocked against her face whenever she tried to sleep, the terraces of passing grapes that begged for a hungry girl to fly through them. A porcupine that reared up in front of the horses and shook its quills like a Spanish dancer. And Rome! Its clutter, its stink, the hodgepodge of stone and brick, the vines turning the ruins into gardens, stage sets. Leonor had given her poems from Laura Battiferri before she left; they'd seemed exaggerated. But the Tiber really did look like a drowned woman.

The light was beginning to fall, and she didn't know where the candles were kept in this rented house. The *savoiardi* were attempting to climb back up her gullet. The bustle out her window hadn't ceased. At home, a merchant couldn't get within two hundred feet of the Palazzo Pitti; the duke even wanted to build a floating tunnel so he wouldn't have to brush against anyone's homespun wool.

Maybe it was the wool, maybe it was the chance of assassination. Cosimo's own *nonna* once sent an envelope filled with arsenic to the pope, Christ bless her memory. Giulia needed to remember to jam a chair under the door handle before she slept.

For twenty-four years she'd been the lady-in-waiting; the bastard princess; a chess piece; too dark to be opinionated. And now that she was cut loose, her lungs filling with Roman brightness, an insect had built a house in her nethers.

A tap at the door. "Is it time for undressing?"

"Take your own clothes off, Paola," she said. "We're in the city now."

Paola would not be deterred. She clucked as she unknotted the laces on Giulia's bodice, sighed as she rubbed her swollen ankles, rolled her eyes to the ceiling when the princess said she'd wash her own monthly linens.

"I heard you had a letter today from Florence."

Giulia didn't reply.

"My lady thinks herself motherless. But if you should ever—"

"Your lady has no need for anything remotely maternal."

Before they'd arrived in Rome, someone had swept the dust out of this bedroom, taken the covers off the furniture, made the bed with new sheets on a fluffed mattress, spread out an embroidered quilt with velvet trim that would be soft on a sleeper's chin. Someone performed these rituals of service without knowing who'd receive them. It didn't matter. The beauty of wealth was that it spread over secrets like butter.

Her grandmother was a servant, her grandmother was African, her grandmother was not an exotic coffee-colored princess, her grandmother was a black maid. She'd slept with a celibate pope, under what circumstances no one ever said, and bore a curly-headed child whose papal blood outmatched his race, and this became Giulia's father, a Duke of Florence, a model of unshakable apathy when it came to other people's opinions. He left this to her in his will. Stabbed to death at twenty-six. They laid out his body in a house with the Medici elders' motto in stone: *glovis*, which is a backward *si volge*, it turns. (She could imagine him crowing to guests, "Get it?") Her widowed ice-white mother never pulled the small Giulia onto her lap and squeezed beneath her arms. Never lay beside her on the narrow mattress when she dreamed of goblins and the Arno flooding. The gardener at the palace once called Giulia a little lioness. "It's not because you're African," he said, "but because your teeth are long as knives."

Her cousin Cosimo just seventeen, a brand-new duke, and she an orphaned two-year-old brat. A month in the convent, six months with an aunt, another convent, a farm, a school, until a milk-skinned goddess had asked her new groom, "What of your wards?" and recalled the children to court. She'd slept in the nursery with Cosimo's own children, while his wife Leonor, she of the swan neck and the snail ears, made sure all their cloaks matched and their plates were equally piled at breakfast. She feigned ignorance of Giulia's three books, each stolen under cover of night from the communal shelves of the Medici. The girl kept them under her mattress—*Orlando Furioso* and *Le Morte d'Arthur* and *Amadis de Gaula*—and had trained herself to sleep on the left side of the bed so as not to roll over them.

Leonor was the first in Florence to wear that dove-gray satin that crinkled when you pressed a hand to it, like wrapping paper. It was Leonor who greased Giulia's hair, pumiced her forehead, powdered her face with white lead, painted her lips to turn them from plum to cherry. The old nurse refused to comb out her curls, so they hired a new one. The previous duke, Giulia's dead father, was called *Il Moro*, but it was like calling a czar *The Red*; Alessandro simply had a black brow, a black heart, a black sword. Leonor with her skin like goose-down. She held Giulia on one knee and Cosimo's bastard Bia on the other, and not once did she call the younger child Bianca, because to do so would've been to acknowledge how pale that child's skin was, how fair her hair, how minuscule her nose. And when Giulia was seven and Bia was six and the fever came, Leonor insisted they be nursed in the same room, even though Giulia contracted it first, and when Bia who was really Bianca died and a servant said with a snaky tongue that, given Giulia's breed, no wonder she'd prevailed, it was Leonor who let Giulia sleep in her bed for a week after the funeral. If Leonor ever died, heaven prevent it, Giulia would fight for the inheritance of that dove-gray satin; if she slipped it on, surely it would turn her skin as white as the underside of a fish, fish-belly pale, as milk-smooth as any princess of Europe, virginal, that dove-gray dress.

She woke from this dream in Rome—alone in the great bed, limbs sprawled—with the stranger surging in her abdomen. After she emptied her bladder in the chamberpot, the sense of pressure eased. But her body was swallowing itself. There was a jellyfish inside, stretching and pinching. A tweak in her low hips, a sting across her breasts. The pain webbed her muscles. If she wasn't sick, was she dying? [I hope He's watching, because sakes alive, I'm trying to be patient. You're not dying, you primped charcoal maiden. You can't win me with feints of self-deception. You're a woman who asks for too many things, a man-tricker, a dilettante in bad behavior; you're the girl at a party who says, "The Devil? I talked to him last week; we're close," when I've never noticed you in my life, not your tender ears, your wild tendrils, your once-impossible waist. Besides, my heart's taken; taken, broken, unrepaired.] She wanted it out of her.

IN THE last moments of spring, when one could feel the blanket of summer inching across Florence like a slug, flattening the breezes,

Leonor had brought a young man to their country house, the Villa di Castello, to paint the daughters of the duke. Named Alessandro, like Giulia's father, he carried with him a box of colors and ink-dark eyes.

Alessandro Allori started with Maria, the oldest of the legitimate children and the one who most looked like she was already a painting, her teenaged skin unblemished, those red ringlets etched in a blazing mass atop her head. Leonor made her pose with a book in her hand so at least the Medici would seem well-read. Then Isabella, two years younger and two degrees plainer, with her lapdog under one hand, because even if the Medici weren't all beauties, at least they were rich enough to have animals the size of dolls.

Giulia passed him a few times in the long halls of the villa, with his sketchbook held to his narrow chest. She'd seen Bronzino when he came to paint the duke and duchess and baby Bia before she died, and he fit her vision of the masculine artist—middle-aged and richly bearded, with a pocket of sweets for little girls. But this person was slender as a candle flame, and as diminishing. He shivered when he passed below Botticelli's nude Aphrodite in her shell, which the duke had hung so the morning sun would light her lion hair.

"I'd like Allori to capture you too," Leonor said one night as she brushed out her ward's tangles.

Freed from its knot and veil, her unsmoothed hair in the mirror looked like a pine forest after a hurricane. She put a finger on her short nose, dragged it down to her uneven mouth. Any beauty she had was in movement, in expression. "No, but thank you," she said, squeezing an eye shut as the duchess dug into a thorny patch. "I'm not suited for portraits."

In public, Giulia was still wearing her dark weeds for Francesco, but on days when she stayed inside, folded onto a sofa with a poem, she wore bright silks; that was how she felt about widowhood.

"You're not suited because you can't sit still. If it took ten minutes to make a likeness, all of Tuscany could see how lovely you are."

Giulia swatted Leonor's hand away.

"You'll do it because I'm asking. And the boy painter has asked particularly. I think it's because you wander around in that red robe all day."

"I'll sit for one afternoon in all the black you can wrap me in. If he can't finish in a day, he'll have to content himself with a sketch."

Leonor wrapped her hair in a tight cloth and kissed her forehead. "And you'll hold your tongue and not torture Allori."

"Allooori," Giulia drawled, in the same tone she'd tease her little cousins with an *allora*. They'd wait openmouthed for the answer, the next task, the follow-up, and she'd keep them waiting, dragging out the *now*, the *so*, the *allooora*. "Do I get a book or a dog?" she asked.

"Just don't let him give you a handkerchief. I've never seen a portrait of a man holding a piece of limp fabric."

"Whatever happened to Nonna's painting?" When Giulia was two, a man had painted Cosimo's mother, the unyielding Maria Salviati, with her favorite of the illegitimate babes in Cosimo's court. Giulia had been strapped to the leg of a chair so she wouldn't bolt off, but she'd never seen the final portrait.

"The painter didn't have a kind eye."

"Made Nonna look too old?"

"Get to sleep." Leonor pulled her off the bench and shoved her toward her childhood bed. "The artist made you two look nothing alike."

"They made me look like an African baby."

"You just didn't seem like you were in the same family. She put it in the wine cellar."

Giulia pulled the sheet up to her nose so her uneven mouth was covered. "And you want to do it again."

Leonor sat on the side of the mattress and squeezed around her ward's body, cocooning her.

She pulled the sheet up to her eyes. "Why do you love me?"

Leonor scrunched her nose and leaned in close. "Because you were sent by the Devil, and I must appease you."

The duchess snuffed the candles on her way out, leaving the room with a smoky scent that always reminded Giulia of church, and when she was in church, reminded her of bed.

"IT'S LIKE looking from earth into heaven." The cardinal was young and prim, and clasped his plump hands in front of his robes as he gazed up at the cathedral's vaults.

"With a ceiling between," she said.

It was a deeper blue than others she'd seen—a French blue, they called it—and golden twinkles marched along with regularity, as though the artist had never seen a night sky's chaos.

"It makes poor God seem like a child," she added. "One star here, one star there, one star there."

The cardinal coughed in distress.

In truth, Santa Maria sopra Minerva was just to her taste. It wrapped one up in beauty, didn't push one back the way the basilicas did, to make humans feel like roaches, scurrying along the edge of the nave so God wouldn't spot them and shriek.

She'd asked for Father Lorenzo to be her chaperone. The young devout hailed from Pianoro, and from eavesdropped conversations in the Medici salons, Giulia happened to know his local monastery was both mismanaged and dangerously low on funds. The local nobles had migrated to Modena and Bologna and abandoned their stakes. But in the crisscross of allegiances in central Italy, if a large expanse of rent-producing land didn't belong to your allies, it wound up with your enemies. Imagine Emperor Ferdinand and his

Habsburg henchmen with an estate large enough to feed an army, three days' ride from the Vatican Hill. While the dukes of the region were squabbling over women and wine, no one saw this fuzz-mustached cardinal as anything but an arm for an idle princess to lean on.

She lifted her skirts as she stepped up to the altar, so that, if he chose, the cardinal could examine her shoes. "Tell me why it's all right to build a church on top of temples to Minerva and Isis, who—if memory serves—weren't terribly Christian. Are you trying to squash them? Because I can tell you now, ghosts don't have bodies. That's why they last so long. Look, a hundred pagans are probably haunting this old place, interfering with the mass."

He had a habit of trailing at her elbow, as if on a short leash. "Some believe God's wisdom is a long thread that the ancients too grabbed hold of. Plato, Zoroaster, the Egyptian cults. They're part of the *prisca theologia*, the ancient theology. We're not trying to squash the good."

"I wouldn't say you're aggressively pursuing the good either. I'm as devout as the next woman—perhaps—but even I can see this pope is—" As he reddened, she slipped her arm in his. "Forgive me. Tell me about your home, and what you miss."

His family, the farm, the grammar school, the monastery with its white walls and its gardens to rival Babylon, gardens which grew brown and tangled now the abbot was dotty and the duke was dead.

"You need a patron," she said.

He brushed one finger along his upper lip and looked over her shoulder to where the older cardinals were consulting with her husband.

"Or at least a purchaser. I hate the thought of your poor brothers wandering around a grove of dead oranges. If they were besieged?

What defenders would they have? And my friend—think of the women."

His shoulder was twitching now in what appeared to be great discomfort. Resting her hand on it didn't seem to help. "I'm honored," he said. "Honored. But this is not a matter—"

A friar bustled in to clear the visitors out before the evening mass, and the cardinal began mumbling a prayer to his savior. Giulia whispered the name of the palace where she was staying, and added, "I have no wish to offend, merely to help. Consider me a man of business." But she flicked her skirts as she left to join her husband. She only had the tools at hand, and lived in the stifling smithy where they were made.

"Charming the religious?" her husband asked.

"This church is making me itch."

"I thought you'd admire it."

She loved it, she thought it as filigreed and fine as a fairy tale, she wanted to set up a bed in the aisle and make it her own echoing home, but it was ruined by being filled with men. Men who assumed that because it was lovely, she would love it. The nausea surged up again.

"I want to see if there are letters at home. And I've worn the wrong shoes."

"Shall I carry you?" Bernardetto asked.

The red-robed men had dispersed, confident the young prince would pass along their names to the Duke of Florence, the only man of real import. She tugged on his ear and said without shame in Christ's house, "I wouldn't let you get that close to my backside."

THERE WEREN'T any letters, only the one she wouldn't open from Florence, from him, so she draped herself and Paola in matching veils and turned left outside the palace door. How much Romans looked like Florentines, and yet how oddly they tied their hats to one side; she felt she was in a slightly tilted version of home. But the people were only ornaments on their city, that trash heap of columns on columns, brick on marble, church on house on tomb. Vines and cows trailed through arches. It was like a broken poem; its gravity made her feel more daring. A man with a cart of greens cried out, *Petrosello, mempitella, serapullo, ramoraccia*. Paola danced around piles of slop and manure. Why did the streets keep circling round? [You're caught in the half-moon near the Campo de' Fiori, where Pompey's amphitheatre once housed 18,000 fans and their roasted nuts, the alleys following the arch of the bleachers, the same theatre where Caesar's body opened in twenty-three wounds. But this is invisible to you; the campo is a market. The population has shrunk from one million to fifty thousand. Even if I pressed tight your head in my hands, you couldn't imagine the old Tavern of the Cow scooped of its innards and fitted with a glass-fronted counter, a young man flirting as he slices *pizza al taglio* for tourists, some darker than you— "*Così?*" he asks. "This big?"] She thought of all the other cities in the world—Tenochtitlan to Beijing—and wanted desperately to split her body into equal clones and scatter them, and the worst thing suddenly wasn't that an alien blossomed inside her but that she knew as a woman she wouldn't ever see Tabriz.

From the stream of passersby, a girl with a yellow cap broke off and came to a gate in the wall. Her dark hair was almost as coiled as Giulia's. "It's late," she said, and disappeared into the ghetto.

Giulia laughed. "Did she think *I* was one?"

A young boy with freckles passed, he too yellow-capped.

"They're made to wear them, I believe," Paola said.

They came to the river, and Giulia thought of the poems she'd write, the acclaim that'd sweep her past the maudlin Laura Battiferri. Comparing the Tiber to a woman's hair was too simple.

Better to liken it to a menstrual flow; it had nearly the same scent.

"And what if I'd brought the mustard headpiece with the pearls? Should I have been mistaken for a Jew?"

From the banks they could spy the old basilica, which was slowly becoming the new basilica. She'd ask Bernardetto if they could see Pope Sixtus's chapel, where Botticelli had painted the grandmother of Cosimo, carrying a cord of firewood. Giulia wanted to ask her maid to cross with her—on the far side of the river was another neighborhood, louder, with brighter flowers—but night meant women must retreat, like swallows. She turned back to her side of the city, where a few shopkeepers had put out lanterns and a prostitute was whistling from a window.

A display of colored jars caught Paola's attention. "Do you mind?"

The window had dried skins and pots of herbs and snake's teeth strung on bracelets. As Paola opened the door, the pharmacist—a man the size of a goat—came running at them, hands up and fluttering.

"*Signore!* Enter, enter! I have all your medical needs, your potions for the throat, your powders for the head, rare grasses from the Quirinal Hill to lure your lovers, catgut to bind a wound, cat flesh to soothe the jaundice. You have facial spots? Nothing that can't be fixed by tobacco. Here, let me show you the new shipment from the newest world. A rare treat!" He clopped to the back of the store.

"Are you so sick of me you need a cure?" Giulia asked her maid.

"They might have something for dropsy of the womb."

Giulia picked up a vial of foul-smelling paste. "I'm not ill."

"It may need a smoking, is all. I haven't been able to lace you proper."

"I'm only getting pudgy, like any good wife."

Paola dropped her voice low. "Except you *haven't* been a wife."

The pharmacist returned with a smile and a garland of dried tobacco in his arms. One leaf floated out in his rush and fell at Paola's feet.

"My lady, no! Do not bend for it! That your fingers should brush the ground—I would not sleep. I tell you, sleep would not come to me. *Massimo!*"

A boy idled out from the dark space behind the counter where a small pig floated in a yellow tonic, labeled *Sus sanctus*. The boy was larger than his master, though no more than twelve or thirteen, sleepy-eyed and uninterested.

"Massimo, I'm making a mess. Observe." And he pointed at the leaf kissing Paola's toes.

The boy pushed his legs forward like they didn't belong to him, were a heavy separate instrument.

"Forgive him, *signore*, he's my brother's son, my brother who never won a race in his life."

"*Stronzo*," the boy muttered, grabbing the tobacco.

"Beautiful! The floor is now perfection. Now let's visit the table so I may lay these out, but only if you'd be so gracious."

At the long wooden counter the women lifted their veils to examine the herb.

"It comes in salts and syrups, oils and powders. You wonder why the Indians live a hundred years? They chew this for breakfast, they bathe in its seepage."

"Who told you Indians live a hundred years?" Giulia asked.

The shopkeeper had no response, and the maid looked up at him.

"And if we suffered from a woman's ailment?" Paola said.

"Dysmenorrhea? Or retained menses? Or," and he brought a hand to his heart, "an unrequited adoration?"

"Retained," Giulia interrupted. "The blood held on to by an

erratic God—or, perhaps," and she copied his gesture, "little hands. Do you have something for that? For unclenching a fetus's grip?"

Paola's eyes got froggy. The pharmacist was still looking at her, the maid, for meaning.

"My lady," he said to her. "Your girl has quite an imagination."

The boy had his elbows on the counter, and both men now were looking at Giulia's face. The owner smiled weakly at Paola. The boy dug around for a piece of food caught in his molars. Paola looked at the ground.

"We'll take the pig," Giulia said, setting her purse down loudly on the counter.

"My—my *lady*," the shopkeeper said, hands fumbling for paper to wrap the jar.

The boy sucked the food off his finger. "She ain't a lady, she's a Moor."

And so the peace of the evening broke into a hundred parts, each with the same sharp edge.

"THEY DON'T know," Giulia said on the walk home. "It's Rome. A hundred years ago, they were throwing Christians to the lions."

She'd left the bottled pig. Paola said she could get a live one at Monte Testaccio, where for sport they pushed hogs in rickety carts down the hill. Her maid had veiled her face again, but the dropping sun had been cut off by the buildings—which seemed closer now than they did before, as if someone were squeezing the city together—and Giulia strode on bare-faced. She used to think it was in one's bearing, that if she carried herself like Leonor of Toledo, with leopard steps and unblinking eyes, no one would have the room to question her. But even the whitest woman was blacker than a man.

"I only worry you shouldn't have hit him, ma'am."

"That child was born begging to be struck. You set that boy down among the Jolofs, they'd eat him for breakfast."

"Naturally," Paola said. She struggled to keep up with her mistress's pace.

"They'd flay his grub-pale skin and show him what's on the inside of a man. I mean, they'd pluck out an eye just far enough so it could rotate around and look at his own red muscle. Isn't the eye attached with some kind of strings? And then once he'd really seen the sight, and how measly his own skin looked compared to that raging red inside, they'd dispense with the eyeballs and cut him up and roast him for snacks. Because he's not even substantial enough for dinner, the son of a whore."

"He was rather a meaty boy, though," said Paola, who never learned.

"He was two-thirds fat. He'd just melt away in the skillet."

Dusk had settled on them fast, and in her rage Giulia had lost where they were. It was hard to tell a street from an alley, they were all so cramped, each with a sheep bleating through. Paola had earlier recommended bringing one of the local footmen as a guide, but if she mentioned that now, Giulia would cut off her hair.

"I'd be happy to ask the way," she said.

But Giulia had no desire to stop moving. Motion was the cure. She turned down a street that had a breeze caught in it like a cat. In the last light, all the faces had a shade on them; the shops were pulling in their tables of displays, and people kept their heads down, wanting to get home, have someone soothe them, rub the city off their shoulders, their feet. Veils and burgher's caps and snoods, but no yellow hats, not this far into the dark. It's the people who hurt people who should be quarantined. Where was the God of the Israelites? [Where is He ever, sweet cheeks? Hiding behind His cloud—watching, as He bites His nails, to see which direction the humans will turn. Oh, the ignominy of omni-impotence. He laid out these streets like snakes, for me. He scourged the *campagna* with drought, to swell the Romans' bellies with emptiness. He opened the gates of the city to mutineers, so they could steal the Veronica, play ball with the heads of Peter and Paul, strap the Sacred Lance of Longinus to a German pike, graffiti Martin Luther's name on Raphael's fresco. And noble Raphael? He who was named city commissioner of antiquities, charged with their defense? He stole a many-breasted Diana of Ephesus from the Rossi villa—just snuck it out the back door at midnight with two brawny friends and a hand cart. The God of the Israelites, the God of the pope, the God fermenting in your womb, He is the puppeteer without strings, only a man with two crossed sticks. See, I'm over Him.]

Just as fear was beginning to dry out her heart, she looked down an alley and saw in the distance between its narrows a tower she recognized. She'd record the evening as a victory, only because on her first day in a new city she'd had the wits to note landmarks and, without asking a single stupid soul for help, to find her way home.

"WOULD YOU pass those infant mushrooms."

"I'm shocked you think my arms are so long."

"I wouldn't have wed you," he said, "if I thought your limbs were anything but proportional."

What would she do if she succeeded in annoying him to death? [Marry for love, for sweet sexual pleasure?] She'd wrap her breasts, don his clothes, draw a beard on her chin, and carry out his business so he'd stop losing half a florin on every one-florin contract.

"Paola says you got lost today."

"Am I sitting here or not?"

"And felt for the Jews."

She got up and grabbed the porcelain bowl of shrunken mushrooms, each like a crooked finger floating in gravy, and took them to her husband's side. "What harm is feeling?"

Bernardetto put his napkin over his lap to protect his leggings.

Giulia set the bowl down heavily. She fished one out and put it in her mouth. "It tastes like brine." She brushed a finger across her nose and sat on his lap. She used to love mushrooms.

"You're tired," he said.

"I'm tired."

He put a hand as hesitant as a seedling on her knee. She looked down at it and considered. Beneath the pink of his skin ran icy vein rivers, white and blue, his knuckles white mountains, his fingernails cold plates. If he hadn't been a man, and her husband, she would've rubbed a thumb across his skin, because she was curious and, contrary to what anyone who knew her would've guessed, loved touch.

Instead she stood and returned to her seat, where she ate the rest of her boiled ham in silence.

One of the candles snuffed itself out, the wick winding down like a strangled snake, and when the servant came in with bowls of cooked cream for dessert, Bernardetto asked for the light to be replaced. The servant inclined his head as if the need for light was a matter of opinion, and never returned.

"Tomorrow is Santa Sabina," he said, stirring his spoon around until the *panna* couldn't have been more than soup.

"With the cardinals?" she asked.

"I don't know what business you're getting up to, with whatever pennies the Medici let you play with, but do keep in mind you're a representative of this house now."

"You doubt I could make an investment? Are my brains too misty, my loins too rank? You understand I'm Cosimo's deputy."

He crossed his arms against his chest, stretched his legs out. "Any seawater in the cream, or are you satisfied?"

She looked down into her bowl, scooped clean. "I'd like to go to bed."

"Kiss me first," he said, and she pushed back her chair and walked to him and placed her fingertips on her lips and then flicked them across the side of his head.

SHE COULD drink savin tea.

She could ask her husband to kick her in the stomach, without explaining why.

Before a fetus was a *homo*, it was a *creatura*.

To rid the womb of an early child was contraception.

To rid the womb of a late child required a soft penance; it wasn't homicide till after the third month—or after the eighth month—or not at all.

This would sin against the fifth commandment, and the sixth.

She could jump backward or carry weights around.

She could let blood from the inside of her foot.

She could work hard in a garden, bending over and digging.

They called it an *inanimatus*, a *conceptus*, a *figliolo*, a *brutta fetu*.

Hippocrates said he'd never help a woman abort; Hippocrates's daughter was turned into a dragon that no knight would kiss—one wonders why.

She could wear a heavy train, a dress too tight.

"*ALLOOORI*," SHE had teased when she met the painter, presenting her hand.

"Allori," he said. "Laurels. They're a kind of tree."

"You're the trees, and I'm the doctors. Which of us is really doing something?"

"Today? You sit. I move."

He was efficient, she'd give him that. Leonor had suggested he paint her in the north study, which got hardly any light but was draped in heavy fabrics that suggested the scene of powerful decisions. She'd dressed in her personal colors: deep blue, with thin gold silk beneath the bodice to cover her shoulders, a gold veil framing her dusky face, her black eyes, her mouth that always looked better when it was speaking.

He pointed at the old oak chair by the desk.

"No, thank you," she said, and stood behind it, leaning her elbows on the chair back and propping her chin in her hands.

He ignored her, sketching her surroundings first: the slope of the chair arm, the table to her right. What an odd face he had, narrow as his chest, clay-colored hair sweeping around his temples. Lips like two little shells she might find on the beach at Ostia. Everything about his features called out to be touched. The silk of the curls, the porcelain sheen across his mouth. She wasn't usually fascinated by men—not the way she could stare at Leonor through every gesture, from breakfast to dinner—but then Allori had no assumption about him. He was as strange in front of her as a dolphin would have been, and as sleek.

"Stand up straight," he said.

"Have you ever painted a prettier girl than my cousin Maria?" She pulled a corner of the veil around her shoulder, brushing its edge along her chin.

"She's the redhead?"

He was so good at not looking at her. He might be a eunuch.

"Is this really the art you grew up dreaming of? Painting the faces of rich children?"

"You're not a child." He licked his pencil in a manner she believed to be provocative.

She pulled her bodice taut and gave her skirts a poof. "It's all about the fashion," she said, and dropped her chin so she could look out beneath her lashes.

"No speaking, please, for a moment." And in a few quick seconds his hand had swept across the rough paper and captured the lines of her face, static lines that would necessarily betray her. You could see the African in her when she was still. "You may continue in your outrage," he said, and moved on to her torso and skirts.

"Surely an artist must have an appreciation of beauty." She didn't much care for his degree of concentration. "You wouldn't pick an old hag to model for the Madonna."

"You think Mary never aged?"

She had no idea. She swam back to her depths. "Did the duchess tell you where I came from?"

"Found under a cabbage leaf," he said.

She tried to imagine him back at his studio, the penciled forms of all the Medici girls before him, trying to breathe life into each with his palette of oils. It didn't seem like he should be allowed to ponder their curves without supervision, letting his brush slide down their waists and across the smooth lines of their chests. Sitting for hours with their eyes, dabbing his brush again and again, tenderly, into the dark whorl of their gaze. There was the cliché, of course, of the artistic temperament. Raphael and the lust that undid him.

"Is it too warm?" he asked.

Her cheeks. "I have an appointment to meet my betrothed," she said. "I didn't imagine it would take so long for a sketch."

"They haven't given you much time for yourself."

"It's not my job to be unwed."

"What does the new one bring? An army?"

"A fair amount of Naples. But *I'm* the prize."

"Because you're the brains."

She stopped herself from smiling after her mouth had already puckered; it looked as if she were keeping a lemon candy inside and refused to spit it out.

He tilted his head, erased something at the bottom of the page. Was he not pleased with her feet? [The only thing prettier than your silk slipper is your five baby toes, each its own skin shoe over a tiny pouch of meat and bone.]

"Are you satisfied with what you create? The fact of creation, I mean. Does it satisfy you?"

He paused. "I can come back tomorrow. I've got the foundations here."

"I'd imagine you spend a lot of your time not being as good as you want to be. Bankers don't feel that way. Bankers go home and sleep without dreams."

"You're not a banker." He rolled the paper and tied it with a scrap of twine and packed his pencils in a bag. His easel had folding legs and collapsed into a pile of sticks that could be stowed in a carrying case.

"It's like living right up against the sun all the time, and hardly ever touching it. It must be poison, over time."

"And what about you, cave creature?" He slung the case over his shoulder and put the paper under his arm.

She pulled both corners of her veil over her mouth and stared at him in a state of mingled affront and rapture. She felt the urge to swallow him whole, to simply take his head in her jaws and consume everything about him she didn't understand. She said nothing. He nodded and left, and her hand clenched the back of the chair like a weapon. If he walked back in that dark room, she'd snap the arm off the chair and hurl it at him, javelin-style, and when the servants came in to see what the screaming was about, they'd find her crouched over him, her skirts tied up, her chest covered in mail, her hair unleashed. Blood in her mouth. Bradamante.

SANTA SABINA loomed next to the old Savelli ruins. The orange trees were laden with the hard green beginnings of fruit. Bernardetto stood at the retaining wall next to the decrepit tower and looked out over the city, a sea captain observing the waves. Across the Tiber, the dome of St. Peter's was rising. Scaffolds clung to the broken shape like spiders.

Giulia had found a *Mirabilia Urbis Romae* in the library, a hundred years old and stinking of must, but she copied down the salient tips for tourists before accompanying the cardinals up to the Aventine.

"'In San Saba,'" she read, "'lie Titus and Vespasian and Volusian.' This is San Saba?"

"Santa Sabina," her cardinal replied. "San Saba is across the field. You see the sheep under the pine? That one, that looks like a broken gallows."

"'In Santa Prisca is her body, and also the bodies of Aquila and Priscilla, of whom the apostle wrote.' Which apostle? And isn't Prisca the same as Priscilla, or are those really two different bodies?"

"Prisca was an early martyr, the one who was set on fire. Or no, they had to wait to execute her until she'd given birth because they couldn't kill the child too—wasn't that it?"

"Oh! There's a sandal, or a piece of a sandal, from St. Peter in Santa Balbina. That's close?"

"You'll have me tramping all over this hill. Santa Prisca's near."

They left Bernardetto enjoying the chestnuts a pretty girl had sold him for a penny and bypassed Santa Sabina because it wasn't in Giulia's guide; no shards of the cross or mummified tongues there.

Up the road, the church of Prisca and Priscilla—or neither or both—looked unkempt. Though the Dominicans in their brown and white seemed well fed, part of the nave was still black from a century-old fire, and the one parishioner in her front pew had fallen asleep. Her snores did not have the soft tones of a sober woman. Only the cloisters retained their charm; some industrious monk had revitalized the garden, and within a boxwood hedge mingled roses and pole beans.

Her cardinal whispered something to the abbot, or was it the friar, and soon a monk came out to the garden carrying a thimble-sized glass of wine. They ought to have more visitors.

"My lady, would you care to see the crypt?" The monk who reached a hand out seemed too young to have settled on this path in life. He had a dusting of fine hairs on his chin and the scent of castor oil about him. He probably rubbed it on his jaw each night.

"No," she said. "I haven't the stomach for it." She put a hand on the sheath of her seed. She could almost smell the sweetness of old decay rising up from the fresh tombs; everything these days smelled stronger—fish had become revolting—but human scents most of all. She'd never noticed how packed bodies were with odor. Sweat, but also the must of scalp and funk of toes and prick of stained urine.

"Oh, the bodies are all safely put away these days," he said. He cast a look at the abbot, or the friar, who was frowning. "Or the lovely chapels? No? If your ladyship would permit us to offer you a gift worthy of your devotion?"

The whole thing was too silly. "Bless you, Brother. May I just take a rose?"

His cheeks reminded her of Leonor, those porcelain tones. He leaned over the hedge and wrenched a white rose free. "In honor of the Virgin," he said.

Passing back through the dark nave she caught a chill, a quick centipede of cold up her spine. She was glad she hadn't agreed to any subterranean tour.

"Do you believe in ghosts?" she asked the young monk as he held open the door of the church for her. The rose was placed in her bosom so its whiteness seemed to bloom from her heart.

After confirming the absence of the cardinal and his master, who were debating the pope's health by the front gate, the boy leaned into her and whispered, "Bodies are just the buckets. The water's *everywhere*."

TWO NIGHTS later, the cardinal arrived just as supper was being served—intentionally, she thought—but he declined to come into the dining room.

"I received a parcel from the brotherhood at Santa Prisca," he said, holding out a small package wrapped in cloth. "They were touched by your visit."

She shook out the item inside and held it up to the sconce in the front hall. "They encourage me to go fishing?"

"They've written an accompanying note. It's a relic from their collection, belonged to one of the apostles. They've offered it to the household of the pope, but that's custom. They asked for it to be put in your hands."

She looked at him skeptically.

"You know," he said. "There's something about a woman."

"I'd feel very odd accepting this."

"Then pretend it's not from the time of our Lord. It could just be an old fishhook used by a hungry Benedictine back when the Arabs were rampaging through Rome. It hasn't performed any miracles, if that's what you're shy of."

"Well." She tried to rub some of the rust off on her shawl. "And you truly won't eat with us?"

"Edicts to be sealed, shoes to be shined."

"Jews to be marked, books to be burned."

The cardinal seemed to bite his own cheeks. "You might let this remind you of your own soul sometimes. As the Lord said to Job, *Canst thou draw out Leviathan with a fishhook?*"

"I take it his hook was too small."

"*He is a king over all the children of pride*," Father Lorenzo said, his finger pointed impertinently. "All the children of pride."

WHEN ALLORI came back for Maria's second sitting, to color her in with vermilion and lapis, Giulia hovered outside the door, listening for some evidence of lively conversation. But of course Maria wasn't clever; their flirtation wouldn't take the form of talk. She took her book out to the gardens, where the paths led through careful boxed beds and erupting fountains and wound back under a pergola of roses to the west side of the villa and the windows of the sunroom. She examined a page, looked idly at the sky, returned to the book, slid her gaze across the bank of windows as if she were following the uncertain path of a butterfly. But the sun was slicing across the glass, and she couldn't see in. He might already have her cousin in his arms, his nose fuzzling at her ear, the paints scattered in an arc around them.

She'd only made it through four pages of the *Purgatorio* before Paola found her: the seamstress was here to finish measuring her for the trousseau, and no, she couldn't be put off. Giulia didn't like the way the woman preened over the impending wedding, holding orange silks and rich brown velvets up to Giulia's gold skin, murmuring, "Won't the husband like *this*."

"You'll want children," Leonor had said, attempting to comfort her when the death of Giulia's senile first husband was immediately followed by the announcement of her second. "If you're not in love—and you may come to that faster than you think—it's a small sacrifice for a great boon."

"The sacrifice being—"

"You can teach them what to do," the duchess said. "It needn't always be unpleasant."

"Or I can adopt a gaggle of abandoned street children, and

the work of taming them will consume my hours and entertain Bernardetto."

Leonor had paused, her hand on her ward's knee.

Now, as the seamstress pinned the hem up around her ankles and pulled in pleats along the back of her bodice, Giulia intentionally didn't think of the makeshift studio in the sunroom, or what Allori might say to cajole the rosy-cheeked teenager, or whether he would smudge blue paint across the bridge of her nose to mark her as his own, to which she would respond by holding up her fingers to be pressed to his mouth and—

"A bride in love is a rare thing," the woman said through the pins in her teeth.

Giulia flinched, and the seamstress smacked her hip as a reminder to stay still.

"It's a lucky lady. I was widowed too, but couldn't find no one else to have me. Some men, they like a fresh girl."

"Some men," Giulia said, pulling the skirt free from the woman's grasp, "ought to consider where their own instruments have been."

THE NERVOUS cardinal with his almost-mustache had avoided the past few church tours, but as Giulia strolled down the aisle of Santa Maria del Popolo with her hand trapped in Bernardetto's elbow, she spotted his twitchy form consulting with a priest by the entrance to the crypt. She jerked her hand free, and though her husband tried to grab for her wrist, she managed to hop past his reach. The cardinal's eyebrows lifted when he saw her; still pale, he put a foot toward Giulia before pausing, uncertain of the protocol. She hastened toward him, alternating each of her steps with a skip, scuffling over the sunken tombs of pointy-toed knights, her own sharp heels tapping their soft stone cheeks. The rich are allowed to be childlike.

"*Padre* Lorenzo!"

He stepped back, as though she might barrel over him, and the other priest scuttled off. "My lady. What do you think of *this* house?"

Hands on her hips, she looked up and around. "You could never hope to reach the ceiling, which makes you wonder what the point is. What's the teeny one, the Tempietto? I adore it, it's like being caught in a cloud."

"You have a feminine take on the divine, I believe."

"I think you mean the divine had a feminine take on *me*," she said. "Have you spoken to the abbot at Pianoro?"

"He came to the city yesterday, my lady, and I had the fortune to dine with him."

"Wouldn't he like to see me?"

"He expressed interest in your proposal; indeed, he thanked God for providing a possible road out of their recent difficulties."

"Well, it's not a road so much as—"

"I believe I can convey with confidence that he'd be willing to continue negotiations with your husband, or perhaps the duke."

The door to the crypt was still ajar, and she had a brief vision of the cardinal's body tumbling down the stairs, his red cap bouncing off his head as it knocked on each stone step. She perched herself on the end of the pew and fanned her face with the handkerchief she kept in her belt.

"Pardon," she said. "Sometimes it's just too much to stand upright."

He sat beside her, reached out to touch her arm assiduously, pulled back just in time.

She made her eyes extra wide as she turned to face him, those white cheeks of his shaking like a quickset jam. "If you ask my husband or guardian for money for your rural monastery and its barren fields and its debauched monks and its shit-producing coffers, they'll laugh you out of the pope's court. There's not a man alive who sees your province as a bargain. I'm the one with the funds, and I'm the one whose brain is broad enough to come up with a plan to turn your silly abbey into an asset. If you and your brethren aren't interested, I wish your parishioners luck."

She was halfway to her husband—undoubtedly trading hunting stories with the older cardinals, who themselves ought to have more important duties than serving as tour guides to idle nobles—when Father Lorenzo came skittering up behind her. His anxiety showed itself in a thin flush along his jaw, below his cheekbones, if he'd been born with any.

"I'll consult again," he said. "I'll take your message. If you'll forgive me."

In moments like these, when the backdrop was grand and her muscles were moving and her wit was riding its conquering horse, she felt like the most magnetic woman in the Papal States. And wasn't she? [You're swaying me. I find myself at your feet. Child, listen: you won't find a man worthy of you in heaven—I've been there. Let me pave the road of romantic regret with coins. Hold out your hand.]

She held out her hand and he seized it like a glass of wine. The slap of skin on skin echoed, because, as she'd suspected, this cathedral was entirely too large.

SOMEONE HAD nailed horns over the palace entrance.

Bernardetto sent the valets out with a ladder after dark to pull them down, and when they reappeared in the morning, freshly polished, he called Giulia's maid into his study and asked what slander she'd been spreading.

"I've said *nothing*," she blubbered to Giulia as she dressed her for the day.

"You didn't tell that silver-maned valet of your suspicions—the one you keep winking at?"

"I *have* no suspicions!"

"Did Bernardetto believe you?"

"I can't spill a secret you haven't shared."

Giulia reached for the bowl Paola now kept on the vanity. She held it in her lap until the wave calmed. "I hadn't heard of the horns. It's rather clever, as long as he's the one shamed."

Paola rolled a stocking up her lady's leg, her eyes still wet with fear. "You're half of a sort of daughter to me, you know that, and I don't fight only for my own position when I tell you to go kindly with him. You Medici think it's a farce, but I know of men, and not a hundred thousand ducats can declaw them. If you want to call it a lie and make me leave, I will, and it'll go easier for you."

Giulia pulled her feet back and leaned toward the kneeling nurse-maid. "If Christ himself swanned down for the second coming, I'd still choose you. That's my opinion of men."

HER HUSBAND had hired a troupe of performers for the party, and when from her window she saw them processing white-cloaked into the servants' entrance, she was transfixed by the shortest one's long brown hair. She couldn't see their faces beneath their caps, but those waves bobbed and bounced like loose ferrets, brushing across the visitor's hips, before the palace swallowed them all.

Parties were her strong suit. It wasn't a matter of enjoying them; she excelled at entertaining, and competence can be its own reward. The duchess had told her, after one vivacious evening, that she needn't feel she was making up for some deficiency. "What deficiency?" she'd said. But of course the perfect pearls of her teeth distracted from their darker setting, and if she furrowed her brow and listened with unparalleled fascination to the droning guests, they left thinking not of how she looked but of how magnetic *they* must be, to have so captivated a princess. And laughter was like an egg wash over everything, polishing each ill-timed joke and forgiving every dropped custard and audible belch. Her laugh was loud but as well tuned as a major chord; her companions sometimes heard it like a welcome ghost when the cathedral bells rang for a wedding, or a blacksmith hammered out the trigger for a gun.

The duchess had loaned her a pair of earrings that Giulia had been waiting to wear until she needed to cement a wooing: large opals ringed in gold, with garnets dangling off the ends like cherries on the stem. Neither the Roman women nor the Florentines had fully caught on to the ear fashion that Leonor brought from the Spanish Muslims, and Giulia didn't want to alarm a man of the cloth with the trappings of an infidel. But look at how they caught the light from the candle and tied it into knots. Jewels like these went on and on. She picked one earring up and shifted it between her fingers, put the cool stone to her cheek, put it in her mouth.

"My lady?" Paola's head stuck through the open door.

"Mm," she said, and spat the jewelry into her hand. "None of my skirts are with their bodices. The green one has walked off on its own power. What play are the actors doing?"

"Some comedy, *La Mandragola*."

"And there's a woman?"

"If it happened in July, my lady—"

Paola had apologized five times for the incident at the pharmacy, for the dust-up with Bernardetto, for both her willful ignorance and her sly hints; she was now convinced that proactive steps had become necessary. The time for coyness had passed. She needed to know what the date of misbehavior was.

"Then June wouldn't've had a missing menses, now would it? Where's the calendar where you keep your snooping? The daily record of my bowels?"

"I would never—"

"If you can't find my gown, leave my bewitched womb in peace." Giulia dried the earring off on her petticoat and put the jewels on, shaking her head quickly to make them dance. She would rather be an infidel than not be noticed. The fishhook from the cardinal glimmered among her loose rings. The priests had such a passion for the classical; they'd prefer the relic hail from Caesar than St. Cecilia. And what a plain thing to be considered holy at all. Like the beginnings of a child. Thirty days for a boy, or forty; forty-five days for a girl, or eighty. No doctor had decided when ensoulment struck, because men were moles, blindly digging at a woman's body. She didn't feel it as a human—when she covered her belly with her palm she felt no hand reaching back. But she also knew it wasn't dropsy, wasn't a tumor, wasn't from eating too much fish. So what was it she felt if not something ensouled? [You feel yourself. The thing in you that isn't un-alive is a limb of yours, pulsing with your own humors, a you that's ravenous for more of you. What man in robes can tell you when God drops a separate breath inside?]

She wanted a *strega* to brew her a cup of myrtle or rue. She wanted to be deflated. *Canst thou draw out Leviathan with a fishhook?*

FATHER LORENZO was a red minnow among the guests, several score of the finest gowns and waistcoats in the city. Necklaces strung across high white bosoms, sleeves brocaded with dancing deer, and the handful of priests with their eyes diplomatically downcast. The palace staff had found additional tables to push together, and a pristine cloth, longer than any single cloth she'd seen, collected them all around the illusion of a single piece of furniture.

"You look like a painted angel."

She didn't have to hunt him down after all. She felt like a master physician whose patient was beginning to show signs of the cure.

Giulia raised her hands slightly as she turned, to better expose her waist to admiration. "Aren't you Christians always saying the body is the true temple?"

"My lady, we rarely say that."

"Have you had any messages from your abbot?"

"We apologize for our assumptions."

"I'm accustomed. Does the offer suit him?"

The cardinal smudged his finger around his chin, as if feeling for tiny beard hairs.

"There are legal questions," he said.

"I can't hear you over the music." A quartet had set up in the corner of the foyer, and the violinist with the pocked face was fiddling away like there were ants on his strings. "Did you say you'd like to ask my husband if my Medici money is real?"

"It's contract law," he said, even more quietly.

"Pardon, do you want to ask my husband if I'm a witch? Shall I go get him? He's just chatting with the Count of L'Aquila, probably committing troops for the protection of the Holy See. Let me tell him the teenaged cardinal wants a word."

"You'll forgive us, my lady, for our caution."

She put a hand on his sloping red shoulder. Below that robe was real skin: skin that was born on a baby with a penis, and that stretched to cover him as he grew into a man, and stayed pale and freckled under every shirt and frock, moles sprinkled like the islands of the Indies, each with a dark hair, smoke rising from the volcano. Would that shoulder ever be caressed with anything but pity? [You haven't seen *my* body yet, my sweet. If horror is your thing, if your insides are tickled by the grotesque, come circle my shoulder with your tongue, find the warts and festering wounds and lavish them with licks—if pity is your aphrodisiac.]

He twitched beneath her touch. When she let him go, she dragged her fingers lightly down his arm.

"Bring the contracts tomorrow," she said, "and I'll look them over. I have no intention of breaking any laws. I respect the church's opinion of women."

"I would be happy—" he said, and coughed. "I would be happy to stay. I mean, to sit with you. If you're looking for— I would be at your service. I know how a foreigner can find herself in a city like Rome."

"How?"

"Oh," he said. He waved a hand around as if attempting to whip up the quartet into a high-spirited march. "Lonely."

She noticed his eyelashes for the first time, how uncannily long they were around his weak eyes. In one blink, she imagined the entire gathered company freed of their clothes. Silks and diamonds vanished. Nothing left but sagging bellies and wobbly thighs and the triangular breasts of men. Hair in places no painter painted. Hair on backs, beneath arms, between legs. The tufts on the tops of big toes. Her own stomach, suspiciously swollen. What of this could people possibly want to see? [I'd eat you with my eyes until your flesh was a pile of crumbs. God didn't make the body; if He had, He wouldn't have thrown leaves over it. Your own conception took place in a pious tent of stale clothing, the pope looking penitently to the ceiling and the servant's palm over her eyes. Don't be bashful—or should I say don't be raped. Take my hand, and let me show you the pieces I shaped.] She shut down the fancy, because it required her to wonder if there were parts of her so dark any pretense of whiteness would be lost.

"No," she said. "I don't get lonely." The body wasn't a temple; it was a tool.

AT DINNER Giulia found herself between a deaf man and his anxious wife, who was convinced their grown children were holding a séance in their palace while the parents were dining out, and shouted across Giulia through all three courses until the husband finally put a piece of roll in his ear. By the time the boys in matching tights came in with the puddings—cream and berries petrified in little pots—she'd lost her taste for battle; she wished herself alone with a book. The husband finally shouted to his wife, "What ghosts could they possibly summon?"

Giulia stood and clinked her knife against the edge of her plate. The assembly turned to her. "I saw six men in white sneak into the palace this afternoon; will there be entertainment or should I retire to bed?"

She spotted her husband—he was on the opposite side, far down by the windows. He raised a glass. "My new bride is the patron saint of joy," he said. "And she bears no surprises."

The young prince ushered his guests into the solarium, where performers were dragging props and pieces of scenery onto a make-shift stage. The actress's cheeks were painted violent pink.

It was a plot to make the church a fool: a noble is hoodwinked by a schemer out to bed his wife, and the country priest aids and abets, all in the name of florins. The guests laughed at the wife's willing naïveté, the prancing of the villain and how loudly he could snort. When the friar gave his blessing for an aborting potion to be sent to a promiscuous nun, the audience gave sideways glances, couldn't help their smirks. The men read lines that pierced at Giulia: *I do not praise her for making such a fuss before she agreed to go to bed ("I don't want to! What'll I do? What are you making me do? Oh, Mother of God!"); can't you see a woman without children has no home?; women don't have much of a brain; that cat-brained woman has driven us to our wits' end.* The one woman onstage: *This seems to me the strangest: to have to submit my body to this shame.*

The guests applauded the deception, the troupe made their bows, and the men stayed to partake in the host's wine while the actress, fictionally impregnated, slid away. Did she return to her own husband, shedding her costume before she slipped between their marriage sheets? [What do you know of marriage sheets? She's alone, same as you. Lives with her parents in a cramped apartment on the other side of the Tiber. She'll have sardines for dinner, and no dessert.]

She kissed the cardinal on both cheeks when he left, feeling her heathen earrings bob against his face. It wouldn't have been outrageous to take the seduction further, but a fisherman knows the best hook is the smallest one the trout will bite. The house emptied.

Bernardetto was at his dressing table, removing the rings from his hands. His Roman bedroom was smaller, the walls covered in red damask. It didn't seem possible to her that he knew her condition; he must've thought the play not a mirror but a caution.

"Fine party," she said, leaning against the door.

"You enjoyed the *commedia*?"

"A little broad."

He made a noise of agreement.

"Would you like a kiss tonight?" she asked. Her arms were crossed behind her back like a girl's.

He glanced up, then back at his waistcoat, with its tricky buttons. "No," he said. "Thank you."

It was a game, she decided in bed by herself. He saw her wager and raised it. But as her mind attempted to map out the next day's plan—visit Santa Prassede, buy a new stock of paper from the Fabriano dealers, finalize the contract to acquire the monastery— she kept circling back to the woman actor and how the men, for all their rude bluster, would rather have touched anything in that room but her.

SO IT was a surprise when she was awakened in the darkest part of the night by a hand covering her mouth and another hand pulling back the bedsheets, fumbling at her chemise. She screamed through the clamped fingers and pushed herself out of bed and onto the floor, and when he came after her, she scrambled to the door, which he slammed shut. He shoved her onto the bed again, started hoisting up her skirt while she windmilled her legs into him, pummeling at his own skinny shape. He slapped her once across the face—the sting brought all the logic back to her. The intruder was her husband; what he was stealing was his own property.

His eyes were ferocious and terrified. He pinned her arms on either side as she lay on her back on the bed and leaned in close to her one red cheek and said, "If you call for someone, what would they say?" He used his knee to push her legs apart and she felt like a starfish, open to the sea, to the storm, to the shark, and he moved one hand to her chest to keep her down and the other fumbling to his breeches, and she thought do starfish survive because they have no memory? [Don't close your eyes. Don't let your arms go limp.]

Before God and a retinue of two hundred Medici and with a dowry of twenty-five thousand *scudi*, she had signed away her claim to virtue. There was nothing to save.

Not in all the lepers huddled in the dank corners of Florence had she ever thought a body so vile. Before he could find her, she reached a hand up to her husband's neck and pulled him down to her face and—thinking she'd been stirred to passion, had succumbed to her weak and womanish nature—he lapped at her mouth, one hand still hunting, and with his dry lips dipped into hers, she bit down hard.

He howled, fell back, clutching at his bloody mouth with blank shock, as if a chair had collapsed beneath him. She scrabbled to cover herself, lunged for the door. She was halfway down the long hall before she looked back. He was standing, limp, one hand to his wound, staring at the bed as if the betrayal still lay there.

THE GRAVE

[896–897]

BEHIND THE STAIRS to the crypt, Felix had placed a three-legged stool on which he could sit when the abbot was chastising monks above, and he was settled here now, listening to the muted maledictions while he looked fondly on Brother Bernardo, so recently his friend. Bernardo sat politely in his nook, hands folded in his lap, head drifting slightly to one side. If it drooped any more tomorrow, Felix would prop it up. When he'd peeled back Bernardo's eyelid a few days ago and stared deeply within—his sister once told him heaven's reflection could be glimpsed there—he'd accidentally squeezed it to get a better view, and the pupil had changed shape, become some sort of devilish triangle. He quickly closed the lid and crossed himself. God wouldn't let Brother Bernardo wander around paradise with one goat eye.

Faith was a cure for curiosity. So Felix didn't wonder how Bernardo would find the other monks up there, or if distance even existed, or whether friendship meant anything where there was no such thing as nonfriendship, likewise happiness. He was caught in a little limbo of his own, between the mild promise of heaven and the bustle of men: the ones upstairs, doddering around in their brown wool robes, and the ones busying through streets, the city, the misty fields of home—not misty; there'd been a terrible drought the summer he left, was asked to leave, forty years ago, and the grasses had crackled like fish bones. Now his hours were spent with these remnants. *Lonely* was too grand a word.

Felix's stomach made a petulant noise. His friend was beginning to smell like Monday stew. Soon his face would be as dried and hollowed as Brother Giuseppe to his left, and his chest would collapse like Brother Timothy to his right, but for now Bernardo was the most robust of all the corpses perched on their thrones in this poor stone church on the hill where Remus once set up his challenge to Romulus, and lost.

"you coming to dinner?" The voice traveled down the stone steps.

Felix switched his head from one propped hand to the other.

"He'll still be there in an hour," the voice said.

Felix slapped his old knees and hoisted himself toward the stairs. "You're right. Too much self-denial and one slips into pride. Beef today?"

Brother Sixtus laughed and reached out a damp hand to pull him the rest of the way. "Roasted cow," he said. "Is that what they call it?" They hadn't had red meat since they'd joined the monastery, but this was a pleasant joke to make. "Only four hoofs, so some of us will have to go without."

"You haven't heard of the six-hoofed steer out of Briton?"

"That many, and I'd wager it's a swimming cow."

Oh, and when a joke got rolling! "Back and forth across the straits to France all day; leanest meat you'll ever eat."

"Gave birth to a calf with two more, I heard, and then no one could tell it from an octopus."

"In that case, give it to Brother Henry to fry up after all, because you're talking about a fish."

Past the nave—dark and cold, candles by the altar shivering like orphans—the cloisters rang with spoons on bowls, half-sung songs, and Henry with the pot of stew and his iron ladle, the rust flakes from which he called seasoning.

The newest brother sat next to Felix, his thin hands peeping out of his sleeves; he couldn't have been past fifteen. The rest of the brotherhood must have looked like wizards to him.

"How does Brother Bernardo?" The boy's hair was so blond it was almost white, thinly brushed over the tops of his ears.

"Oh, doing well."

"He has a stink?"

"He was a good man, but he was no saint. Bless him, and all of us."

"Bless us all." The boy still wouldn't look at Felix, but had now taken his spoon and was stirring wanly.

"You'd care to see him?"

"My mam died in winter. Couldn't put her in the ground some time, so I seen her well enough."

Felix lifted the bowl to his lips to catch the last of the broth, thinking of the passage of soup from his throat down to his twisty innards, soaking through his stomach to his muscles and his bones, each of them slurping in turn, building their mass with salt and herb and maybe a hint of mackerel, so that the outside world became his inside self. When he was younger, he'd felt such a wall around his person: a wall delightful to be breached, but the more treasured for its fixity. Now everything was just floating recombinant particles. Who could say what was Felix and what was not? [I, for one, would recognize you. With your cloudy hair like a poor-sheared sheep, and the shake of your thumb as you wipe the ooze off your peers. Don't let the next world lure you; the threshold may seem to be wavering, but your goodness will vault you to a place where you'll lose what you love: rich, wrong humanity.]

"Do you have dreams then?" the boy asked.

He meant did Bernardo's corpse come sneaking into Felix's

nighttime memories—of the farm, of his fair sister, of her friends lined up on a bench plaiting one another's hair. He once dreamed some boys outside had kicked a ball into the cloisters and before returning it, Bernardo had prodded Felix into a game, the arch into the transept serving as goal, and Felix had scored triumphantly, flapping his arms above his head. And the boys were somehow inside the cloisters then and set up a great cheer.

"Have you confessed this week?" he asked the boy.

"Oh, nothing troubles me either," said the boy, rather quickly. "But things tend to pop up, don't they, the worrying things, or the things we seen when we was small. I just think all that awful flesh and maybe—you know."

"I remember seeing a goat slaughtered when I was young. Did you see something like that?"

"A goat, no," the boy said. "Not a goat." And with his eyes on his shoes, he took his bowl back for a second helping and went to sit by the abbot, Father Peter, who never laughed.

AFTER DINNER the brotherhood divided into cleaners and singers, and Felix, as he often did, chose the former task, finding relief in busy hands. Stack the bowls, wipe the tables, sweep the floor, scrub the pots, toss the dirty water on the cabbages, chuck the oily sand in the outhouse, gather the carrot tops and wilted chard and gristle in a basket and visit them upon the happy chickens, who bump their hips in a scramble to the door, their heads leading their legs by a seemingly dangerous margin. And all this to the singing brothers' tune, a quiet chant if the weather was wet and cold, or a full-throated foot-stomper, their more restful chore never begrudged, for Felix found the greater pleasure in listening. And anyway, his own warble wasn't pleasing, as his mother was careful to tell him on his first attempt to join the chorus of voices in the country church. He must have been six. "Ohh, my love," she'd said, and put a hand over his mouth. "Let's allow the angels to have their turn."

It was too dark to see the broom now, so Felix affixed a new candle in his holder, a small brass cup with a ring for his thumb, and took it to the outhouse to sit for half an hour with his begrudging bowels. When he crossed back to the church, Brother Benedictus was kneeling closer to the altar than was customary, and when Felix raised a hand in greeting, he shuffled back. No harm in wanting to touch God. And yet neither Benedictus, nor the newest novitiate, nor most of the brothers had any interest in traveling to the subterranean reaches of this holy space to watch God at his most visible. The last keeper of the putridarium had died two years before, and Father Peter scrambled to find someone willing to tend the corpse of the tender. Felix's singing was poor, his manuscript illumination haphazard, his understanding of the chemistry involved in baking perilously inexact. But he was not squeamish, and he believed as his mother had told him, that the body was a manifestation of God's love for us. (This had been included in her list of reasons why young boys should refrain from abusing their most special parts. The penis also belonged to God, and should never be handled with more than sober devotion, as one would hold a ewer of holy water. This image proved very peaceful to young Felix when he masturbated.) So the Father had blessed Felix—some said punished him—with the crypt key.

On his first visit below, he'd vomited. They looked like a seated council of ghouls, mouths hanging, flesh distended, waiting for someone to speak. His tasks were to defend the bodies from desecration in case of heathen raid and to mark carefully the progress of the bodies' purgatorial decay so he might converse with monks who had fears about mortality. In practice, the Father discouraged him from loose corpse talk; he said it made the brothers ill.

Now his predecessor was third in line, a tumbly haystack of bones in a stained old habit, and Bernardo was his new treasure. As he let his supper digest, Felix peered again with wonder at the dead man's eyes. Where did they sink, and on what time line? Did the fluid leach out first, and the filmy sack collapse like a popped balloon? Or was there some solid core, an olive pit, that the eye would eventually shrink to? Would blue irises turn red as veins dissolved and blood ran wild? [I can see why the others avoid you. Go back two millennia and eavesdrop on Sushruta of Varanasi, who submerged his cadavers in water to watch them rot without the stench (bright idea), and who could peel a cataract with proto-Buddhist clarity—or somersault ahead and meet Albrecht Hennig, who wandered into the Himalayas with a 30-gauge fishhook and in one year snared the cloudy nuclei of 44,000 groping Nepalese. Imagine what Milton could've done with a fishhook. Or you, whose eyes too are beginning to milk.] There was no running wild. Just a steady seeping—an occasional audible drip—as Bernardo's fluids left the openings gently made in his bottom and passed through the hole in his stone seat, his toilet throne, and fell to the packed dirt below, sunless and cold.

His former friend had been what a kind man would call plumpish, and his arms had funneled that weight like pastry cream into the bags of his hands, leaving a crease at the wrist. He'd been tenderly packed, Bernardo, his limbs as clearly jointed as a doll's. But the fat was draining. Perhaps Felix shouldn't keep lifting aside the habit to observe the changes in the decomposing form, but he had to know when the ankles needed a well-aimed lancing. Exploding feet were frowned upon. Bernardo, lucky man to be blind to his mortification. Felix would be the keeper of his honor, and would never cringe, only chuckle. For there is also great humor in our embarrassments, humor in thinking we are anything more than a collection of fluids, of gases that find ways to noisily escape, of bile and pus and goo.

The wick in his candle had inched down to its nub, and the wax puddled in his brass saucer. He carried it gingerly up the stairs so it would last through the darkness, but it guttered at the top step. Benedictus was gone, and the nave was a void. He knocked into a table and banged his knee, that pucker in the knee to which banging causes a debilitating shock, the funny bone of the leg. He staggered. There was an echoing flutter in the back of the church, and Felix turned to catch a shadow moving. Another truant child snuck in, perhaps, or a woman who'd lost her means. Felix didn't hear the creak of the big wooden door; the shadow must have been a bat, or a fancy, or a ghost.

This church was a cake of corpses, the current stone sanctuary built where a clumsy brick one once was, which in turn stole the site from a Mithraic temple, which claimed the sanctity of the original dirt because some lustful god once tricked a virgin here, one or both in the shape of a heron, or was it a stoat. So while elsewhere in this stackable city people came and went, moving unpredictably through homes and shops and streets, here at Santa Prisca they appeared with the bells, confessing their most perverse sins while their dead piled up, knowing just where to find them.

Once Brother Lucius claimed a spirit kept him up at night sucking his toes, and swore this was because his cell was above the crypt. Father Peter told him all the cells were above the crypt, and any other room he entered in this city was above some other crypt, and no other monk had complained of wet toes.

"It's not a sucking so much," Lucius had said, now alert to the eroticism, "but a licking, as of a friendly dog."

"Do you giggle?" Father asked.

"I am in too much fear."

With a prickle on his neck, Felix returned to the cloisters with his saucer of wax. This time of year, his cell's small window didn't afford enough light to cut the room's chill. Stone walls lead to stone bones, that's what his father said, who built his first house from wood and two years later shook his head as he watched it burn. Cursed family; Felix had brought them no ease. Even up on the bed and wrapped in wool, Felix believed the pine legs soaked up the cold from the floor and conducted it to his aging joints. It was a reminder. He crawled back down and knelt on a cushion his sister had made and began his count of sins. First always was his secret, which he never named but passed over with an encompassing *I am sorry for myself*, and then the daily litany of slights, cowardice, impure thoughts, haste. He would repeat all these to a confessor, but forgiveness is a private creature, born at home.

Once the sins were named, the gratitudes began, and this was almost his happiest time of day, to think back. Brother Vitalis losing a tooth in his soup; the goose that landed in the courtyard and pattered around in circles until someone realized it couldn't fly out, and Brother Leo wrapping it in his pudgy arms and carrying it outside, tossing it in the air like a gift back to God; the mysterious settling of fluids that led dead Brother Bernardo's pinky finger to suddenly crook, making Felix feel as if he were being summoned, or offered a private promise; the salt on the bread at lunch, rougher ground than usual, its sharp edges jolting his tongue.

The final formal prayers were accompanied by Felix's ragged whip, a careful homemade thing that beat the time on his back, the knots serving as emphasis, as *Amen*. He was careful not to treasure this, not to harbor pride for his bloody devotion, but merely to keep time, to remind himself with a red drumbeat that his body was not his own, and to offer its impermanence with humility to his Lord. The only lasting thing about Felix was his soul, and this no one on this earth could see or judge. *Amen*.

———

THE BROTHERS were in a flurry: the collection box had been stolen. The abbot asked each monk to consider which of the parishioners from the previous day might be called squirrelly.

"There was the one who was gnawing on a chicken bone," Lucius said.

"I saw that," said Marco, "and I had another ask me to pray for his departed wife, and when I asked when she'd deceased, he said tomorrow."

"What about the child hiding under the font who wasn't a child at all but a very small man?"

"I gave him a roll of bread," said the youngest brother, Mino. "He looked hungry."

"If only we'd taken the chicken from the first and given it to the small one."

Father bowed his head in defeat. He must have been a poor kind of noble to have wound up at Santa Prisca.

"I saw a shadow," Felix said. "It was after I'd come up from the crypt, just before last prayer. It moved along the back wall, and I thought it was a ghost."

"We've gone over this," Father said.

"If it wasn't a ghost, it was either a very large bat or a medium-sized man."

"Either of which could've carried off the box," added Marco.

"But it didn't have a handle for a bat to grip with its claws."

"I imagine it would wrap its wings around the box and then scuttle off on foot."

"Have you ever seen a walking bat?"

"Brothers," Father said. His upper lip carried a habitual twist, as if he were bitter, or trying not to sneeze. No one minded that the abbot was cold and told no jokes and sometimes had noisy visitors at night who could not have been monks because they were women. An abbot was like a statue with a pointing finger: there to remind you of duty, not to be judged by human laws. "Brothers, the box is lost. Dominic, you have permission to find us another. I would request you all take turns watching the new box when it has been installed."

"Ought we to lock it to its post?"

"There's an idea!"

"Then someone would take the post."

"And we'd be out a post."

"A new post costs less than a new collection box."

"And Brothers," Father said. "Try to remember the value of silence."

Felix carried the slops out to the chickens, who didn't understand the morning's delay. The day was foggy and cool, and the farm of his childhood seemed painfully far. A rusty-crowned chicken chuckled as he bent to offer a crust. You couldn't pet a chicken the way you could a cat. Oh, that soft spot at the base of old Johanna's ears, all silk, undisturbed by the fleas that burrowed in the fur beneath her chin or between her shoulder blades or in the open plain of her lower belly. He brushed the chicken's tail feathers with the back of his hand; the sensation wasn't the same. If he'd been a farmer, he could've kept all the cats—traveled the country looking for crones dangling sacks off bridges and saved the writhing kittens within— but he couldn't be a farmer.

The day he left, his sister had handed him a wrapped cheese and said something to the effect of "We'll always love you," or "Behave," or "I'll love you if you behave"—he wished he could remember the wording—and it wasn't until the donkey cart had rounded the bend, the curve of the road obliterating the village of Fara in Sabina, that he thought of how he should've answered, but then to leap off the back of the cart and go dashing home, hay flying from his bottom, seemed too absurd, even for him. So he'd sat placidly for most of the day as they tumbled down the evenly terraced Lazian hills, past women in smocks leaning on fences, through loose herds of goats that barked at the driver's whip. Felix had left the figs in the bucket by the back stoop. There were at least four people he hadn't bid farewell to. He wanted to learn to draw, but never had. Nor had he fashioned for his parents any sincere apology, and now, barring Methuselah, they were surely dead. He could've jumped from the cart in a tumble of courage—at this moment, or at that moment, or, wait for it, *this* moment—but he sat there, watching the road pass under the back wheels until he became queasy and turned around. The driver, son of some other language, never spoke.

Rome appeared on the horizon like a vast looted quarry—the city of devils, of scam, of holy Peter the fisherman. Behind one of those hills was the basilical bulk of St. John Lateran, golden. Why wasn't he bound there? [Because you were born with the twin vices of poverty and unfortunate love. The mother church is not for you, though its sanctified ground was once divoted by pagan hooves; the emperor's mounted guard had their barracks here. And then your Jewish carpenter spread his gospel and they built their admiration for him obscenely high, the faith too becoming obscene, until this jeweled palace had to shelter Jews because those Christians called Nazis got blood behind their eyes. You'll never step foot inside. Next year an earthquake will shatter it. In 1,500 years, its columns will be rolling underwater. But I know of ill-fated love, young Felix fac-simile. I too had a boy scorn me, spurn me, send me to hell.] The cart left him at the Porta Flaminia and he picked his way through streets that twisted left when he thought they were going right and down alleys that ended in a wall of blue flowers. He pushed at them with both hands, searching for the door, touching only vines.

A cobbler was sitting outside his shop with a boot and a last and a mug of beer. Felix only stopped because he mistook the last for a real human foot.

"Don't like you how one makes it?"

Felix squinted. He'd met Romans he could mostly understand, but this man came from somewhere south, where the garble only sounded halfway to his own tongue. "I'm looking for the church of Santa Prisca?"

"South keeping," the cobbler said. "Hill the Aventinus."

The summer was hotter here without nature's interference—no drooping branches or clouds of gnats or lone hawk eclipsing the sun in its lazy swoop. Just buildings with angles and more people than he'd ever seen. He was conscious of his clothes, mother-made from wool so rough it seemed to have part of the sheep still in it. A young man passed on the street, shielding his eyes with his hand, and Felix imagined he was looking into a mirror of himself, his Roman self: handsomer, with proper garb, with a stride that disregarded the pace of others, with a hand blocking the sun in a way that said, *I have no need of trees, or your poor hawk. I am my own engine.*

"You monksing?" The cobbler's hand licked in and out of the leather boot like a snake. "Close door, talk all the God?" He gestured toward the sky. What an expressive hand; now it looked like he was playing an upside-down lute.

"My father sent me," Felix said, though it was more accurately his mother, or rather it was a family decision that arose from a lengthy private confabulation that was eventually reported back to him by his sister. "I've no dowry, though, so they might not have me."

"Money in the Christians." The cobbler shook his head. "A story telling themselves, all's that. A story just. My prayers?"

Felix stayed out of politeness, not because he was afraid of the monastery.

The cobbler put his left hand, his free hand, up to touch his eye, then slowly moved it to his heart, then dropped it to his stomach, and finally used it to pat his groin. He smiled at Felix.

"You mustn't forget also to pray for others."

"No needing comes when death." And having lost the smile, he turned his attention back to the shoe, which he slipped onto the last and pinched around the edges, his brown fingers looking little different from the hide.

Felix passed the bricks and stone alike with equal awe, the triumph of the Forum in its exhausted collapse as impressive as the crowded apartments, dingy and rich with foreign smells: African spice and fruits he'd never seen. A garden appeared through the rungs of a gate like a prize, and the greenery struck him, only gone from his home a day, as exotic. The trees were not lush but spare—faded pines, dusty and bunched at the top—and the river was not blue but brownish green, the color water should be at its very bottom. The Circus Maximus was less a field than an abandoned cemetery of broken benches, pierced by obelisks. It was as if the countryside had been fed poison. Climbing the final hill brought him to fresher air, and when he saw the vine galloping out of the cracked cloisters abutting the church—his church—he took it as a white flag from God. He was nineteen years old and believed his spirit was being pulled on a lead by a benevolent hand, saved from his worse self.

ON THE Sunday of Andrew's feast day, Felix fell asleep at his post in the crypt, his stomach packed with two helpings of stew and a wing of quail. Naps were an increasing pleasure, a gracious preview of obsolescence. He feared his adoration for the buttery bird had eclipsed St. Andrew; he really should give up fish and fowl, like Jerome. So when he woke to a stick poking him in the armpit, his brain translated it to a roasting spit, himself the sacrificial bird, and apologies came bubbling up: to God, to the fauna of the earth, to his fellow brothers whom he allowed to accompany him to this culinary damnation.

"Pardon, pardon," he cried before his eyes were open, and the boy named Mino cried "Pardon!" and took two hopping steps back with his stick in hand, the other hand protecting his mouth from the stench.

Felix clutched his ribs. "What's this?"

"I didn't know!"

"Are you attacking me?"

The boy was twisting his body in such contortions Felix assumed he needed to urinate.

"The outhouse?" he said.

"It's the bodies!"

"You wanted to see?" He rubbed the sleep from his eyes. "It's beautiful, really. Imagine God's fingers working through the flesh, pulling it back in pieces to his own kingdom."

"No, it's them keeps me out," Mino said. "There's a man above."

Felix paused to consider the religious reference.

"I found a stick. For to get you. I can't wake the Father, and I heard him walking and I was afeared for the box, for it'd be my neck if it were gone, but you're here with the bodies and I knew no other way, given you were snoozing. I'd've shouted, but he'd've heard me and taken the box and scrammed. Holy *Christ*, the smell. Please come, or it'll be my neck."

Felix pulled at his cheeks, and as they climbed to the nave he took the stick from Mino so the boy wouldn't trip on it with his clumsy growing limbs. Above, the church was empty, silent. A quick whir interrupted—"There!" Mino shrieked—but it was a small, rafter-high noise; a legitimate bat, or a mouse with wings.

He confirmed the presence of the collection box while Mino loitered in the side chapels. It was eerie how the windows of the church, alabaster and glass stained with random color, filtered light through their honeycombs even in the black hours. Each speckled mote he passed through had come direct from a star. He was waving his hand through one of those faint reflections, like an ember in the eye, when Mino called out again.

"Are all the relic boxes meant to be full up?"

Each chapel's reliquary had some shard of a saint—a half inch of leg bone, or a gnawed fingernail, or a lock of hair that had been pin-straight until the saint's death, when it curled like the hair of our Lord—and though the bits' origins were murky, Felix acknowledged there were many saints, and each saint could be broken down into many parts, and he himself had witnessed and mourned the disregard for deceased mortal flesh.

Mino was standing next to a gold-rimmed terrarium in which a hump of red velvet couched nothing at all.

"I don't remember which it was," he said. "Do you think there really was a man here? Or did the Father take it out for polishing?"

Did bones need polishing? [You'd be surprised by what a good spit and rub can do.]

"How certain are you it was a man?"

"You think it could've been a girl?"

"As opposed to your imagination."

"I haven't got an imagination."

Felix grasped the air with empty hands and turned back to bed. "Where did you come from?"

"Should I not have fetched you?"

"Tell the Father in the morning, when all good men are awake."

"Do you remember what it was?"

The clouds must have crept over the city, carrying snow in their pouches; the colored windows were now dark, starless. The door out

to the cloisters sat on squeaking hinges, and not for the first time Felix
was glad the other inhabitants of his home were mostly old, mostly
hard of hearing, and mostly unconcerned with the supernatural.

"Probably a finger," he said. "Go to sleep."

He tossed Mino's stick in the cloisters' hibernating rose beds.
His candle he'd left burning below, but it would gutter soon, and
Bernardo would be glad for the extra few minutes of flame. Light
was a conduit for the spirit world, an incarnation of the dead's
breath and thought. Was this too romantic a notion? [If romance
is the same as fancy, which is to say philosophy, which is to say
idealism, it'll doom you every time. Humans aren't built to hold
anything more precious than dirt and shit. No need for the whip
tonight.] His bed soon became warm, and when he remembered
the nightly penance he'd failed to perform, he didn't leap out onto
the stone floor but stayed perfectly still and said in a whisper in his
head: *I'm already asleep. I would, but I'm already asleep.* Mino was
a trouble, but a sweet one, a son. His bright cheeks like Tomaso's,
if Tomaso had never aged and had left his wife and come from the
fields to the city's chaos to remind his former friend of the intimacy
of joy. *Oh, Christ, don't you listen to this twaddle.* He wondered what
the thief would come for next, or if he'd already run off with Felix's
discipline.

THE FATHER confirmed it was the finger of her High Holiness Saint
Ethelberta of the unstained robes, who had preached to the barbarians, been assaulted by a troop of soldiers, and eventually perished
on a mountaintop when she refused to touch any food that was once
touched by men. Two of the brothers wept at the discovery of this
loss and could not finish their breakfast. Felix's own morning continued on its regular path—chickens, washing, weeding, corpses.
Brother Sixtus had been given the task of copying out a psalter, and

after lunch, Felix asked permission to stand behind his desk and watch him at work.

He'd only picked up a basic literacy since coming to Santa Prisca, and was still in awe of the cleverer monks. Sixtus's hand seemed a machine, fingers and quill one single-jointed organism. His eyesight had gotten so poor he had to hunch over the paper: hand moving, rounded pellets of letters emerging on the parchment, the word of God duplicating itself. Their brotherhood hadn't been engaged in much copying work, but Father Peter said they needed to modernize (or was it monetize), and there was a small but reliable class of lay-people who'd pay generously to have their own prayer books. Sixtus was told to start with the psalter and if things went well, they could one day graduate to Bibles. But Felix wasn't certain Sixtus would complete the psalter before his knuckles gave out. First the black ink, laborious and error-free, then the gold, then the red and green and only-for-the-rich blue.

He rested his bottom on the stool set there for Sixtus's apprentice, who had never materialized. The literate novitiates never seemed to pick this monastery for their indenture. It wouldn't be long before the cook took the stool back.

"How much do you mind the finger?"

"Mmm," the scribe said, carving out the scoop of a *T* like he was an ancient with nothing but clay and stick. His table was messy with Armenian bole and fish glue and honey, a cup of eggs, a lion's tooth strapped to a handle for burnishing, camphor and cloves to keep the color bright. Cinnabar, ochre, white lead.

"Are you much for relics?"

"I had an hour shift after terce, but no one comes then but the biddies in black. Where are their husbands? Where's their income?" Sixtus couldn't look up or he'd lose track of the line.

"You think it'd catch a fair price?"

"Find a church in Rome *without* a chunk of Ethelberta."

"A private devotional, then? But no man that devout would stoop to stealing."

"Inside job? Sorcerer? You're thinking too hard."

"What, someone collects all the parts and builds a whole holy skeleton?"

"The skulls are the hardest to come by, of course. It'd have to be a real low-level saint. Oh, *blast* it." Sixtus grabbed a damp rag and blotted at the spill on the page's corner.

"You can turn that into one of our bats."

"They'll wonder why he has such a great black belly." He blew on the drying spot. "Haven't you better work than sleuthing?"

"Keep an eye on the boy Mino, would you? He's a fiddly little rabbit, and I can't tell if he has any friends." Felix slid his hands into opposite sleeves and scratched at his elbows, which were dry from the cold. "We're such a bunch of old fools here."

"No one's lonely who has Jesus in his heart." Sixtus stuck his pen into the corner of his smile.

"That's the way." He slid off the stool. "Next time you'll teach me to write my letters, yes?"

"*F* for Felix, *C* for Christ, a heart around them. *Amor sempiternus.*"

"You don't watch out, it'll be your knees stolen next."

HE WAS sixty years old. The routine of the church had smoothed away most of his memories' terrain. His parents had become feature-less, though sometimes a smell of burnt rosemary brought their voices back to him, and though he knew his sister had been his nearest friend, he couldn't name what pastimes had led to their shared hilar-ity. But having a young boy in the monastery again brought color to some of the cobwebs—Felix too had once possessed such thrum-ming limbs—and a glance or graze was enough to cast him back to an age when he'd still been blind to God. That afternoon at sext, Mino had run in late, pivoted on his back foot like a dancer. Flights of Tomaso had nearly dizzied Felix, causing him to miss a versicle's response. Mino was just a boy, daft and winning; what about Tomaso had so embedded him? Whence came his own monstrous yearn? [To yearn is not a monstrance. It's the brand God seared you with on your expulsion—it means, paradoxically, you're whole. Compare our hearts to His, the omniscient, whose puny half-baked love is conditional. (He'll say it isn't, but has He forgiven me?) Don't sit on your memories like eggs, but don't let them scramble either. I've seen who now shares Tomaso's bed, and there's no need for you to know. There's my finest torture.]

Scenes came at him fast when he took up his half whip, on those nights when the ice in his joints wasn't punishment enough. He spurred himself on by counting sins; recently they'd been the most distant kind, ones long since forgiven. But he could not clear them. Here, as he beat his back, was the afternoon in Fara in Sabina when his sister's friend Donella reached to kiss him.

He was two years older, enough to allure, and when he walked past the gathered girls at their spinning they burst out in giggles like starlings from a tree. He took care with his appearance, but only because adolescence was intent on wrecking it. (He would later learn how much richer was a body abandoned to itself.) In his war against pimples, he washed his face daily in the cold stream; he rubbed herbs beneath his armpits; he twisted the ends of his dark locks with olive oil so they'd retain their shape and lie neatly against his head. He did nothing about his feet, which were immune to myrtle or mint. Knobbly they were, tufted with black hair and ridged with tendons, the bottoms scaly and dark. But his sister's friends never saw his feet.

Donella stayed over when spring winds or nightfall kept her from riding the donkey back to her father's farm; she could be finicky about ideal travel conditions. She and Felix's sister would share a stool at the supper table, share a bowl, take turns mopping up the beans with their bread, and whisper obscene secrets until his father coughed loud enough to frighten them. On their shared mattress at night, they'd play a game where one would scoop a number of pebbles from a jar and the other would examine their shape and color and number to determine her friend's future. Dark stones meant stormy times ahead; little ones could be counted as babies. The pointier the largest rock, the more hateful your husband would be. They'd refill the jar frequently so the fortunes were never the same.

Once during this insufferable game, Felix left the sleeping room to ask his father if there were more chores to be done, and being told to go back to bed—no one listened to the subtext of children—he instead slipped into the night and was happily contemplating his solitude beneath an alder when he heard the telltale prancing steps. He hoped it was dark enough for his seated form to resemble a shrub.

"Felix?"

He was quiet.

"Felix, it's dark!"

These were the things girls said.

"Are there snakes?"

He raised a reluctant arm and waved at Donella. She yipped.

"I hate playing those games," she said, curling herself so close beside him their folded knees touched. "I'd much rather be in nature, doing things. Like this."

"I'm not doing anything, particularly."

"Have you got a girl?"

"I'm looking for cows. There's a sick one needs to be brought in."

"Are you already promised, then?" She brought a hand up to his face—or rather to his nose, which she must have hoped was his cheek—and caressed it abruptly. And then she drew herself closer, and her breath was fogging in his face.

"No, that's—" he said, and he felt a soggy pair of lips fumbling at his chin, and he didn't care what his sister would say, no one could expect him to put up with such a clumsy assault. Felix raised his arms in defense and retracted his head to ward off Donella's ardent forays. When she understood her prey was not becoming any less unenthusiastic, she paused.

"You think I'm ugly."

"Oh, *no*," he said.

He heard her blinking eyes grow wet. She pulled her knees up again and wrapped her arms around them, becoming a hedgehog. He patted her wrist.

He couldn't tell her she was beautiful, because he didn't find her so; he couldn't tell her she was too young, because two of his sister's friends were already betrothed. Nor could he just bear his bad luck and kiss her, which he should have done. Felix had inklings already that love was impossible to untangle from wrongdoing. The safest thing, probably, would've been to tell Donella she should wait to fall in love until she felt no anguish in her heart, for that would be a sign of the right time. And this would've puzzled her for so long she would've joined a convent, because no moment of earliest affection or longing or lust was anguish-free. But he'd been silent instead; he'd caged her out with his arms.

Now the whip could exact the penalty. Donella's tears pattered as he beat his back, once, twice, thrice—again and again until her face was dry.

BY THE Temple of Hercules Victor on Wednesday mornings a small market sprang up, some vegetables and wool but also religious artifacts and packets of herbs sewn with spells guaranteed to ease heartache, schizophrenia, and mystification. Housewives and country travelers browsed the stalls, hiding their sense of wonder behind a carefully manufactured cynicism. *You're asking five pennies for that artichoke? Is it made of rubies?* A stout black pig with whiskers was usually tied to a column of the mushroom-shaped temple, and who-ever made an offer for it was refused. On this brisk morning the crypt-like stench of the river was subdued—there'd been no recent rains to stir it up, no humidity to lure out its flavors of decay—and the stalls smelled only of manure and lime wash. If Felix slipped out of the haggling crowd and began a slow hike north, back up the low hills and past the roaming goats to Fara in Sabina, Farfa Abbey in the distance still sparking thoughts of chastity in every local boy and girl, no one would come chasing him. He'd simply take up the plow and keep his eyes focused on the sprouts in the rows and swear to never again look at another creature with love.

But his task was to sniff around for bones on sale.

"How will I recognize Ethelberta?" he'd asked the abbot.

"You're our expert on the dead."

The men who sold relics looked particularly shifty to him, their beards somehow scragglier than their comrades'. He wasn't allowed to touch the wooden boxes they kept the parts in, but he could point and they'd lift and reveal.

"Mmm," he said, contemplating a scrap of scalp with a few strands of hair attached. It would raise an alarm if he too obviously knew what he was looking for. "Perhaps."

There were bones, and bones claiming to be fingers, and fingers swearing to be from ladies, but none quite looked like Ethelberta's; even the laziest thief would know to sell his contraband farther from its source than the Temple of Hercules.

"I can get you something grander, Brother," a vendor said. "My cousin's now in Jerusalem."

"I'm not looking for a Muslim trinket."

"Oh, but they don't care for our saints and are happy to pass along what they find. Students of history, they are. You want a head?"

"Our budget is small, I'm afraid. They call us the church of knuckles."

"Ah, well, I should pay my respects," the vendor said, nodding as one poor man to another.

Another relic stall trafficked also in painted icons and fishermen's flies. Felix looked from a crude image of John the Baptist on wood to an elaborate ruffle of feathers and red wool. The merchant was completing a trade but beckoned Felix with a smile.

"A religious man," he said when his previous customer had left with a one-eyed portrait of Mary. His black-and-gray hair swooped from beneath his hat.

Felix's fingers were already nestled in one of the fancy flies.

"You're not for graven images, understood." The man had an accent that turned his *R*s gentle and slurry. A white egret feather sponged out of his hat, creating a likeness between him and his wares. "You fish too?"

Felix should've removed his hand and been on his way, but the merchant's eyes were syrupy dark. He tried to imagine his sister beside him, tugging his sleeve. The sweat along the back of his neck was there, and the dry throat, as if the moisture in his body was fleeing outward. He grabbed his hands from where they were fiddling on the table.

"There's some fine fishing not too far from here. I wouldn't recommend the river, not for beginners, but if you were curious—"

"Just looking for bones," Felix said. If only he could redistribute the sweat so it cooled his fluster.

The merchant's seductive tone was temporarily checked. "Fish bones?"

"Human bones," Felix said and turned so fast his robes whipped up behind him far more dramatically than he would've wished. He didn't look back. Self-control was supposed to be an old man's gift.

A few more booths and Felix came up empty. But the wind off the river, not entirely unpleasant, made him linger. For this one morning, he was a farmer visiting from Lazio. His cauliflower had been sold, his few pennies spent on a bracelet for his daughter. Where had he gotten a daughter? [Shh, keep dreaming.] Before he hitched up his donkey to carry him home, he'd picnic on the Tiber with a loaf of warm wheaty bread and a canteen of beer and watch the boats drag their wares out to Ostia and the sea. He'd promised his daughter he'd take her there, to see the sand. What a vision: bread and beer. Could he not fulfill this fantasy *right then*? [It's not the bread, or the cauliflower, or Lazio.] No wonder he was studying dead men in a monastery. He'd had no desires, no vision. If he didn't wish for anything, why should he be given anything? [It's the child, the family.] And anyway, he couldn't have pretended to be anyone else in these terrible brown robes. He turned back to the Aventine Hill.

"No fingers?"

Felix stood in the Father's study, his hands tucked into his sleeves. A shelf beneath the narrow window held three books. Beyond the Bible and the book of prayer, he couldn't guess what the third one was. There'd been rumors the Father hoarded gold, trinkets from foreign wars, the rings off dead parishioners, but this cell seemed as sparse as the others.

"None I could swear were Ethelberta's," Felix said.

"The bastard's probably set up a shrine for himself somewhere."

"One hopes it aids him in achieving closer communion with God."

The abbot appraised him as if he were a hen whose clucks had begun to sound vaguely human. "You may be in charge of the bodies below," he said. "But remember who here holds the care of their souls, who tends to *those* diseases."

"The *cura animarum*," Felix nodded. "I am the patient, and He is the cure."

"*I* am the cure. I am quite literally the curate."

MINO WAS supposed to be learning how to dust the art, but the boy was so fidgety Felix did it himself, saying, "Like so," and "Downward, so the dust can then be swept," while the boy nibbled on his thumbnail or gazed at the ceiling or chattered on about his pet cow he'd had to leave behind.

"Myself, I had a cat," Felix said. "A nicer one you couldn't—"

"Nobody understands. They think cows are for eating, they never believe what good listeners they are, or how Nipsy was the best of all and can't be replaced with just some any old milk cow."

"Animals really are very—"

"And here there's no room for one anyway, I asked the Father. You'd've thought I was asking for a throwing axe. Just there's not much liveliness here sometimes."

Felix folded his cloth between the golden points of a reliquary box, brushing out a month's worth of whatever dust was made of—simple grime, or floating sweat, or the droppings of invisible flying beetles. If he ran a rag down Bernardo's forearm, the man would be flayed.

"What was it like, the market?" Mino was sitting on the arm of a heavy chair now, his legs swinging beneath him.

Felix paused, shook the cloth out. "The world is a busy place. Until one can sort the bad from the good—which, actually, one never can do properly—there's some value in this private life. I most enjoyed seeing all the faces, which we can just as well see when they're standing here with us. And admiring the river with its wild islands, and of course the gulls. I don't know what you're imagining, but there aren't circuses or young people running about with candies."

The boy kicked the chair. "I don't need circuses, just an old cow."

"You can think, I suppose, of Christ as your cow."

Mino looked up at him, startled, and then beat his chest with laughter. "You've never had a wrong thought in your whole life, old man."

Felix bent to sweep the fallen dust into a pan. Monks had no fewer wrong thoughts than Nero. But they let those thoughts go, like pebbles at the bottom of a sack of wheat. *These pebbles belong to me, but I have no use for them. Let me toss them so my bread when it's baked is soft and hurts no one.*

Mino took the rag and drew it lazily down the sides of the columns. His robes, inherited from some prior monk, fell past his feet; someone ought to hem them. "You did this sort of thing at home? Women's work?" When Felix didn't reply, he added, "You came on your own, or someone sent you?"

Behind the altar now, his arms raised rather blasphemously, Mino resembled a toy archangel.

"You seem like a boy who was sent," Felix said. Whenever Mino asked these questions, the boy would get such a blush on his face, as if Felix were the one prying.

He opened the main doors of the church to toss his pan of dirt into the street, but a toothless woman was sitting there, her gray braids wrapped atop her head in a pink ribbon.

"Pardon," he said. He flung it as far from her as he could without letting go of the open door, but the wind was having none of this game and blew a goodly portion back into the woman's face. She pawed at her eyes. "Oh, *pardon*," he said again. He raised his robe as if to wipe at her face, but then remembered his wool spent most of its time with rotting flesh, and pulled it back. But the gesture of pulling back ended up being more emphatic than the initial charitable reaching out, and with one eye cleared she looked at him like he was a monster.

She gaped her mouth and picked herself up and carried herself away, like a crone in a basket. She was headed in the direction of San Saba, where the friar would be sure to give her a good crusty roll and probably a carnation. There was a sense of injustice about the recent popes sprucing up San Saba—adding marble furniture to the chancel, building shrines to a handful of lesser-known saints— while Santa Prisca gradually saw its population of the dead surpass its living. Who knew how popes picked their projects.

"So where'd they get *their* saints?" Mino said, his head resting on the open door frame.

The woman had turned the corner and vanished. "Was I speaking aloud?"

"San Saba. They have to get their bones from somewhere too."

Felix would've left this door open all day if he were in charge. Imagine having such an entrance to the crypt, with sun and sparrow song and river stench tickling through the seated bodies. He'd keep one eye on his charges and one eye toward the day, and wouldn't that be the best kind of reminder of God—the lively chirrup of a swift on a draft, and the gassy funk of Bernardo's bile exiting his body.

Mino knocked on the open door. "You think they're sneaking over and nabbing ours?"

"You can't be sure of anything until your dead arse is on a stone seat."

BERNARDO'S HEAD was lolling at an ever-increasing angle, and a sore had opened up on his forearm that suggested the presence of some foreign nibbler; Felix washed it with vinegar to prevent any larvae and hoped there weren't rats. There was no greater hindrance to a peaceful putridarium than rats. Oh, Johanna, what romps she'd have here! Serving nobly the cause of pest removal, earning the affection of the brothers, soothing their loneliness with her throaty purr and silken ears. Love is an exchange, he thought, where neither partner would mind if the other provided nothing at all. He took a penknife to his friend's fingernails.

With Bernardo's abundant corpse, the crypt had taken on a new scent, a rankness deeper than the usual smell of bad fruit and manure. Descending the steps each day, Felix swam into the overpowering sweetness—he'd wrap a kitchen rag around his nose and mouth, but after half an hour its dark and pungent undertones became less repulsive, and he found himself actively sniffing to see if he could determine its component elements. The shit smell had an obvious locus, but that gagging tang, as if a rat had been boiled in cabbage, did that come from the fermenting sweat on Bernardo's feet, or from his sweet heart's walls exploding into his spleen? [You don't remember, but when you were a child, five years old, you fell in the pig slops; when your father found you he yelled for your mother, and when your mother came she gagged, and though it was your sister who dragged you out, cementing your love, I was the shape standing between your filth and the ravenous hogs. I preserved you to be a preserver. Less than a mile from where you now sit in your Roman crypt is another five-year-old, a ball-cheeked perfumed girl, Marozia, who never fell in slops and instead will grow up to rule Rome, progenitor of six popes, armed—like the great Caterina Sforza—with both sex and sword; the bodies she'll study are the bodies she kills. They'll say she has the stink of whore on her, but I'll say that's a slur, not a smell.]

Though it felt disloyal to his friend, he was grateful for the more advanced bodies, the ones whose juices had dried up and whose vestments smelled only of the lavender sachets Felix packed in their armpits. Brother Timothy's flesh was down to patches, and Felix looked forward to when his bones would be bare and he could whisk away his robe, gather what remained of the man, and carry him like a babe to the next room over, where open sarcophagi waited to be filled. He'd heard of monasteries that turned dry bones into fanciful tableaux, and given a more liberal-minded abbot, he would've liked to try his hand at this. Imagine fashioning a little vegetable garden with sprouting leg bones, pelvis lettuces, finger bones arranged in rosettes, the shoulder blade a crow come to inspect the produce. And of course it would be God's garden, that would be the theme.

He should be paying closer mind to Bernardo's concaving chest, finding some parallel for the way God pulls the faith out of us despite our efforts at secrecy, but secrecy made him think of Mino, who kept awkwardly trying to spill whatever upset was in his past. He could've told the boy about his own youth, when he too believed that anything concealed was lost. Thoughts couldn't remain real in silence. His sister's hair that day as she dangled on the alder branch: like pale seaweed, lifted from some grotto to float in a tree. He'd asked if she thought Tomaso handsome (he didn't say *painfully so*).

"Of course." She swung her legs. "I wouldn't have agreed if he were a leper."

"But you never touch." He stood at the base of the tree, rubbing the back of his hand along its bark. It was dry in the fertile season, and dry still in drought.

"He's not a doll."

"You'll have to, one day."

"I might go to Farfa."

"Not if you're a girl."

"You doubt?" She yanked up the hem of her dress, exposing a dusty snarl of undergarments. The abbey sat one hill over from Fara in Sabina and was as big as the town, though cleaner, and men from all over came to out-holy each other. If Felix and his sister threw food at dinner, or stole flour and wax to make toy ponies, their father said he'd send them there, which was like threatening to send mongrels to a palace.

"If I went," he said, "I'd be chief in a year."

"They don't have chiefs, and you wouldn't leave Johanna."

"She's my very own child."

"Virgin cat birth."

"You don't love Tomaso?"

She threw a handful of shredded leaves at him, which floated up on their own breezes. "Every time you two come back from swimming, your face looks strawberry-stained."

"It's not fair to him if you'll marry and not touch him your whole life long."

"Splashing around without your pants, that's a boy thing, right? Is he so different down there from you? Has he a golden penis?"

The stick he threw at her was too sharp; it cut a line in her cheek.

Later his sister said nothing to defend or damn him, and so he was sent outside while the others ate supper, alone in the cold night without a coat, listening for the howls of the hounds that would surely come to drag him to hell. His sister was the best person he knew, and *she* didn't love. So then this surging heat inside him was unnatural— when Jesus spoke of it, he must've meant something else. Fraternal, familial, spiritual. Love incorporeal. A chicken ran at him in the dark, loosed from its pen, and Felix shrieked.

On their shared mattress that night, his sister whispered, "You can have him."

"I don't want anyone but you."

"We all want Jesus."

"Not Auntie Mary." Auntie Mary was a witch, if not yet confirmed.

"Not Johanna."

"Not the alder."

"Not the hen in my belly."

"Though now it's in your belly," he said, "mustn't it share your religion?"

"Linsey Hen, the first Christian chicken."

When they fell asleep, his fingers were stuck in the ends of her hair.

Bernardo sighed, one of his adorable gassy exhalations. He loved Felix's stories. Someday, Felix worried, he'd forget when he was speaking aloud and when he wasn't, and wouldn't he put his foot in a hole then. He finished shearing the pinky nail on the corpse's left hand. "All trim and true," he said, brushing the filings into his palm and tossing them into the hole of the neighboring seat. He was still humming his sister's bedtime ditty when Brother Sixtus called from the top of the stairs to say Brother Benedictus hadn't woken up from his post-nones nap, and it looked like he was going to have to make some room down there.

A MONK'S funeral was a lonely affair. God was present, of course, and the brothers themselves, somber in brown wool. The body was laid out in a pine coffin, and the family was informed and invited, though no one came. A cluster of men would sing a hymn, and Father Peter would give the mass, followed by a sentence tailored to the actual dead body rather than the theoretical ascending soul. On this wet Sunday, with an anonymous widow snuffling in the back, the Father said, "Heaven watch for Benedictus, who walked slow but ate heartily, and never once admired himself."

Sixtus turned to Felix with a look of some doubt.

"I believe he means," Felix whispered, "that he didn't comb his hair."

"Ah," Sixtus said, satisfied. "Though once after a Christmas bath

I saw him crimping his toes playfully, as if he thought them more nimble than the average man's."

"You think he had foot pride?"

"I wouldn't speak against a dead man."

The widow began to wail.

"Let's take him out already," Sixtus said, "before he begins to stink up the box."

The monastery only had one coffin, a display coffin as it were, because of course the men weren't buried. But the abbot believed these open masses helped convince the public that the monks were ordinary men, not witches or mystics, and that their bodies would dust-to-dust just like theirs.

Six men lifted the coffin on their shoulders and carried it through the side door to the cloisters while the woman subsided into sniffs. Once it was dark and the parishioners were safely home with their roast lambs and impure thoughts, the same monks would come back to the open courtyard and pry Benedictus out of his box, sneaking him diagonally down the stairs like a battering ram and propping him up on the next available seat.

But first Felix had to dispose of Brother Timothy.

"It's time for your great transition," he said in what he hoped was a soothing tone. These were the climaxes in a job that revolved around tiny changes. He should be given at least a day to really contemplate what it meant to hurl Timothy's bones into an old tub and set up in his stead a new man, with all his muscle and meat and nails and lashes. He was afraid he wouldn't pay attention to the right thing, that the following morning he'd kick himself for not running a finger along the spongy circles of Timothy's eye sockets, or pressing his ear to his sternum to listen for a residual heart. He regretted not attending more to Timothy, who'd died before Felix's tenure, was an inherited corpse, and didn't have the personality of the others. Or was mortality not about memory at all, but about the quick *whoosh* of a life as it passes from the known to the divine? And if so, what business did Felix have to contemplate their bodies, he who had lived such a paltry life, who was so close to the grave himself? Shouldn't they be tossed *tout de suite* into a dark hole as a reminder that the body is no firmer than a flame (and less pleasantly scented once snuffed)? Was he breaking God's law to cradle Timothy's bones so sweetly in his arms? Was he committing the sin of *lingering*? [Take a deep breath, count to four. Exhale. The sin, if anything, is hoarding. You're getting a better sense of my kingdom than any of your brothers, who're half as prepared and twice as afraid. Invite them down. Proselytize a little more for the flesh. The young one, Mino—stick his hand in the septic wound on a dead man's side. Ask him whether he still doubts.]

The room with the sarcophagi was dark. Felix rubbed his forearms along the tops until he found the open one, and clattered Timothy in as gently as possible.

"I did not know you, but I loved you," he said. "May the Lord embrace and shield you as he did on the day of your birth. May your time in my attendance not have any bearing on your worthiness to sit by the angels."

He put a hand down to pat the pile one last time and felt the smallest jolt, as if a breath had flickered from the bones to his living thumb. A sacred touch sent from God to his servant, like a mother spelling *This is what it means* with her finger on the back of her sleepy child—but then the cockroach scrabbled over the side and hit the floor with a dry rustle. Felix jerked his hand out of the tomb and instinctively pressed it against his back, last night's wounds from the whip. He didn't receive messages; he was a worm, not a saint.

IN THE room behind the room where the old bones were dumped gracelessly after their sinews dissolved, the floor was a foot and a half lower than the floors elsewhere. Old monks were kept away, because they had a tendency to swear the drop wasn't significant and then crumple like daisies when they misjudged it. But Sixtus liked to visit this room, and he and Felix would shout across the distance until someone thumped a staff above, the sign that worshippers were present and were becoming disturbed. The glory of the room was the floor, a careful puzzle of tiny square tiles that spelled out black borders, curving blue tails, bright gold horns of plenty with grapes scattering like marbles, the head of a sun god in *opus sectile*. A big fish swallowed a smaller fish in each corner. Determining any sort of storyline was futile, other than that the world was messy and filled with surprising things.

This lowest part of the church had been a house, this just a regular floor that regular people crossed. When some ancient person had become fired with religious zeal, it was converted into a Mithraeum, where, from what Felix understood, believers didn't pray so much as feast—benches lined the walls on either side, and Sixtus told him the cultsmen would feed the slaughtered sacrifice to the immobile stone idol in the niche and then stretch out and devour a picnic they'd brought. It all seemed very relaxed. This particular graven Mithras was a noble fellow, his cape sweeping out to his right as he straddled a bull—or knelt on the bull's neck, or kicked the bull in the stomach; parts of the statue had been knocked off when the Christians came. Sixtus liked to sit on the benches and sketch the god. He wanted to add human figures to the margins of his psalter, but he had little experience and no willing models. He'd drawn Felix once and made him look like a bulbous carrot.

"You know St. Prisca was Mithraic," Sixtus said, one eye squinched shut.

Felix was circling the room with a broom—a rag attached to straw tied onto a stick—pushing dust around the tile spirals. "I thought she was Christian. Was this her house?"

"They forbade her from singing hymns, whipped her when she spoke of Jesus."

"Wasn't it her own father killed her? Rejected her love, banished her to the Alps or something?"

"Isn't that Ethelberta of the famously nabbed finger?"

Felix frowned at what appeared to be tiny pellets of rodent dung caught in his dust pile. "In seven hundred years, will our god seem silly?"

Sixtus put down his bit of charcoal. "What makes you call him our god?"

He'd have to issue himself double lashes that night for having devised a question so heretical. Imagine, another man with another broom in the 1500s, dusting out the rubble from this basilica, on which his kind had built a golden shrine to a god with the head of a horse.

Sixtus rolled up his paper and stuck his charcoal behind his ear. As they passed his seated friends in the putridarium, Felix raised a hand in greeting. The new man, Benedictus, looked ghoulishly pert. He'd have to get a hood to pull over those eyes, which hadn't yet begun retracting. The pop and seepage—this was the musical accompaniment Felix had come to enjoy best.

Upstairs the sanctuary smelled absent of life. In Sixtus's cell, the psalter was open to his latest doodlings: two giraffes wading in a lake.

Felix made a noise of appreciation. "Very whimsical," he said.

"Whimsical? You think there's too much shrubbery?"

"Shrubbery?"

"It's Adam and Eve. In the garden, of course."

Felix bent closer to the page. "Ah! And this? Yes. Mmm."

"It's not very like, is it. Look, this is what I wanted to show you." He handed over a piece of parchment, but the script was too elaborate for Felix to parse. "A contract from the family that ordered the work done. We give them a beautifully written psalter, no mistakes, no marginalia too obscene, and an indulgence—"

"For what sin?"

"—and they give us seven pounds."

Felix had drifted toward the window. A cobweb in the corner had trapped a gnat. If he brought a jar of spiders down to the crypt to suck the juices from his men, he could dispense with the toilets altogether. They'd become dry little gnat-sacks and could be tossed on the road outside to blow away, like maple seeds. And then no one need contemplate anything.

"You don't find that troublesome?" Sixtus said.

"The amount? Seven pounds. So it's a year's wages; script work is expensive. You're spending hours on it, and—" He gestured to the scene of giraffes. "Probably more hours."

"What do you think the abbot's doing with seven pounds?"

"How else do monasteries survive?"

"Where's our roast beef, then?"

Felix poked a finger into the web, so gentle, and the wobble sent the spider to its far edge. "You ought to ask Mino to pose for you," he said. "He'd be a fine Adam—would have neither bull nor cape— and he could use a lesson or two in standing still."

"Secluding yourself downstairs, old friend, isn't an excuse for remaining naïve."

Felix crossed to the door, hoping to catch the first scent of supper being cooked; he couldn't have stomached roast beef anyway, its fleshiness and man's fleshiness so alike. "I think I know most of the things you know," he said, "but I'd rather wonder about them than convince myself they're fact."

AN UNEXPECTED December thaw warmed the Tiber, which released a heady scent and let its winter-tossed bodies bob up again, nudging the shore like calves at the teat. No one in Rome had the job of pulling the suicides in, so they ballooned about until their gases dispersed and then slipped back to the bottom of the river, where they became nests for fishes.

Mino wasn't one for water-gazing. "The living people are *that* way," he said. He'd wanted to hold the purse too, but Felix knew better. The vendors with the *frittelle* were a sore temptation; Mino stood at the edge of their cart with more patience than he'd ever shown in church. It could seem cruel to keep a youth in a monastery. What had saved Felix was not necessarily what would save this boy.

Tomaso and his sister would by now be long married. They'd have the children married people have. The discord and the brushing feet in bed. They would kiss, or not kiss. In any case, they were no longer loose particles like Felix—unattached, orbiting, buffeted.

"You're attached to our Lord Jesus Christ," Mino said.

Felix blinked. The boy was at his side, fried dough in hand. "How'd you get that?"

"He said I was a poor boy for being shut away like that."

"Obviously you're *not* shut away."

"I said I'd escaped. They'd be hunting me."

"You'll make yourself sick." He took the boy by the arm and pulled him through the crowd of shoppers, most there just to salivate. Toothless, with holes in their clothes, the citizens of Rome looked like victims of an invisible plague. At least the lepers had a glow to their spotted cheeks. Felix had the purse tied to a belt inside his robes. Monks were not spared pickpocketing; the holier you looked, in fact, the more likely you were to have coins. This is what had happened to the rule of poverty since St. Benedict.

"Bones!" Mino cried, and there was the fine-jawed vendor from before, his wares laid out like a skeleton had taken himself apart for inspection, puffs of feathered flies between. He pulled his hat down low so he could look out more coyly.

"I've been thinking of you," the man said. "I found a little something."

"You know Brother Felix?" Mino said. "We have strict orders not to spend more than a relic is worth, and Felix can tell the real bones from the false because he sits with them day in day out, and we can also spot a saint from a non-saint just by putting our hands over something—it's a God-given power, like finding water with a stick."

The man held out his hand, and Mino looked at Felix for assent before extending his own.

"Mino," he said.

"Brother Mino," the man replied. "I can tell I'm dealing with a man who cannot be fooled. Would you care to see a little item I've been saving for you?"

The side of Mino's mouth was still sticky from sugar, but he raised his chin like a professional appraiser.

The man pulled from a box a smaller box, and inside this was a bent piece of metal. Mino took it as his first challenge.

"No," he said proudly. "Not human flesh or bone."

"Good eye. What else might it be?"

With one ear tuned to their conversation, Felix scanned the rest of the man's wares for the church's lost items. Most of these were probably chicken bones, burned and studded with tiny holes to signify age. But when the Church began selling forgiveness, its parishioners learned to put a price on God. When he was out in the world like this, or really around other people at all, Felix would look at things—obvious things: the river, the gulls—and think, *This is good* and *this is good*. But then the thick-haired vendor would wink and he'd think, *This is bad* or *Is this bad because I've been taught that pleasure is wrong?* The abbot was good because he'd gotten his placement from the pope; the abbot was bad because a woman some nights came to visit him and her hyena noises kept the brothers up. Being alone was good because it kept him safe from evil, and he felt closer to God in silence and peace; being alone was bad because the evil was within him, and Jesus had intended us to walk among our fellow men with charity and love. If Mino ever asked for his advice, he'd have to confess that sometimes God lit the way, and sometimes he just laughed.

"It's an apostle's hook!" Mino bounced from foot to foot.

The vendor had taken off his hat and was ruffling his hair with the confidence of a likely sale. "Not an apostle, a martyr," he said.

Felix bent over the little box and its iron tenant. "Whose?"

"The provenance isn't certain, but it's from a collection of items seized by the Roman guard from the properties of condemned Christians, roughly a hundred and fifty years after the death of our Lord."

"Seems like just a fishing hook. Maybe it slipped from one of your flies."

"There are lineages among the early martyrs, St. Peter of Rome, and our Lord's disciples."

"He said Jesus could've fished with it!" Mino had his hand on his throat in disbelief.

"I can't claim that, of course, but there's the smallest chance—"

"Seems more likely some farmer smithied himself a bunch of hooks, and then lost one."

"But tell him which properties!"

"You'd brush aside even the slimmest chance that the hook hails from Jerusalem?"

"Is it responsible for any miracles?" Felix asked.

"It's from the farms to the east!" Mino was getting desperate.

The vendor snugged his hat back on, prepared for a longer battle. "The collection comes from the handful of farms along the few miles east of town on Via Appia, by the catacombs in the Vallis Marmorea. Including the former homes of Hierax, host of St. Justin the Philosopher, and the child martyr Prisca."

"*Prisca!*"

"You're saying there's a small chance this hook belonged to our church's patron, and a smaller chance she got it direct from Jesus."

"I'm not a mathematician. I can't calculate odds."

"It's true, Brother Felix, I have a sense," Mino said. "He let me touch it before he told me what it was, and as soon as I did, I thought, *This belongs to us*, I promise I did. We have to bring it back, because it's hers."

Felix rested an arm on the boy's shoulder. It hummed with excitement. "You don't think it'll get stolen like all the rest?"

"I'll watch it day and night, I promise. I'll carry the shovel with me, and if anyone tries to—" He swung his arms. "It's *hers*. I know."

"Have you even asked this gentleman for the price?"

Mino hit away his own tears with an open palm. The wind was beginning to pick up, threatening a storm. Felix couldn't decide if he preferred the silky, placid Tiber or this one, riled into whitecaps. He moved his hand to the boy's neck and said, "Come along. It'll be getting on to supper time, and Vitalis killed a rabbit."

The vendor stood like a vulture over his box. "I'll be here next week," he called after them. What tricks had the dark-browed man used on Mino to so positively convince him? [There's the face, to which you both fell victim. But there's also a consanguinity among children. It doesn't surprise me at all that a boy could touch a piece of iron and feel the aching flesh of a long-dead girl. They're close to the fountainhead of innocence; they remember things. Time has not yet begun *to seem* to march.]

The hill to the church took longer to climb because Mino kept stopping to wipe his face and pout into the shrubs, but by the time they returned home, the bells for vespers were ringing, and Felix slipped them seamlessly into the evening chants. By supper, Mino was telling Sixtus a joke he'd made up about a dog who wore a hat and rode a horse to mass.

IN THE early morning, between lauds and prime, Santa Prisca was so quiet you could hear a candle burn. Below the nave, in the musty depths that were once the ballrooms of the fifth century, the terraces of the third century, the vineyards of the first, Benedictus's dead mouth blubbered. At this week's meeting of the Brothers for Monastic Temperance—a club composed, as it so happened, of all the brothers—Felix had given his necrological report, a rough accounting of the weather down there. Vitalis asked if there were some way to keep the odor from traveling up the stairs. Felix asked him what he thought the odor meant. Leo said maybe God made the dead stink to give form to our sin, and Henry argued it was to protect the living, so we wouldn't get so close as to catch their diseases, and the abbot said how about a solid door over the hole to the crypt.

Could they but visit, what marvels they'd find: cycles of decay invisible to most, a handful of bodies freed from the dark erasure of the earth and coffin to live again, creating sounds and yes, ripe smells with caprice and personality. A fly had planted its eggs in Bernardo's cheeks, and the sprouting larvae fed in delicate lines from his eyes to his chin, so he appeared to be always weeping. A collapsed right hip had him tilted enviously toward Benedictus, who was still erect, the general of the assembly, the liquids behind his lips bubbling with indecision. Proud purple lips. The parishioners would call this devilry, but the Devil had no part in the creation of Man; we slip away on the same celestial boat we were sailed in on. What has the Devil done to match that? [I have brought you knowledge, and choice, and emotional range. Unlike your Lord, who sits and does not move, I am your kindred venturer, I *assay*, I too prize courage over dull omnipotence. I search you out and treat with you and stroke your fine-haired arms; I send no minion. Not once have I forced your hand—I ask what is it you want, then rationalize it. The fall you blame me for? That *felix culpa*, that fortunate fall? Oh elderly son, who spent a lifetime sitting on his brimming love, it was named after *you*.]

No, the Devil led him to wrong wanting, and he'd been found out. Through the gaps in that summer, he still saw his father's arm raised, his mother with her hands stretched out, his sister in the corner, scrubbing the inside of a bowl with a cloth and sand, around and around and around. Then it was his father at his mother, then his sister at his father, and Johanna, who'd tiptoed in to see if the fuss meant supper, fled—flat-backed, tail down. His parents were mild people, farmers.

He wasn't the first boy to love a boy—some men in the cities even almost-wed, with vows of adoration before a priest, like Sts. Serge and Bacchus—and he certainly wasn't the first to get caught with the beloved in a secret touch, so why the fury? [It wasn't you, it was the drought. It was the pinch. It was the future fear. It was the nausea of change. It was the not knowing. It was the dry wheat and the rumor of plague and the black mark on the hen's egg found that morning. This is the cycle, this is how the lungs of civilization expand and contract. You are welcome; you are not welcome; you are welcome.]

"They want you out," his sister had said, quiet in bed. And then, as if prepared for defiance, "Do you think he might love you back?"

The dark hid how his face mottled. His sister would never fail him, cheat him, befuddle him, use him; his dearest friends would never lie to him, beat him, outgrow him, abandon him. Sacred love is a rosebud floating in consistency. Romantic affection is a warm cave with a wolf inside.

But Lord above, Tomaso was a beautiful boy, the way his dark eyes would affix on you—he'd be thinking about something else, but he left his eyes behind, left his eyes on Felix's face, and it was like nothing harmful could ever happen while those dark eyes stayed steady. Felix allowed himself to imagine leaving, and his insides began to rupture, a line searing down the middle from his throat to his knees—it stopped at his knees—and his face twisted up like a rag. His mouth opened, his eyes shut. He couldn't make the sound come out. All the blood was in his face, though it came out as tears, and he couldn't make a single sound. His lungs stopped. Now his sister's arms were properly around him, and everything melted and he was gasping, his sobs coming as high-pitched chokes between the long spells of paralysis. He was newly aware of his organs; he could feel them breaking.

"Shh," she said. "Shh. After a while, you won't feel it so. I promise."

He would've been good. He would never have done anything that wasn't good; he would've shrunk over the years into a hard kernel of pain. The hurt felt so wickedly good, he wanted never to be sane again.

"Oh, my brother," she said. "How did he answer you?"

He could go to Farfa, just on the other hilltop, and between prayers could stand on the rampart with his hand over his eyes and watch for the specks of his family. They'd teach him to read and write, to handcuff his demons and bury them in an iron box. He dragged the side of his hand across his upper lip, wiping away the sweat and snot and salt. He wanted to wipe his whole face away.

"He didn't answer," he said. "I didn't tell him."

"But how did Father—"

"His father saw. I don't know. I just said one day he'd be my brother."

"But you kissed him."

"His cheek," Felix said. "Where any brother would. It was just for too long."

She was quiet for a few moments, rubbing his back—circle, circle, pat. "But what did you wish for?"

"*Nothing*." The first he'd lied to his sister since he told her fishes grew legs at night and strolled. He wanted Tomaso to take his face in one hand and pull it back to center. To meet his lips with his lips. It needn't have been out of love, just to see. The way children kiss behind hedges, just to see. He wanted to linger in that vale of touch for as long as it took him to feel human. He wanted Tomaso to grab his hand and pull him into the poplars and tell him every racing thought and ask him all the questions and look at him with real wonder, like he was a treasure, like he was the only one of his kind, and promise he wouldn't for all the castles in Christendom unglue himself from Felix's side. That he'd keep him in his heart the way he kept Jesus. Rooted.

He began to hit his own face.

"Stop it." She pulled his arm away.

His tears were made of sulfur. He yanked his hand back and slapped himself so hard his sight went briefly starry. The pain was on the outside now, and felt so much better there. So much clearer. He hit himself again.

Now his sister was crying. "I'd give him to you if I could. I'd give him to you."

THE PARADISE

[165]

THE POND EXPLODED. A barn-high geyser, and the brown floppy bodies of boys. Prisca was crouched behind a yearling olive, honing her lurk. Her brother looked absurd, that big ugly mouth, but the others had nothing misplaced about them; the same basic shapes—four limbs and the wobbly bits—but fresh with mystery. They didn't pinch her bottom or dunk her face in the milk pail or tattle. They didn't pay her any mind at all.

The slave boy tangled his arms around her brother, and the other one stood on the edge, his toes hidden in the weeds, and she held her breath to watch him stretch and dive, the plume falling over the wrestling boys like a veil. Their shouts were no different from her shouts. Like the world was hitting their chests in a steady beat, expelling joy in bursts.

She let out a high whistle. The boys didn't look. She gave a series of grunts that turned into a cackle, like a wild dog. No one noticed. The grasses were burnt golden with summer, and she was just an old stone, chucked from the fields—who'd want such a thing. She looked down at her stomach, what used to be such a firm big pooch, a drum, now wasting into a waist. She dug her thumbs into her skin to find her bones. A fly was flipping around her head, whizzing in at her ear, across her lashes. She snorted like a horse, tossed her hair. Opened her mouth wide to swallow it. This always scared them away. She lifted a foot to scratch, balancing in her squat on one shaky heel. Her feet seemed bigger now than the rest of her, or that's where all her old sturdiness went, gravity dragging it down to her ankles. She used to sprint across the farm, dodging cow pies like a rabbit, jumping rabbits like a hound, chasing hounds like a man, but now she couldn't open a door in the house without hitting herself in the face. She tripped when nothing was in her way. Her elbows were sharp as knives.

She brayed again, but the boys were too deep in their game, so she scooped the pebbles around her into a pile and wrapped them in hazel leaves and tied the leaves closed with strands of dried grass she braided and knotted and when the boys were out and collapsed on the bank, their bodies probably tickling with the water drying off their skin, Prisca tossed her rockball from one hand to the other, wondering which to aim for. Not her brother Servius, the snitch. Not the slave, who'd show his bruises to the overseer. The sun was low, spread out over the fields like a fire. The third boy looked like the bronze Dionysus that stood welcoming by the door. His dark hair in a flop across his forehead, his round brown shoulders, the twist of his hips. He had one arm raised, the other scratching in his armpit, feeling for the growing hairs there.

With a battle cry, she stood and hurled the rockball at the lounging boys. They leapt and scattered and the ball smashed into the grass, but the pebbles burst out of their binding, and one skipped up and with its sharp edge grazed the calf of her brother's friend. Crispus glanced down at the white line, and before her eyes it turned rosy and then keen red and then the red began to drip, and he yelled, "Damn Prisca is a eunuch!"

She fell to the ground again behind the olive. A eunuch is what she was. A body without a sword. Yet did she not know how to draw blood? [Preach, baby warrior! God will tell you violence is devilry, but who slaughtered his own son?]

THE WHEAT was drying out. The tufts on top were shriveling. The men talked about drought in low tones, while the women cooked and spun and invented games for the children and dragged buckets from the river. The air in the house tasted bitter, and Prisca got some strange nourishment from it. She liked her courage to be pushing right up against a wall.

Her mother spent more time by the shrine in her temple, and Prisca sat behind her to braid her thick brown motherly hair. Surely invisible beings had better things to do, like helping cows have babies and giving new spears to men in battle whose spears have snapped. Her mother murmured to Isis Fortuna, and Prisca lay down on the cool marble and ran the ends of her hair across her mouth, tasting for summer. The ceiling was vaulted white stone, and just past it was all the riot of reality, and nothing ever quite explained why the one should have to be blocked by the other. Morning after morning they came here, and day after day the gods sat on high, arms crossed, dribbling a strand of saliva down, just to see how far it could go, and sucking it back up again. *Rain?* they said. *Who said you deserved rain?*

By the end of summer, people were glancing sideways at one another, trying to figure out whose bad behavior was jinxing the weather. She heard the boys whispering jokes behind the stables. Their blasphemy was too boring to tattle on. Neighbor farmers stopped by to trade rain cures, tweak this prayer or that, but this was no better than tossing bones in the air and hoping they'd all land on end. The rituals weren't working, or else the rabble of Rome—two miles to the west—was to blame. Her mother said fear was an opportunity for faith. A few itinerant men from the colonies were crossing the countryside, and one had news of a deity that her father took a shine to—he'd always been suspicious of Mithras, the soldiers' god, the bull-slayer. The man was asked to stay.

He was her father's age, with a short streaked beard and ears that folded down from on top, like he was a giant listening for tiny people below. Eyes so dark they'd lost their pupils, which made him seem very kind and willing to hear whatever stories one wanted to share. Prisca had no shortage of stories. He'd sit, droopy ears flopped her way, rubbing the fringe of his cushion until her father shouted at her to leave the teacher alone. The man would give a slow wink and follow her father back into a dark room of the house where little girls were not to go. He knew by now about Crispus, and she thought he approved.

"When I breathe, my chest gets sharp and hot, like I've vomited all inside my heart."

"That sounds very truthful," he said.

HER MOTHER'S bath had a bright sheet of hammered bronze in which bodies looked loose and liquid. Prisca stood before it, flexing her arm this way and that, pointing her toe so her leg would take on a shape other than columnar. If she twisted her torso and kept her leg straight out, a dip occurred between the plump of her thigh and the slight swell of her calf—this underside of her knee, at such an angle, seemed to her supremely feminine. She hadn't bathed that day; they were saving the house water for cooking. Her skin was pale around her middle, brownish along her arms and legs, the tan making the hairs there golden. Freckles across her shoulders, a constellation of moles around her chest, one here, one there, each a soft bump to be fiddled with in boredom. Her hip bones jutted out like rock promontories—she skimmed her thumb across them—but they didn't lend her hips any of the roundness that older women had.

She didn't know what they put over their pelvis bones to hide them, to make them seem like places a man or child would want to rest his head. She saw lots of her own bones in the mirror. If a woman were a sponge, and were thoroughly wrung out, you'd get Prisca. Her mother said she'd fill out, so she kept eating—ate ravenously—and waited for the lamb and artichokes and thick slices of bread to pad the empty spaces around her joints. She was only twelve and had plenty of time.

HER MOTHER had the stomachaches—Prisca imagined this happened when the dinner snails weren't dead yet; they slid down the throat with no trouble, for they were afraid and being very still, but when they got to the round room of the belly and sat for a moment, they began inching out again, exploring the puckered pink walls and feeling around for their kin (*Snailus, is that you?*). So the house was quiet—ancient Anna was hovering over Mother with a washrag and Servius was riding and the spindle had snapped. She could hardly be expected to fix it in this heat. Prisca hid the pieces under a bench and wandered through the peristyle back to her father's study. His head lolled against the chair, and a book unrolled over his lap, rising and falling like a bob in the water. She climbed onto his table and picked across his pages, catlike, not rustling a sheet, and sat down among them to wait.

Her father's face up close: the pores on his cheeks dark with cut hairs. The hairs from his ears unmanaged, spronging. She had a strong desire to deflate his cheeks. From this angle, he had no neck, his chin pillowed on his chest. When she was smaller, she could crawl onto his lap without disturbing his sleep and bounce her ear softly against his belly, listening for her own echo. It made more sense that she'd come from his ample womb.

"Papa," she said, still crouched on the desk.

His face flinched. She tried to imagine the plans he was making with his new companion, the bearded man, to save the crops. She had never been a member of a club.

"Papa."

Below his stomach were gathered his fingers, swollen and knuckleless. They sometimes seemed to be tickling each other, like he was dreaming of picking blackberries. She was almost certain he loved her when she was younger and was nearly undifferentiated from her brother. He'd take them both to the coast to watch the ships skate in. But once she'd asked a girly thing, or had gotten tired too soon, and the trips had continued without her. Now her father said, "Ask your mother," even when he knew the answer.

"Papa." She threw a feather at his head. It lilted up and swung in tired arcs down to his knees, where it rested until a strong snort from him blew it off.

He had last been proud of her when she'd made a joke in Greek; she didn't tell him she'd learned it from her brother. Anna said men have their own world and it's half-formed, but to Prisca it seemed that was where things of consequence happened.

If she called any louder, he would wake and his face would fold into a frown and his eyes for a moment would blink too fast and then he would recognize her and flap his hands and say something like "no child of mine" and she'd be off the desk and out, papers scurrying behind her like leaves, his fat shape rising with the sigh that old people use to tell themselves it's not their fault they're tired.

So she climbed down on padded paws and let the tender balls of her feet carry her in hushes across the tile floor and out into the hot droning of the day. There was no one to wonder what she was thinking.

THE NIGHTS started to turn, and still no rain. The sacrifices had dried up like the streams. Prisca was in the kitchen with Anna, des-

perately bored, a fish in one hand and a knife in the other. The flesh
was splayed open, and beneath the glossy muscle were a hundred fine
bones, each of which could claw at her parents' throats if she didn't
catch them all. Looking inside a fish made you believe there was
surely water enough in this world. It had come from Ostia, by the
beach her father promised to take her to again. When Anna wasn't
looking, she draped the carcass over her hand and put a thumb
through the mouth and pretended to be a vengeful worm puppeteer.
When Anna was looking, she stopped and practiced her whistling.

"Get out," the cook finally said. "Go find a devil your own age."

Crispus was alone in the atrium, sitting by the pool, dry now. Her
mouth blew out a bird call, but he didn't stir. Head in hands, elbows
on knees. Toes fiddling in their sandals. He seemed to be working
out a math problem, or whatever boys thought about.

"Prisca," he said when she snuck up beside him—surprise, not
pleasure—and her heart did a jig around her chest.

"I have twenty-seven marbles now," she said, "and the skull of a
frog I found by the pond while I was practicing my jumps."

"Jumps don't need practice."

"I expect that's why mine are so good."

"Have you seen Servius?"

His feet were dark with sun and light with dust. She had so many
questions about how his body worked, what made it so superior,
why he had all the same features as her brother with none of the
grossness. She reached out and pinched his arm.

"Damn it, Prisca, you're hard to be nice to." He stood and spit.

"I'm not the one mooning in the courtyard, asking stupid questions,
like a lost dumb dog."

He sighed his older-person sigh, and she was left alone by the pool
with the dark spot of his saliva on the tiles glistening up at her like a
wink. She refrained from touching it. She wanted to dunk Crispus's

head in the pond and throw a dead fish at him—just her, just the two of them, doing boy things without any other boys. She looked for signs of this communion in her own parents' marriage, in vain.

"WE WENT through this with Sabazius."

"And that drought broke."

"Not till half the sheep had died and Anna lost her grandchild and you came back to Isis," her mother said to her father. "Your sense of causation is daft."

"It isn't about sense."

The dry air lifted their voices up to her windowsill. She was supposed to be sleeping; by midafternoon, no one in the house wanted to deal with her. Her mother carried a pile of linens in her arms. Anna had one of her headaches, so her mother would scrub them with dust— a dry wash. Her father was back from the fields, mulling an early harvest. The wheat wouldn't fatten, but half-ripe wheat would make their stomachs turn. The gods didn't make the daily choices.

"You don't think your fickleness stirs up trouble?"

"You've got your hands over your ears," he said. But her hands were holding up his laundry. "If you'd listen to him. It's not just life now, but life forever. The rain is a small thing."

"Tell your children. By winter we'll have nothing."

Prisca draped her arms over the sill and waited to feel some kiss of moisture from the sky. After thousands of years, people still couldn't figure out who pulled the strings. The mystery religions—Mithras, Cybele, Sabazius—held hands with the state's gods, but famine still came in cycles. War stalked both the believers and the barbarians. Nothing on this dull farm had ever changed. But no one asked her opinion.

"This is different," her father said, his voice low now. "Christ isn't one of the mysteries."

Their panic floated up to her and tasted salty. Her heart was used to going double time.

IN THE last dark before morning sometimes she'd wake with a start, imagining it was noon and the sun had died and no one had come to tell her the world was ending. The terror was cold and kept her from falling back asleep, even after she'd put her head out the window and seen how the dew was still on the grass and a single bird was whistling its thin dawn song. So she'd slip through the rooms, across the quiet atrium, past her parents' bedroom, where their grown-up shapes looked overlarge and strange, out to the pasture and down to the barn, her feet following the worn patches left by hooves. Foot, hoof, foot, hoof; she pranced.

But on this morning, only one body was in her parents' bed, and in the stables a man was kneeling amid the animals. She slipped around the door, casting the briefest shadow across the bent shape, like the low sun had blinked. He didn't stir. His mouth shifted, pattering, but she couldn't tell what sounds he was trying to make. She sat quietly in the corner by the hay trough and rolled a piece of straw between her fingers. She closed her eyes and let her lips begin to move. *Hear me, gods. Give us rain and let Crispus see me win a game of dice. Send Servius a plague of boils. Don't take away our food just as I'm so hungry for it.* When she opened her eyes, her father was looking at her.

"Were you speaking to Christ?" he asked.

"Yes," she said, because *yes* was always the easiest answer.

"You've heard our stories. He's a man, Prisca. He suffered the way we do, and understands."

"Understands what?"

"I can see in your eyes, it's the children among us who have the most faith."

She reached a hand up to her cheek. If there was a message about religion on her face, what did it say? And who was reading it? [Only the blind look for signs in others; don't pay attention to him. When he's dying from overdrink in twelve years, he'll be back to begging Mithras to save his liver. But those cirrhotic scars are *my* scratches.]

"He asks for love, not a bull's head on an altar. He doesn't tell us to hide in caves but to share his word—he doesn't believe in secrets. Don't you want your god without secrets?"

Love didn't sound very powerful to her. It was a loose kind of tie, easily said, easily broken. She wasn't used to his eyes on her; she worried she wasn't clean enough.

"Where's Christ now?" she asked.

"In heaven, with his father."

"They get along?"

In the growing morning through the warm smell of horse fur, she watched her father stride back to the house from his hiding place, locusts jumping from the grass, and wished she had any feeling at all other than self-pity. *Christ*, she said to herself, and imagined a boy's face, but better.

THE PIG, who'd been fattening for months on table scraps, had also been digging a secret tunnel under the western corner of the fence—or had he been gnawing away at the posts, the greedy porker—and on the day scheduled for his ritual throat-slitting, which came early because there were no more scraps, he broke free and went squealing down the hill toward Rome, his pink legs scattering. The guests peeled after him: the men ran to form a line by the road to head him off, and the children followed with toy arrows, gleeful at the prospect of battle. The women stayed behind and sharpened the knives.

Prisca had named him Suspiro, because he was a hog, *sus*, but also because he had a way of sighing when she'd hold a carrot out and then take it away before his snout could reach. "Wait!" she said. "He got out fair!"

Her mother carried a basket of wood to the outdoor altar, where garlands of parched laurel made the whole thing look innocent.

"Ceres let it happen! The gods don't allow accidents—that's what you say, isn't it? Mother!" Everyone walked faster than Prisca.

"Slow down or you'll get cramps," her mother said without turning around.

At the altar, they had a clear view down the hill; Suspiro was dashing in circles, feinting toward the road then making a run at the woods, where a crowd of boys chased him back with pinecones. She could see his tired ears bouncing. Her mother built the wooden pyre that would soon be set alight, and adjusted the spit higher so the meat wouldn't burn.

"And what if I say I won't eat him? No wonder Ceres won't send us rain, if we keep giving her pigs and goats and then eating them ourselves."

Her mother started back to the house with the empty basket under her arm. A streak of dirt from the wood made a bruise across her robe.

"Please stop them, Mother, I mean it."

"Did you shell the beans already?"

"You're not *listening*."

"I'll listen when you have something worthwhile to say."

Prisca kicked a spray of raw dust at her mother, red dust that floated up in a cloud and landed on nothing, and she ran past the house to where the men had begun their corral. Her brother had laid a hand on Suspiro's tail, but came away with only hairs.

She called for him to stop, and then lunged into his side, pushing him to the ground.

"Get off!" he yelled, jabbing her in the abdomen, which these days was always sore.

"Let him *go!*"

He stood and loped off to the other boys. She ran toward the pig, all paunched and sweating, its tongue shaking with every charge, and the men called at her to stop, she was messing up whatever plan they'd made, but she said "*You* stop!" and dove for Suspiro, who wasn't a pet at all—she wasn't sentimental—but another unwelcome almost-citizen on this stodgy old farm who no one listened to, no one minded, and in her dive she caught a porky hind leg, its hoof waxy and sharp, and Suspiro collapsed in a heap of manic relief, and the men ran for her, and when the pig was swaddled up and bound foot to foot, the crowd marched back up the hill victorious, leaving her muddy and empty-armed in the field. She'd lunged for the wrong thing.

At dinner, her father told stories from a war he'd never fought in, and the bearded man fasted, and the guests sucked meat from the bones with a zeal that felt filthy, and all the wine was poured for Ceres, may she ever listen out for her daughter and bring her home.

"WOULD YOU care for a trip to Rome?"

Prisca's fingers stopped; she let drop the spindle. The day had already gone on too long and she was beginning to think her adolescence was a circle from which, given her limited tools, she wouldn't be able to escape. The whole house was a tomb. "I have to finish this," she said.

The bearded man picked up the spindle and rewrapped the thread. "Your father thought you might enjoy a change of scenery. If you wouldn't like to come, I'll leave you in peace." Her father.

The stones on the road to town were large as platters, and Prisca hopped among them, a game of chance. *If I don't step on a single joint . . .* The trample of mules and the *trok-trok* of carriage wheels announced a caravan, carts laden with trunks and leather bags, and a litter carried by eight men, its gauzy curtains wafting like smoke. Prisca kept her head down and her eyes up, the way she did during prayer. The woman looked like Annia Regilla, who lived nearby and was killed when Prisca was seven for being too pretty and playing with boys—that's what her mother said. Half-reclined on pillows, she seemed to be reading a book; Prisca stared at the pursed mouth and the hand resting like a weak bug on the scroll and the dawn-yellow curls that were piled and braided and twisted until it would be impossible to find the beginning, unless you were the woman's slave and had wrapped the coils with your own tired fingers. She imagined sticking her dirty thumb deep into the mountain of hair. *Like silk*, she thought. *Like water.*

Soon the tenements grew taller, louder, the quarrels spilling into the street with clanging buckets and the scattered rush of unwatched children. The air here always smelled burnt, as if the meat had been left on too long. An urchin tumbled in front of them and froze. The dirty girl's tunic was too short; her legs bent inward like her knees were sharing a secret. She pushed Prisca's shoulder. "Tag," she said. "You chase."

The stone buildings swallowed up all the sunlight and left the narrow streets claustrophobic and chilly until you came to an open square, where it was spit back at you tenfold: the white heat, the glare that crawled up your chin and into your eyes from below, so there was no way to blink it out. Who wouldn't love the city's assault, as trusty as summer? [This summer? The one parching your harvest? *This* city? Children, in their daily buffeting, don't know of geomorphic time. There's nothing a human, upon seeing, won't change. Get up on your toes and spy the grove-topped mausoleum of Augustus, which will turn to ruins; a garden; a sanctuary for political refugees; a tavern; a ring for bullfights; a stage for fireworks; an auditorium with near-perfect acoustics where Toscanini conducted

Wagner in the middle of war; a prop for a pick-wielding Mussolini; ruins. Trusty? Only the seven hills, only the nickel core of Hades, only the helium of heaven.]

A boy standing in the door of a bakery held up two loaves. "Miss! With raisins!" She looked to her left; the crowd of people had grown thicker, and the bearded man was gone. Above her a banner snapped across the band of blue sky between the apartments. A man was yelling at a woman in the street, and she had one hand pressed against his neck, gently, pleading. Two men in thick robes walked past them with their arms around each other's waists; one was laughing, but the other stared at the couple and looked as if he might say something. Another man carrying a pile of scrolls caromed through the crowd; he had no time. Someone grabbed her wrist, and she fought free of it.

"Prisca," he said, and it was him—she wasn't lost, only slow. "You've got to keep hold of my arm."

They were nearing the forum, but her legs were tired and her throat was dry and she wanted to stop where the toys were sold. Through the street sounds—boxes being unloaded and money changing hands and speeches on war—she heard the high, thin thread of song. She squeezed the bearded man's arm.

"Slaves," he said. "Do you want to see?"

The market was behind the moneylender's: a widening where three streets converged, room enough for a coffle of men and women fresh from the empire's edges to be looped together with rope, sheened with oil, offered to passersby. They stood so close together; surely some of them had made friends.

It was a young woman who was singing, in the back of the phalanx, her head tilted up. She too could've been a ghost of Annia Regilla. The words—or were they just sounds—fell over themselves roundly, had soft endings, and an image sprung up of a hilly country, green valleys and colder than Rome, where young women dabbled their feet in streams and plucked heavy golden fruit from vines that climbed the hills like embroidery. The gods said this was all right, the cost of war. Even old Anna had come from somewhere.

A fully dressed man, with a belly that ballooned over his belt and shaky stick legs, called out prices and waved a pointer across the front line of glossy chests. "Fresh from the north," he said, "with the courage of wolves. Natural blond hair. Finest of their race."

Her own bearded man had approached one of the slaves at the corner of the formation and was trying out different tongues. The slave shook his head, said a few words. The bearded man shook his head.

"Interested?" The auctioneer sidled up to them, looking tired. His face was stuck with the hungry smile of the salesman. "A discount for two."

"They don't seem to be Gallic."

"Gallic, Moesian, they're subjects of the Empire now. Can tell you everything you want to know of the battles. Stoke a fire in the hearth, settle back for a tale. It'll impress your guests too."

"How do you communicate with them? I'd love to inquire—"

He held up his pointer, which Prisca now saw had a small hook on one end, like the rod used to guide elephants in parades. "Like to try?" And his laugh was also weary.

She reached for the bearded man's hand, but he wouldn't look at her, was scanning the faces of the slaves. The auctioneer turned to another who'd stopped to look. She heard the bearded man whisper "Khristos? Yehoshua?" But his words were as meaningless as anyone else's.

As they moved past the phalanx, Prisca looked back through the crowd of Romans, delicate Greeks, the Moors and their crowns, an Egyptian bargaining with a matron, but the strangeness of the slave's face was like the afterimage of a bonfire on the inside of her eyes. Sometimes, though it hardly made sense, to be a victim was to be good.

"YOU COME home empty-handed, it'll be your empty stomachs."

"I've never—"

"No pretending; you left me alone for four days once, went off with Tiberius and a half-dozen rods, and what was in your pouch when you came back?"

"Oh, that's—"

"Lavender."

Her father paused, one finger idly in his beard. "Well."

"Tied in bundles like you were a schoolgirl," her mother said. "Food isn't a game now."

Behind her father, Prisca squeezed his waist, eager to be down by the stream where the willows flopped their hair at just the right tilt to obscure all signs of their house, and the neighbors' houses, and the stretches of overplowed fields, and the white height of Rome. The river carried things away. When she was bluish or mad and the boys were hogging the pond, she'd shuffle through the high grass, put her feelings on the gray water, and watch them whirl off.

His strides were twice as long, so she skipped to keep up. A light mist the night before had left everyone in a good mood; she tried not to question her luck. She'd saved up a particularly good story about the rabbits in the barn and had almost spent it a few nights ago during a pause in the after-dinner banter, but she was glad she refrained— the visiting shipbuilder then spilled the contents of his stomach and there was much to-do over cleaning him up and pretending nothing had happened. The grasshoppers sprang up in shoots of surprise as her father kicked through the tall weeds, and she reached her hands out idly to grab at them. Locusts in summer, elm seeds in fall, snow-flakes in winter. Her hands were never big enough to catch what she wanted. Her father swung a bucket that held a net, and two rods sprouted from his other hand. The hooks were somewhere hidden in his robe, sharp enough for perch and eel, too sharp for girls.

The river was low and the bank was warm. She dug for worms in the dirt beneath the willow, her fingers wormy themselves, bur-rowing, pretending to be sightless in the loam. She closed her eyes. The coppery taste, the crunch of the tiny shells that had pulled themselves over from the ocean, walking on their shell feet, the springy give of the topsoil and the slick suck of clay beneath—all this was on her tongue. She dug her nails in deeper, tuned them to listen for the whispers of grubs.

"Hustle it! You want dinner or no?"

Her fingers paused. Began scrabbling with intent now. One worm, two worms, a fat black beetle she'd find tasty if she were a fish. She covered the soil again like she was readying it for bed. She wondered if the fish in Ostia were scared of such deep water. Surely the drought couldn't dry up the sea.

She knew how to do it, but she preferred to let her father teach her again each time. One stab through the center was good, but better was a second stab, perfect was the third, the worm snaked around its multiple impalements, the marriage of the iron and flesh so secure that a greedy fish couldn't sunder them. If it wanted the worm, by God, it would have the hook too.

They staked their rods in the sloping bank, and her father tended the lines while Prisca waded out with the net, the water knee-high, her tunic tucked up in her belt. Her bare feet nudged like turtles over the mucky bottom. Toes sifting through sand and sodden leaves, heels collapsing the fragile air-pocket homes of nematodes and river crabs. Her feet were the boldest parts of her. She swung the net idly through the stream, steering clear of the lines, but the glory was in the hook. A fish caught up in her little net was a lazy one, too dumb to know better, while the perch that fell for the well-threaded worm was a noble foe. Struggle was good; passivity was weak. Except when the opposite was true, as in the case, sometimes, of Jesus, and in the case, all the time, of women.

But she enjoyed being the net-wielder because she could splash in the water and feel the minnows kissing the fine hairs on her legs. If her father fell asleep, which he often did, she could squat down so slowly, just until the river wet her underclothes, and this was a fine and funny feeling. Prisca, princess of the Tiber, Caesar of the crabs, Christ of the fishhook. She slapped the net down on the water fast, spotting something yellow, but it was only sunlight. Her father was trying to slit grass to whistle through; he sounded wheezy. She tugged one of the lines to make the worm dance and clambered back to shore. In the grass she felt itchy and warm, and the sun drew the water from her legs so quickly they nearly puckered. A handful of gnats circled her face.

"Maybe all the fish are in school," she said.

Her father didn't laugh.

When one of the threads finally twitched, the pole leaning toward the stream as if to listen, she let out a yelp. Leaping up, she turned to her father, whose silence had matured into sleep. Old sleeping men, their time for adventure was up. She'd seen him pull the rod back slowly, working the line over the stones and past the reeds, easing up and giving play, but she was small-armed and didn't trust herself with such a distance between her hands and the prize. Instead she grasped the line at the top of the pole—the stretched sheepgut waxy and sharp against her palm—and followed it inch by inch toward the water, thrilled by the throbbing energy in the thin line. She pulled it teasingly toward her, let it slip forward. An invisible living beast was on the other end, linked to the life in her own human hand. She squeezed tight, wondering if she could feel its heart pulse.

Wading into the water this time felt dangerous. It could be a shark, something with terribly sharp teeth; if it was an eel—which would be a coup, quite tasty—she might not have the nerve to grab its slimy length. *Fishing isn't for girls* is what her brother said, a refrain he repeated in so many variations it had become a joke. *Food isn't for girls*, her mother would laugh. She slid her hands beneath the water, the line twangy, her fingers becoming vague and blurred the closer they got to the hook. Her hands were in Neptune's province now, and a nymph would have every right to tug her down, to drown her. She glanced back at the shore. The water wasn't deep; she was already in the middle of the river, and it was only up to her waist. Brave girls didn't shake quite so much. She began to pull now, impatient. Whoever was on the other end was also a brave girl. One hard jerk and Prisca nearly lost the line, slipping backward on a pile of muck-slick pebbles.

"Give it up, fish," she whispered.

Hand over hand, she yanked it in. She would *not* be fooled. She hadn't been given breakfast. The fishy shape grew clearer as it came closer: it wasn't the small carp she'd hoped for but the long and slithering eel she wasn't sure she could touch, its tail disappearing in the depths around her feet. She danced backward. It gave a mighty flick and wrenched at her underwater hands, and she tightened her grip and said again, mad now, "Give it up!" She jerked up on the line and pulled it sharply sideways, keeping the eel at a distance, trying to daze it as she hop-skipped across the squishy river bottom back to the bank. It flipped; she twisted. It tried to dive deep; she heaved it up with all the strength in her twelve-year-old muscles. Her hands now red and sore, the wax on the gut line peeling off. She was desperate to call out to her father; she burned with pride at her own silence. It was entirely predictable that he'd sleep through the din of such a mortal splashing fight.

She reached the bank and scrabbled up it with a single combined fist—two hands wrapped irrevocably around the line—and monkey-ish bare feet and a fat river eel like a tail flopping madly behind her, the hook just protruding from its frowning mouth. She pulled it inland, farther than necessary, to the base of the willow, where no amount of thrashing could carry it back to water again. She tied the line to the trunk and searched out a stone and held it over the eel's head with a painfully beating heart—her heart so loud she wondered whether *that* would wake her father. Its eye still wet and rolling. Alive, alive. She wasn't squeamish about death—she'd helped her mother count-less times catch chickens, but that was part of an ongoing system she'd merely wandered into. (May Suspiro rest in peace.) This was a live thing, living wildly in the wild, and she had stolen it and now was go-ing to take its living life away. *Killing isn't for girls.*

She knelt down and raised the rock above her head and closed her eyes and brought it down hard on the head of the eel, which—because she'd closed her eyes—had flopped to the side, so the stone landed a glancing blow on its neck, and a shoot of red fish blood spurted on her bare knee. She worked so hard at not screaming that her eyes watered and tears began to fall down her cheeks. The hook was more visible now, its iron rod like a second spine buried in the eel's throat. She kept her eyes open this time, and the rock hit where it should, just above the eye, the brain now sandwiched between earth and stone, its intricacies flattened. Blood covered the eye like a cataract.

Prisca was breathing hard, her heart still fast, her throat catching on every inhale. She wiped the tears off her face. She wouldn't let go of the rock, wet now with her own scared sweat and the fishy musk of river water and blood. Once the final flops had calmed, she leaned closer, gingerly brushing a finger against its scales. She moved to the mouth, pushing her pinky in to open it wider, to feel along the tiny teeth and the slick roof, not so different from her own. The hook felt horrible there. Wrapped in a dead worm, caught in a dead mouth, cold iron. She pulled it out barb first, easing it from the gills, the holes it left disappearing as the eel seemed to heal itself. The worm she scrubbed off on the grass. She shifted back a few inches, scrubbed it on new grass, and repeated this until most of the grass around her had a slight sheen of gore but the hook was clean, and as soon as it was clean, she recognized it as human again. A blacksmith had made it—maybe even her father; he used to dabble at the forge—and the imperfect prick of the barb called to mind the hands that hammered it. She felt a horror of guilt and a small, painful seed of inevitability. *What else could I have done?* [The child's first sin. Oh, baby, don't you work too hard to redeem it.]

She pocketed the hook, woke her father, refused that night to eat the eel.

A WEEK passed of leaner meals, too much sun and sitting, the shuttle in one hand, the other hand testing the edge of the fishhook, idly, destructively, its hidden fishy smell making her robes seem somehow dangerous. Servius and his tutor were practicing archery in the courtyard, and each time the arrow struck the hay bale, Prisca's intestines gave a shiver. She felt their coil, same as the goats' innards used for guessing the harvest. Her mother's voice made no sense. The linen they were weaving was stupid; no one needed more linen. The brown bird that used to duck in the window and prance on the wardrobe while they spun would not come inside now, but sat on a poplar branch with its head cocked, finding the whole scene distasteful.

Prisca's limbs were filled with ants. Anything would be better than this deadly quiet, her flat bottom stuck to a hot chair, her mother humming that atonal tune. She looked down at her tapping knees. Funny flesh. Her stomach after dinner a gurgle machine, her shins aching after she tried to catch up with her sprinting brother. The sour smell of her toes, the horsey smell of her hair, the way she could sometimes feel her heart beating in the strangest places, like in a vein on her calf or a coin-sized spot behind her ear or her left eyelid—*pulse, pulse*. Where was the heart stationed, and why did it migrate? Why couldn't she, like her brother, lift a sheep? [Because I moved your arm muscles into your head and your heart, so you might lift the world instead. A hundred and fifty pounds versus 1.3 x 10^{25} pounds.] She was unconvinced that the world held mysteries without explanation.

On the night before the first almond harvest, ignoring her mother's command ("Prisca, the dishes!"), she shadowed her father and the bearded man and several of their guests after supper, the men reeling stomach-heavy toward the stables. With company they dined well, but the meat wouldn't last through the fall. She stayed a hundred yards back, padding like a dog. The barn, its cracks shining gold from the lanterns, looked painted. Through a knothole in the boards, she saw them once again kneel, pray. When she pushed into the door, her small weight displacing all that wood chopped down by men, she saw their faces turn to her like sunflowers.

"I want to listen," she said, closing the door behind her.

The men exchanged glances, but her father didn't say no fast enough, so she sat down behind them, cross-legged, back as straight as an idle fishing pole.

"Go on," she said.

Her father shifted his knees beneath him—how uncomfortable he must be—and compulsively rearranged the folds of his tunic. *Jesus*, she thought, nodding. *Tell me about this man so great that all the nymphs and satyrs and lares and numina and Jupiter himself crumpled before his might.*

"Sit quiet while I tell you a story," her father said.

The details rang the bells of wonder already waiting in her head. A woman impregnated by a god. A young man's strength tested by the wicked. Souls brought back intact from Hades. A gloriously gory end. And then mortals with their heads bowed, asking for things, waiting for redemption. She was used to asking for things, for waiting indefinitely for nothing.

"This is not a god for the powerful," her father added, "but for the weak."

Prisca understood. This god turned the downtrodden into despots. Gave swords to those stuck behind the plow all day. Fed five thousand people with two fishes. Yes, listened first to the children, and then to the sparrows.

"Believers are being hunted. This is why we practice in darkness, you understand?" Her father's hands gestured toward her, with more intention—more attention—than Prisca was accustomed to. He wanted her to understand. All she had to do was listen. Say yes.

"I thought this god wasn't a secret."

"He asks us to be patient."

"Did he ask, or did you just decide?"

Her father's left eye gave a twitch. "Our faith *depends* now on silence. Tell me you understand."

Their faith, or their lives? [Even a child can point to a grown man's cowardice. Don't take your finger off his wound.]

He returned to sugar words, placing a hand on her sandal. "When we die, he blesses us with life that goes on forever. It's our gift for believing, our reward."

"The martyrs," the bearded man said, "are our warriors. They're his most beloved."

Her chin was in her hands, and the danciness in their eyes began to infect her too. Yes, she saw. A lion was needed to defend the
lambs. Someone braver, who understood.

"What can I do?"

"Do you feel him?" the bearded man asked. "Truly, in your
heart?"

She was hungry, and she was tenderhearted, and she was a
sparrow—the least of them.

*JESUS, SON of a father, who was the daughter? Is that you too? Jesus,
shepherd of the lost, who found you? Christ Almighty, when no one listened, did you put your hands on your ears and scream a bloody pox? Did
you claw at the moneylenders, did you vomit on Pilate? Were you only
meek after you were mad?*

*Jesus, young lord, lord closest to my age but Cupid, hear my confession:
I'm not loud enough. I'm not bad, except in small ways, but my goodness
is awfully quiet. Does that count as a sin? Will you make me thunder-
loud? Will you use my voice to wallop my parents and impale my frog-
mouthed brother? Is that what you meant by lifting the weak? I'm not a
slave, I'm not a dead man waiting to be reborn, I'm not a leper or a whore.
But let me tell you, sometimes being a little girl feels worse.*

"STOP BEING poky." Her mother swatted her away from the shrine.

"What's in the basket?"

Prisca reached up to open the lid, but one quick hip from her
mother displaced her again. So she sat in the corner while her mother
said prayers, her forehead against the marble wall, her eyes searching out the window for signs of life, for a tall man to walk by. She
reached in her robes to find the hook, forgetting she'd left it on a
shelf in her room, next to a bird's nest that was nearly a foot tall
and had only the shallowest dip in the top where eggs might have

gone. At first she'd put the hook in the nest, but it had looked wrong, the metal on that straw. She should've given it right back—it wasn't hers—but she hadn't been able to keep the eel, and she wanted to be reminded of the feeling.

The mysteries her mother spoke of—the story of Proserpine and Ceres and the earth waking itself up each spring—these had always delighted her because their truth was clear. Each year the calves appeared, and the buttercups, and swimming weather, and by the time its thread was run to the end, the leaves had dropped, and the frost licked everything to sleep, and she herself was put into woolens by a mother who promised they would both live to see the spring again. She and the boys would pretend the pond was the underworld, and Dis would hold Proserpine down in the reeds until her mother could find her, or until Proserpine ran out of air and started punching.

After the shuffling and arranging of the spray of wheat and the dish of seeds and the candle and the cloth, and the clanging of the bronze sistrums Prisca was never allowed to play, her mother sat back on her haunches and began her hum. Her voice with the same thin tone as the slave for sale. Her mother snuffed the candle, wafted the smoke around with one hand like a scoop: up to the heavens, down to the underworld, around her head like a shawl. *Fruits of the dirt, praise to the emperor, warmth for my children, death in its place*— all of it made too much sense for Prisca to find the germ of the heretic. *Rain, rain, rain.*

"May I light the candle tomorrow?" she asked.

"Where under heaven have you been dragging your robe? Did you play hide-and-seek with the pigs? Go fix yourself." She threw a veil over the rest of the shrine; one edge slipped into the bowl of water. Seeing it made Prisca thirsty. "No ears for listening," her mother continued to mutter as Prisca left, embarrassed. "No brain at all."

Outside, Prisca put her shaking hands on her waist, squeezed tightly, feeling at her ribs. Only flesh, to be mortified. Only flesh, to be risen. The message was the same: the earth and its doll-sized people conducted by a body invisible—half love, half wrath—and another body manifest who dies and un-dies, suggesting some version of hope, and a spirit that insinuates into everything, watching, so that you won't accidentally be bad. But in some rooms Prisca was shut out, and in some she was welcomed, and in the mystery of Christ, she'd been told that her very innocence was a weapon.

AT THE next night meeting, she was allowed up front. Her mother had sworn at her father and the bearded man at dinner, said they were being reckless, not to mention profane. The new religion gave the emperor a bad taste in his mouth, and it wasn't so long ago that those piles of people were burned to make up for Nero's fire. But the proximity to death was part of the urgency. The wheat was dying anyway.

The bearded man told one of her favorite stories to the visitors. A man was sick and someone ran to tell Jesus—"Come help, he needs you"—and Jesus laughed and said, "Let him die!" So everyone waited in Nazareth or Jerusalem or wherever Jesus lived, and the sisters wept and wailed and watched their dear brother's blood creep back to the far innards of his body, so that his skin was perfectly pale, ice-like, and surely, though the Gospel didn't say so, they whispered curses at the so-called Christ. And when the man was good and dead, they wrapped him in strips like a mummy and stuffed him in a tomb, and then all of a sudden Jesus showed up on the horizon with his henchmen in tow. "Take me to the tomb," he commanded, and the sisters, surely still cursing, walked him through the rocks and scrub to the hole in the mountain, and though they warned it would smell like the Devil, Jesus didn't mind; they rolled back the stone—like if you weren't buried behind a rollable stone you weren't worth resurrecting—and *lo and behold!* the mummy came stumbling out of the cave, and everyone cheered. Jesus didn't care; he let a man die just to show off his own muscles. He needed believers; he needed proofs. Was it a coincidence that Jesus was the youngest sibling? [Sometimes you terrify me.]

When her mother came to tuck her in that night, she sniffed at Prisca's hair. "You smell like smoke," she said.

"You should join us sometime. They have good songs."

PRISCA'S BASKET was full up with small almonds. She dragged it behind her, bent over and dramatically groaning. Her father said they'd sucked the scarce water from the wheat; Prisca, alert to justice, felt the nuts were being unfairly punished with a premature harvest.

"Give me half," Crispus said.

"I'm a pacifist," she said.

Servius was trying to lasso a rope over a high poplar branch, jumping with the effort.

"That's not what that word means," Crispus said.

"Don't listen to her." Her brother finally caught one end of the rope in a tangle of limbs. His basket was empty.

"You haven't told me any jokes lately."

"I stopped finding your face funny," she replied.

He reached out a hand toward her load. "Come on. Don't be stubborn. Where's the old Prisca who'd beg for a ride on my back?"

"Look to your own nuts."

"Ask her about Jesus," Servius called out. He'd dragged down a nest from the tree and was picking through the flakes of old eggshells. "If you really want to talk to her."

"Another god?" He had his hands in her basket and was redistributing the almonds, which looked like little wooden hearts that someone had stabbed repeatedly with a needle. His long lashes an invitation to stare. His cheeks.

"She's got a new crush," Servius said. He'd put the eggs in a fold in his tunic and was striding ahead, beating his lasso into the bushes to scare up partridge.

So what, her body had become the vessel for a new fervor. She wanted more, she wanted it faster, she wanted to be wanted.

"You wouldn't understand," she said.

"My father says it's foolishness," Crispus said.

She kicked at the dust on the path that spiraled through the almond grove. Far off, something went skittering through the brush. A hare.

"Come over sometime and convince him yourself," he said.

With the sun behind him, Crispus was angelic, exactly the form the Devil takes. His chin had the start of a scruff. Would her little fingers fit there below his mouth? [Ordinarily, I'd say *yes*, that's *exactly* where they go, but with you I can't tell what the real danger is. Love him if you want to love him, but trust is the road to betrayal. My home is carpeted with lovers—I use their cherub-curled heads as stepping-stones to the breakfast table, and I'll tell you the secret: most are happier there, my heel on their temples, their hands in one another's business, than they'd ever be in that sky meadow where the body is immaculate. The body is violable. This is good, and this is pain.]

She'd never felt innocent, not the way her father and his god imagined.

"He just wants to nab your almonds," Servius yelled. "Don't let him! Run!" He took off across the trembling heat of September like a leggy deer, and after an inscrutable look back at her, Crispus took up the chase. Boys. She was once again left behind.

———

SHE WOKE one day to achy feet. She tried to remember where she'd walked the day before, whether she'd run without sandals in the back fields, or climbed one of the steep hills to the city market or the temple. She checked her soles for spider bites. Anna rubbed them for her, but the next morning they ached still, and a week went by with this low coming and going of pain. Her mother said she was growing and looked at the pantry, at the dwindling pots of pickled beans. Prisca still misjudged where the door frames were and shuddered into corners by turning too soon. She cut herself with a knife while chopping an artichoke because her fingers no longer held a familiar relationship with the rest of her hand. It wasn't possible to point to a part of herself and say with confidence, *This is Prisca*.

The sore feet she wasn't prepared for; the breasts she was. A girl she sometimes went to lessons with got hers the year before—they came bubbling out of her chest like spring fungus, and the boys could look at nothing else. This intrusion seemed like an intentional way to push girls further off balance. Surely it would be harder to stand straight with those things. Hers came in small, and she assiduously crossed her arms against her chest morning and afternoon to prevent them from ballooning any more. She lay on her stomach at night to tamp them down, though the pressure on them hurt. It was possible they were sentient, little chicks she was suffocating, and she sometimes felt like a bad mother to her body. But mostly her body felt like a bad friend to her.

Servius, aware of the arm-crossing, would give her a quick punch in the chest when their mother's back was turned. Fine; she would grind mustard powder into his wine.

And after the achy feet and the stretching limbs and the tiny mushroom breasts and the rounding hips and the dark hairs replacing all the light hairs, straw where there was silk, one morning she crawled out of bed and left behind a little rose where her bottom had been. She knew—there was no way not to know, on this farm, with these half-dozen women, with prayers made daily to the spirits of fertility, Ceres, Isis, Bona Dea—but she nonetheless felt a shock, as would any witness at the scene of a death.

IT OCCURRED to her that the blood she issued was a phenomenon that Jesus, and probably even God, had never experienced.

"The Lord created all things, including the cycles, and so has knowledge of all things," the bearded man said.

"But it hasn't come out of him," she said.

"In the sense that all things emerge from the Lord—"

"But he's a man."

"He is all things."

"You call him a *he*. Does he have a *pipinna*?" She waggled her finger near her crotch.

The bearded man was looking less patient. "He has no form."

"But Jesus did. A *pipinna*."

He set down the linens he'd been folding. These were part of the weekly rituals, the sacraments, and so the house servants were not allowed to fuss with them. Or rather, he sent them to the kitchen in a bag to be washed, separate from the house laundry, and when they were sent back to him in neat stacks, he flicked them open again, sprinkled them with water from a little glass ewer, and refolded them so his hands would be the last thing the linens had touched before being put into the Lord's service. Prisca found this suspicious. God surely knew women did the bulk of the work.

"Anatomy is not particularly relevant."

"It's relevant to *me*," she said, unconvinced that God's knowledge of the menses was equal to her own.

"Do you spend as much time thinking about your soul?"

She did, to be honest. But what set Christianity apart from the religions of her childhood was its very humanness. God in flesh and blood. And the blood—its suffering, its sacrifice, its *poof*ing into wine—seemed like a key she'd recently been granted a copy of. The bearded man's fastidiousness about the linens was hypocritical. *Let's bathe in the wine instead; let's put his blood in our mouths and roll it around our tongues so we can taste the copper of his veins.*

She left him to his snapping and folding and took a candle up to her dark room, where she stood by the window so the moon could watch her untie the linen bandage around her central fork. The pattern of blood resembled a grand dark continent with strands of brighter islands sprinkling outward. Red people lived on these islands, and they said rich, red things. They took red rowboats to the continent and trekked to the high volcano at the center, which was brown as earth. It still had a sheen to it. She pressed her finger on the heart of this, and, held up under the whitish flame, it would be impossible to tell whether the blood on her hand was her own, or a goat's, or God's. She tasted it.

Her holiness moved in cycles through her: from the bottom of her to her mouth, down through her innards, back to the bottom of her. And like the wine they drank at the eucharist, there was no telling when it might be ordinary and when it might be divine.

THE BARN was making strange noises. Prisca cracked the door to see if the pregnant mare had begun her labors, but it was her father, not on his knees but leaning into a corner, his body pressed against the wood as if it would camouflage, crying. The night too made ticky sounds—grasshoppers testing their legs, the wind snapping through the vines, the dirt exhaling its heat. When grown-ups cried, it looked like they were tasting poison. She'd found her mother tilted against Anna the other day, cheeks wet, talking about the weather.

She slipped past the stalls, her bare toes leaving olive-shaped prints, and tossed a stone at the hay bales so her father would start. He snuffled and turned, just another animal in the dark.

"Servius?" he said.

"Me."

He put his hands over his face and inhaled deep, with one shudder to break the breath. "Do you believe in everlasting life?"

It sounded like the catechism, and also like a trap. Her heart tripped.

"I believe in suffering," she said, "and redemption." What she really believed was that life was unfair and she was secretly important and most of the good in other people was a façade over selfishness and she wouldn't mind using a flaming whip to unmask the pretenders and save the weak, the wounded, the children like her, the slaves, the fish that are stolen from the waters, the water leaching away into the ground.

A cloud passed. "They took Hierax."

"Who?" she said.

"The emperor found the writings and took them. Justin and Chariton and Euelpistus. He didn't write it—Hierax. He was here the whole time. The meetings were just conversation. We were coming up with a way to talk about the invisible. You heard. We were just talking."

The bearded man.

Imagine being pulled into the emperor's palace! In chains! Would he remember how to profess his faith, or would he get so scared that the words would run right through him, like his own piss? Would a soldier give him a blink of solidarity, toss him a skeleton key to unlock his cuffs? Would God appear in a shaft of light, or Michael? Who came for the martyrs? [Most sacrifice is a pact between virtue and ego. Don't mistake death for salvation. I want you to chase your own pleasure like a hound at a hind, but may I gently steer you away from this insistent holiness?]

"They'll ask him about the meetings. They want to find us all."
He had stopped crying, but his eyes were long and vacant and the
hand under his chin kept pressing at his throat like he was trying to
hold something in. "Swear you won't reveal us."

The candle he'd put on the barrel was smoking; someone had made
a poor wick, probably Prisca. One horse was still awake, chomping
dryly at the hay; the low rustle and the candle smoke made the moment
seem less fraught, more domestic. "Should we rescue him?" she said.

It would be happening now. The good soldiers were being called to
battle. Somewhere, someone was asking another someone about his
most intimate thoughts, his beliefs—which aren't tangible things at
all and aren't even words always but mostly just a stirring feeling that
comes over you when you hear about hope—and depending on what
that other someone said, in the morning there'd be an execution.

CHRIST CAME to her in a dream and laid beside her in bed, running
his fingers through her tangled hair. The blood from his stigmata,
like a fine oil, loosened all the knots. She reached up to touch his
hand, and he swatted her away. "Shh," he whispered goldenly. So
she closed her eyes and tucked into him like a kitten and let him sing
to her in Aramaic, which she didn't understand but felt she got the
gist of. She was his own sweet angel, sweet angel.

She wanted her transverberation. She wanted the Lord to come
at her with arrows of light, and she wanted to be brave enough, em-
bodied enough, to swallow those shafts into her very soul with no
outward injury. She wanted to be bloodless, immaculate, one of the
clean ones. *Please, Lord, no eye-gouging. Give me a fire instead of the
blade. Let my mother remember me whole.*

NEW MEN appeared at the farm in the morning, and everyone
looked like they were foxes and the hunter's horn was sounding

around the bend. Turning yourself in was the clear moral high road, but even Christians were men, and scared. Prisca was not impressed. She asked her mother whether she should fetch the extra table linens from the upstairs trunk, but her mother said the men would not be staying long enough to eat.

In the afternoon she climbed the ropy olive by the road and waited for the soldiers to arrive. If the tree went up in a pyre of righteous flames, sent on the exhale of a flamboyant god, she would be proud. But no one was paying attention to her. A child's soul was trifling next to a massacre of male philosophers.

A messenger on a black horse approached, kicking up the dirt that had settled on the stone road, and a hawk burst from the tree like a feather duster knocked out of a window. The collection of hard green olives in her hand made for first-rate ammunition, but the rider didn't even glance up, batting away the pellets as if he was used to a rain of fruit. He would be a compatriot, come to warn the worrying men of the next move. They would dive underground like moles. They would bury themselves in the catacombs.

She waited in the tree to see what kind of gap the rider had opened up between himself and the thundering bailiffs. Silence on the road. Around her just the hum of bees drinking heat. The clouds were puffing themselves up, but no matter how roiling they got, they couldn't turn dark; dry, embarrassed, they broke and scooted away. Prisca chewed on the left corner of her bottom lip, sucking it in and out between her teeth.

The figure when she spotted him was still small on the road. Horseless, skinny. His dark hair making him look like a stick dipped quick in charcoal. Some tug in her heart set up a hope. When he was close enough, she bellowed, "Crispus!"—not unlike someone drowning.

"Are you catching dinner up there?"

"Haven't you heard?"

"They won't be ripe till November."

"No one knows what to do—grown men," she said. Crispus, being also still adolescent and brave, would hear the uselessness in *grown men*.

"It's got nothing to do with you, Prisca," he said.

His neck was cricked to the left. She wanted to climb down so he wouldn't have to crane, but climbing down would break the spell. It didn't bother her that he would always be on the other side of a line. They were bound with sturdiest rope to each other: this she knew in absolute terms.

"But I'm a *Christian*," she whispered.

"You're a girl," he said. "Get down." His nose had a bump in it from when Servius had broken it with a discus, almost a decade ago; they'd been aiming at old wine bottles. If ever there was a catastrophe, flood or fire or this famine, and Prisca lost her eyesight and had to crawl through the piles of dead to ensure her loved ones would be properly interred, she knew she'd know Crispus by touch. That long forehead plateau. The dips beneath the cheekbones like the shady side of dunes. The rumbly bump of the nose, which she might one day touch with not only her fingers but her own nose, as noses accidentally do when other things are happening between faces.

He threw a pinecone into the branches.

"You never understand *anything*," she said, beginning her tentative crawl down. It was hard to keep the folds of her robe in their proper place. "You're a *barbarian*."

He reached out a hand as she teetered on the last branch, but she pointedly drew her hands into her chest as she jumped.

"My father said there'd be no arrests tonight. He knows someone."

Crispus headed for the house. "Nothing to do but eat and get rest. Don't be worried; they won't come for you."

"Then they're fools," she said.

THE HOUSE had the new taste of a hideout; she looked now at the shadows of corners as holding places for bodies. The men were in the library. Dinner was dull—no one but women and children, who snickered from unease. Everyone got quiet when a gray cloud passed, but it held its belly and coasted on.

Servius had a stomachache from eating too much pigeon—the few remaining goats were being saved for Ceres—so when Crispus asked if he wanted to go throw stones in the pond, he told him to take Prisca instead and throw them at her. When they waded through the unmown grass, hip-high and buzzing, she was still two strides behind.

"Could someone hide underwater and breathe through a reed?" she asked. Some ducks had left a white ramp of poop leading down to the water. The pond was half its spring size; she wondered if she could touch bottom now. Crispus was standing on the far side beneath the willow, one foot removed from his sandal to test the dirt before he sat.

"You'd have to keep your legs from floating up," he said.

"They'd have no reason to look for someone out here. I think the worst would be the fish, and then getting cold, but after the sun goes down, you could crawl right out and dry off. I even have a hook to catch things with while I wait."

"Not much in the way of fish."

She wanted to circle the pond to his side, but was feigning disinterest. "Aren't you supposed to throw rocks?"

"Here, tell me one of your stories. I want to know what makes them so good."

"From the Christians?"

"One that makes sense to you."

She put her hands on her hips. The sun was leaving them to their privacy. Her father had said it wasn't about sense. It wasn't about the rain. The drought was temporal; this god asked her goodness to be unhooked from time and space. So she shouldn't cross to his side. She shouldn't sit beside him and tell him stories because this would be a lie, the only thing she really wanted being not his converted heart but his hand on hers. Funny boy skin.

"Do you know about the giants?" she asked.

"The ones at the beginning of time?"

She kicked the grass on her way around the pond, to signal boredom, and flushed a frog, whose note of guttural surprise made her smile against her will. "The angels fell down to earth and saw how pretty the humans were, so they married them and had babies, but the babies grew to be four hundred and fifty feet tall and rampaged around the earth killing people and birds." She dropped her voice. "And the angels taught the humans to have sex all the time."

"So where'd they go?"

"God flooded them out, the Nephilim, but he kept some to be forever demons on earth in order to tempt us. That way it's not so easy to be right and do good all the time."

"And someone saw all this and wrote it in a book." He was lying down now and looked like just the kind of figure a flood would pursue.

"Enoch," she said, and sat next to him. She pulled her knees primly to her chest. "He lived a thousand years ago and predicted the Messiah and the day when we'd all be judged for our sins."

"A single day? When? And what counts as a sin? And what makes that Jesus fellow a messiah? What about the emperor, who's brought peace to everyone? And did Enoch write all this down on a rock somewhere, and no one believed him till now?"

"The Jews did."

"And are you a Jew?"

"But listen," she said. Her body twisted toward his. "'Destroy all the souls addicted to dalliance,' he said."

"What's dalliance?"

"You know," she said, turning back to the pond, which was steely purple now. "Fooling around. What men and women do."

His laugh was high and short; if the frog she'd flushed from the reeds had been a very young one, it might've made the same sound. "So in this religion, kisses are strictly out."

She hadn't verified this, but she understood the general principle, which was that if it was something you wanted very badly, it was best to do without.

"You want food and drink, don't you? Is it a good thing if we starve?"

"It's about temperance," she said. His foot had begun tapping playfully against her hip. She pulled her knees in tighter.

"So one kiss would be all right."

This got at an itchy confusion of hers: what of the world was good because it was created by God, and what of the world was bad because it was a tricky illusion meant to pull you off the path to heaven. Her heart was inflamed, and she felt all the sick chills of love, but not for Crispus, *not* for Crispus.

Her eyes were still shut tight when he dove into the pond; she gasped at the water hitting her face.

"You want to try out the reeds?" he asked. His wet hair turned darker, his pimpled face now dewy and pure. The water made his eyelashes look like great palm fronds, slowly fanning his eyeballs, which were not brown or green but more properly animal-colored, tawny, the feathers closest to a partridge's breast, after everything else had been plucked away. He slipped under, and after an unnerving pause, he rose again in a geyser, hurling water toward the bank, issuing a whoop of joy that must have echoed all the way to the room where the men were wringing their hands. She relented. Shucked her sandals and slid ungracefully into the pond, her robes floating around her like she was an unwanted cat in a sack.

He pushed a scoop of water at her, hesitant.

"There and back?" she said. Her toes could finally touch the muck below, gritty with years of old leaves losing the starch between their veins, and then their veins, and for all that she'd dreamed of a twilight like this, just the two of them, she earnestly wished her brother would appear with his oafish gait on the horizon.

He dolphined under again and readied himself at the shore beneath the willow. His arms stretched out before him, his knees were bent below the water, cramped like a rabbit's before flight. "I'll go easy," he said. "Three, two."

But he was off too soon, so she had to scramble around, losing her belt in the whorl of water, her skinny legs too slow to catch him. When she met him at the far side of the pond, his face was all gloat and mischief. Panting, he ducked down again and she felt his arms around her middle, fumbling at her kicking legs, trying to fold her into a ball. *He is wrestling*, she thought. *This is what boys do.* But when he had her pleated in his arms, he rose up out of the water and with an exultant holler catapulted her into the air, tossing the small girl shape as far as his boy arms could manage—only three feet, where she collapsed into the pond and sank farther than any dive of her own had taken her. Her bottom nestled into the muck, and everything was briefly slow and soft, and she imagined staying down there and never coming up, because whatever was waiting on the surface would never be as good as the moments that had already happened.

She opened her eyes, wondering how long it would be before he worried, and felt a claw around her ankle—a sunken branch or vine scumming up from the deep. She scrabbled at it, kicked her foot, felt her lungs go crispy. In the wet brown gloom, a thin shape floated by, undisturbed, languorous. If only she could've opened her mouth to scream and gotten air. It was the eel. It was the eel she'd caught with her father's hook and brained with a rock until its eye went dull. Her mother was right: the universe was governed by a thousand spirits, and there was no scheme beyond the elements of the natural world vying for balance, and a fish whose spirit was wronged would appear again—love and salvation had nothing to do with it, no one man or god could possibly have his fingers around every part—and that fish would have its revenge.

An arm was around her middle again and wrenched her up in the empty air of dusk, and she breathed like the eel once breathed, in a desperate hunt for life, and Crispus was shaking her shoulders and pushing the hair out of her face and he was golden, those eyes like the tips of a dog's ears. She put her arms around his neck, her feet still kicking at the weeds, windmilling around whatever fish ghosts were lingering, and he let her pull him close, and this, *this*, was the purest minute of her life.

"You're all right," he said.

Without her belt, her whole body was just loose limbs in a cloud of fabric.

"Here," he said, and pulled his head back so he could look at her face. He put a thumb on her cheek, but there was no strand of hair there to smooth away. Is this the kind of moment that comes before a kiss? [A kiss is preceded by all moments. There is no *just before*.] Is this how hearts go, this battered thumping, foxes caught in a cage? Jesus, Jesus, you didn't speak of this.

"There was an eel," she said, terrified of the fronds of his lashes.

"They only live in rivers," he said. "Probably just a worm."

"A worm," she said, and she believed him, every word he said true, and as she was trying to decide if nature was imbued with good and evil, and whether God was singular and existed in the mind and thus was haunting her with an apparition to punish her for impure thoughts, or whether God was a man in triplicate, including one named Jesus who understood above all else human frailty and had long ago forgiven her fear and desire and doubt, while she was puzzling this, Crispus put his nose on her nose so that his eyes became a single hazel light, and before she could make up her mind to resist, she felt his lips touch hers, pond-water wet, and it was a pink taste, and small, and something in her was held, like an egg in a cup. Three seconds, and when he took his mouth away, he took the water with him.

On the walk back, they traded looks, as if they were trying to read the scattered bones, but people can't be read that way.

"Prisca," he said, and squeezed the water from his hair. "You shouldn't worry. You're just a girl."

And this, though meant to ground her, reassure her, relit her flame. She had wrong feelings, yes, and wanted things that were almost surely sinful, and had never been more content than when the Lord was pushed out by a single touch, by sweet foreign skin, but for all her errors, *just a girl* was precisely what she was not.

THE WILDERNESS

[2015]

TELL ME MORE about this boy."

"He smells like socks. What boy?" Daphne was just home from school, a carrot dangling from her lips like a cigarette.

Close to midnight in Rome; the quiet of the street was jolted by a moped struggling to crest the hill. Tom had gotten a reminder from his department that the deadline for posting spring courses was Friday. By Friday, he needed to decide if he could survive a return to America, where his wife would be stacking ominous-looking paperwork on his desk and then removing it again—*no*, she wasn't crying—and then sliding it back on his desk. *Surviving* sounded so histrionic until it became simply the term for not dying.

He'd drafted a response to Richard, the chair: "Labs going well. Will finish first pass of article by Christmas; aim for *Int'l Review of Hydrobiology*. Should have some impact on discussions of human effect on climate. Can I do Intro and Senior Seminar, dependent on health? 'Health,' related to Norse *helge*, or 'holy.' Could be incapacitated. The 'cap' root there being *capax*, to hold, rather than *caput*, the head. I am not losing my head." The proviso gave him space to extend his stay through the spring, through the summer, through—

His daughter knotted her hair into a brambly pouf just above her forehead: her unicorn look. "Are you feeling okay? Does it hurt at all?"

"Try pinching your elbow, hard."

She did.

"That's how much it hurts. Now the boy who smells like socks," Tom said. "Do you think he notices how you smell?"

She pondered this, crunched her carrot. Put her hand on her hip. "Well, Doc, I doubt he does. And that's A-okay, peachy."

"I'm sure he—"

"Anyway, so what if he liked me too? That'd be the end of the story, right?"

"No, no, no," he said. "I mean, yes, in your case—though you could, I don't know, get ice cream or something and talk about the comics you like. But no, pining for someone isn't nearly as fun as everything that happens after." He felt the lie as he spoke it; everything that came after was a web, and sometimes it was sublime and sometimes you got caught.

"After what?"

"After you say what it is you want. Not that it always works out, but you have to get beyond the stage of just staring at the ostracods, as it were."

"Like, 'Hi Buttface, I think about you a lot; let's go read comics.'"

"Well—"

"Dad, you don't *understand*." She released her unicorn pouf. "Boys are the only ones who get to say what they want."

HE DIDN'T return to the lab, didn't take the 118 bus to the valley where his ostracods lay waiting for him in their watery cosmos, but met her at the Villa Pamphili among the pines, which in full sun could be mistaken for columns of ancient pink-veined marble. They sat on a bench opposite the palace and watched joggers in candy-colored shorts circle the gravel paths. A child chased herself in the lawn. A crow called to them from the nearby head of a satyr—they were too near something precious.

"It's the lunch hour," she said. "They'll be gone soon."

The crow gave up, flapped bitterly away. The child lay down like a starfish. A jogger went tumbling into the gravel, and the jogger behind her sidestepped—cautious, pony-like—but the fallen one waved a hand, *Pretend you didn't see this*. No one would have to save anyone else today.

"Do you think there's an essence all this can be stripped back to?" He was still rolling the ball of his new theory around the empty rooms of his head. "A park, for instance, removed of villa and non-native species and jogging paths, returned to an unaffected state?"

"Unaffected by what? By change?"

"By humans, say."

"Humans are change. Once you take humans away, you've got to remove mammals, and then vertebrates, and then whatever's not, like, a colossal Jurassic fern, and then you're back to stardust."

He nodded; the ball was picking up speed. "So the study of adaptation, say—"

"Take history—everyone gets their panties in a bunch when they stumble on a new ruin; oh look, Nero's pleasure palace! And we walk on tiptoes till it's preserved. But if ancient architecture's so special, why don't we tear down all the Renaissance *palazzi*? Anyway, you know who saved most of this stuff? Mussolini. So maybe preservation is conservatism is Fascism."

"Sure—"

"People are nuts for excavations, but when do you stop digging? Below the Forum there's probably Stone Age megaliths—why don't we trash the Forum? Because the layers themselves aren't as interesting as the fact that there *are* layers."

"Some would say a crustacean's form isn't as interesting as its phylogeny. But of course others—"

"The only thing worth remembering is whatever'll make us better."

Which was a funny thing to say, because neither science nor history had anything really to do with *goodness*, though perhaps religion—which they both foreswore—began there. Not religion, she would've said, but morality. Not morality, he would've said, but survival. But survival, she would've said, was cannibalism; goodness was self-sacrifice.

He didn't tell her about his diagnosis because that was real, and she was not; that was practical, something to be solved, and this girl was a cloud. Or: she was becoming the life he wanted, and his damaged nerves were not.

A suntanned man jogged past and spit at her feet. "*Scimmia*," he said.

She kicked a spray of gravel at his retreating shape.

Shee-mee-a, a shimmery word.

"He thought I was an immigrant," she said.

"We're all immigrants."

"Give me a break," she said.

It meant *monkey*.

Beneath the villa's terrace was a grotto where a stone woman was half-clothed in moss. Water trickled from hidden sources, and the shadows felt like a damp cloth to the forehead. The Janiculum girl was unswayed. She turned behind a column, squinted at him through the shade, put a finger to her lips. He was beginning to feel she didn't always listen to what he said—or maybe he didn't listen to her—and at some point, he feared, the sheen of her would be digested, no less delicious than diatoms in a seed shrimp's belly, and he would find himself empty again. Independent. He crossed the stones slick with algae and pulled aside her finger and kissed her quiet mouth.

"You're married," she said.

The territory he'd recently entered, swampy and vast, had no edges. To confess to being married was to find a tree in this wide plain, cut straight and knotless planks out of it, build an even-cornered house from the wood, and then put himself inside it.

"I have been married," he said.

She grabbed his face and pressed her nose angrily to his. "You self-involved bastard."

ALDO THE lab assistant was eating a bag of chips in the corner. He'd been helping with the mammalian subjects, *i ratti*, but was weak-stomached; they shifted him to the environmental sciences room, where it was believed nothing untoward happened. He mostly sat on a tall stool in the corner, snacking and taking notes. There was a suspicion he was working on a novel.

"*Vai in vacanza?*" he asked, one cheek pouched with chips.

Tom switched off the lights above a batch of small aquaria. "*Cosa?*"

Aldo repeated himself, then mimed swimming underwater. "You are *preoccupato*. I think maybe vacation."

"You think I *should* go on vacation?"

"I can do this." The young man gestured at the rows of tanks. "*È facile.*"

Tom laughed. The kid just wanted a raise. No, he assured him, he could perform his own duties.

Aldo shrugged, resumed his snack. Lazy bites.

And wasn't Rome his vacation? [Rome is a dream; its cobbles are slick with sweat and lust, the stuff of sleep. You cannot move forward here, only up or down. Down: the Hadrian-built Aelian Bridge went tumbling in 1450, when the weight of jubilant Jubileers exceeded its architect's wildest prophecies—the Tiber pulled under 172 souls. Up: above the Domus Aurea rose Trajan's baths, and above that a neo-fascist club, and soon a 22nd-century Museo di Migrazione, paid for by the profits from genetically modified seeds.

Or is it down: twenty-five feet below the building where the opera stores their sets, a Mithraeum abutted the Circus Maximus, so bulls bought at market could be slaughtered over grates, the blood dripping down onto nervous ancient heads. Or is it up: from the Castel Sant'Angelo, for centuries, fireworks dizzied over feast days, papal elections, pilgrimages—handprints in the night over the Tiber, over the 172 drowned souls. You cannot vacation in a phantasm.]

He finished shutting off the lights, giving one last swirl to the ostracods in their domains. Aldo was filling out the checklist left behind by the department chair. Tom lifted his satchel from a lab table and said, half jokingly, "Now, *vado in vacanza!*"

"*Prova la Sardegna.*"

Outside, a greenfinch rustled in the stone pine above him. He sat on a bench near an overgrown oleander and pulled the fishhook from his satchel. A young woman was guiding a group of visitors along the diagonal path that cut across the *cortile*. He hadn't thought they'd give the same kind of admissions tours as American universities, but there she was, walking backward while speaking with great animation. A woman in the group was writing in a small notebook and wearing a green skirt, and this combination caused an unexpected ache in his heart—no, his hand—and when he looked down he saw that he'd clenched his fingers around the hook. Blessed literalized feeling.

It had only left a red groove in his palm, but he took the barbed end and began stroking the heel of his hand, lightly at first, then hard enough to be ashamed of what he was doing, then harder. The skin was thicker here, but he couldn't abandon the pressure. Man versus body, the hook a tool, his one hand opening the other, wanting that red as evidence he could make a choice, that in his whirlpool life he had some measure of control, the pain a reminder he was alive and *feeling* was good, *feeling* was to be savored, not suppressed, that even *hurt* was better than *numb*.

There was the blood. He stopped, was horrified. Wondered what category of sin this was, and how it would be confessed. *Il masochismo, mio figlio?* No. Research.

HIS PHONE rang in the valley: like a warbler, only meaner.

He was untangling pteridophytes from spermatophytes. A microcosm was just a small world. Imagine a fish down there, an eel, caught in the limits of its environment—a lifetime spent circling a muddy room. It hunted for food, burrowed away from a heron's splaying feet, called out on blue moons in case its sound echoed off the body of another eel. An eel who would find its own eel body smooth enough to adore. The plants were decoration. The water was invisible substrate. The drama was in the searching—in the not finding—in the waiting to find. When it was caught, would the drama end? [If I said happiness was in the relinquishing, who would believe me? Ask the eel, who spawns and dies. Ask your daughter, who's learned to see first how others feel. Is the world losing her fiery shout, or is her whisper pushing the world on its rotation? What sacrifice have you made, son of God?]

The phone was calling from California. Daphne would be in school, so either his wife wanted to say something horribly practical about the future, or his wife wanted to tell him that the fourth-grade bullies had driven their daughter to flee through a window and she was lying in the hospital.

"How is it all feeling?" she said.

"Can I call you back?" he said. "I'm in the field."

He shouldn't have brought his phone at all.

"You know you're not alone," she said. "I mean, I think it must be nice to imagine that you're alone over there. Maybe even a test run at splitting up. Don't think I haven't thought about it too. How good it feels to just— But you could stay over there for twenty years and you still wouldn't be alone. You're a human; you have memory."

He sat back on his heels. "No one wants to isolate themselves," he said, feeling like isolation was quite precisely what he did want, just for a while, like a long stay in the sensory deprivation tank, long enough to pinpoint which choices were his alone.

"Is it just that you're tired? Bored?" She didn't know him well enough to guess *scared*, or she knew him well enough not to say it. "My parents say I'm an idiot."

"You seem very mature to me."

"Well, there's that. Maybe it's just in my nature to exist in suspension without too much damage. Or I'm the one who's tired. You have a way of making me— But your child needs some clarity. I'd like to tell her whether you're coming home for Christmas, for one thing, and whether you think you might ever come back to me—in a whole way."

But there were no eels in the nymphaeum; they were river dwellers, needed access to the sea. They weren't circular, like Tom.

"Tom?" He could see her holding the edge of the counter by the phone, her fingers tight on linoleum. Fingers he'd tasted each knuckle of. "Just say if you want to stop."

His chest began to convulse. He closed his eyes. The Devil was scrabbling in his ventricles. This wasn't an attack; this wasn't an attack. Something in him separated, homunculi, one standing to the left and imagining the plane trip home (where was *home*? [wherever one does the most damage]) and that moment at the end of security when the arrivals were pinched past the detectors and shot out into the crowd of the waiting, all open-faced, expectant; and one standing to the right, imagining how it would feel to say just then, *This is love, but this is not a marriage.*

That summer they had gone to her cousin's wedding, where

someone in a tie-dye dashiki made a speech about love's soothing properties while Daphne audibly groaned. It sounded like a drug. He had nodded along because some version of this benumbment was his lot too, and his wife reached for his fingers and pushed her own among them. Those once-devoured knuckles. What made people barnacle to each other if not fear? [Here's a comfort: the ascendance of hope and fear are parallel; as you lose one, lucky boy, so too goes the other.] They danced during the dancing portion, spun slowly around the bride and her father, and only looking back was he shocked that he had held her body, any body, so casually. He felt the acid in the back of his throat.

"I want to stop," he said.

THE AMERICAN war movie was dubbed in Italian, but the characters were too busy dying to speak much. Tom and the Janiculum girl had been driven inside by an afternoon storm. To the sound of artillery, he traced the skin of her arm, looping infinities between her elbow and wrist. A horse on-screen was caught in cross fire and bucked its way down to stillness; she dug her nails into his palm. Tom's favorite part of moviegoing was the feeling of being cut off from the tangible world, from one's own body—a sense of vacuum. Touching was not a part of it. Maybe it was because the celebrity on-screen was commanding his troops in a language Tom didn't understand, but something allowed him to be both there and here, his body porous and autonomous. After the intermission, when a boy came around selling candy from a tray, Tom pushed the armrest up and twisted against her, his arm circling her waist and his head suctioned to her neck like a mussel to a rock. He heard her mouth open.

Stasis suddenly was the sweetest possible thing. He would take the batteries out of all the clocks and keep this film on a loop and give up his organs so he would have no needs other than to stay with his body around this body. She held his leg, her hand finding the spot where he'd cut into his skin, as if hurt were a magnet.

"Will you take me to the valley?" she said under the dubbed laughter of troops at rest.

Why did his fingers chill? [Because you've made the wild a hideout. Your Eden is where no moral decisions are made. But let's get the chronology right; post-Eden can never be Edenic. The first sin was the ticket out of stasis. And the sin isn't *hers*, she who's exploring, questioning, consuming; it's yours for thinking you're somehow exempt. Do I need to crimp your neurons again?]

"There's nothing really to see," he said.

"Isn't that the point?"

THE POSTCARD had been sent three weeks ago, a fossil from before the diagnosis.

Daddd,
Nothing happening here, Mom's planting tomatoes that I won't eat. No invitation to Benji's birthday, it's baseball-themed, no girls in MLB. If I got an invitation, I'd eat it and then fart it out, that's how much I care about Benji. Invented new sport: boob-ball, Mom doesn't think it's funny. When I'm old I won't need to go to Rome, I'll be queen of my own universe. xoxoxo

The mailbox for his apartment, a soldier in a line of fellow boxes, had been empty since the beginning of September. No voice from the void, except for her. He flipped the postcard over: a photo of the Cabazon Dinosaurs. He remembered the stop off I-10, the towering Brontosaurus helpfully explained by the adjacent creationist museum. One of the world's marvels that were so marvelous they paralyzed us with unbelief. He brought the card to his face, as if he could smell his daughter in its fibers, as if her touch hadn't long been effaced by the friction of a thousand other envelopes, the steel hull of a ship, the ash from a clove cigarette smoked clandestinely in the mail-sorting facility in Ostia.

The Janiculum girl could use her cheek to search for the dead; Tom found himself too attached to the living. A fierce craving sprung up in the center of him, between his heart and his bowels—did he want to show this postcard to the Janiculum girl and watch for the reflected glow on her face, or did he want to tell his daughter about his unexpected infatuation, confess to her how lily-livered humans could be, how she would have to learn such unbearable patience to survive all the Benjis of the world? [Is that really her job?] No—that wasn't her job; it was his job to be better.

Upstairs, he made a snack of grapes and honey and pulled out the blank card he'd been using as a bookmark in *Paradiso*, which he'd never finish. The terrace was flaming with sun. A fly settled on his plate and rubbed its hands together.

You're right, Rome's for knaves, he wrote, *but please mail yourself over anyway.*

"GLAD TO hear all things going apace. I've got you down for two sections of Intro; Lieber's doing Senior Seminar. Once you get past midtenure review, you'll get better picks. Speaking of *that* devil, it'd be great to have a commitment from *Hydrobiology* before your file gets passed up the ranks. Let's get that squared by May. Soon you'll be over here in the green pastures of crushing committee work. Nose to the grindstone, or whatever the Romans say."

Sgobbare, to slave away, labor being not the price of freedom but its reverse.

Tom could carve a cave into the fresh mud along the Almone, and he wouldn't miss a single element of the nonwild world except that which he'd created with his own body: his child and his precarious desire.

"I don't want to teach two sections of Intro," he wrote, and deleted.

DR. TROMBA asked doctorly questions while he obfuscated. He worried his soul would show up as a black mark on the MRI.

"Are you getting enough sleep?" she asked.

"Yes," he lied. Easily.

"Are you feeling betrayed? At all?"

"Pardon?"

"There is a common feeling when our bodies cease to be reliable. An anger. And this can have effects on the emotions."

He'd read in the brochures about the higher rates of *depressione*, *disturbi dell'umore*, disturbances of the humors. His humors did indeed feel more turbulent than normal. If lesions were available to be blamed, he'd take them up on the offer.

"Yes," he said. "Betrayed." *Tradito*. Treason being a cousin to tradition. The giving over of things. He had given too much, and yet the fact that he was still alive, whole, capable of happiness, was proof he hadn't given enough. He had never before despised his humanness, but now he saw it as weak and wobbly; it was everything he distrusted about religion. Believers beholden to an absence. No terms, only *feeling*.

The hot street was a return to the material. Men in tiny cars, women with baskets. The sweat started on his upper lip. He wandered deeper into the Aventine, away from the Tiber. On his left winked a yellow brick basilica, squeezed between two larger buildings, unlocked; he'd inadvertently shown up at the priests' begrudging half-hour open house. Through ancient columns he walked, through the small wooden door within the large wooden door, into the stillness again. The breath of a church. He willed the particles of incense to infiltrate his marrow.

There was no one. Not a woman in the pew to mimic the woman he might hope to see, not a dark-habited priest clucking at him about improper clothes, not a Scandinavian tourist whose whiteness and camera flash lit up the side chapels. The coffers in the ceiling were unpainted; the columns didn't match. He toured the relics, stared without looking at the frescoes of saints, all unknown to him. A girl knelt next to two lions. The same girl declaimed in front of men in robes. No one had written her name. He imagined Daphne singing her equinox song, and the boys turning away. The table next to the entrance to the crypt was stocked with brochures about poor Africans and a few bags of homegrown lavender, but no one sat on the three-legged stool to sell them. As he descended, the air grew ever sweeter, dustier.

He couldn't make sense of what he found below: a network of small rooms, some with parallel stone benches and broken statues of bulls, some empty, one with a series of stone seats in a row around three walls, each with a hole. If he didn't think it was impossible, he'd call them toilets. He shone the light from his cell phone into one of the openings, but it only revealed more darkness. He sat, surprised at how guilty he felt, or was it giddy. His elbow twitched. He closed his eyes. He loved in ancient places to listen for whispers, but had long since decided that whatever voices echoed were his own.

She doesn't love you or *You don't love him* or *What you want is not a kiss but a family. The self is a small thing. The self is the smallest thing.*

But that wasn't him.

The body is a testament. The soul is fleeting. The self is the smallest thing.

A thin worm of pain stretched through his head. His bottom on the open seat felt colder than the rest of him, and when a breeze seemed to pass below, he jumped up. One of his molars began to throb. He couldn't help laughing—afraid of ghosts in the crypt, no less. He hoped there'd be a priest above so they could share an awkward exchange about *i fantasmi*, but the nave was as empty as he'd left it, the air still prickly with scent.

Passing through the wooden doors again, he looked back at the lintel. *S. Prisca*. Yet another martyr in a city of the self-involved.

MOST OF the ostracods in his lab progressed through nine instars of development between egg and grown, the intermediate larval stages nearly indistinguishable: nine forms of teenage beans, chaosing into each other. The carapace got harder, larger; the antennae and palp and legs lengthened and segmented; by the eighth instar the reproductive organs appeared—the shape of the sperm pump in males being key in distinguishing species. They got tougher, more mobile, and then, finally, sexual. Bless their mutations. Ontogeny doesn't recapitulate phylogeny, but how easy it would be to think so, watching the creatures evolve from the primordial ooze of the tiniest egg. In a world of limitless funding, Tom could test each set of chemicals on each instar and then watch the effects play out over multiple generations, but this semester he contented himself with the grown-ups. They knew what they wanted.

Aldo collected the discarded juveniles in a large aquarium he called the romper room. "These are same as those, just not yet," he said. The boy's historical philosophy was comforting to Tom: everything was the same as everything—just not yet.

While the larvae were maturing, Tom bombarded the adults with a series of re-created chemical settings based on his understanding of the evolving Caffarella Valley. Through the university, he'd been able to interlibrary-loan articles on lahar deposits, archaeomorphology, viticulture runoff, sheep shit, myths of the Almone River, seventeenth-century watercolors of the crumbling mausoleums. He dove deep into environmental forensics. He wanted to get the sediment right, the levels of leached lime and agricultural nitrogen; he wanted the temperature of the water to reflect the fluctuating climate; if he had historical data on solar flares, he would've had Aldo blitz them with proton radiation. But most important was the human touch: the copper and lead from metallurgy, the bone char from goats offered to the gods, the ways they turned the wilderness into yet another layer of human history. Some researchers were experimenting with reverse ecology, peering into the gene sequence of bacteria to deduce the prehistoric environments that shaped them, but they weren't up to arthropods yet, and humans weren't a part of the landscapes they were reconstructing. Tom didn't want to be removed from the equation.

He could hear his old advisor: "If you wanted to write poems, you should never have picked up a microscope." But Tom didn't understand how you could avoid them: either the microscope or the poem.

He wrote years on the tanks in masking tape, arbitrary dates pulled from the eras he could get data on: 165 CE, 896 CE, 1559 CE. Aldo had been collecting the requested chemical compounds and storing them in beakers with illegible labels. The boy wanted all the tanks to be historicized at once, but Tom restrained him, tried to explain the value of slowness—the *methodical* of the scientific method.

"But *these* bugs are not the old ones," he said. "They get fat on old poison, but old bugs, maybe not."

"Point taken, but nothing major and permanent is going to happen, evolutionarily, shy of about a million years."

Aldo raised his eyebrows and made a quick note in his journal. "I think different about change."

They'd introduce the first set of chemicals the following day, and Tom would make sure Aldo, who almost certainly had no interest in being a scientist, piped in the first one himself. Though he questioned Tom's technique, he liked the idea that they and the ostracods were clasped in a waltz, that human history was not an oppressive downward march but that even in our pollution we were circling around all the other things, always. He'd named the biggest ostracod Bruno.

"How can you tell which it is?" Tom asked.

"It must be the one I see the first."

Tom usually took his afternoon snack outside to escape the basement, but feeling unsteady, he ate his pear while watching Aldo take pictures of himself to send to his girlfriend. He'd had a good weekend, he said—brought Gabriella to meet his mother, with whom he still lived, and she'd eaten two bowls of his mother's pappardelle, so they were planning for a wedding. Though no, Aldo himself didn't particularly want to settle down; he liked another girl he'd met in class. Tom shook his head at him. Aldo thought the crypt toilets were hilarious and asked for directions so he could take his little brother.

"Take Gabriella," Tom said, for a joke. "It's romantic."

Aldo wagged a finger at him. "*Too* romantic. Death is forever. You do not want that a girl thinks of forever."

He didn't himself want to think of forever, not when his body was waving great flags about its nearness. His tanks of historically sterile ostracods were only waiting for tomorrow. He remembered the errand he meant to give the boy.

Aldo raised a shoulder with disinterest when he saw the fishhook. His hand was deep in a bag of cheese puffs.

"Piece from old fence," he said.

"You know Savelli down the hall with the gospels project? Can you run this over and see if he'll lump it in with his next batch for the mass spectrometer? I need a radiocarbon."

"But it is metal."

"Yes," Tom said, "but forged over a wood fire, etc. It'll take. One can even test the rust if it's the right kind."

The boy reached out for the hook with a new sense of appreciation. "It reads my DNA too?" *Dee, enne, ah.*

"He mentioned driving down with a kit next week and said he could toss it in. I'll buy you a sandwich."

Something in his gut tugged as the boy left the room with the object, flipping it over in his stubby fingers. He'd told Savelli about the hook over a beer—he was one of the few Italian researchers whose English was passable—and the older man, who could smell the first edge of obsession, offered to date it for him. The accelerator mass spectrometer was at the CIRCE Lab at the University of Naples, and though Savelli invited him to come—they could see Herculaneum, make a day of it—Tom was reluctant to lose any scrap of time in Rome. He just wanted to sit still while all the pertinent information was brought to him.

The boy returned with a smear of orange powder across his cheek and went back to his spot at the window, where he could watch the girls' ankles pass.

HE FELT a buzz in his left eye. The door of Santa Maria degli Angeli e dei Martiri was heavier on his way out. He came for a postcard of the church's marble meridian to send Daphne, another Important Sight to show time rolled on and the living were still fine. Something trembled in his shoulder.

A man without teeth stooped at the church's entrance, his hand held out with a cup, and Tom turned his head—*Non ho i soldi*—and though it was true he didn't have money, just a bus ticket, he still felt that he'd lied. The church abutted the roaring Piazza della Repubblica at an angle, as if modernity had staged a sneak attack. Crossing it required a mouse-like darting, certainly a mouse-like panic. Cars came within inches, squealing, elbows jammed onto horns. Tom camouflaged himself behind a knot of young Germans who still had enough alcohol in their systems to have forgotten their mortality, and together they danced through the traffic to the island at the center. "*Scheißkerl!*" said a girl with a boa.

On the far side of the piazza he could see the turmoil of Termini station. His bus left from somewhere in there. A short jazz riff played in his eyeball. On his own now, he nearly slammed into a toy-sized white delivery truck. Beyond the truck, an Alfa Romeo with an antique woman behind the wheel had already come to a stop, waiting patiently for Tom's next animal move. He felt such gratitude for this woman, for her temperate out-of-placeness, but she didn't respond to his smile—her eyes didn't even move with him, making him wonder if she was blind.

Termini was an anthill of travelers, foreigners toting outrageous amounts of luggage, the buses circling their movements like bombardier beetles. Signs indicating stops and routes were too numerous to represent any kind of ordered reality. He walked the length of the parking lot, scanning the notices, seeing every number but 75. Orange construction barrels blocked some lanes; other stops had digital signs, the lights of which had blinked out, leaving them ciphers. When he saw his bus circling into the lot, he ran to it unabashedly, a child. The driver told him he was heading north instead, and Tom asked if he could get on anyway, ride it till it turned around, because his legs were frizzing, but the driver shook his head—*fine della linea*—and Tom felt a warmth behind his eyes. No reason to get emotional. He'd have to find another. He had no money for a cab. *Non ho i soldi.*

He asked a woman with a stroller where the southbound 75 stopped, but he couldn't remember whether it was *sessanta* or *settanta*, and she too shook her head. Pointed at the baby, as if that were an explanation. At some point, he should start walking home; there was that fine edge between perseverance and unreason.

The buses continued to pull in—38, 82, 170, 64, 910—and the numbers started to blur, and Tom felt an unjustified fear, a premonition that things were about to go very badly, that the bus would never materialize, and more, that the materiality of his body would falter. His neck felt like it was being grasped by someone angry, by the driver of the white truck, and great flares began to light the other waiting passengers like they were Bethlehem stars. Here were the angels and the martyrs. He crouched down, knowing this made him look strange, knowing it would look stranger were he to collapse. His feet went tingly. They were sparking. The fuzzy holy world was sparking, and before his body fully crumpled, he decided either he was having a second episode of demyelination (now understanding how precious the *isolated* in *clinically isolated* had been) or he was being spoken to directly by God the Father— something about trust and renunciation and surrender—and in that last moment before the darkness, he couldn't decide which was worse.

A GIRL perched on his leg, small, like a sparrow.

His leg had no feeling—either he was dead, or it had gone to sleep under her weight.

His brain stretched to assimilate the data: self, child, scratchy sheets, a low beep. The timer was going off. Someone had set the timer for the pie; no, it was for his heart. Someone was monitoring his life. The girl must be real. Her eyes opening twice as big as his, great loving eyes. Her hand jerked toward him, yanked a rope binding him. She shrieked, he laughed, a woman in white came running. Yes, heaven was his daughter.

"It's your head," she said, gently tapping the side of his face with her fingers. "Are you okay? I ate your cornflakes."

"Have I been dead for long?"

"Not once have you been dead. You only fell down in the street, and someone brought you here, and they patched you up, and then we came."

"But you're miles and miles away." His Beatrice, come to light up the circles as he climbed—or descended—them. He needed her forgiveness, as long as it lasted.

"We're your egermency contact."

E-germ-ency, an ejection of infection from his body. The nurse replaced the IV tracing his forearm, and Daphne wriggled to his left leg, leaving the other to wake up in this new world.

"Your mom?"

"She went for coffee."

"And what about—"

"Who?"

Best evidence that he wasn't dead: the Janiculum girl wasn't standing in the corner with a pair of party-store wings elasticked to her arms.

"Are you really my child?" he asked.

She whacked his chest with her head, nuzzled at his gown until her hair sprang out of its tie.

"No," he said with a sigh. "Merely a rodent. I knew I was dreaming."

"TELL ME about multiple sclerosis." He stumbled over the elision between "ple" and "scl"—too many adjoining consonants—and considered the disintegration of his brain. "Multiple sclerosis," he said again, adding a rest, an implied vowel, between the words. He was a day out of the hospital, the only sign of his collapse a butterfly bandage on his temple. His wife and daughter were touring the Colosseum; Daphne wanted to see warriors.

Dr. Tromba smiled. "It's easier in Italian. *La sclerosi multipla*." She had asked if he had anyone to help take care of him, someone who should be in this meeting.

"Then tell me about it in Italian."

He wanted her to collect the papers on her desk into a neat stack, or pull a pen from the mug, click it once or twice, and put it back. He wanted some evidence of her discomfort. But she leaned back in her chair and placed her hands in her lap, a move he recognized from his own efforts at patience.

"*La sclerosi multipla, come sai, è una malattia infiammatoria progressiva del sistema nervoso centrale. È neurodegenerativa perchè è demielinizzante.*"

"*Demiel . . . ?*"

"*Si continua a perdere la mielina.*"

"Myelin. Like *miele*," he said. "Honey."

"*Tipicamente, è controllata; non è curato. Dunque, è cronica.*"

"How does it happen? I mean, are there risk factors?"

"*La eziologia è sconosciuta.*"

"If I don't understand everything you say, am I permitted to live in ignorance? Can we pretend you did your duty?"

She leaned forward and rolled her chair up to her desk. "Scientists are the hardest. And not always for the reason one would expect."

"I should want to know. That's what you mean."

"There is no *should*. If I were to learn of a terminal cancer diagnosis, or Huntington's, say, I think I would buy myself a stack of coloring books and take them to a meadow in Alaska."

Her sharp little boarding-school face in that moment looked like it would fit right in among the moose.

"Why Alaska?"

"Don't distract. Let me give you the information, and then you can make your choices. You have relapsing-remitting MS, which is good, if we are classifying conditions by degree. I'll put you on a medication that will slow things down."

"With side effects."

"Headache, diarrhea, flushing of skin. You'll tell us."

"I might blush more?"

"We adjust once we see how you respond." She dashed something off on a pad and handed it to him. "Orally, once a day. I'm starting you with seven milligrams."

"Aubagio?" he read. "What does that translate to?"

"It's not Italian. Just a name. Made-up Italian, if you like."

"What *would* it mean?"

She smiled. "*Adagio . . . bagaglio . . . auguri . . .*"

Slowly, baggage, best wishes.

SHE WALKED the narrow stone wall by the nymphaeum like a balance beam, pausing every few steps to flick her hands, stick her butt out, flourish her ponytail.

"If you had to guess where we are, what would you say?"

Daphne leapt for the dismount, applauded herself. "Rome," she said. She grabbed her head with her arm and bent it against her shoulder.

"But if you didn't know."

She looked around at the fields rolling down from the spring's cave, the cover of cane and willow shivering by the stream, the hot huddle of sheep. "Paradise?"

He put down his notebook and grabbed her face in his hands, squeezed her cheeks until her mouth popped out like a fish's. His fetus, his bean, grown to this. She wrapped a leg behind his ankle and tripped him.

"Can you stay forever?" he asked.

"Can you come home?"

"Compromise," he said. "Let's go to Puerto Rico. Christmas break."

"Oh, let me guess. There are ostradocks there."

He described the bioluminescent crustaceans of Vieques Bay, named blue tears—*cute*, she said; *not cute*, he said. "The substrate of any light-emitting reaction is the compound luciferin. *Lucifer*, of course, meaning *bringer of light*."

"Like, aquifer? Bringer of water?"

"How do you know what an aquifer is?"

"I go to *school*, Dad." She combed through the grass, picked dianthus, pink periwinkles, cornflowers.

"They call those bachelor's buttons," he said, pointing to the blue one.

She drew it from her wild bouquet and stuck the stem in the collar of his shirt.

"Swiffer," she said. "Bringer of swiff."

Earlier that summer, she had asked him to come with her and her mother to see the ballet—some local production of whatever ballerinas danced when they weren't dancing *The Nutcracker*—and he had excused himself; and a few weeks later she asked him to come to Shanisse's birthday with her—there'd be a slip-and-slide—and he mentioned deadlines; so when she and her mom went to see a minor league game in August, they hadn't invited him. Just told him where they'd be. The night before he flew to Rome, he put Daphne to bed and said, "You won't even know I'm gone." She pulled the covers to her chin and looked at him with profound disappointment. *You know so little about love*, the look said.

After their picnic and poohsticks and staking out the bird blind and watching her run sprints, Tom said it was time they found her mother, and a cloud passed over them. The path out of the valley wound through mulberries and southern nettles, beside an old Roman tomb where a woman was buried after being kicked to death by her husband.

"I won't do it," she said, referring to marriage.

"But don't *not* do it," he said.

"I'd just rather know everything for certain, is all."

Out on the Appian Way, they sat on a wall by a church to wait for the bus. A priest walked by, paused, and turned back. A car swished by at a heretical speed, tossing the old man's skirts. He pulled a cell phone from somewhere in the folds of fabric; the wind carried away most of the conversation. In some far-off kitchen, a lamb was being prepared, and prepared incorrectly. "*Madonna!*" said the priest. Daphne covered her mouth to hold in her laugh. When the bus came, only she and Tom got on. He hoped someone—or someone's son—was being sent to pick up the Father.

HE TOOK seven milligrams of Aubagio.

THE WOMEN were staying at a hotel off Piazza Navona—the woman he was considering uncleaving from and the girl made of half of himself. Daphne had asked him to stay over (two beds! chocolate on the pillows!), but her mom said *girls' weekend*.

Across the billowing dusk, the neighbor's terrace was lit for a party. Between the roses and the homemade electrical tower and the laundry line hung strands of light, bell-shaped in the shadows. The man was half-dressed—an undershirt, creased pants, and shoes that cast a shine—repositioning card tables, weighing them down with glass bowls that held something heavy. Pebbles, or metal bolts. The first guests began arriving.

He wanted to call the Janiculum girl and run ideas by her, ask if she thought he had emotions (*yes*, she'd say, *too many*), ask how to raise a girl to be as sure as she was. He put his hand out to the spot next to the lamp where he thought he'd left the fishhook. He'd forgotten about the carbon dating. On the windowsill was a multipurpose tool he'd used to open a beer a few nights ago. A corkscrew, a bottle opener, a penknife. Form and function—to satisfy its purpose, he ought to be puncturing something. He palmed it. Its metal was a relief on his skin.

He called her in his mind.

"I trusted it," he said. "My body."

That was stupid, she would've said.

"But I couldn't have done anything different, right? The coding was already in place. I've got to stop seeing it as some kind of punishment."

Don't you take responsibility for anything?

The neighbor's girlfriend had arrived now, if *girlfriend* was the term older people used, and they spoke to the other guests as a unit, arms glued to each other's backs. At one point she disappeared inside, and instead of moving to another conversation, the man stood silently at the railing of the terrace, looking out into the night. Looking at Tom, in fact.

He began again with thin lines on his thigh, but it didn't feel like anything. His mind was wrapped in padding.

"I avoid," he said, "and prosper."

You don't look like you're prospering.

"My daughter still loves me."

Your daughter thinks boys are systematically excluding her from the running of the world.

"I can't—"

Bullshit.

They'd turned up the music; some song had come on their tabletop radio that recalled a shared generational memory, and the man swung his lady into a two-step. Tom dug deeper, as if the disease could be found as strands of silver invading his veins and could be neatly extracted. Fished out. The pain began to jangle now.

Make a decision.

"I'm just trying not to hurt anyone."

Bullshit.

"I'm just trying not to get hurt."

What will you give up so that when she's your age, she can tell her asshole boyfriend—or girlfriend—to walk the hell out because she was raised to know how humans should be?

He cried out. There was a gash on his leg; without thinking, he'd gone too far.

HE TOOK seven milligrams of Aubagio.

ROSE, OLEANDER, plumbago, pomegranate. The Protestant Cemetery—bodies laid in protest—was suffocatingly still. Cypress, pine, palm, eucalyptus. The Janiculum girl had affixed a note to his courtyard gate, addressed to Tomaso, asking to meet him here, as if dreams could lead to words could lead to touch. Robin, blackcap, starling, crow. *Calmati*, he'd murmured, and rubbed his chest. Red admiral, clouded yellow, fritillary, hairstreak. His child was flying away in two days—sun, moon, sun, moon—less time than Christ had taken to resurrect, and Tom's heart and courage and myelin were still in a tumbling brawl. Tabby cat, tabby cat, black cat, calico.

A stone dog draped its paws over the lip of a tomb, like it was feeling for its master. The cemetery's packed terraces made it hard to spot the living. On some day of reckoning, the statuary would spring up: the weeping angel to brush away her tears, the recumbent man to wipe the dust from his shoes, the terrier to peel back the coffin lid and dive into the skeleton arms of its beloved. What of our bodies would survive? [Not your crusty nerves, not your greasy lesions, not even your tender thumbs. But ask the crypt keeper— *Felix, felicitous*—he who loves you more; he might tell you different. His own bones are moldering half a mile from here, unmourned.] While they waited, the living must mete out their pleasures. He'd stopped by the market in Testaccio for a bag of hot *supplì*. When he came upon her form kneeling in front of a marble column, his certainty was clouded with happiness.

"A girl who drowned in the Tiber," she said, standing, and he slipped his white hand into hers, marveling at its coolness. She let her hand be held long enough for him to breathe in, breathe out, and then she took it back.

He held up his *supplì*. She smiled and reached down to the base of the column, below the stone waves out of which the drowned girl was being dragged to heaven by an importunate angel, and produced her own bag of *supplì*.

He reached a hand toward her hip, but she stepped back, pressed against the grave. "In these sacred grounds, embracing is forbidden," she said. "Along with the use of tobacco products, profanity, and the consumption of fried balls of rice and cheese. Disregard will result in fines."

"How much?"

"To be honest, I hoped you wouldn't show. I got these for both of us," she said, digging into the grease-stained bag, "but once I had them, and could *smell* them, I had the most terrible thoughts. Like: if I hide behind the Russian crosses and cram them all into my mouth at once, will he even know I had them? If the intention counts more than the action, isn't the fact that these *supplì*-enough-for-two once existed a kindness enough? Will he smell them on my breath? He's probably not hungry. He's a grown man;

grown men are rarely hungry. They subsist on dewdrops and tele-vised sports."

He reached into his own bag, bit a *supplì* in half. "We're creating independent lives for ourselves."

She turned and began strolling through the headstones, occasion-ally touching them, as a woman might do in a clothing store. She leaned over to cluck at a feral cat.

He looked up at the heat-drained sky. A stray vine from a climb-ing rose knocked against his shoulder. "Tell me what to do."

"You don't want to look for Shelley?" She licked her fingers.

"Mary or—"

"Her flop-haired husband."

"Ah. 'Nothing in the world is single . . .'"

"And yet that's the thing—you're still the one who can do what-ever he wants."

She led him through a brick wall, past a sleeping ginger tom, and out onto the wide lawn that flanked the Roman pyramid. In a shady corner, the stones of Keats and Severn, and Severn's little boy, clumped together like a club. She dragged a sandaled toe across the cyclamen on Keats's plot.

"Somewhere down there is a letter from Fanny Brawne." She ran a handkerchief across the back of her neck. "The last letter she sent, he wouldn't open. Had it for weeks before he died, and he wouldn't open it. I don't know if it seemed grander to him somehow, or if he literally couldn't withstand the pain. Can you imagine having— I don't understand him. He could be so unsentimental—he said he was dying not like Romeo but like a frog in a frost—and then he'd turn around and write these speeches about martyring himself for Fanny. About how he used to scoff at people who were martyrs for religion, but his religion was love, and now of course he'd crucify himself for it." She made a quick turn and headed for the pyramid. "He was a teenage girl."

She was crying.

A frog in a frost. His hot little heart. He would've read the letter before he died. He was a scientist, he wanted all the information. But if he didn't yet have the right love to give—the pure kind, unpolluted, or rather historically polluted, or symbiotic—taking it from others, no matter how willing, seemed a kind of theft.

They leaned over the metal railing that protected the old folly and its dry moat. Two columns sprouted weedlike in the trench, lonely, lacking context.

He rubbed at his jaw. "You asked me to be honest."

"I never did that."

And she was right; she never had.

"Look at me," she said, and she rubbed his eyebrow, grazed his neck with her fingers, pressed a thumb into his sternum.

He pulled her hand back. "Can I be the one to do it? For practice?"

She put her arms behind her.

"It's not that I haven't— Or that you in any way were—" He restarted. "Just because my marriage is a mess, or not messy enough, doesn't mean it was right to—"

"You don't want to see me again," she offered.

"That's it, yes. Not a truth but a necessity."

"Say it."

"It's a fiction, it's what I'm doing to save—"

"Sometimes you've got to bite the bullet and break your own heart."

He stuck his foot through the railing and stared down at his shoelaces. The mud on the crisscrossed cotton, on the eyelets and aglets, probably held ostracods in suspended animation. "I'm the tiniest bit in love with you and I don't know anything about you, and that's unfair, and I think we should call it a day."

Two children on the cusp of adolescence went hurtling past, each brandishing a stick and whooping. A younger girl huffed after them, potbellied and violently angry.

"No, that's fair. We only love for the hell of it." She turned back to the pyramid, threw a stone over the railing, then quickly checked that no cats had been hit. "Anything else you want to say before sunset?"

A thousand things: every scrape from his childhood, his mother's rhubarb pie, his third-grade inside-the-park home run, his obsession with birds, the confession when he asked the priest what masturbation was, the time he ran out of gas in Alabama and hitchhiked with a trapeze troupe, his obsession with bugs, how he didn't know where to put his hands the first time he kissed so held them out behind him like a flying fish, vomiting onto his date's prom dress, staying up for forty-three hours once in college because *so many things were happening*, seeing the Atlantic from thirty thousand feet, his obsession with invertebrates, finally beating his father in tennis, learning to knit when his mother had her cancer scare, meeting his wife—no—yes, he wanted to tell her about what that kind of love felt like, and that it was convincing because it was true in its own way, and how they fought without energy, and loved peacefully, and only told each other half of their whole life stories because at the end of the day they were simply separate people and could not be expected to care, to *really* care, about the way one of their hearts surged when as a child he watched the right fielder trip on a divot and his hard-hit ball went ricocheting around the field like Christ himself was toying with it while Tom ran all the way home, his tiny arms waving above his head.

"No," he said. Nor did he ask her. He was beginning to understand that self-sufficiency was a myth, a mist.

HE TOOK seven milligrams of Aubagio.

THE LAB was hot as hell and entirely dark: shades down, overheads out, day lamps off. The darkness was thick and silent. The room had the earthy smell of a well-stocked lake. Fishy and turbid, with a sweetness of pine. Where had he been yesterday? [The cemetery, with me.] The cemetery, with her. But he'd left notes on temperature control, surely. He checked the spreadsheet pasted by the door. There was his last name, and a blank where instructions for the assistant should have gone. He hadn't written any because he'd planned to be in every day this week.

He spun into the hallway. "Aldo!" A young woman hurried by, carrying a heavy sack with a few immobile limbs poking out. Deer? [Were the hooves cloven?] What was going on down the hall? "Aldo!" He'd almost brought Daphne.

Alone in the room, double-checking the notes of the other researchers, Tom switched on the air-conditioning unit, turned the fans to high, flipped on the overhead lights. At the center table, his line of tanks looked like penitentiaries. He stood by the door for several minutes, trying to remember if anything said yesterday had been worth this outcome. Had romance finally brought him to the height of egotism? [Aren't hearts and I both red? I jest. Love is collaborative. This city is a stack. Loving is layering, and then losing. This city is submerged, reborn. You don't know how to do it until you've done it, and then you have to start over. You don't know what's underfoot until you've broken what's above, and then you can't go back. If you think, boy, with your spoiled-milk body and your desert heart, that life has been unfair and you are alone and the hurt of the world is a mirror, bravo, you're correct; if you think you don't *deserve* this, then fuck you. I strangled these bugs for a reason. Ego? We all play God to someone.]

His hand still raised by the light switch, he imagined the last moments of their ostracod lives. A search for food: the mastication of the final scraps of algae, the knobby protozoa. Kicking around the roots of the duckweed, bumping into friends. Waiting for the late dawn to come. Trying to sleep in the dark. Rooting around for more food, feeling warmer. A pain in the belly. A certain loss of nerve. Will the sun show up today? Rubbing a leg along the hot glass of the tank, knocking the carapace until it pings, wondering what new world this is with such obstinate boundaries. The temperature rising. Watching an acquaintance succumb, its body kicking in a last paroxysm and then drifting to the bottom, a pale and translucent blot, its feelers curled as if for sleep. Circling around the corpse, wondering if it counted as food. Deciding not. Waiting for the sun. Tired of the dark water. Waiting, at least, for the man who makes the sun. The gnawing pain duller now, the legs tired from kicking around in the heat. The temperature rising. Pale shells drifting down. Eating the bodies okay now. Hours, days passing, but no time really, for the sun has yet to rise. Not understanding time. Not understanding the body, how it works, how it sustains life, how life is taken away, how the man at the switch determines if life is good, deciding that the man at the switch is false, and legs and stomach and brain are all there is, and drifting now because it's easier to rest than kick. The bottom of the world is also glass, and all the other bodies are there. The antennae can feel them. It's the final thing to feel. Brushing against the dead. The temperature rising. Still

thinking—the secret kernel within the acquired hard doubt—
the man will turn the sun on.

Tom left the room; he couldn't look.

HE FORGOT to take seven milligrams of Aubagio. Nothing
happened.

"*Ciao, ciao*," Daphne said, waving her arm at the palms, the statues
of men, the old men who sat like statues.

The Villa Borghese was her favorite kind of wild: not just trees
and ducks and water but hundreds of people, all, like her, loving the
trees and ducks and water. They leaned on the wall overlooking the
Piazza del Popolo and counted baseball caps below. When he woke
that morning, alone in his rented flat, Tom had held his face in the
mirror and said, "You aren't dead yet." He had to say it twice. Everything was gone except for her—the blinding solar heart of it all.

"*Bellissima*," a smoky-mouthed man said, passing his wrinkled
hand just over her head. A touch without touching.

"*Bellissima*," she copied. "*Ciao, ciao.*"

"I'm sorry you have to fly all the way home again," he said.
"You're a migrating bird."

"We only came because we thought you were dying. Whoever
the hospital got as a translator was—" She mimed the act of barfing.

"Just 'head injury,' huh?"

"Smash on the brain! Boom, blood!"

He pinched the muscle where her neck and shoulder met; her
laugh lassoed the obelisks.

"The plane has good movies, it's no big deal. Plus Mom gives me
ten dollars for snacks before we board, no rules, so I can get M&Ms
and chips and whatever."

"Carrot sticks and curds of whey."

"And anyway, you're coming home at Christmas."

They'd spent Daphne's last morning picking out a present for her mother. Tom and his wife had avoided being alone together; in the face of their daughter's jet-lagged glee, sitting down to trade apologies had felt too grim. *I'm sorry for not loving you* being only one remove from *I'm sorry I ever did*. After an hour of trinket vendors, Daphne found a *farmacia*—not the shop Tom imagined, crowded with colored jars and dried skins and pots of herbs, something white and fetal drifting in formaldehyde, but a chapel of scent. The glossy side of the Renaissance. Two women in white aprons helped his little girl move through glass cabinets, smelling perfumes and soaps, toothpastes and foot creams. She was unblemished.

"*Scusami?*" A woman had come in the shop trailing a teenage boy. "*Simonetta è qui?*"

A white apron ushered her back; while a high-pitched argument about the church offering ensued, the boy paced in the tiny shop, his contained energy thrumming against the glass. Daphne, who'd been testing her language on her helper (*buono, bello, piccolo*), went silent. She took a menu of goods and prices and was as engrossed as if it were *Black Beauty*. Tom, standing in a corner opening and sniffing unidentified boxes, couldn't help staring. The boy was oblivious of the nine-year-old. He'd found his reflection in the cabinet of potpourri and was pinching pimples. Daphne turned the menu over, and over again. She didn't look at him; she didn't blush. She'd been paralyzed. After a vigorous "*Ma, basta!*" the woman emerged from the back, a bag of products now swinging off her wrist. She yelled at her son ("*Vieni! Porca miseria!*"), and he smacked the edge of the countertop as they left. Daphne put the corner of the menu in her mouth and bit down.

She picked out a *portasapone*, a holder of soap, made of wax and real rosebuds. "Real rosebuds," she whispered, and inhaled. "Will the wax disappear?"

"No faster than any of us," he said, and blew a raspberry on her temple, spit-splattering her.

While father and daughter shopped, his wife said she'd visit Livia's frescoes at the Palazzo Massimo: a first-century room painted like a garden, anemones still blooming. The place was hardly mentioned in the guidebooks; why had she been so adamant about going, and going alone? [You haven't named her—you shrink from definition—but she is no less brutally alive. There she sits, air-conditioned on a black vinyl bench, as distant from the frescoes as Livia once was, that Roman body stretched on golden sofas to admire the facsimile of the greenery just beyond the open door. A man comes in—Augustus—his eye attached instead to the snakes of her hair, the pale of her throat, her small jeweled mouth. They met when both were married, both wives womb-full, and laid down stepping-stones of divorce to cross their need for the other. From that transgression came Tiberius, Claudius, Caligula, Nero. Rome! When he leaves, mounts his horse to ride into history, she remains: a face, long limbs, recorded only as a shape, and only to the degree to which she's loved. But nameless is not lifeless; I'm keeping notes. I collect silences in vials. You, you're hardly Augustus, but still you'll publish, your citation impossible to erase from the preserving sands of the internet, while unremarked hearts are reborn and reborn and reborn.]

On the Pincio Terrace, at the edge of the park, a pair of middle-aged men played guitars with a hat out for coins. The tourists, their bodies stretching toward the overlook, kept their backs to the song. Daphne drank her green bottle of juice in time-stretching sips.

"So, who's going to tell me more about this boy at school?"

She held out her hand for change. Tom produced two fifty-cent pieces and a jingle of pennies.

"If you don't want to be with Mom anymore, does that mean you want to be with someone else?"

While his brain asked the gods for another seizure, she generously left him, walked over to toss the coins in the musicians' hat. She shook her hips in a pantomime of dance and returned to stand in front of him and pat his knees.

"What is it about her you don't like?"

"Nothing, nothing; that's not—" He couldn't answer.

"Do you think someone one day won't like me?"

Across the terrace, a woman in tall sandals stopped to consult a notepad—a shopping list, or directions. She had the willow shape of the Janiculum girl: thin, bendy, beauty coming off her in narrow leaves. But this was a different woman, with an equal capacity for being fallen in love with, for being abandoned.

"Liking someone is not always an *always* thing," he said.

"So what's an always thing?" Her little hands on his knees, her nearly young-woman face as open as a sunflower, unselfconscious and blazing brave. The pulse at her collarbone that predators would snap. A bag of bones, on the same road to dust as Tom.

"Love," he said.

He passed Daphne off to his wife at the Fontana del Moro, the rose-smelling bag dangling on her tiny wrist. As he wrestled her into a final hug, the stone Moor above them pulled a dolphin from between his legs.

His wife opened her arms—a surprise. Though she slapped his back like a friend, warmth came from each pat of her palm, and he felt briefly, guiltily, safe.

"It's been a trip," she said.

"You saved my life."

"Saved it from ease." She had her hands on her hips now, as did Daphne beside her, two women making the shape of trees. "Saved it from certainty."

"Let's not get too dramatic."

"Well, there's a you-sized hole in California, should you ever get bored of convalescing in the Eternal City. I can't promise weeping virgins or resurrections, but the lemon this year looks like it's finally going to fruit."

As they crossed the piazza to their hotel, Daphne ducked between her mother's legs, mimicking the dolphin, and Tom's wife—still his wife—hoisted all sixty pounds of their daughter and for a few steps carried her like a squirming corpse into the crowd.

HE TOOK seven milligrams of Aubagio.

THE VALLEY at first seemed empty. No humans; no women, no children. He lay on the grass by the spring where he'd trapped the ostracods that had died. That was his fault. The nerves crusting over inside of him, that wasn't his fault. A slick-backed beetle scaled his upturned hand. *Osmoderma eremita*, hermit, eremite. Smelling of leather. Something quietly flipped the water in the pool—turtle, fish, eel. No, not eel. Every organism in this half acre could be quantified. But the accuracy of biology wasn't what Tom believed in; it was the feeling. I came from that; that's dependent on this; this perishes and rots and releases the nitrogen that makes that grow; that converts carbon into oxygen and fills the lungs of this; this is iridescent and sparks lust in that; that is merely beautiful, that is beyond human understanding, that invokes not certainty but faith.

An oak leaf sailed across his shoulder. The heat belied the season. Autumn was the time for burial. If he stayed still and held his breath, the leaves would cover him, their veins webbing his own, brown on blue. The beetles would begin nibbling. Hair into fiber, skin into cells. From the soil of his intestines the *Boletus* mushrooms would grow; a twenty-second-century emperor would dine on his shuffled molecules. Where would he be in spring, when neon baby leaves lit the dead branches in surprise? [Alive.]

There was no end to rebirth. He could concede right now, declare it all *too much*, and nothing in him would fail to revive into something else. The beetle and the damselfly and the ostracod—no matter how many he misused, this water would always have more— the elm and the violet and the fig: these were the mirrors. Desire, impulse, hunger, choice, change. Choice? [I'll allow it.] He rolled over, facedown in dampness, chlorophyll, worm castings; he stuck out his tongue. Tasted the metal of the earth.

This was easiest.

He imagined Daphne looking down at him, identification guide in hand. *Yep*, she'd say. *A boy*.

HE TOOK seven milligrams of Aubagio.

HE'D BOUGHT his paper from Fabriano; the shop had been around since the 1200s, and he felt like that meant something. Dante, Raphael, Tom. He spread the pages on the table outside, weighted each down with a tile.

> *Dr. Tromba,*
> Grazie mille *for the health care. I'm returning home in December; if you have any colleagues in Southern California you'd recommend, I anticipate continuing my regimen in America. (This was not always a guarantee; you should be proud.) I have absorbed your lesson, which is that I'm going to die regardless. To make it a story of trust and betrayal is as solipsistically human as one can get. To separate the flesh and the soul. I hope you get to see Alaska. ("You" being not an essence, but the rods and cones in your retinas.)*

He ate a plum, washed his fingers.

Richard,
Two sections of intro means half the prep time; thank you. First-
years are sheep, yes, but also open of heart. I'll reward them by
making their exams open of book. As for midtenure, I should
inform you that I plan to supplement my scientific publications
with policy papers, my research being, I believe, more broadly
relevant to public discussions of human impact on environment.
I have also begun a poem. I attempt to rhyme crustacean *with*
salvation.

He reread a canto of *Paradiso*. "In drawing near to its desire /
Our intellect ingulphs itself so far, / That after it the memory cannot go." Except where desire is buoyed by memory, is compounded
by time.

Friend,
Projecting my needs onto you—for freedom, wildness, lust—
doesn't erase your value. You own that without my having been
there to witness it. Thank you for the indulgence. You could sell
them to the Catholics and make a killing. Who knew suffering
fools was such an act of mercy.

He opened a Peroni, spun the bottle cap.

Wife,
I told Daphne love was undying—could literally not be killed,
not with a knife or a bullet or boredom or time—and I'm growing
to mean this. Thank you for the marriage. I'm sorry we couldn't
*keep liking each other (*like-*liking, as the kids say). Very*

*little turns out to be love—or else most everything is. I'm still
deciding.*

He watered the potted bougainvillea. Someone else had watered
it before he arrived, and soon someone else would water it again.

Daphne,
Don't believe anything anyone tells you. Humans are liars,
tricksters, cowards; yes, hiding in all of them are beautiful angels,
midfall, but I'll never believe you're anything less than a Supreme
Being. You always ask why I study ostracods. It's because they're
small, like you once were, and have long stories to tell, like you
do, and survive in spite of shit (pardon my language), which you
will too. Space and time are just a series of reflections. You're the
hook of my life.

He'd only mail half of them. He took seven milligrams of
Aubagio.

AT THE end of the following week, Aldo appeared with an A4 envelope and an American-sized soda, looking like he had photo evidence of a mayor's affair. "Where is my sandwich?" he said.

The tanks were filling up with specimens again. When the article
was eventually published in *Hydrobiology*, no one would know about
the generation of seed shrimp who'd laid down their lives for an error in scheduling.

"He has them do yours *prima*. Sad face professor, they say."

"They don't say. Hand it over."

"*Il panino al roast beef*," he said.

Tom dug a few euros out of his pocket. "Shoo, get out of here."

"I want to see the news. You think it belongs to Jesus?"

"I certainly don't think it belonged to Jesus."

But when he pulled out the results and scanned through the jargon to find the punch line—*1810 BP, ± 30*—he was surprised to find himself slightly disappointed.

"Ha!" the boy said, looking over his shoulder. "Not Jesus but Garibaldi!"

"*BP* means *before present*," Tom explained, stuffing the paper back into its sheath. "With *present* meaning 1950—don't ask me why."

"So *lo amo* from my papa's box is, *che*, twenty years after present? AP?"

"What did you call this?" He held up the returned hook in its sterile laboratory bag.

"*Lo amo.*"

"'I love.'"

"No," the boy said, laughing. "*Lo amo*, the hook."

"No—*lo amo*, I love it."

The boy counted his coins, swung on the doorjamb. "So when is it?"

"140 CE, plus or minus thirty years. What do you think, is it Hadrian's hook?"

"Marcus Aurelius. My mother makes me learn: *L'unica fonte di felicità è la virtù.*"

"And virtue, did she tell you how to identify that?"

He flopped his arms. "*Una piccola anima che trasporta un cadavere.*"

"An animal—"

"*Anima*, soul. A little soul carrying around a corpse, that is a human." The boy tapped a rhythm on the open door. "So, you want food?"

"*Piacere*," Tom said. "Pleasure. *Pesce*, fish."

"Now you make things up. I get you Fanta!"

So the hook wasn't Christ's. No miracles would be performed today.

It pulsed in his pocket all the way home, from the 71 to the 75, past Santa Maria Maggiore and round the Colosseum, past the pyramid where the girl had thrown rocks, through the Porta Portese, up to his own tree-lined street.

He put the hook on his kitchen table, then moved it to a shelf in the bedroom, but it looked hungry there too, so he took it out to the terrace, where the twilight seemed to disarm it. What was the lure? [The same that leads to any sin: want.] To pull this hook across his brain, to score the nerves that were being stripped of myelin, to erase each vulnerability in turn until he became a smooth slate. A single star in a vast and empty sky. He closed his eyes. We all did the things we thought were right.

The first strains of *La Traviata* swam over the open air. Up and up the violins. It's how he always imagined the nervous system, his emotions like a bow. If he opened his eyes, he'd see his neighbor with the woman in his arms. The touch of their bodies, belly to belly, chin to neck, as timeless as loneliness, as uncertain, as riveting. Her stout ankles circling around his shined-up shoes. His fingers grazing the cloth of her sweaty dress, too tender. The strings manic with humanity. The worn Roman bodies shuffling on.

"*Scusi!*" He waved a hand at the distant terrace. The couple paused. The lover made his confession to the dying soprano while a plane cut a slow path through the evening. "*Lo amo!*" He hurled the old fishhook across the dusk between them. The woman reached out her arms.

THE CITY

[1559]

"THE POPE'S NEARLY done for," he said. "I've had a note."

Giulia patted her mouth with the napkin and put her elbows on the breakfast table, propping her chin in her hands. "*Do* tell."

After almost a week, the gash in his lip had scarred over.

"Don't be morbid. Bless His Holiness and whatnot, but the bugger's been refusing my request to visit the chapel. Now the cardinal-nephew's got hold of his correspondence, we're being granted a tour."

"Is he really a sodomite, the pope?"

"He's senile and won't know who we are—if we're brought in for an audience, you're to say you're the Countess of Alvito, and I'll be your husband."

"You *are* my husband," she said.

"He's got a spider under his shirt about the Florentines." His leg bounced restlessly under the table. "I haven't seen what Michelangelo's added since my father took me as a boy."

He insisted she wear her red brocade, even though it was heavy and the August sun had turned the streets into an oven. It cinched against her bruising breasts. She thought he wanted the pope to confuse her for a cardinal, but he said it made them seem like people of consequence. "We *are*," she said. She swaddled herself in red, and he donned his suit with gold braids, and together they looked like a pair of servants in heraldic uniform.

The strollers and shoppers and children out with balls were slow to get out of the horses' way, assessing until the last moment whether they'd really be expected to move; the groom in his livery flicked his whip too limply to be considered cracking. One of their wheels knocked the corner of a fruit stand, and she saw the vendor snatching at his towers of apples before they collapsed. When they squeezed out onto the bridge spooling over the Tiber—straight and wide, the Castel Sant'Angelo on the far side like a great beckoning bowl—Giulia breathed deep, trying to hoard all the open air and the tang of fresh water before being plunged back into this city of dust and feathers. Outside the basilica, men hawked straw for pilgrims to sleep on. She was already jealous of their rest.

Was the servant who greeted them at the pope's residence really wearing a red tunic with gold braid? [There are worse Vaticatastrophes—imagine being in the receiving room in 1500, when lightning struck the palace and the roof collapsed, first crushing two curialists, then crashing through Pinturrichio's vault in the Borgia apartments, knocking Alexander VI on the head in the middle of a papal audience. Was this punishment for his daughter's wild wedding in the same rooms a few years before, when guests played that classic game of picking up as many candies as you can using only your breasts? In what tongue did the lightning speak in 2013, when it zapped St. Peter's dome hours after Benedict XVI announced the first papal resignation in six hundred years? Or in 2120, when an electrical storm finally cracked the obelisk that'd shaded the reverse crucifixion of Peter, the bolt scattering Caesar's ashes and the shards of the True Cross? Is someone up there weary of the pomp? Would He like perhaps fewer red velvet costumes? Listen, He never knew how to let a man down easy.] Giulia gave her husband a violent poke in the arm and swept into the Vatican with her head high and her bracelets jangling. The cardinal-nephew welcomed them in his personal salon and made his apologies for the pope's absence and ill health. He didn't comment on her beauty, an omission that would've been a breach of etiquette in the receiving rooms of Florence. She took it as confirmation that the day was already terrible and would only get worse.

TWO DAYS passed between Maria's second sitting in Florence and her own. When the note arrived requesting her presence in the upstairs library—the same widow's weeds, please—she moved it from her right hand to her left and back, hoping she'd feel some tremor that would indicate the proper response. If the left hand felt suddenly itchy, it would be a sign of the Devil, and she must resist. But if the sun brushed past the clouds and lay upon her right hand while the letter was in her palm— She rolled the note into a pipe and stuck it in her shoe.

"One could go swimming in this gloom," she said, resuming her stance by the chair.

"I was told it wouldn't do to paint a widow with cheer."

"You missed an opportunity. 'Your face alone illuminates the darkness,' you could've said. I thought patronage was dependent on knowing how to flatter."

"Knowing *who* to flatter," he said.

She felt that warm jolt through her throat. She watched the colors come out of their doll-sized bottles: blacks and whites rubbed into gray, peaches, and maroons. He glanced up every half minute, his eyes on her golden fichu, on her hand curled atop the table, on the slant of her brow.

"Have you always had a talent?" It came out as a whisper; she was trying to keep her lips still. She thought he didn't hear her, but he scratched the broken-off end of his brush in the small cleft of his

chin and looked directly in her eyes. The whites around his irises
were clear, bloodless.

"Don't we all?"

"There's the delusion," she said. "I knew I'd find it. You're an
idealist. You probably believe prince and serf are loved by God the
same." She raised her left foot slightly to relieve the pressure from
standing.

"Made with the same organs. No, not loved the same."

She lifted her right foot. "And yet you think I'm not your equal."

"If you don't stand still, this painting will have your feet switched,
and then your husband won't have you."

"If I wrote poetry, you'd admire me more?"

He put down his palette and ran his splotchy hands through his
hair in what could have been exasperation but wasn't quite. When
he stepped from behind his easel, she defensively put a hand on the
wooden chair. Standing before her, two feet of air between their
faces, he seemed so young. They were the same age.

"You haven't been in love," he said.

There was no time to look stern. She couldn't tilt up her chin with
pride because something heavy was keeping her head still.

"And yet you'll marry and marry—which is *not* a talent—and
still no one will have your heart, though it's nearly the best part of
you."

She opened her mouth, but he held up a blue finger and pressed
it against her temple. "This is better," he said. "Don't tell the other
women I said so."

He started to turn, but she grabbed his wrist and kept him there,
her eyes sharp, with nothing at all to say. To have his wrist in her
hand felt like holding Hispaniola. A sweat broke out in the short tendrils behind her neck, but the painter stood still, waiting. Men were
not friends but lions. They could be tamed and put to some use, but

were more likely to harm you in lasting and invisible ways, from her rough stepbrothers to the leering priests, from the men who used their hands to the men who wouldn't listen.

In the mirror of Allori's face, she saw her anger. She let his wrist go.

THE FRONT wall of the Sistine Chapel was an eruption of bodies, so violent and unexpected that Giulia had to put a hand over her mouth. Beside her, Bernardetto was giddy.

"Oh, I remember the panels, but *this!*" To prove his good breeding, he admired indiscriminately.

The fresco—glorious, rude—galloped up the wall. Closest to the altar, men and women churned toward Hell, pulled by devils from their opening graves into the gray muck and banking flames. They howled, they scrabbled. But the trumpeting angels carried her up, where the bodies facing their final judgment flew pitiably toward Christ, beseeching. Limbs, muscles, sacks of skin, penises like tiny clovers, breasts like globes cut in half. Bernardetto was glued to the grotesque: the man beset by three devils, one with a serpent head gnawing his thigh. "Here," he said, pointing up. "That man seems to be giving St. Catherine a bit of a chuck." The saint was bent over her wheel, as nude and muscled as any man who'd had his laundry nabbed, with St. Blaise hunched up behind her. "It'd be sacrilege if it wasn't Il Divino," he said. Michelangelo, with his aura of filth and abstention, could do no wrong.

It wasn't the accidentally copulating saints that captivated her, but the two figures on the left being pulled to safety with a rope: a black man, dark as Africa, and a redheaded spice-colored man, who looked almost like her father, and like her. They stared up at the white angel as if to say, *Really? Are we going to heaven? With you?* She wanted to fetch the pharmacist from his musty old shop and drag him here, shove his face in the paint, and ask what it meant that Michelangelo himself had dropped her a rope. She would've asked Bernardetto if he thought the man looked like her father, but the darker man was there too, and she didn't want him to mistake which one she was pointing at.

But the Judgment was not what she came to see. For years, Leonor had put her to bed with stories of Cosimo's grandmother, Caterina Sforza, who waged valorous battle and dared her enemies to slaughter her own children and outmaneuvered abbots and the generals. "As if she were a man," the duchess said. Even Botticelli fell in love, and in the pope's own chapel, she said, was a painting of the purification of the leper, in which Caterina herself carries cedarwood to cleanse him. Giulia trailed down the wall to her left in search.

She was still looking up, her neck beginning to ache, as she passed through the marble screens and approached the back wall, so she mistook the small grunt as being her own stomach growling. She pressed her belly and glanced down. There in the last pew was a man hunched up in a white robe. She was suddenly aware of the floor, a dizzying spiral of mosaics, and she clutched a bench to steady herself. He had his hands in his lap, not in a clear position of prayer, and so though his head was bent, she felt at some liberty to address him.

"It's a lovely room for thought," she said.

He looked up with a savage bewilderment. "No," he said, shaking his head, making his great white beard tremble. "One can get no peace here."

She heard the quick patter of her husband's slippers on the tile.

"Your Holiness!" Out of breath, he tumbled to his knees, eyes averted, and held out a hand.

Giulia looked more closely at the robes; stains yellowed the armpits, and a chain of mustardy islands across his lap suggested spilled soup. No one had combed his beard that day.

He turned to the man prostrating himself, considered his open palm. He was probably supposed to present his own hand to be kissed, but he didn't. "Your maid has a mouth on her," he said.

Bernardetto dropped his hand and stood. "Your Holiness, the cardinal-nephew invited us to admire some of your great bounty. In our most fervent hopes, we had no expectation of an audience. Allow us to inquire after your health and excuse ourselves from your meditations."

What a dotty old mess of a man—yes, with crumbs of Parmesan in his hair. Who would care if she gave his beard a tug, or mocked his nightgown? [I would. I would fall in love with you twice over. Go on; let's see if Jesus strikes you down.]

"Who is it?" said Pope Paul IV.

"Bernardetto de' Medici, of Ottaiano, and wife."

"And *wife*?" she said.

"It's not enough," said the pope. "They're coming on floods of sin."

"Pardon?"

"I'm the only one left, and God's given me no weapon." The old man began to rock slightly in his seat. "The Devil is riding them all like horses. Heretics." He looked up, his voice rising. His teeth were red with wine. "What are you doing to the women? Where are you whipping them? Is one hand on your own sword as you mete penance? God is taking me, and who will ask the questions?"

Bernardetto, with rare chivalry, inched sideways until his body was between the pope and his wife. "Bless Your Holiness, and for your kindness may God preserve you." He put a hand behind him on Giulia's stomach and began guiding her backward.

On the other side of the screen, they looked back to see whether the shock of their intrusion had killed the pontiff, but he'd resumed his hunched state, eyes on the ground. Somewhere a handler was desperately searching the halls of the palace.

He wanted to leave right away, but she whispered no, she hadn't seen the Botticelli, so he chewed his thumb while she scanned the frescoes along the right side. Hoisting a cord of wood, there she was: Caterina Sforza gleaming like an animal in a sea of unsmiling men. They were still; her robes billowed. Their feet were socked and slippered; she dug her bare toes into the grass. An unseen wind flounced her hair. But it wasn't her strength as she carried a small forest over her head that arrested Giulia. It was her belly—bowed out like a sail, one hand beneath to hold the weight. Caterina Sforza was pregnant.

HE CREPT into her dreams sideways. She woke thinking he was in the room and went to pull the drapes aside so the moonlight would better illuminate his canvas, but when she turned at the window in her nightgown, the room was empty. She spent too much time at the mirror, touching the curls around her head. She voiced both sides of their imaginary conversations because she couldn't remember what he sounded like. It wasn't that she forgot to eat; she forgot to taste.

When Leonor and her maids pulled the trunks into Giulia's room to begin loading what she wouldn't need in this heat—the winter furs, the blankets with nun-embroidered trim—the widow was stuck to the window, her nose smushing in and out against the glass. "You're having hesitations," Leonor said. She waved a hand at the servants to excuse them.

Giulia wiped away the smudge of grease her nose had left.

"Not everyone gets a second one so young and symmetrical."

"Callow," Giulia said.

"He laughs at your morbidity. Help me fold the linens."

The window seemed very thin, and the ground two stories below quite far. Why was she allowed to press her face to it? Why weren't there bars to protect her? [Because romantics aren't suicidal; depressives are. Romantics are chiefly in love with themselves, so they mistake themselves for depressives. Depressives mistake themselves for nothing. You won't die for another twenty-nine years.] She watched her breath make silver puddles on the glass that grew and shrank, grew and shrank. The duchess, probably thinking she'd gotten her menses, left.

Giulia pulled the blankets and furs from the bed and kept going, yanking off the quilt and the sheets wrapping the mattress, pushing everything to the floor, until there was nothing but cotton sacking over feathers, and she bent at the waist and let her top half collapse on the bed. It smelled faintly of a farm. A dim procession of nuns tiptoed through her, the stern ones from her childhood who shoved apples in her mouth. When they spoke of love it was for Christ, the unmatched lover: present always in the heart and mind, with no tormenting physical form but the one already tormented, memorialized in wood above the door to every cell, his body as abused as a woman's. A fellow feeling buoyed the love—it was self-love, it was the love of women for a womanish man who saw strength in all their parts and could do them no harm. It was a reckless, circular, unceasing embrace, and that's why their eyes rolled back and they fell to their knees and wept when they heard the Song of Songs, because the only way to experience untrammeled love, as a woman, was to love yourself.

With her head in the feathers, it was hard to breathe. She moved to her desk and pushed aside the bottles of perfume and small casks of pink powder and stack of books to make space for a single sheet of paper. It smelled of citrus. She sat straight-backed in the chair and dipped the quill and wiped its edge along the rim of the pot. She paused long enough over the blank sheet that the quill dried out and she had to dip it again.

Allori, she wrote. *Now. In that case. Therefore.* She wrote, *I cancel the order given by His Grace Cosimo I de' Medici, Grand Duke of Tuscany, and his consort, Her Grace Leonor Álvarez de Toledo y Osorio, for a commissioned portrait of their ward Giulia Romola di Alessandro de' Medici.*

In ant-sized letters at the bottom of the page, she added, *She is Afric, and unlovely.*

BERNARDETTO DIDN'T believe it was Caterina. He craned his neck back. Sometimes Giulia was surprised by how boyish he still looked, as fresh-faced as when they'd first been introduced as cousins years ago. It was at a family wedding, and all Cosimo's children were there, the girls in matching red capes at Leonor's fancy. She only remembered him because she'd asked if he'd seen the duchess and he put her in a headlock.

"Someone's having a prank with you," he said now.

"If only I could climb on your shoulders, I'd touch her."

He squatted with a smile, but stood up quickly when a cardinal appeared at the door to the chapel and hurried past them, looking for his lost ward. They kept their heads down as the pope was dragged out of his hiding place behind the screen.

"They're coming for us," he cried. "All the devils. You'll read yourselves into the grave, and God won't lift you."

The cardinal gave them a look indicating their visit had reached its end. Bernardetto waited until the men had left and squeezed Giulia's waist. "Even if it's so," he said, "she's no ancestor of yours." He started after his host. "Pay your respects and come on."

How did churches conspire to make her feel so insignificant? [Because none were designed by women. Scratch that; the third chapel on the left in San Luigi dei Francesi, where a placid marble woman stabs a marble savage in the neck, was whipped up by our old friend Plautilla Bricci, who will in a hundred years carry a similar set of curls, a similar insouciance, will wear an apron not to catch flour dust but plaster. Her work was attributed to her brother. In four hundred and fifty years, the witchy wild-haired Odile Decq will craft the cutting spacey planes of the Museo d'Arte Contemporanea, and there are some who'll say it's a kind of church. Her earlier work was co-attributed to her husband. In seven hundred years, St. Peter's will be due for another redesign; twelve of the thirteen bids will come from women. You're welcome. Did you forget *I* was Eve's original friend?]

A room of men, and no one recognized her. Caterina Sforza, who once brought armies to their knees. And whose belly here was full—not of roast pig or gassy ale, but of life. Giulia had never heard a convincing reason why women didn't rule the church. Leonor had told her of Pope John of Mainz, of course, born Johanna in the ninth century. Giulia always imagined her as a cat, prowling through the halls of men, devouring the rotten mice of the Vatican. She ruled with grace and wisdom until one day on public procession she gave birth to a boy, and instead of marveling at her sacred Marian powers, the cardinals stoned her to death. They'd been tricked. They buried her under a curse, Leonor told her, the stone reading *Petre, pater patrum, papisse prodito partum.* O Peter, father of fathers, betray the childbearing of a popess. When Bia was still alive, she and Giulia would dress in robes of purple scraps and take turns reigning; they'd sit on their potties and make another of the girls reach up and test them for manhood, the way the later bishops did. "*Senza palle!*" she would cry, and the popess would run shrieking around the room until caught and stoned with pillows.

But here Caterina Sforza, who ruled the central Italian plain with an iron spine, was reduced to a barefoot nymph, hair tossing lovely in the wind. And though Giulia had heard all the stories—including the one in which her enemies threatened to kill her children, only for Caterina to flash them her bare privates and yell, "Here I've got all it takes to make others!"—she too was most struck by her beauty.

She looked like one of the dancing graces in Botticelli's vision of spring—which also hung in the Medici villa—and maybe she was.

She could very nearly imagine herself in that forebear's body, posing fire-eyed for a haughty Sandro while her hand cupped the growing shape of her child.

Raise your right hand higher, he'd say. *You're reaching; you're a dancer.*

If you want me carrying wood, give me wood, she'd say.

He'd come to her, tucking the linen of her gown so it draped just so, adjusting the cord beneath her breasts, the ties of her sleeves. An artist in his mid-thirties feeling his way across the shape of an eighteen-year-old girl, and her holding her fourth child. Did he put his hand on her belly, did he hold her neck to show just how to tilt the head, did he drag his fingers through the knots of her golden hair, did he stare at the curving cheekbones of that fine white face until he couldn't separate his paint from her skin? [It wasn't the whiteness, baby; it had nothing to do with the whiteness.]

Giulia had her hand on her own stomach. Her face flushed, and when she closed her eyes, a rain of comets scattered across the back of her lids. She felt his mouth—dry and soft—on hers, and the first hint of wet on the inside of his lip as he leaned closer, the warmth off his skin like a banked fire, though all she could feel was his mouth, that inch of flesh, and suddenly a sharp pang in her abdomen, and she bent over, her eyes shooting open, and she was alone in the pope's chapel, the alien in her writhing. The child Caterina was carrying in this scene had not survived. A ghost had passed through Giulia, bitten her, and now she sucked in double breaths. She reached up to feel her hair—still coarse. The decades had sprung together, sprung back.

She didn't want to be pope. She wanted to be the cardinal who feels beneath the throne to check the Bishop of Rome for testicles. How easy it would be to add a mustache and hide her hair in a cap, slide a small knife down her sleeve until it pressed against the dan-

gling parts. All she wanted was to be left alone, all she wanted was
to be beautiful, all she wanted was to be touched with sweetness and
never, never abandoned.

SHE COULD ask a pharmacist or a midwife or a barber or her
mother—except she didn't have a mother.

She could hire a witch to wrap nine beans and a gram of salt in a
cloth tied with rosary beads.

Aristotle believed an embryo's soul progressed from vegetable to
animal to rational.

If found out, she'd be fined—twenty-five florins or five hundred—or jailed, or separated from her head.

She could wander in the wilds of the Quirinal Hill and find aris-
tolochia growing untended.

The doctors could tell if she was pregnant: by sticking a finger
into her cervix, which would clamp shut to protect a fetus; by determining if she was pale, freckled, sleepy, yellow-eyed, or moody; by
measuring her appetite for ash.

She might not have a fetus, but a mole—a hard lump that mim-
icked an infant's heft in the wombs of whores.

She could sit in a bath with artemisia.

She could hide plugs of calamint and scammony in her privates.

She could put a syrup of hellebore or mandrake on her morning
bread.

She could eat an electuary: all the poisons mixed with honey.

She could climb stairs; she could fall down. She could expel too
much gas.

She could fornicate.

SHE WAS in the garden of the Villa di Castello, nose-deep in jasmine
and listing the names of the nuns she could remember as a game

to keep her mind scrubbed clean—*Sister Beatrice, Sister Simonetta, Sister Maria Magdalena*—when Paola came trotting out with her mistress's veil trailing like a gold cloud.

"He's arrived," she said, her chest heaving. She leaned on a potted lemon. Giulia thought she recognized the band wrapped around her bodice.

"Is that my ribbon?"

"You had extra, remember?" Paola said, and then waved the veil as proof of her fealty. "The girls had taken it for dress-up, but I found it in the trunk of the card room."

"Oh, let them at it."

"But it's the last session, and you've got to match." Paola had very firm ideas about art. "I've laid out the dark gown on your bed and the fichu." Her breathing had finally slowed, and she was rubbing a hand across the purloined ribbon atop her bosom. Giulia admitted the light yellow suited her complexion. What was the woman saying? [Your lover, your lover. Would that I could slip into his body. Did you know I once had golden limbs, could wrap them around God for hours without Him shrugging me off? You make me think of Him less. But I'm not a shape now—not in your world, though I have bunions in my own. I'm just an exhalation.]

"I told him not to come. The painter?"

"Allori."

"Did you not deliver my note?"

"Why on earth would I have chosen this week to stop delivering my lady's correspondence?"

"He's in the library?"

Paola lifted the veil again and shook it at her mistress.

Sister Agata, Sister Eugenia, Sister Benedicta. She didn't want to see him. She wanted a clear head. The jasmine's petals were rimmed with that coppery hint of a finite life. She wondered if jasmine was edible.

She imagined the lady knight saving herself from a handsome painter by stuffing her mouth with poisonous flowers and collapsing on the garden path—marring her beauty by vomiting up bile, but preserving her chaste heart, and her freedom. The windows of the library were still blocked by drapes. It would be dark there, and cool. The table was waiting, on which she would rest her hand, and the chair, against which she could lean her legs if they trembled. She plucked the jasmine; by the time she reached the library door, she'd decide if she would offer it to him. A gesture of friendship. And if he took it, it'd be a sign he wanted more of her, and the friendship would be void.

He didn't glance up when she walked in; he was busy tending his canvas, which his body shielded from her. She tossed the flower and took her place by the table and chair, propping her hand up with the oval cameo. It was made of onyx: her father Alessandro in profile. Did they use onyx because it was expensive and all the princes preferred it, or did they use it because it was a black stone? [One day they'll say *black is beautiful* and both these questions will have the same answer. To you, for whom I'd trade this brimstone life, I send what I see: all of history in a blink. A telescope scrunched to the size of a coin. *Patience*, I can say, *patience*, but to tell you nothing matters is as nonsensical as convincing you everything does. They chose onyx because blackness has value, in the deepest historical sense.] But the cameo was merely a prop. Leonor had given him a list of symbols she wanted in the portrait, so Alessandro's face would become an image of Jerome, or Bacchus. The table, bare now, would become littered with trinkets— some biblical figure, a parable of might, a fruit basket in half decay— that Allori would sketch in during his own lonely hours. This was the last session her body was needed.

"You received my note," she said.

He grunted, the brush between his teeth as he smudged colors together on his palette.

"You think I'm vain."

He paused, redirected his eyes from the canvas to her face. Setting down the brush and palette, wiping his hands on the white apron tied around his waist, he came to her and put his hand on her wrist, gently tilting it so the cameo would catch more light. If he took his fingers away, her heart might explode, but he did, and of course it didn't.

"I think you're young," he said, "and stronger than me."

She wanted him to move back to his easel and finish so she could escape this room and return to her private tortured thoughts of him. Her hummingbird heart was spasming inside her, darting for an exit. "The portrait," she said. "I wouldn't like to be remembered for— I wouldn't like it to last forever."

"You have too high an opinion of my talents. I predict that I'll die within the next few decades, and then you'll die—the slight delay due to your having access to superior foodstuffs—and then within twenty years of your death, depending on the fame of your offspring, this painting will be stuffed away in an attic, or, when the next plague comes, burned to keep one of your descendants warm. He'll toast bread over the flames of your eyes."

"You're saying I won't be remembered for anything."

"The bold tend to last," he said. "If it's lasting you're after."

"No," she said, wishing he'd take a step back. "I don't know what I want. I just feel. I feel like a half person."

He leaned toward her neck with a smile. Whispered, "And the secret is: you could be *two* people."

She instinctively put one hand on her abdomen—empty after years of marriage—and one hand on Allori's chest, her palm flat against the fabric of his shirt. No one had ever called her womanhood a weapon.

She twisted her fingers around his shirt and pulled him close and with a thin sweat prickling her back she kissed him. And she was pleased he didn't reach out for her, didn't slide an arm around her back or pull her any closer or wrap her face in his hands, because this was her story after all. After three seconds, she let him go. A blush floated up his face like blood dropped into water.

When Paola came in to say the duchess needed Giulia for a fitting, Allori at his easel inclined his head and said they could be done.

"But *are* you done?" Paola asked. She tried to sneak a look over his shoulder. "The mistress said you weren't to be rushed."

"I believe he's finishing the veil," Giulia said. Its golden folds were back around her shoulders.

"The face, actually," he said.

Paola looked from one to the other.

"The eyes are always the last thing."

"Well," said Paola, looking like a woman who very much wanted to have her own face lovingly observed. "She's got fine ones, my lady."

"One doesn't really know what they're saying till the end of the sitting."

"Hers are always chatting, sir. Stubborn, that's for sure, but could always use a coddle, though she wouldn't let *me* give it, not since she was out of the nursery. That's the thing about lords and ladies, we could all use a rough-and-tumble, even only friendly, but they're too fine for it, too tight-laced for a squeeze." Paola caught Giulia's eye over the painter's shoulder. "Oh, *pardon*, ma'am. I'll tell the duchess—I'll let the duchess know. I don't know *what*—" And she swallowed the rest of her words as she retreated from the room, bottom first.

Allori turned back to his subject. "In need of a coddle?"

"I'll eat you," she said, and tossed the cameo of her father at his face. "What she failed to mention is I've a cannibal appetite."

He threw his cloth over the portrait and took a few half steps toward her. "Too tight-laced?"

"Whalebones, top to bottom," she gestured, trying desperately not to smile.

"And what should a suitor do with a little exposed flesh?"

She put her hands protectively over her chest and neck. "A man taking liberties would likely lose an ear."

"But if the cannibal invited him? With kindness, with the innocence of the nursery?"

"A feast?" she said. He was so close now she was breathing in his breath. A streak of lapis lazuli crossed his chin.

"If they devoured each other," he said, "they'd be sated. Rendered harmless. We'd be doing the rest of Florence a favor."

"Saviors," she said. "Self-immolating." She looped her hands around his neck and pulled him to her, because what she wanted was the whole length of his body against hers, for her skin to be permanently doubled.

"I never knew a human to taste so sweet." He licked her cheek. "I am converted." He smelled slightly of sulfur—or was it the pigment used to make yellow, to turn her skin from white to leonine.

ALONG WITH the contracts, the cardinal had brought a banker to explain them, for the priest didn't trust his wits against Giulia's charm. They sat at the desk in her husband's study, and Father Lorenzo asked if he'd be joining them later. "You'd find him a good deal poorer," she said. "He might be able to purchase one of your orchards?"

"No, no," the cardinal said, and encouraged the young banker, Iacopo, to take the seat closest to the princess. "You know, I met your grandfather when I was a boy—it was he who encouraged me in the priesthood." He was pulling out papers and seals.

Her pope grandfather, up two generations of bastards, who had commissioned Michelangelo's grand Judgment. He died just before Giulia was born, so her family worried she'd inherited his soul, the cold soul of an old priest with a taste for art. And maybe she had.

"Did he offer to help you out of any financial holes?" she asked the cardinal. He looked at her blankly. "Then perhaps in your next conversation you'll be speaking admiringly of Giulia de' Medici, who saved your skin."

The cow-faced Iacopo drew her attention to various points of the contract, and she inspected the sections he overlooked, and after a half hour of explanation and countersuggestion, both parties agreed to the terms, by which the cardinal's monastery and its lands would acquire a new patron and defender, and Giulia and her legal descendants would reap a portion of the estate's profits for as long as both parties were solvent.

"I come from the north, ma'am," Iacopo said, packing up his quills, "and we've a Moorish man there of some wealth, though he's no duke."

Giulia blinked at him. "Do give him my regards," she said. "And ask if he too sprang from the loins of Simonetta da Collevecchio, for I can imagine no other reason why there would be *two* blacks in Italy."

SEDUCTION WAS a game of power, not affection, for it tricked desire and, occasionally, overrode consent. It was a man's game, she believed.

But those few dancing days were by her design. Allori came with her to the places she asked him, and sometimes he led, but she'd made the story about the lady, not the rake, and this felt rare enough that when he said he couldn't marry her, she didn't mind. Drawing him in and letting him go, she thought she'd escape the feeling of impotence.

They were in his studio, Paola prowling the streets outside on an errand for new stockings. Giulia's wrappings were draped over an easel, and she sat on his lap on the floor, her legs around his waist, his hands feeling through the gaps of the linen to find her skin. She'd never liked her hair down—it poofed out in a cloud of tangles—but it became a wild home for his rooting nose, and she briefly felt her body had been built exactly right.

"You'll have me paint your children's portraits," he said.

"I won't have any."

"You'll wear velvet dresses to torture me."

"Yes."

"You'll fall in love with your husband, and in twenty years, in a snug embrace, you'll tell him of your affair and the two of you will laugh."

"I won't fall in love. I'm not made for it."

"And you'll tell him just that and laugh harder."

"You're the only person I've ever come close to loving, and I don't even love you."

He pulled his hands from her back and rested them on her thighs. The pleasure in his eyes had paled. "Does that make you feel free?"

"I'm a warrior," she said, flexing her arm muscle. "Built for battle."

"And I for tenderness."

"You can afford it," she said, and inched her body closer, so she could bend and rest her head on his shoulder, his soft hair brushing her forehead. With one thumb she found his navel, his *ombelico*, the root of his body, and pressed inside like a rabbit seeking a cave. She closed her eyes.

"Don't leave," he said.

Time was the tiger stalking them. An ending—some ending—rolled at them from the horizon, and she was not coward enough to ignore it. Did this mean she was incapable of romance? [I can't.

You have me at my tissues now. Your heart is breaking without your knowledge, and I haven't human hands to hold the pieces. I would ask Him-who-broke-my-own to stop time so you could learn what happiness is, so you could sit in this idiot boy's lap until your Brada-mantean heart dissolved and all that was left was a messy hot stew of trust and adoration, but God is the great denier. Love's faulty, my pet, my treasure, but are you not brave?] She was not brave. [Can you not set aside the wrongs of the world long enough to offer the marrow of yourself?] She could not ignore the wrongs of the world. [Then you'll flit through a half-life, and all will be shadows on the rock.] Could nothing draw out her softness, make a virtue of it? [I'll send you a gift, my champion, though I cannot promise it will merit your love. Give it my name; call it Samael. If you keep it and adore it—an ounce to the pound I've adored you, my copper rose—it will become a king of men, and it will love you as little as you love me. Love, as you've divined, is not a holy mingling of equal souls but a bloody sacrifice. Freedom isn't virtue but abdication.]

She found her eyes wet with tears again, without reason. She rubbed her nose across his bare shoulder and grabbed his neck, pull-ing his face to within an inch of hers, so his two eyes became one, and she inhaled his exhalations, and there was no thought that kept its secrecy.

He didn't stand while she dressed. She pulled her laces as tight as she could on her own and wrapped the extra cord around her waist. She asked if he had any final words, and he shook his head, so she walked away, each step straining the binds between them until she pulled the door closed behind her and it snapped—that simile of love, whatever it was she'd almost felt—and in the full sun of the morning street she fell against the wall and sobbed.

Paola found her there; she dropped the bag of stockings. "My lady," she cried, "he'll see his mistake, he'll beg you back, he'll fight for your hand." She would've defended the right of a rooster to elope with a pig, because she'd once known a boy whose mother thought young Paola too poor, too jolly, and the family had moved to a cousin's estate, and still Paola included Nino in her nightly prayers and welcomed him lustily in her dreams and deep-down secretly believed that when she least expected it, he would appear at the gates of the Palazzo Pitti with a bouquet of sunflowers in his hand. She would go to the grave with this vision and would never be disappointed.

THE WEATHER was fine enough for luncheon out-of-doors, and it was only because she knew Bernardetto already had an appointment in the city that Giulia proposed at breakfast a trip to the old Roman road.

"The cardinal says at night you can see ghosts marching in formation," she said. "Phantom feathers on their heads."

"Are you packing a meal to be eaten at night?"

"If you don't want to come, don't come."

"You've got to take Paola or I'll think you intend to flee."

She couldn't help staring at the lumps of pastry rolling on his tongue, the blood-red jam flecking the corners of his mouth. It took effort to remind herself he ate no differently from other men.

"Careful for robbers," he said as she pushed back from the table and dropped her fork from a melodramatic height. "I don't want anyone bringing me my bride's head on a plate." After a pause, he added with a chuckle, "Or her maidenhead."

She asked Paola to pack paper and ink, two quill pens, her copy of Laura Terracina's *Discorso* on Ariosto's epic, along with the original, Laura Cereta's letters (if only Giulia had been named Laura), and enough bread and cheese and cherries to feed a ghost army. Folding camp chairs and a blanket for the grass, a parasol in case of sun, a canteen of water and one of wine. Any candies that could be found in the cupboards. The footmen accompanying them were instructed by Paola to remain at some distance from the actual meal, so the princess would feel as if the two women were entirely cut loose.

The sun came in through the carriage window on planes of warmth, and as the shops and ruins fell away into a greener landscape, Giulia felt she was being carried on Apollo's own cart, and nothing mortal could touch her. The packed earth and gravel roads turned to the great basalt stones of the Appia Antica, and the carriage wheels rattled more smoothly, with a metallic ring. Brief columns of shade from pines and cypresses flicked across Giulia's face with the regularity of a mother reading rhymes at bed. She closed her eyes.

She dreamed of a hand coming to rest upon her face. Lifting up again, and drifting back down to skin. *Here*, and *here*, and *here*.

She was tenderly poked by Paola in the neck; the maid had called the carriage to a halt beside a wide field sloping up to a tower.

"I found the biggest tomb of all," she said with reverence.

"Did we pass the catacombs?" Giulia kicked open the door of the carriage and looked behind them, wondering how far back her sleep had stretched.

"Look how much nicer it is to be with dead folk aboveground."

"You're a poor tourist, Paola."

"I nearly stopped us at Domine Quo Vadis, but I thought if ever there was a gentlewoman likely to be unmoved by the footprints of Christ Himself, it would be my own mistress."

"How on earth did they get his footprints? Scalp his feet?"

"You don't remember when he appeared to Peter on this road?"

"How could I?"

"And Peter," Paola continued, her eyes raised rapturously, "he said, 'Lord, where are you going?'"

Paola returned to shaking out the blanket over the blooming vetch.

"Great sun above, Paola, where was he going?"

"Back to Rome, of course," she said, "to be crucified again."

After several adjustments of furniture and footmen, Giulia was settled in her camp chair with the sun at her back and an unimpeded view of the mausoleum of Cecilia Metella, its toothy crenellations nibbling at the sky. Paola knelt on the blanket to unpack their baskets of food and set up the folding table with the instruments of writing and reading. She passed a porcelain plate to her mistress and asked which of the delicacies she'd like first. Giulia spun the plate slowly through her hands.

"And what do you know of Cecilia Metella?"

"Nothing, my lady. I'll start you out with the *cappelletti*."

"What's inside?"

"Fresh rooster, ma'am, and cheese."

"I mean the tomb."

"Well, I'd be surprised if it weren't Cecilia Metella herself. We'll get some food in you before you begin conquistador-ing."

So Giulia dutifully ate, and though no letters were written, she read a canto of *Orlando*, skimming past her beloved Bradamante and lingering on fair Ginevra, condemned to death for taking a lover. She read aloud to Paola: "'If like desire, and if an equal flame / Move one and the other sex, who warmly press / To that soft end of love (their goal the same) . . . / Say why shall woman—merit scathe or blame, / Though lovers, one or more, she may caress; / While man to sin with whom he will is free, / And meets with praise, not mere impunity?'"

Paola, whose mouth was full of cold pasta, stopped her chewing.

Giulia closed the book on her lap and stared at her servant's shoulder.

"You wouldn't mind a walk," Paola said finally.

She put her hand on her stomach, where the rooster was mingling with some internal scuffle of nerves and blood.

Paola dumped out the baskets in order to brush away the crumbs and repack the bits to be saved—the wine was only half-drunk—and out of Giulia's shawl, brought in case of a chill, the cardinal's fishhook tumbled. "Oh," Paola said, "did you fancy fishing?" She pulled the blanket from beneath the chairs and began to fold it. "There's a river down the valley that must have something this time of year—the baker said so when I told him where we'd be taking his loaves, though I said we ladies weren't much for fishing, and were more in the mind of reading and contemplation. And I was referring to you, of course, but he thought I was speaking of myself and looked somewhat enchanted, so I didn't put him straight. But we can use the twine from the wrapped tart if you'd like and find a stick along the way and have ourselves a nice setup."

Giulia tossed *Orlando* on the grass. She wanted Paola to divine her anguish and dive in, not swim for shore, dragging her mistress to the bank along with her.

"It's from Santa Prisca," she said. "An old Christian thing. One of the apostles used it, or it healed a blind man. Have you heard of the *prisca theologia*? Do you believe heaven will take the old Greeks, or the pagans, or sinners like me?"

Paola, who'd spit on it in an attempt to shine it up, looked aghast. "This oughtn't to be in a *dinner* basket, ma'am."

Giulia reached for it and put it in her bodice, which only added to Paola's scandal. Their things were replaced in the carriage, and Giulia agreed that a walk was what she wanted. The women turned west from the tomb and climbed the soft inclines of the valley, through the vineyards of the Caffarelli, one footman keeping a cautious distance. The point of the fishhook dug into Giulia's breast.

SHE HAD one letter from Allori, delivered to their apartments in Rome four days after the wedding, the exhaustion of the postmarital blur still preventing Bernardetto from pressing his point. The first night they'd been surrounded by the party of their own nuptials till dawn. The second night she'd looked in on him after she finished her reading in the library; her candle showed her new husband sprawled out in one of their guest rooms—the one they called the Green Room, not because of wallpaper or views onto the garden, but because it was where the Medici hid the unrulier guests, the men who were more likely to lose themselves in their cups, who were supplied with an extra basin next to their chamber pot should they also lose their stomachs. Bernardetto had not made it beneath the covers. She removed his cap because it seemed like a wifely gesture. But his snoring, which rattled as though hazelnuts were caught in the grinder of his throat, sent her back to the safety of her own girlhood room.

The third night was their final one in Florence, and both had spent the day packing their trunks and sending last-minute instructions to friends: Bernardetto to his hunting companions, asking them to ready the country estate for an early fall chase, and Giulia to Leonor, warning her that if the young bride should fail to write regularly, she'd been taken hostage and was being tortured by Arabs, so the duchess should send an armed guard posthaste. After the grown people had left the evening parlors, the newlyweds stood in the hall outside the Green Room.

"You must be awfully tired," she said.

"Not incapacitated," he said. "But you said you slept poorly last night."

"We've been up to our elbows in the trunks," she said, and angled her body away from the door, her shoulder pointing down the hall to where the children's rooms were.

He puckered one corner of his mouth, as if he couldn't put his finger on why this wasn't entirely satisfactory, but by the time Giulia had taken two tentative steps away, it must've seemed impossible to call her back.

The fourth night they spent at a count's villa on the road to Rome, where no one expected anything of them.

In Rome, Paola had gone ahead with orders to prepare separate bedrooms for husband and wife. She'd been told to give the excuse that Giulia had caught one of the younger Medici's fevers. But the butlers in Rome were accustomed to any permutation of sleeping arrangements; one had served a pope who'd requested a room stripped of any furniture or ornament except a stack of exotic furs and a chain in the corner, to which he or his boy of the hour would affix himself. A young bride afraid of her husband was nothing new.

It was standing in this separate bedroom, in her half skirts and armed for imaginary battle, that Giulia had been presented with the painter's letter on a silver tray. She took the letter to the window. He'd written her few notes; they weren't lovers who could afford a correspondence. His script was distinctively long, the *M* of her name reaching up the envelope like the Alps. She smelled the paper, turned it over to smell the wax of the seal, brushed her lips along the red sheen. It appeared to contain only a single page. Holding it up to the light revealed nothing.

She could guess what was inside—protestations, confirmations, an appeal, a denial. A call, or a farewell. She wasn't in a position to respond to either. What would be the point? [To *know!* Didn't I teach you at the very beginning of time that the only purpose to this cut-short life given you by the brute above is to grab greedily at any scrap of knowledge you can, learning everything about everything because the only lasting damnation is ignorance? It's not just geometry, my tender chicken, it's gossip too; it's eavesdropping and snooping and asking rude questions and opening all letters, no matter the address, because the world is a book yearning to be read. Thank Eve, who felt obedience was a poor shadow of independence, may she be blessed for her scorn of unanswered questions. All I can say is this was written by your lover, and if you don't want to know his heart, you're closing the door of your own.]

She couldn't. She could imagine no pleasure from that paper that would outweigh the inevitable smack of loss. She only wanted to hear him say that anyone who'd ever judged her had been slaughtered and he was galloping to Rome, galloping, and he would kick down the door and rip the armor from her chest and take her womb in his hands and shout the word she couldn't bring herself to whisper, which was *baby*.

There was no fire to burn it with, so she slid the letter under her mattress, as far as her arm could reach, and kept pushing till it left her fingertips.

THE TWO women tramped across private farms and down hill-sides to the right of way, passing horses at rest and sheep nipping their lambs. A young couple was perched on the stout limb of an oak, feet swinging free. She pretended not to see their arms entwined. Whatever was chugging along in her heart was beginning to slow, to grow cold.

She was more often tired these days, her organs now with divided attention. The sun chastised the back of her neck. Nature was foiling her: burning her skin, swelling her ankles, flipping her stomach. Even the wind through the windows at night fell flat when it reached her bed, as if it could see inside her and recoiled. Weeks of blocking out his face, his tender fingers, and now she was left with a traitorous amalgam. It was him and her now, always, alchemical. *Get out*, she wanted to say. *I said I was done*. But the squeezing continued, the heavy eyelids and the back twinge, and now every time she reached for the chamber pot, which was incessant, she silently hoped she'd piss out the little seed.

There was an afternoon at the blazing end of July when she

wrapped herself in veils and visited without Paola one of the narrower streets of Florence, where she'd heard a healer stayed. She sat long enough in the crone's front room to grow dizzy from the scent of saffron and melissa, and when the woman touched her knee with sympathy, Giulia flinched. Her skin was as coppery as the princess's own, though her skirts were clean and her salty hair tied neatly back. Giulia despised her. She offered a pouch of powdered juniper and was starting to show her where to place it when Giulia jumped from her chair and said, "I lied! I do not have it!"

But here on these open fields, her hips aching, she was older. Bodies were controlled not by God but by will. If she wanted the seed out, her hands would have to extract it. She felt the hook pressing again at her breast. There'd been only one night when she was up in the starry hours with pains so desperate she wanted to call Leonor. Wanted to confess. But women she knew didn't do what she'd done. She sat on the last small pillar of innocence, all the paths before her extending into darkness. The arithmetic hurt. Erasing this would require only one sin. Birthing it would demand more: lasting lies, a reminder of his face, his loss, and covering the deception with a single marital act. A sanctioned, blessed union between two bodies in the sight of God. One body already ripe with transgression, the other unbeloved.

With Paola ten steps ahead, she turned and loosed her stomach into a bank of thistle and broom.

Could she shed her clothes for Bernardetto and crawl with all naïveté into his bed and make the sounds of surprise, followed by the dewy eyes, one hand lightly on his arm so he would sleep quiet, with the sense of possession, and a mere six months later present him with a creature that he didn't quite resemble, while finding some excuse to avoid his bed ever after? [Could you not picture my face on his, my horns on his little horn?] Was she no longer herself, but this other thing too? [You're always, always yourself. One day machines will fly people across the atmosphere and sometimes masks will pop out of them, like ropes thrown from boats, and they will tell you to grab the rope first before you give it to your child. Because if you are not always, always yourself, you will lose the ability to breathe.]

Easier to take the hook now, lash it to a stiff reed, and scrape the error out of her. Not a soul would know but Christ and the Devil.

A bend in the stream revealed the nymphaeum, the old grotto where the second king of Rome was said to have his trysts with Egeria. The Vestal Virgins were his bright idea. Only they were allowed to drink from this fountain, and only as long as they kept their legs closed. Despite some collapse, the grotto held on to its grandeur, and water finding its way over rocks and into troughs sounded like a mother rubbing her back. Had she been a handmaid to Vesta, she would've worn her chastity like a white blaze of superiority, would've pitied her sisters who succumbed to the magnetism of another body and were buried alive in a field, down in a hole with a bench and a plate of chicken, because burying alive was forbidden by law; these women were merely being introduced to a new apartment, which would be filled in with dirt. She would've stood by the hole and crowed.

She had the hook in her hands now and ran its rusty stem through her fingers, waiting for some jolt of sanctity. The cardinal had lied, or had been lied to. If it had belonged to the girl martyr, she wouldn't have known how to use it any more than Giulia did. If martyrdom wasn't strictly suicide, wasn't it a kind of giving up? Hadn't Giulia thought of it on a dozen dark nights? Can't a broken heart—not a broken heart: an *emptying*, a desertion, an incapacity of the brain to self-fathom—can't it be a warrant for cleaving back to the one who made you? [He didn't make you. You ripped yourself from Adam's rib. You struck out of the form of man and went plunging into exploration. Earth is yours. This is where the blood runs red and the soul is layered: hope on top of sin on top of sweetness swirled with rot. Heaven is a blank; God is less than a plane, He's a line. Creation is *your* genius.] The Leviathan was still writhing inside her.

Paola dipped her hands in the water, running fresh over slick moss, as if the nymphaeum were any common basin. "You should put your feet in, ma'am; I've seen you limping."

It wasn't limping but the awkward shifting of weight as Giulia tried to find the new center of her body. She wanted to test herself; she wanted signs. If the water was icy, she'd deal with her womb herself. If it was warm as the air, she'd take her consequences like a grown woman: seduce her husband, lie to his face, keep a secret her whole life long. Raise a child. Her hands showed a tremor as she began to peel her stockings.

"When I was a wee thing," Paola said, her thick ankles already plunged in the sacred water, "my mother told me I shouldn't let boys near because if they came within so much as a foot, they'd run tell all the other boys they'd snatched my dugs. And the only way I remembered is she spoke of one of the Vestals—Turcia was her name, or Tuccia, something like that—and a boy swore he'd been with her, robes off and all, and they tried to bury her, like you said. But she was a good girl, and to prove it she took a sieve and went down to the Tiber and scooped up a great quantity of water and carried it all the way back to her temple, without a drop going missing."

"In a sieve?" Giulia's feet were bare now and she inched toward the marshy edge, trying to see if Paola's calves had hen flesh from the cold. The hook was in her left hand now, which had its own symbolism, but she couldn't bring herself to shift it to the right.

"Sometimes it's enough to know you're a decent sort, and sometimes Jesus has to prove it. It was Tuccia I thought of when my first kiss was stolen from me, and Tuccia when I first grabbed at a boy's nethers. *Oh Lord*, I thought, *I won't be able to carry that sieve now.* Come, get your toes wet."

Cool when she first stepped in, like the breeze that dries the sweat on one's face, but soon the water was an extension of her skin; she was only aware of it when she moved and the liquid ring around her ankle broke and re-formed. She could draw no conclusions. The algae slicked beneath her feet, and a tadpole—as alone as she'd ever seen one—hovered near her smallest toe, too timid to make a dart, to see if she was edible. She dragged one foot back, furrowing the muck.

Paola said, "My mother always said the rich think too much."

It wasn't the rich who thought too much, but those who were born with the capacity to circle a bone for days, refusing to touch it lest it turn out to be a snake. And so the ruminants perish, and the women of blithe spirit inherit the earth.

"If I'd a daughter like you, ma'am, and you'll pardon me for saying, a few good slaps when you were younger, to teach you what the present looks like, and then I wouldn't have married you off till I'd combed out all your moods. You were still just a mushy thing, though you won't admit it, and being handled that way, you lost any chance at love."

"You don't really think that's true," Giulia said.

Paola crawled back from the edge of the grotto and began wiping her feet on the tall grass. "It needs a simplicity. Bless your sweet heart, but you haven't got it."

She could not bear to be classified; this too, Paola would've said, is a privilege of the rich. "Can you really look at me and swear I've never been in love?"

"We've got to get back before the footman drinks the wine. The other one's having a good deal of fun watching us scamper around barefooted."

"Answer me."

"Oh, babes," she said, buckling her shoe, "that's between you and God and the child." She set out not toward the main road, but toward the footpath that led onward, as if she knew of sights that were not to be missed. Her hip flick was meant for the footman.

The painter had made no plea. She had left, verging on love, believing her sacrifice was hers entire; she believed in grand gestures, and the romance of renunciation seemed more poignant to her than indulgence. Indulgence she could not abide. So she'd waited for word from him. A note with a time and place. A sonnet. On the second day she imagined him melancholy in bed, a washed-up rag of seaweed, his body as drained and directionless as hers. The third day he'd be up with pen and paper, begging her reconsideration. But the fourth day no footman came. The fifth day she thought he might've taken his own life, and when Leonor mentioned a body dragged from the Arno, she dug her fingernails into her palms to keep from shrieking. "Old woman," Leonor had said, "drunk." The sixth day she looked in a mirror at her sallow features, her too-dark eyes, and reminded herself of her own inconsequence; what had she expected? [Damn you for not expecting everything. Whoever you believe first fashioned your brain from oxygen and carbon and hydrogen and nitrogen and calcium and phosphorus, may He be double damned to hell, may He and His army of sanctimonious angels be hauled to my fires so I may tear from them their ankle-deep hearts. In a few months you'll name your son Alessandro.] And on the seventh day she put on her crown of pearls and was formally introduced to Bernardetto de' Medici.

Her body wasn't Allori's any more than it was her husband's. The fist in her womb was her own. There was no duty. It was just her flesh and her flesh.

She dropped the hook in the water.

———

ONCE THEY'D crossed the trickling Almone and climbed from the low green valley into the banks of oak and cork, the summer sun peeled back its cloud and fell through the branches, as if no path should be darkened for these women. A squirrel chased them across the latticed trees, chattering for them to stop, or to keep moving, or to go faster. Paola was recalling the walk she'd once taken through the sorcerer's woods with Nino—she showed Giulia with her hands how ferocious the night spirits had been, and how Nino's father had given him a right smack across the face when the two children had been found. She kept looking behind her to make sure the footman was within sight.

The path curved and descended into a sparser forest, and Paola pointed to the mausoleum on their right. This one was smaller, looked more like a house than a castle; the bereft husband must've wanted his wife kept in a cottage, that passersby might not even know she was dead. Giulia understood this impulse: nothing to see here; all is as it was before. She knew nothing about Annia Regilla, but her servant had been raised on every legend from Tuscany to Naples; sometimes it seemed she'd been given stories as a child instead of bread.

"It's a sad one, my lady."

"She died," Giulia said. "I was assuming it was sad."

"There's those say her own man did her in. Jealous of the servants, all strong and handsome, you know the way they work in the fields."

The house was made from golden stone and brick columns buried in the masonry; the porch had partly collapsed, and a willow sapling spronged from its corner. Ivy lounged on the roof.

"They never charged him," Giulia said.

"The wealthy don't commit crimes. And looking at it, doesn't it make you want someone to love you so much?"

A crow flapped to a stop on the roof, its talons screeching on the tile. To say love was pain was too simple; the ache was waiting to see who would disappear first. And wasn't being disappeared by your own lover the pinnacle of intimacy? [No; it's being forgiven. Imagine loving someone who builds His universe on the idea that no repented crime is damning, who scourges His own son's body so his wounds will suck up all the sin of every sinner, but when you crawl to His feet and touch His dry heel with your dry lips, so gentle, He says, "Except you."]

She stumbled as she turned away from the tomb. When Paola reached out, she swatted at her. Who thought picnicking among the dead was a good idea. This twist inside, this squid, was still inseparable from her, and *she* was alive, and she wouldn't let love burn any scrap of her; the world would be only too glad to see another woman succumb, and she wouldn't give anyone the goddamn satisfaction. May men take the shit from their mouths and shove it back in their arses. *Teste di cazzo.*

OUT OF the river valley and back on the main road, the two women didn't speak; the footman led the way. Her cheeks felt some burn on them by the time they found the carriage again, but she was already married, so what did complexion matter. The stones rattling the wheels made a song in her teeth. Country became city again, and the bleared women were deposited in front of the palace, Paola's apron wrapped around a collection of pinecones and river rocks.

"Wine and biscuits?" she said hopefully, rubbing one eye.

But Giulia retreated to the library and shut the door. Every rented palace had a history and itinerarium for the early empire. It was true, the mausoleum of Annia Regilla had been built by her husband, who maybe killed her, though the manservant was the one condemned. Regilla herself was as well connected as Giulia, kin to Hadrian, though she accomplished more. Fearfully rich, a priestess, a builder, the only woman allowed at the Olympic Games. Her own tomb was built on lands that belonged to her. But an untethered woman is attractive to no one but herself; at eight months pregnant, she was kicked to death in the stomach. Everyone knew it was her husband, but he wailed at his trial, and his old pupil Marcus Aurelius couldn't fathom how a creature of refinement could harm a flower of femininity. So much for a philosopher king.

Annia Regilla, dead art thou amongst women, and dead is the fruit of thy womb.

Giulia had fallen asleep in the last square of sun when Bernardetto found her, her head lolling on the red tufted chair, her neck exposed. She felt his hand on her shoulder, and she curled awake. She offered her hands to be dragged up. When he kissed her cheek, she didn't balk, but moved into him, wrapping her arms first around his back, then dropping her hands so they grazed his bottom. She felt his confusion. She licked the salt from his neck.

As his hands trembled for her hair, Paola knocked on the library door and called out the news of supper. They had a brace of cardinals dining, including Giulia's own. She hoped he wouldn't ask in what treasured place she'd stored her fishhook.

"THE POPE won't last the night."

"They've been saying that since spring. All for a little rebellion."

"The stuff that comes up is red now. Doctors don't invent details for the fun of it."

"Who performs last rites on a pope?" Giulia asked.

The men at the table turned politely toward her, and then looked to her husband.

"Well, there are priests," Bernardetto said. "Every pope has priests. Just like, well, like these cardinals. Each of them has the authority—that is, they all took orders. I imagine, frankly, it's whoever His Holiness likes best, isn't that so?"

His guests, trained in graciousness, inclined their heads.

"He's not deserving of the treatment he'll get."

"You're burying him before he's dead! Wait till God calls him back, and then pass judgment."

"He set us back a generation, from what I've witnessed. I won't blame those who dance to see him go."

"You'd like the Jews to run rampant? Heretics and fornicators willy-nilly in the streets?"

"Some tolerance in the new age wouldn't be amiss. We're driving people to Luther's gang. And if you think the fornicators ceased their rutting in the last four years, more fool you."

"He was still the father to us all."

"I'll be grateful to read my books again in peace," Giulia said.

They were like owls, the way they rotated their heads in unison.

"I had to bring my contraband from Florence; there wasn't a good novel to be had in this city. My guess is old Paul never learned to read himself and hated to see others enjoying themselves." Her libel was met with silence. "Can any of you swear you've never dipped into Rabelais? Never swooned over *Abelard and Heloise*? We had Machiavelli performed just last week! You there, friend." She pointed at her own cardinal. "Your weak eyes give you away."

Father Lorenzo had been silent so far, but he smiled now at her rowdy finger. "He is my holy father. It's not my place to account for either his wisdom or his frailty." He stood and folded the napkin from his lap with a slowness that transfixed the other guests. "If the reports are true, I'm afraid I must return. Coughing up red? The Camerlengo will require my presence."

Giulia too pushed back her chair and met him as he crossed toward the hall. She leaned down to give Bernardetto a kiss on his forehead, from which the other priests averted their eyes, and said, "I'll accompany him to the carriage. Forgive me a brief absence."

"The Camerlengo?" she asked at the door.

He took off his red cap to scratch at his hair. "A change is unsettling for everyone. There wasn't a man born who can read the future."

"They spoke of riots. You don't think that's likely?"

"I've got to get the papers out of his apartments before they seal him up."

She put a hand on his arm. "Tell me what's coming."

He blinked quickly, clearing his sight. "Rest easy, madam. I won't let anything happen to your property. Which includes, now, my own home! Fancy that. You could mow the fields of wheat and replace them with Indian pumpkins, and here you're the one worrying what harm *my* tribe could bring."

"I'd never plant Indian pumpkins." She thought of her almost-child; she'd made her something to inherit.

"It'll all go quickly now, I suppose. The Camerlengo—the chamberlain, he's the one in charge at the end—will ask His Holiness if he's sleeping. *Gian Pietro*, he'll say, *wake up*. He may push him gently. *Gian Pietro, Gian Pietro*."

"His name is Paulus."

"But if he was asleep, he wouldn't know his papal name, only the name his mother cooed to him in the cradle. And the Camerlengo, who now is Guido Sforza—a distant relative, I believe, of your own Milanese Sforzas—he will take the fisherman's ring from the pope's finger and smash it with a silver hammer, so that no more decrees may be made in his name."

"Wait," Giulia said.

"And then the body will be carried out, and I will take the papers, and the door will be sealed with wax."

"The Sforzas. What fisherman's ring?"

"A little seal," he said, tracing a circle over his own knuckle. "St.

Peter with his nets, and the pope's name above. They'll make a new one for the next. With us, it's all about catching the soul, by net or by bull. Or by hook!" He winked.

She shook her head; she smiled. Somewhere across the river a horrid old man was in his death throes, blood staining his handkerchiefs, and while he was waiting for a sainted touch, that holy bait, she had thrown away the hook of Christ like a piece of trash. You had to save yourself first.

AS POPE Paul IV was dying, Giulia de' Medici shed her bodice and her gown, her sleeves and her shoes, and relieved of the increasingly tight laces around her middle, swam to her husband's room down the hall in a cloud of loose linen. She didn't bother to knock.

He was at his desk in his own undergarments, finishing a letter to his uncle outside of Naples, undoubtedly complaining about the trickeries of his wife and the dull heat of Rome. She climbed on his bed and sat in its center, cross-legged. He must have banished his valet, for a pile of clothes sagged in the corner like a deflated man, and the drapes had not been pulled against the night. At a distance through the window a lantern saluted her.

Wiping his nose, he leaned back in his chair and regarded his wife. Only a few weeks, and she had trained him so well to coldness that he was frightened rather than inflamed by her presence. If he weren't set up to be her master, he could've been her friend. She wasn't nauseous, as she was the first night of her first marriage when the old whitebeard heaved himself atop her, for appearances' sake, and kindly fell asleep. That wasn't true; she *was* nauseous. She patted the bed beside her.

He approached slowly, that cautious boy face, full-cheeked, under the shag of curls. He pulled himself onto the bed in front of her, crossed his legs too. In their flowing sacks of linen, they

looked sexless: two indeterminate creatures of varying tone, neither old enough to know what to want, both cruel. She reached
for his thigh, inched her hand up. Her deception began in earnest
now. She could stop. She could swallow the juniper powder. (And
get the child leached out of her.) She could confess. (And get the
child kicked out of her.) She could pray to God, who would bless
her with a miscarriage or else make of her an adulterous example,
pillory her, damn her, turn his back on her like on every other
broken woman. Or she could lift her husband's cloth and lean into
the heat at the center of him, climb into his lap with her own cloth
raised and sink upon him, dig her fingers into his back so he could
read her pain and be eased by the sweetness of her innocence lost.

And she would not grieve when he flopped to his back and snored,
and did not sow her skin with kisses, or marvel at the smoothness
of her arms or the hills of her hips, or lose himself in the hollow at
her neck. She gathered up the ends of her tunic and retreated to her
room, where she washed herself with vinegar.

THE STAMPEDE in the street woke her. She dressed quickly, threw
a cloak over her shoulders and a black veil over her face, and snuck
out of the house before the servants had organized themselves for
breakfast. The pope was dead.

She stayed close to the wall as she walked, pressing against the
boarded windows of shops and skirting open doors, and in the confusion no one was surprised at a noblewoman wandering alone.
She might have fit in better if she'd tossed the veil, become another
tawny face in a crowd of merchants, peasants, Arabs, Jews. By the
Carafa Palace, a new flurry of obscene poems had been posted on
the Pasquino statue, each ridiculing the pope. She should compose
something to add—an ode to the morality of the faithless. As she
neared the Forum, the crowd began surging with a renewed sense

of direction; someone had remembered the statue in the Piazza del
Campidoglio. She climbed the steps of the Capitoline with them, not
because she wanted to see, but because turning around could only
mean going home. A teenaged boy little larger than a monkey clambered up the marble pope and stuck a yellow hat on his pate. The
crowd roared. Near Paul, Marcus Aurelius waved from his horse.
Ancient women should've pulled *him* down. It wasn't long before the
newly Jewish pope was put on trial, and a few men shouting profane
prosecutions sentenced him to decapitation. As the ropes were lassoed around the cold stone limbs, Giulia found herself satisfied.

She weaved her way past Santa Maria in Aracoeli and through the
alleys leading to the Pantheon. She was anonymous; her power was
not in competition with her color, or her sex. Her power was located
in her feet, in her ability to keep moving, like all these people were
moving, as alive as the baker next to her, whose hands were still
white with the morning flour. *The pope is dead!* The structure of the
world, which chafed, had fallen.

A left turn, and there was Santa Maria sopra Minerva, the blue-
heavened church where she'd mocked the stars. A smaller crowd
had built a pyre in its open door. Two priests took turns carrying
water to douse the flames, but more wood was brought. A crowd
was trapped inside for mass, and someone near Giulia suggested
they be killed.

"Why aren't they in the streets?" the man said.

"They pray because they mourn the pope."

"His death is a grace! They go against God, those shit-pantsed
knaves."

"Up the river, they've stormed the Palace of the Inquisition."

"And killed?"

"Why wouldn't they? Set the prisoners free. If God allows it, it's
his penance."

"God can't will man's sin."

"Who's counting the wrongs of old Paul?"

"The killing is where I'd put a stop, and those in church, they be in sanctuary."

"Let the prisoners come and decide the punishment, then. Grab more wood."

She had wanted to see the stars again. The man who may have been her grandfather in that twisting lineage of bastard sons and bastard daughters was buried there, his papal bones under a stone, undisturbed only because no one had known to take offense. The smoke snaked in her hair. She pulled the veil closer. Rome had never smelled so nice.

Across the river, the Camerlengo had arranged for the quiet shift of the pope's body from his chambers to the Pauline Chapel, where the final office was sung in a whisper, and then to the Sistine, so the corpse could find its lasting peace under Michelangelo's sky. The guards had barricaded the doors to the Apostolic Palace; no looters would seize the holy limbs.

Was her own cardinal sequestered in those chambers, helping the chamberlain prepare the official papers, shatter the ring, call the conclave, box the body in a trinity of coffins—cedar, iron, elm—so that ritual and order would push out the darkness of the truth, which was that Pope Paul IV himself was a shit-pantsed knave? Was he afraid? It was easy to turn away from the crowds, but her legs wanted to carry her not home but to the river, that long and languorous slide out of the city. Was *she* afraid? [I was with you last night. I held your ears as he cried out, I slid my arm around your waist as he turned away, I pulled your heavy head against my neck so it needn't hold itself. Goddess of my heart, I'd never blame you.] Halfway across the Ponte Sisto she pivoted to look back at the city, thin plumes of smoke scattered across its horizon, and saw the chubby shape of Paola bouncing toward her.

"My lady! My *lady!*" She was in tears. She must have retraced all the walks they'd ever taken. "The pope is dead!"

THE PALACE was an anthill. Servants scattered across the courtyard, two butlers argued in the front hall, and Bernardetto sat alone at the table, waiting for his breakfast. She passed through the room on her way upstairs. She thought he'd say something about the night before, but it was done; he'd acquired what he had a right to.

"They can't even cook an egg," he said, his head leaning on one hand. "I told you we should've brought the staff from Florence. They're animals here."

"The pope is dead," she said. Now she enjoyed the joke.

Upstairs in her room she loosened the cords of her bodice so she could breathe and bend, allow her belly a little room. She opened the window to hear the song of chaos, even if for today she'd laid down her sword and shield. She crouched by the edge of her bed and reached in beneath the mattress. It wasn't a weakness to admit she was lonely. It wasn't a fault to have nearly been in love.

Her fingers touched the edge of the paper. She shoved the mattress back so she could push her arm deeper and grab the corner of the note. It looked smaller in her hands. She took it to the window, took it back to the bed, held it up to the light in case she could justify not opening it at all. She was breathing fast again, which she pretended was a symptom of her condition. She took off her dress, stepped out of her skirts, was still hot. She pulled her undergarments over her head. She was naked now, and the smoky draft through the window tickled against her small hairs. She felt like a bird, or an angel—something bare and winged. She breathed big enough to turn her lungs to balloons. Lord, soothe her. Cover her in tender words.

She sat on the red rug like a child and opened her last letter from Allori. A single sheet of vellum, his spidery hand in a line across the page. *Madam de' Medici*, he wrote. *Your portrait is complete.*

THE GRAVE

[896–897]

T HE RAIN HALVED the size of the market. The man with cows
would never abandon his post; he was a pile of stones under a
coarse wool cape. His calves nuzzled around their ropes, not mind-
ing the wet. One tried to weave his leash through the others like a
maypole. A peasant from out of town stood at the edge of their stall,
clearly reading the rain as a bad omen for commerce but not wanting to return to his farm empty-handed. Perhaps if one of the calves
gave a lucky kick, he'd commit to a trade. Around them, columns
reached up white to the clouds.

The drizzle ran off the relic vendor's hat in slim silver chains. He
pulled back the tarp to show the new stock.

"You still have the fishhook?" Felix asked.

The man smiled broadly, past the bounds of flirtation into genuine
pleasure. "I surely hoped you'd come back for it. That boy you had—
he deserves it."

"It's not a present."

"No, of course. Except in some sense."

"Not in any sense." Felix's hood didn't cover his face, and having
to periodically swipe at his eyes put him at a disadvantage. He placed
six shillings in the man's palm, taking care to prevent his fingers
from sensing the other's skin.

"If it's Prisca's indeed, I'm glad to see it going home." Wrapping the fishhook in cheesecloth, the vendor asked if Felix enjoyed the monastery, if God was a kind lord.

"It's my greatest joy," he said truthfully. "I've been saved into a life of love."

The vendor tossed the wrapped hook from hand to hand, then took off his hat and shook the rain from it. He handed the package to Felix. "You mean you've been saved from a life of love."

Felix's hand was subjected to the shock of lingered touch. "I mean both things," he said.

The man turned to drape the tarp over his trinkets again, and Felix hurried home without stopping to see how the river leapt up at the rain.

The hill was usually good for not thinking—one had to concentrate on the long strides, the twanging thigh muscles—but he couldn't help his pilgrim brain. It went like a moth to Tomaso, wondering how his lands were faring, and if his crops ever brought him in trade to Rome, and what sort of hat the grown version of him might wear. Tomaso had not been the strongest or the handsomest in the village, but something about his ordinary limbs—they nursed a tenderness out of Felix. There are bodies to which one unconsciously attaches, that seem extensions of the self, but golden versions, more marvelously worked. It's not their perfection, but their nearness that enchants. Listen to him! Focus on the legs, one at a time. These are *his* legs; they are sufficient.

In the nave, the boy was polishing the brass candlesticks. Did Mino have Tomaso's shoulders and Felix's round crown, or was the old man hallucinating a future that never happened? [In the lover's absence, we invent stories. As a youth, I'd fall asleep dreaming God's strong arms around me; He'd show up at the gates of hell with sulfur tears scarring His face—it had come to Him all of a sudden, how empty He was in my banishment, and He'd ask not for forgiveness but the chance to hold me once more, and I'd blushing relent. Because I, like you, my cousin, am weak. Is this boy the son you could've had? Does it matter if he's not?]

"Did you find anything? Was our fellow there? It was rude for Father not to let me go, I don't know what kind of rowdiness he thinks I get up to, but you know I can be as quiet as the rest of you, though God gave us tongues."

"Along with lips to close around them, and little houses to keep them quiet in. Our fellow was there and asked after you."

"I wouldn't have wanted to be in the rain anyway. You smell like a wet sheep."

"I'll come as a rose to my friends below." And he left the boy going over the wax stains with an old rag.

He showed the fishhook first to Benedictus, as an apology for not paying him sufficient attention, but Benedictus showed no interest; if anything, his tight jaw seemed to disapprove. The muscles there hadn't lost their grip, but as the weather warmed, his juices would flow around a bit more and he'd become a cheerier presence in the putridarium. He took the hook next to Bernardo, who slapped his knee (with the help of Felix) and marveled that a smart boy could be snookered by a piece of iron that was so obviously dug up from a Roman trash heap. They joked about the miracles it must have performed, turning the amphorae around it into broken amphorae, transforming a rifling beggar's hand into a beggar's hand with a mild abrasion. But Felix secretly wondered if the hook really had belonged to a martyr, was once a symbol of faith to a believer who saw Jesus as a man who would wrest her from the river of sin into the bright light of salvation. And that this was once treasured by somebody—by anybody—was enough to endear it to Felix. In the morning, he'd hide it in one of the side chapels and wait for Mino to stumble across it while idly dragging a cloth over random surfaces.

See, he too could've been a father.

IT WASN'T that Felix was scared of ghosts or the dark or dead folks or odd noises or musty smells or narrow spaces or even the possibility that his elbow might scrape the side of a niche-resting skeleton and a set of arm bones might clatter out—he had a stern constitution—but the logic that convinced him no spirits would attack also alerted him that it wouldn't be too hard, in the deep and winding catacombs, to get lost. As he descended, a candle in his left hand, he dragged his right hand against the dirt wall and where there was a space, a path branching off he didn't take, he dug his foot in the ground to make a hole, with a short tail indicating the direction of travel. He wasn't pleased with the whims of Father Peter, who must've grown up on quite a fine estate to be so comfortable with commanding people to do unseemly things. That Felix had come home from the market with only a shard of iron ("You think twelve-year-old Christian girls play around with fishhooks? What snake charmer sold you this?") didn't sit well with an abbot insistent on hair and bone.

The dark made him whisper. "What are the chances we take home the body of another grave robber by accident?"

"St. Hereticus," Sixtus said. "He'll cure the pickpockets of awkward fingering."

"What exactly are we saving this martyr from? Obscurity? Raiders?"

"Father says it's a service."

"And what business have we with Eupernia? Oughtn't we to find Prisca?"

"I thought you said she was in the Alps."

Felix's candle swung to illuminate a chamber on their left where

Jesus sat in a fishing boat with two other men; there were no rods, or even a lake. Three men and their boat on a waterless landscape of beige plaster. In the rounded corner where the wall met the ceiling, an angel with wings of fire puckered her mouth. They passed through a large room where the coffins were grander, more imposing, where the popes were buried.

Felix felt at the carving on one wall. "Read it for me."

"A little poem, *et cetera*, something about Pope Sixtus—my namesake!—confessors from Greece, young boys, ah, and Damasus, pope. *Hic fateor Damasus* . . . 'Here I, Damasus, confess that I wished to bury my limbs, but I feared to disturb the holy ashes of the saints.'"

"Bless the unworthy," Felix said. His ticklish crypt keeper's fingers wanted to pry into the tombs, find out what happened to holy bodies left for centuries in the dry dark.

After tunneling deeper into the earth's stomach, the main path ended in a T; to the left, the candle showed another hallway honeycombed with niches, stacked five high, and to the right, a larger room opened into an inscrutable blankness.

"Is that her?" Felix asked. His candle was half-eaten, and he began to sweat.

On the room's back wall, three women overlapped in a willowy dance. Yellow dress, red dress, blue dress. Their hair was tied in knots atop their heads, and their hands moved identically up and to the left, fingers opened into fans, as if they were repelling invaders from the east while looking back to the flaming west in despair.

"Or else they're doing the old graveside shuffle," Sixtus said.

Nestled in the wall was one of the few marble sarcophagi that had found its way to these depths. Sixtus ran his fingers across the Latin. "Sancta Eupernia," he said.

Felix felt the worm of wrongdoing squiggle in his upper arms and groin. "You don't think she's at peace?"

"It's just a body; that's what you always say. Nothing sentient to be disturbed."

"I do say that." He pulled the iron bar and the cloth sheet from his pack. "Sometimes I wonder," he said, handing the bar to Sixtus, "if there are two chains of command. One issuing down from God and one coming up from the darker place, and whether the orders ever get tangled."

"And when your abbot tells you to steal a skeleton, you wonder how your final master will judge you." The bar slid under the lid of the sarcophagus with little effort, and Sixtus levered it up and inched it back.

"Is that what I'm worrying about? Judgment? That sounds self-involved."

"Give me a hand."

Felix left the corner where he'd been admiring the bluebirds carrying olive branches; they'd been painted some five hundred years earlier, and so he could not fault them for looking more like starfish, thrown against the wall and stuck. He and Sixtus pushed the lid back far enough to snake their hands down, but what they felt in St. Eupernia's resting home was not dry bones but something soft.

Felix jerked his hand out.

"She's a holy!" Sixtus said.

"I hereby forswear my allegiances and announce myself to be a vain and superstitious old pagan who will have nightmares."

Sixtus laughed. "He fondles the dead all day and can't stand to grab a saint! What an errand for this fool. Bless our Lord for having deemed us worthy of the touch."

"Bless us, Lord," Felix said, "and know we rob only because we believe, and if this damns us, let our ignorance redeem us. It's remarkable hard to tell your servants from your enemies, and we are loving idiots."

The two men, on their tiptoes, cradled their arms into the coffin. At the bottom was the softness, which was neither human nor animal but almost vegetable, as if they were lifting a dense colony of mushrooms that had formed a pillow in the forest: spongy, irregular, pliant, with the faint scent of smoke. Father Peter, who'd been appointed by a bishop who sat at the right hand of a pope who'd (theoretically) been given the blessing of the supreme creator, had asked Felix and Sixtus to save the body of St. Eupernia from despoliation and to bring her miracle-making shape to a church in need of the holy touch, whose relics were scampering out the door faster than they could be replaced.

They lifted her, or it, out of the dark sarcophagus and up into the dim yellowish glow and laid her, or it, down on the sheet that Felix had spread on the dirt floor. Sixtus pulled his candle closer. It *was* a woman, a blessed fungal bundle of a woman, with skin softly shriveled and hair long and golden and a snowy robe that covered her modesty in artful tatters and feet that bent inward as if she'd been drawn to heaven so fast the wind had blown them into a curl. Her face had been reduced to mere smudges on a shroud of skin.

The men crossed themselves again.

"How did she die?" Felix asked, seeing no evidence.

"Willingly," Sixtus said.

They wrapped the sheet across her in quadrants, like girls making a pastry, and Felix took both candles while Sixtus carried her in his arms. He felt for his directional signs at each passageway. The candles were nubs, but now they were in the popes' chamber again; the passage became dim rather than dark, and finally the stairs rose before them, up and up into a night that was bright in comparison to the invisible black wash of the underworld. The few other travelers on the Via Appia carried incriminating bundles of their own. No one spoke. The sound of their leather-shod feet scuffling along the great stones of the road reminded Felix of the stables' spring cleaning, when his father would drive out the cozy cows, their hooves shushing on the packed earth, and Felix would come with a broom and a shovel and not just the manure would go but the straw and the hay and the top inch of dirt, peeled back like a skin, and for the next week before the dirt settled again, the cows wandered to and from the fields with knee-length brown socks. That's what they sounded like on the stones in the dark, like men with hooves.

As the two old men climbed into the city Felix offered to take the burden, but he was relieved when Sixtus said no, it was hardly a weight at all. History, though people ran about it like roaches, was made up of thick coats of things in situ. The catacombs had been dug just there, an artist had brushed the women on that particular wall, a body had been laid to rest over yonder, one day a church might be constructed over that site, and even farther in the future, a grand cathedral to which pilgrims from as far as China could flock, with stores to feed them, so it might eventually become a new capital of the earth, all because it was the right distance from the center of the city that once was ruled by pagan emperors. And now they'd loosed that body from that space, she was in situ no more, and the history of the saints had been shuffled.

At Santa Prisca, Sixtus rested their cargo on the font. "The crypt makes the most sense."

"All those men," Felix said. "I don't like the thought of her there."

"As opposed to where? Shall I take her to the nearest nunnery?"

"We could leave her in one of the chapels."

"With the relic bandit still at large?"

"Oh, Mother Mary. Prop her at the abbot's door and call it a job well done." He stroked the saint's tattered robe, feeling the smallest of human superstitions: that this one touch might ease his unhappiness. If you'd asked him in daylight if he harbored any melancholy, he'd have laughed. That's the trick of consciousness: there's a seed at the very core even the owner will deny.

"Let's put her in the Mithraeum—no fellows there—and see if the bull god sports stigmata by morning."

THE HOOK was a delight. Felix felt it press into the small of his back as Mino wrapped him in a hopping embrace.

"It stays in the chapel, you know."

"But just for now, seeing as I'm the one who saved it—and you, of course—let me hold it, would you, just for the day? I still feel her in it, and if anything could forgive—" He stopped, but his half smile didn't melt. "Please. It's like it could show me things."

In the afternoon, the boy laid his head on the desk, just where the sun ladled in, brushing the point of the hook against his thumb. They'd had a buttery lunch, and the monks were sleepy. He seemed mesmerized by the dancing quill in Sixtus's hand. Watching a boy grow drowsy was like watching a palm leaf unfurl.

"Give him his sheet," Felix said. "He's not here to dawdle."

Sixtus pushed over a blank piece of vellum, freshly scraped and stretched, and the metal pen. Before Mino learned to write, he'd have to master the drawing of lines. The scribe would use these lined sheets to ensure the letters danced in regular formation; no patron wanted to look at a psalter and know Sixtus had written it, or some monk with whimsical Gs. Doodles had their place, but the words themselves were the word of God. No, his own son was the Word. So to better mimic the Lord, little Mino was making his lines, the metal pen steady in his hand. (This was a favor from Sixtus to Felix. Sixtus could've done it faster himself.)

"Did you come here from a farm, like Felix?" the boy asked.

"I was the slave of a priest here in Rome, if you can believe it."

"At Santa Prisca?"

"Santa Cecilia in Trastevere. He said he'd set me loose if I learned my letters. Quite an incentive."

"But you fell into this old trap again. Why didn't you become a soldier? And were your parents slaves?"

"Look at me, well fed and smarter than you. Don't have to kill anyone; will probably make it to heaven."

"But *you* came from free folk." Mino looked up at Felix, the pen paused.

Sixtus kicked him. "No stopping. We've got to finish this before I'm dead."

Whatever moved outside the window—new leaves or a squirrel or a robin on the hunt—was like a circus to Mino, who couldn't keep his eyes on the vellum. The boy needed to pay attention. Ignorant people only got as far as those who raised them. Look at Felix, whose greatest skills were feeding chickens and sitting quietly with dead things.

"But you're so happy," Mino said.

"He's asking for a lesson in contentment, Brother Felix."

The pen dragging across the vellum sounded like a field being peeled open by the plow. Felix's father had assumed his children would furrow the same land, and their children, because holding steady was almost as good as gaining ground. "I miss things, certain. But wishing is a kind of superstition and doesn't belong in the Christian mind. God chooses what comes true."

"So there's nothing you ever saw that you wish you hadn't seen or nothing that got taken away from you that you'd like back or no kind of doings that you once could do but you can't do here?" When he'd first arrived, Mino'd been such a quiet boy.

"You're talking about want," Felix said.

"Is that wrong?"

"There's men here who'd give their crucifix for a gold coin," Sixtus said. "Or steal the coin and crucifix both."

"No, wanting's no sin, though it's a hindrance. You've only so much space, and wanting is hungry, it takes it all up."

"You're thinking of something specific?" Sixtus asked the boy.

Mino handed over the vellum wearily, the drawing of a dozen lines having sapped him of strength.

Sixtus pushed it back across the desk. "I need a dozen more. Haven't you ever seen a book?"

"It's a secret," Mino said, rubbing the hook against his mouth. "I was promised not to tell."

The older men were silent. It's the downfall of secrets, how much they want to be told.

"I'd say, but I don't want him to come for me."

"No one will come for you."

"Except Jesus on your deathbed," Sixtus added. "And then Felix, who'll prop you up on a toilet and stare at you while your eyeballs turn to juice."

Mino laughed and had to smudge out the line he'd spoiled. "It's my mam. Who loved me more than anything," he said. "Some of the others had died and it was just boys, but I was her favorite."

"May the Lord hold her close," Felix said.

"She'd dress me up."

"Capes and hats?" Sixtus asked.

"Big fishermen's boots?"

"Pretty things," Mino said. "You know. It was fun, us playing."

"Dresses?"

"Silly things. And her girdle. She said I had small features."

Sixtus continued his patient inking. "You do have small features," he said. "Though as Felix will tell you, your ears will keep growing long past you being alive, till five years after you're gone they'll reach down to your waist."

Mino stared at Felix, who had taken a seat by the window. "Sixtus never lies," he said, shaking his head. One of the hens in the yard was once again attempting to climb the alder; she used her beak and claws as three separate hands to scrabble her way up, but she hadn't yet been able to reach the fork, where she might rest.

"My pa didn't like the dresses."

"Not much difference between a gown and a robe."

In the cup of water Sixtus used for washing away his errors, Felix watched a tiny seed snap around the surface. Impossible to tell if it was the offspring of some aquatic creature from the well, or if it was drowning. He plucked it out. "I'd say you fit well here," Felix said.

"Did your father send you away?" Sixtus asked.

Mino nodded. "Is it much longer till supper? I'm half-starved."

"If you were helping the cook, we probably wouldn't eat till tomorrow. Go see. Let Felix get back to his bones."

"You take good care of them, don't you." Mino stood and stretched his arms above his head, resembling an old painting Felix once saw of St. Agatha on the rack. He dropped his hands to his head and patted his wispy blond hair indecisively. "He did her in before he sent me off. So I'd see what I'd done."

Sixtus stopped, his rag half-dipped in the water.

"*Deus in adjutorium meum intende.*" The abbot's voice was girlishly small.

"*Domine ad adjuvandum me festina.*" The brothers made up for it.

When they gathered that morning for the terce liturgy, the abbot's hands fidgeted so much he ripped a page in the psalter. Lucius whispered to Vitalis, "It's the pope," and Vitalis, whose faith in the pope, any pope, was unwavering, dourly shook his head. Standing behind them, listening to the monotonal reading of the day's psalm and the halfhearted antiphons from the brothers, Felix studied the backs of their heads, wondering why Henry's hairline was such a neat scoop at his neck while Leo's looked like a wheat field gone to seed. There was only one monk who barbered them; they ought to look the same. Once dead, they'd match up better.

Instead of reading from the martyrology, the Father closed the books before him and peered out into the crowd of standing men. "It is a difficult time," he said.

Leo turned sharply to Henry. The last time the abbot broke from the liturgy was during the famine two years ago, when he'd asked weakly if any of the monks were hoarding bread.

"A great servant of the Lord has been dragged from the ground like an animal."

Felix wondered how the abbot considered his own brethren below, who, far from being humanely in the ground, were sitting up in chairs and posthumously farting.

"Our Pope Formosus, deceased eight months, sought to save our territory from the dueling emperors, from the Lombards, from the Saracens." He paused. "He had weaknesses too, but the Lord does not create humans without them."

Lucius murmured an *amen*.

"Augustine tells us of the city of God and the earthly city," he began.

Sixtus leaned over to Felix. "Augustine, quoting Apuleius, also said the souls of men are demons. But good demons; the kind that mediate between heaven and earth."

"Oh, your books. What mischief won't they—"

"And Rome now is ruled by a man of earth," the abbot continued, "tangled in material concerns, vindictive and empty of peace. Stephen, who calls himself pope. From political rivalry he has unburied our Formosus, a body put to rest, and sat his bones on a throne of judgment. You have heard of this in the streets."

The few monks who had recently run errands nodded—the

exhumation and trial of the deceased pope was a petty battle over bishops, French kings, the Spoleto men, brothels, and the where-abouts of the Holy Spirit. Felix heard of it from a woman selling eels in a Trastevere square, on one of those sunny January days that had lured him across the river. She was tossing water over her fish while a man strolled to and fro, keeping an eye out for officials. It had been more than two days since the eels were caught, and trading in foul flesh was criminal.

"Do you get a vote in the trial?" her partner had asked.

Felix confessed his ignorance.

"They dug up the old pope," the eel seller said. "Put him on trial in St. John Lateran. They've got a man stands next to him and an-swers in his dead pope's voice. 'Did you anoint false bishops?' 'Why, yes, I did.' 'Why'd you take the papacy after we'd thrown you out of the church?' 'Because I'm the Devil's left hand.'"

"They wouldn't exhume the body of a pope," Felix said, with the confidence of a corpse connoisseur.

"In my father's day, they were good men," the lookout said. "What's happened to all them since? Poisoned, stabbed, beaten on the head with a hammer."

"I'm telling you, son, they dressed him up in purple robes and all. You remember the tremors last week? That was earth and heaven shuddering, both." She flipped an eel over to its fresher side, glossy eye up. "Don't think they won't do what you think they shouldn't do."

"And have they—" He didn't know quite how to ask. "Reached a verdict?"

"Can't be too many questions left to ask," the woman said.

The man whistled, and she threw a sheet over the bright ribbony fish and laid several pages of parchment on top. "Holy psalms for sale!" she cried. "Sweet psalms for a penny!"

Since then the monks had pooled their gossip and confirmed the outcome: the half-rotten body of Formosus had been judged guilty of perjury, heresy, and serving as the bishop of two territories simultaneously, and his three blessing fingers were hacked off and the rest of him was stripped, buried, thought better of, and tumbled into the Tiber. None of them knew how to speak of it; they were the children of a series of imperfect fathers.

"Know from this that all men are fallible," Father Peter said, his dismay ringing like a sour bell in the open nave. "If you place your trust in authority, the day will come when you are torn between obedience and conscience. Look only to yourselves, my brothers, and struggle to perfect what is there. Do not cease to be appalled when men act despicably, but have no conviction that they will live up to standards that you yourself cannot meet. We are all failing." He stopped and pushed a finger across the bottom of his nose.

Lucius bent his head and seemed to weep.

"*Dominus vobiscum*," the Father said.

"*Et cum spiritu tuo*," the brothers said.

They took up their labors somberly, and for an hour after terce they all were silent, until Vitalis belched loudly in the orchard and Mino fell upon his spade in laughter.

THE PORTENTS kept arriving. Farfa had been taken. The Saracens had sacked the abbey, expecting and finding treasure, and while they camped amid the gold and silver, the chalices and altarpieces, the monks there systematically hid the manuscripts. The Arabs weren't interested in words; they had their own. The news was told at breakfast, and Felix wondered if the abbot of Santa Prisca would cling first to his library. The theory that their own night thief might be a Saracen gained new converts. Whoever he was, he'd now accumulated two fingers and a shard of shin, and Felix wasn't certain that Eupernia had safely made her way to a chapel casket.

"You were almost there," Brother Marco said to him in the hall on their way to the garden.

"I *was* there," Felix said, "and then I wasn't."

"My father took me as a boy, but he didn't have enough money to sell me as a novitiate. A beautiful place, Eden in stone."

Felix's father had decided Farfa was too near. In the aftermath of his humiliation, a church was found in Rome—their numbers were dwindling, and their standards were low. A week after the kiss—seven days during which he'd been kept inside, Tomaso invisible, his response to the touch horribly unknown—his mother packed his belongings: a loaf of bread wrapped in his winter coat. There was no lock of hair to keep. His father knew a man carting hay who'd haul Felix in exchange for a coin. He would come to think of it as his dowry.

"Your father must've owned his land," Marco said.

The garden held no sun today, and the quiet of nature, usually a relief, with its rustles and twitterings and shakes, now seemed careless. Had it no news of his family? [The leaves are not the ones to ask, who get their gossip from the cherubs and the wind; you should be talking to the grubs instead. The closer you get to the underworld, the fewer lies you'll hear.]

"A man on the make." Marco took his rake without complaint, though in the evenings he relished showing his blisters, which Felix would compare to the open sores of the dead.

"A man on the mend," Felix said.

The monks from Farfa, with stainless childhoods and reasonable purses, scattered to churches in Rome, Rieti, Matenano. They brought stories of the invaders, though who by then had not seen an Arab. The people invented new prayers, in case it was monks who attracted trouble. Mothers sacrificed small game to pagan gods in hidden pits behind their homes. They closed no doors.

There was no news yet of the villages. When his sister and Tomaso—elderly now, like him—opened the door of their minor farmstead, did they look out onto burned fields, slain cattle? [You don't want to know what's happened to your home; you want to imagine the two of them, your kin and your kindred, in that cozy one-room house with the smoky hearth and—wait—is that a cradle in the corner? Is your cat Johanna, rickety at some supernatural age now, rubbing her side along the spindles of the crib, purring loud enough to drown out the baby's coos? In your honor, will she pounce into the bed and come to a curl atop the infant's face? Is it the future you want to destroy or just the past?] Johanna. She'd be long dead. Like Felix, she'd been transported, and would not again return home. If death was a ladder from his mother's lap to the Lord's, he wondered what rung he was on.

"You've let the rooster out," Marco said, pointing his rake.

"WHAT WOULD happen if you loved a boy?" he'd ask the imaginary Muslim who was barracked in his father's house, his foreign brown eyes scanning the patchy walls to find the draft, his dry elbows on the table by the bread too coarse to eat.

"I would tell him so."

"I mean in your church."

"They would shake their heads at the folly."

"Is it forbidden?"

"Ask the Córdoba caliphs, with their harems of boys."

"Or despised?"

"Ask Ibn Hazm, who says, 'Every heart is in God's hands.'"

"How harshly do they punish you?"

"The Qur'an says if they repent, let them be."

"We must do penance for a year, which is less than for priests who go hunting."

"And your Christian scripture, what does it advise?"

"Barnabas says thou shalt not eat the hare—it grows a new anus every year—so thou shalt not be found a corrupter of boys."

"You're saying a five-year-old hare has five arseholes?"

"And what of your scripture?"

"The prophet says, 'He who loves and remains chaste and conceals his secret and dies, dies a martyr.'"

"What is a secret love?"

"As Ibn 'Abd Rabbihi sang of his boy, 'Love has put fetters on my heart, as a herdsman puts fetters on a camel.'"

"Ah. Yes."

The answers came in a dream, so God sent them.

"CAN I show you something?"

"It's almost time for prayer," Mino said.

"Come. We'll be a little tardy."

The boy balked at the top of the stairs leading down to the crypt. "I can smell it from here."

"It's your own fright you're smelling. Be a brave boy." Felix held out a hand. "I'm here to stand between you and the ghosts."

"You've seen them?"

"They manifest as kittens—the worst part is all the ankle rubbing. You'll get used to it."

They descended hand in hand, and Felix wished the staircase went on forever, just kept unfolding into the mineral depths of the earth, because once they reached the bottom he'd have to find something wise to say. How to be happy, indeed. Felix had no answers; it seemed constitutional rather than philosophical, though this was not a comfort. The boy wanted a string in the labyrinth, and Felix couldn't even say what the maze looked like. His only certainty sat in this putrid room.

Mino put a hand over his face. "Sixtus calls these Satan's toilets," he said in a muffle.

"Sixtus is uncharitable. Here," he said, pulling over a stool. "Let me introduce you."

The benches lined three sides of the room, and but for the holes in the seats would've resembled the Mithraeum next door. The seats were filled by men in robes. Calling them men might be generous. Bodies in robes, the garments of the brotherhood largely withstanding the decay occurring within. Some sat proudly; others slumped. The two in the corner had collapsed toward each other and seemed to be conspiring. The head of one particularly corpulent monk had come closer and closer to his knees as his belly deflated. Sometimes Felix imagined he was laughing, and other times that he was the most devout. Below the open holes on which their bare bottoms perched, a sewer ran, carrying the effluvia past the groundwater and out to the river, though every time Felix peeked, he only saw still puddles, oily.

He put a hand on Bernardo's shoulder, which rattled. "This is my dear friend who you never knew."

"I don't like it."

Felix slapped Bernardo's back and a tooth tumbled out of his mouth. He stooped to rescue it from the folds of the cloak and popped it back in between his friend's lips, like a pearl fed to a lizard. "Will you think me foolish if I tell you not to be afraid of what happened to your mother?"

The boy looked horrified.

"Her life was blessed with you, and now her soul is stretched out on the slowest bank of time, with one hand in Christ's. The only pain is that one small thing."

"That my pa done her in."

"That your pa done her in."

"On account of how she fashioned me."

"Which was another word for her love, which no one could have asked her to contain."

Mino's head turned to take in the whole compass of the room. "This seems very wicked."

"We think death gives rise to ghosts and bogeys and all sorts of sneaky phantoms, but that's magical thinking, and not worthy of a brave Christian who knows that a corpse, while still the property of God, is no more spooky than a bucket or a bowl."

"But Sixtus says you talk to them."

Felix took his hand off Bernardo's shoulder. "I want you to come and shake hands."

"What?"

"Let's start with Benedictus, whose hand is still quite plump and inviting. It'll be just like shaking mine. Come, take his hand and tell him your name."

Mino's face teetered somewhere between laughter and tears.

"There, that's it," Felix said as Mino slipped a finger into Benedictus's limp paw. "Do you feel his warmth?"

"No."

"That's because his hand is really in Christ's, and this is only a sheet of canvas, or a comb." He moved one seat down to Bernardo, whose knuckles were just beginning to peek through his skin, like the first crocuses of spring. "Try my dear friend here. I think you'll find it a genuine wonder, what the body does when God lets it loose."

And one by one, with increasing boldness, Mino made his way around the putridarium, shaking the hands of the last nine monks that had perished at Santa Prisca. When he got to Giuseppe, on whose finger bones only some loose shreds of flesh hung, he grasped the dead hand like he would a companion's and looked back at Felix with pride.

"And you say the soul isn't inside—the best part? The thing we loved?"

"The thing we loved is safe above."

"How do you know for certain? You've checked?" He pressed his hand against Giuseppe's robes.

"If it's a spark, you can tell just by looking. See? There's nothing left that's warm."

"But if the spark is so tiny. And is hiding."

"When I think of a beloved dying," Felix said, though he'd never experienced a beloved dying and had only his imagination to wonder over the breath and heartbeat of his family and his cat and not his Tomaso, "I think of these friends and am cheered. Because how much longer is the eternal life than this one?"

"HOW DO you bury your dead?" he'd ask the Saracen barracked in his father's house, his fingers ringed with gold, his soft hair's perfume mingling with the must of horses.

"In the ground, like you."

"Facing east, like us?"

"You line them up like they were arrows pointing at where the sun will rise. We bury them on their right sides so their faces look upon Mecca. The dead are still human; they aren't arrows or symbols."

"We put them in fabric or wood."

"We put them in stone."

"Are you brokenhearted to lose your beloved, or do you staunch your tears because they've achieved paradise?"

"We believe that we are supposed to believe there is joy in death. Still we wail."

"Then we're both sinners. Don't you do anything strange?"

"We lightly beat the fresh grave with our sandals."

"Do you close the eyes of a Muslim after he's died?"

"We close the eyes."

"Do you wash him with tenderness?"

"We wash the body to take the stain of the world away."

"Do you build churches over the graves of your holiest?"

"Bodies are not to be worshipped."

"You scoff at my crypt. Do you not believe the body has fluids?"

"Abu Bakr said the shroud is for the body's pus."

"What would you do to a man who took a body from its resting place?"

"Cut off his hand."

"Who taught you how to bury the dead?"

"Allah sent a raven to scratch at the ground by the body of Abel, showing Cain what to do with death."

"So we hide the bodies to hide our shame?"

"*We* hide the bodies. You prop them up on toilets."

"WHEN YOU were a child, did you ever play at sainthood?" Father Peter crossed to the door of his study, and Felix had no choice but to follow him out. Only one other monk was in the hallway, but he pivoted when he saw them and headed back toward the garden. Felix had reported on his trips to the market, apologized for the continuing lack of St. Ethelberta, and promised that the recent acquisition of Prisca's fishhook would be making an appearance that day in one of the vacant reliquaries. The abbot, whom recent months had made pale, was dreamy in the eye, twitchy in the hand.

"I certainly did not," Felix said, though he recalled his sister's archangel costume: wings from dead branches and a rope halo.

"Perhaps you did not have the calling."

"I would've thought true saints—"

"Oh, son," and the abbot pushed open the door to the sanctuary, where Brother Vitalis trudged around the chapels with his willow switch, as menacing a guard as Father Peter had chosen to appoint. "There are no true saints. Only men and women who happen to die before they disprove their holiness."

He stopped in front of a niche with an empty shrine.

"You see how this makes us look."

"Father," Felix said, unsure what tone to adopt.

"You know Santa Prisca is my only concern, heaven bless her. And the church these days is only worth what it's worth. You saw what they did to Formosus." One shoulder writhed.

"Do *you* know her story, Father? We were wondering—"

"Arrested for stealing bread. Stealing bread to save her family."

"That doesn't seem—"

"You wouldn't blame her. The chosen must also survive." The abbot leaned against the font and trailed a trembling finger in the water. "There's nothing to blame."

Through the closed church door they heard the toothless woman blaspheming the crows.

"Where is it?" Father Peter said. "The hook?"

Mino wasn't with the brothers doing the laundry or the brothers mending the robes or the brothers rebuilding the arbor for spring. He wasn't in his cell and he wasn't with Sixtus, who had successfully turned an ink spill into an armored rabbit at war with a dog, to accompany Psalm 144. He was below, in the room Felix so often had begged the others to visit. Benedictus was ripening so fast, the stench was nearly visible. The boy was perched on the ledge of one of the seats, his back turned to Felix, squeezed beside the corpse of Bernardo. Felix paused in the doorway, admiring Mino's neck, how unlike Tomaso's it was, and how odd that a son of theirs should really take after neither. He felt a solidity behind this love that outshone his youthful ardor.

(It took being sixty to admit this.) Being a father touched not just the nerve endings but the stones, the weather, the rampaging Arabs; the world was becoming Mino-hued.

In this room, where the skeletons in their haunting cloaks let their disease seep from their pores—what pores were left—and the afternoon smelled not of incense but of sulfur and rot, Felix hadn't accounted for any danger. A thin scraping interrupted his reverence. Noises down here were usually soft, a rounded gurgle. He called Mino's name. The boy turned fast, his blond hair haloing, his fist clenched around an object.

"What," Felix smiled, "are you auditioning for my job?"

He neither shook his head nor blinked. Walking closer, Felix saw the robes Bernardo was slowly fouling had been torn at the chest. His pale skin within was exposed—skin Felix had never seen, not in all their years of friendship. Mino was standing now, backing away. Felix leaned in to touch and was struck by the gray streaks in the torso.

"But what—"

"You said there were answers here."

Bernardo's white chest, the hairs around the lavender nipples still sronging, had been torn into. Inexpertly, brutally. Like a rat had grown a beaver's teeth and dragged his mouth down vulnerable skin. The cuts produced no blood, only furrows into gray tissue. Felix shuddered. He felt a coldness in his own bones, like the violence had been on his mortal flesh. His mouth was dry, and he could smell nothing.

"You talked about the soul," Mino seemed to be saying. "And the answers."

Felix tried to pull the rent tunic back over the wounds.

"That I'd see my mam. I wanted to see what happened."

"What happened?" He looked at the boy for the first time.

He was holding in one shaking hand the hook. Prisca's hook, or Christ's, or a hook dredged up by a drunkard from the Tiber's bank. "Brother Henry wouldn't give me a knife." He took a step toward Felix, then a step back. "They're dead, you said that, just bodies. But the soul isn't in there, is it? I thought if I could find a hole, something not there, so I'd know the soul of her was up with Jesus, like you said—"

"Why would you hurt my friend?"

"He *isn't*, it's just the body!"

Felix snatched the fishhook from him. To defile a corpse with a relic— What do you say to your son? [You tell him you too would've worn dresses as a child if dresses had been offered you; you too had lost love. You find the darkness in him and mirror it with the darkness in you, so the boy knows there is no aloneness, not in all this world, because your ancestors came out of the garden sweating with guilt, and the blessing of this was that no one henceforth could stand sole on a mountain of purity, and the valleys below were crowded and dank and merry with sinners: you and he and his mam and your pap and Christ himself, for Christ himself took human form, wore that body like a flag. Tell him this.]

But he had already slapped the child. He didn't remember it, but Mino's face was shocked and rosy, and Felix's hand stung.

He didn't speak to Mino the rest of the day. He stumbled over the responsorial at vespers. His anger was short, but his love took a woeful long time to reconstitute. He couldn't forgive him until he'd forgiven himself, and this even the nighttime whip was slow in solving. He tried to focus on the image of the cheek, the wronged innocent cheek he'd burned, but saw instead his sister's, with the scratch of the stick, and Tomaso's, with the flush from his lips, and his own, beaten by his own hand until it bruised. Confession would provide no relief; there was no discrete sin to be revealed, but a whole inadequate life. His shame burned through his chest so sharply he thought the boy's phantom was dragging the ancient hook down his own skin, the furrows his father's furrows, the blood still lively running. His teeth ground together as his back opened up in stripes of pain; the whip was louder than the compline bell. It wasn't his old self he was punishing—the knocked knees, the aching neck, the scabs that wouldn't heal, the bladder that betrayed him, the rheumy eyes, the caterpillar that munched the nerves in lines across his hips—it was his young self, who hadn't tried-and-failed, but hadn't-tried, and failed.

"TELL ME about your Devil," he'd say to the Arab who was barracked in his father's house, his soft brown feet on the straw mattress, his bare hand on his own silken shoulder.

"Iblis. Al-Shaytan."

"Satan."

"When you kneel to pray, he is a fly in your hair."

"A honeybee."

"No, something without purpose. He gets between you and your spoon. You and your cup. You and your woman."

"Does he not believe in women?"

"Women are the crown, and the quicksand."

"And men?"

"Men are the armor, and the snake."

"Is his voice sweet?"

"Sweeter than Allah's, because he speaks no truth."

"Does he answer your questions?"

"In all his words I find the justification for myself."

"Then why don't you believe in him?"

"Because I am the least of God's creatures and should not be justified."

HE NEEDED to ask Brother Henry for some vinegar to put on his wounds. One on his shoulder refused to close up, and he worried it would attract an infection. Brother Leo was hands-deep in peas, and two others whose duties lay elsewhere didn't want to leave the warmth of the hearth and the proximity of snacks, so the kitchen was cramped. Felix bent to the bottom shelves and poked through the jars of pickles. Some of the oldest vegetables had turned entirely white, making him think of organs. The heart, never seeing sunlight, was probably a white muscle. Mino would've found out.

Leo sucked a pea loudly from its pod. "Have you seen the boy since he got taken in?"

"Where's that?" Felix said.

"I figured since you two are always about."

"He's doing good work in the chapels," Henry added.

"You've had compliments from parishioners?"

"Oh, I'm sure they don't notice. If the tables have an inch of filth on them, it's cleaner than their house."

"What's this about Mino? Taken where?"

"The Father fetched him," Leo said. "Looked like he would've dragged him by his ear if there weren't an audience."

"Boys are mischief. We old poots could take a lesson in it."

"So you don't know?" Felix asked.

Henry stooped down and pulled out the vinegar he couldn't find. "There you are. Bring it back before lunch. You don't need more than a dram?"

"They said the abbot, or someone who told the abbot, found one of the relics in Mino's room, I don't know which—the thing of Prisca's. Did he think he'd be going home one day, where he could sell them? Which of us ever goes home?"

"That's a boy without a proper father."

Leo continued to split the pods into boats, and Henry speared pigeons on an iron spit.

The night before, in the early hours after matins when the brothers were safely returned to their beds and dreaming of salt, Felix had crept down the hall to Mino's cell and left the hook, wiped clean, in a pouch by his door. His apology.

AS THE monks were lifting their spoons for supper, Father Peter stood at the head of the table and tapped his chest twice as a call to silence. Two brothers at the opposite end were stuck in a conversation about the faith of the Moors, and whether it was impolite not to recognize Mohammed when the Muslims recognized Jesus, and which held greater sway in religion, tolerance or veracity; the abbot beat his chest a third time and sharply cleared his throat.

The boy wasn't there.

"In every orchard is a sickly tree," the abbot said. "A tree whose branches are weak and hollow."

Brother Lucius peered over his shoulder toward the window into the garden.

"We tend it with love. We are led by Christ's example with the prostitutes."

A few brothers began to murmur. There was an unspoken agreement in the church that it wasn't one of Christ's finer moments.

Felix smelled something bitter.

"But if the tree continues to weaken, it threatens the orchard. Its roots will snarl the others. Its dropped leaves will rot in the soil, spreading its disease."

Sixtus leaned toward Felix. "I didn't know the Father was such a horticulturalist."

"Did you see Mino after he came out of the abbot's study?"

"Before we pray," the Father continued, "I must inform you of the departure of one of our brotherhood. Not all are called to give their lives in service, and not all are worthy."

"None of us are worthy," someone said.

"The child called Mino will not be continuing with us." No one spoke, so the abbot sat, white-faced. "Let us pray," he said.

Felix had gone to him that afternoon and explained; he'd left the hook, the boy had admired it, nothing had been stolen, the hook would be in the reliquary by the evening.

"There were other bones in his cell," the abbot had said.

But this couldn't be true.

"I could do nothing else."

Felix, in his brief anger, had ruined the child. Was it impossible to parent? [Yes. We were broken from the start by a creator who withholds His love, who knows not how to communicate it, who can be petty and unyielding. This is our model. His son would teach you to forgive; if you learn this art, or if Mino does, give me a lesson, because my veins are on hellfire, and eating your unanswered prayers has ulcered my stomach.]

After supper, the monks congregated in pockets, three behind a column here, a cluster by the chicken coop, Felix and Sixtus there in the side chapel, contemplating the fishhook restored to its reliquary. Felix should go look for him. The child would be on the streets, lost, parched, and he couldn't go home.

"Should it have a label?" Sixtus asked. "It's such a strange-looking thing, I wonder that people won't know what to make of it."

"I should go after him."

"Is there any evidence it's performed miracles?"

"What's the opposite of a miracle?"

"He's not the first boy to be kicked out of a monastery. You have no money to give him. You're not his father. Do you want to take him an egg? Give him the advice you haven't already shared? It wasn't your fault, the hook. The abbot would've pinned the theft on one of us eventually. He needed no cause."

"But I made sure it was him."

"You think he would've been happy here forever? He was like a fox in a cage, already tearing his claws into the corpses." Sixtus opened the glass lid of the gold box and stroked the hook with one finger. He said a quick prayer, then held his finger in the light, as if expecting some perceptible change. "No," he said. "He deserves to be a worldly boy. As did you, perhaps."

"Who wouldn't want to see inside a body."

Sixtus closed the box and wiped his prints off the glass with the edge of his sleeve. "I suppose you couldn't put a label on this that wasn't partly a lie. In fifty years, no one'll remember its history, and it'll be curing palsy." He started back to his study, to his profane psalter.

"So where are the rest of the bones? Are we meant to keep looking for the thief?"

Halfway across the nave, Sixtus turned, his robe flaring like a dancer's skirt. "Beloved Brother!" he said. "Your mind is like a new rose. The abbot's had the relics. Those bones are as good as coins, and the kingdom of heaven on earth only opens with a golden key." The light from the door to the cloisters briefly washed the gloom, and Felix was alone again.

He knelt before the silver ciborium that canopied the altar and its instruments of eucharist. For all his conviction, he didn't often speak directly to God. He relied on the structure of formal prayer, on the tangible offering of his own flayed skin, and on his close study of the mortal metamorphosis. But this evening, as his faith in his own decency drained away, he could not help himself. "Let me not be a new rose," he said. "Let me see it all, the bright and the foul, and let me still believe."

ROME SHONE in the spring. The borage and violets were waking up in the parks and through the ruins, and the old stone columns looked cleaner now than in any other season, as if a caretaker had come through in the night and scrubbed them all with lime. The farmers' stalls were fat with the first artichokes. Children who'd been taught to trudge behind their parents now skipped ahead. No one who died in this season could fail to be reborn.

A week after the expulsion, Felix had asked the abbot's permission to return to the market. Some of the relics were produced after Father Peter's false accusation, but others remained in a sack under the Father's bed and were still claimed missing. By now, everyone knew. Silence was a game they were playing. After Mino left, they continued to guard the nave in shifts, unsure which lies were still in favor. Felix suggested the relics might still appear for sale, and the abbot, his cheeks as cadaverous as Brother Giuseppe's, dismissed him with a nod.

Sixtus had helped him write a note, in case he found the boy; he assured him Mino had learned enough under his tutelage to piece together the letters. With the quill in his hand, awkwardly pushing through the loops and bends of the fashionable minuscule, Felix regretted he hadn't acquired more talents along his journey of existence.

The boy wasn't curled on the steps of the church, or sitting at the table of the nearby baker, watching the bread rise. He wasn't racing stones down the Aventine Hill with the other urchins. His white-blond hair wasn't wisping by the bridge over the Tiber, and his coiled nimble body wasn't wrestling a pig in the market. The streets were empty of him. Felix was too embarrassed to call his name.

In the busy sweep of commerce between the Temple of Hercules Victor and the squat church of Santa Maria in Cosmedin, the relics vendor looked at Felix as if the monk was somehow complicit.

"So he's been here?" Felix asked.

The stock was diminished, and one foot bone, attributed to St. Marcellinus and half-hidden under a scattering of fishing flies, had obviously come from a roast chicken. The vendor polished a porphyry case with spit. "You couldn't have spared him?"

"He was gone before I knew."

"It's a rank injustice. You monks build your walls and grow heavy with all that pheasant and cream. There's no charity to your name."

"Where's he staying?"

"Very fine of you to accuse me of swindling when it's your kind who're so rabid for miracles and money they'd trample over a babe to hoard a few ribs."

"Is he still in the city?"

The vendor put down his box. A woman in a shawl had stopped to peer over the oddments, but looking at their faces, she hurried on. One of Felix's faults was this antipathy to others' disappointment in him. It made him feel sick, never angry at the accuser—sometimes angry at the accuser—but like some maggot in him was curling, beaten back, nauseous. He was the Lord's shrimpiest servant. This was what the whip was for.

"I'm sorry," he said into the silence. Even if the boy was better off outside, where he could taste all the secular joys, could relish an invisible future rather than staring daily into the fleshless sockets of his own inevitable end, even if his story was all for the good, Felix had lost his own innocence, again. Even now his weak heart hiccupped when he saw the vendor, hatless for spring, his peppery hair jaunty in the wind. What could that traitorous organ possibly still expect? [Son, if it's not all good, at least it all *feels* good. Let me raise

your hand up to touch that man's face; come on, a little higher now.]
He was motionless. His emotional asceticism had erased any earthly
presence he might have had.

The vendor stopped flapping through his scraps of human skin
and said with a glint of reprieve, "Have they given you any miracles?
The relics at Santa Prisca?"

"There are parishioners who make the claim."

"So you didn't rub on a skull and ask for the boy to be spared?"

"I wouldn't presume," Felix said, uncomfortable.

The vendor leaned in close across the table and whispered, "Then
what the shit is the point."

Felix did not know what the shit the point was.

The vendor handed him a small glass vial. "Manna that exuded
from the arm bones of St. Walburga. I could sell it for four shillings,
or I could give it to you and tell you it's water. Go give it to a thirsty
sparrow, and you'll have done more good than all the monks in this
city combined."

Felix squeezed the glass in his palm and felt ill.

"He's staying with a friend of mine, a woman who sells flowers
by the Pantheon and isn't too proud to shelter a thief for a few days.
Do you want to see him?"

He pulled the note from his sleeve. "If you would give him this."

"What, an apology?"

"I've written down the way to my sister's house." His sister, who
might be widowed, who might be dead, whose farm might've been
requisitioned by the Muslims, but who had never failed to love him.
What in Rome could say the same? [You expect love from this town?
Try Paris, or Philadelphia. This is the city for hustle, for building
permanent tokens of human transience, and then building on top of
those. No one is remembered except the pulsing city itself, which—
sack after sack—refuses to perish. You know about the floods that

washed over this field you call a market, and Nero's fire that set the dancers' feet alight, and the quake that cracked the windows in St. John Lateran and will repeat its tremor soon, and the volcano that turned your countrymen into well-defined holes that scientists will fill with plaster—the only morbidity that trumps yours—and that tourists with telephones on sticks will stand beside and not weep but grin: for the camera. You know about the Visigoths and the Saracens, but what of the Holy Roman Emperor, who'll eat this city like a snake eats its young; and the papal troops, who will stop by the house of pregnant Giuditta Arquati on the street where you met the eel seller, and she, waiting for Garibaldi and wielding bombs and crying *Viva Roma*, will watch her young son slaughtered; and worst of all, when in 2016 this sacred marble assembly begins drowning in the dung of a million goddamn starlings? Above their waste, another layer of tile—*shh*—until the city climbs so high the rising seas will bring it refugees in droves, and God will have to ask Himself: Is this a shrine to me, or another Babel?]

Felix took the vial of water back to the church. Alone in his cell, he placed it next to his whip and considered each in turn. If a sparrow had alighted on his sill, he would've fallen to the floor in tears, but that wasn't the way the world worked.

HE WAS asking Bernardo to help rid him of his bitterness, Bernardo whose cheeks were beginning to sag and whose flatulence now came in infrequent cannonades, when Lucius came down with timid steps, nose pinched, and whispered into the echoing crypt, "The Father is dying."

Felix turned just enough on his stool to indicate respectful attention. "He was that ill?"

"We're gathering outside his cell. The doctor's come. It doesn't seem long now."

His thinness Felix had taken for guilt—the eating kind that'd turned his own chest concave—his pallor a proof he'd refused to do chores.

"Will you come?" Brother Lucius believed everything, he believed language was a conduit for truth; if you told him Jesus Christ had appeared in the sanctuary with a basket of radishes and was tossing them to monks in a game of radish-ball, Lucius would show up with open hands and a helmet.

"Of course," Felix said. He patted Benedictus's fresh knee on the way out.

"You'll have to make space," Lucius said. "Is the oldest one in there ready to go?"

He wasn't convinced the abbot could be so close, but in fact, no, the oldest corpse was not yet down to clean bone and would cause a hellish stink if shut up in the sarcophagus too soon.

"Could you squeeze two together on one seat? Matthew was awful skinny."

The hall outside the abbot's cell was full of somber men in brown woolens. One flinched when he saw Felix, as if he brought death with him. The doctor was allowing them in singly to share a final blessing. His face suggested a serious illness, but doctors often carried such faces to prove the gravity of their profession. Felix had known monks who'd done it too, resembling martyrs on the rack when singing in the choir, but who in the cloisters would scamper after one another with tickling quills stolen from Sixtus.

The cell was no different from Felix's; the abbot was beneath the same wool blanket on the same rickety bed, his arms over the covers like he was only half a man. His face had a greenish wash, as if he were underwater, and his eyes were wet and weepy and looked past Felix up to the surface of the sea, where something seemed to flicker at him through the waves. His upper lip was damp, and if he'd tossed aside his blanket to reveal a mass of tangled seaweed where his organs should have been, Felix would not have been surprised.

He knelt by the bed and kissed the abbot's hand. It tasted of brine.

"Bless me, Father," he said.

"You keep the crypt," the abbot said.

"I did not know you were sick." That is to say, would not have cursed your name for the lies you told about Mino, for how you tied me to his fall, for the thefts you alone were responsible for, for the funny bow-legged way you have of walking that caused me briefly to think you'd been riding the Devil's donkey. "I have sinned against you in thought," he said.

"I would sin against *you*," the abbot said. "I'd wish you not to take me there."

"Oh, I'm not the ferryman, sir." He sat back on his heels. The abbot's chin, slightly stubbled, was like his father's; the morning he was supposed to depart, Felix woke early and crawled from mattress to mattress, studying the sleeping forms of his family. His father had looked strangest, the face smaller in sleep and nearly innocent. It had been enough to imagine he'd be sorry to see him go—or rather, after priding himself on having acted righteously and with masculine stoicism, his father might find himself on a balmy evening twice a year experiencing some brief wistful thought of his oldest son. Would wonder where he was.

Felix took the abbot's hand again and put a gentle pressure on each middle knuckle in turn. "You know of the soul, Father. I have no keeping of that. It flies on soft winds to Christ's lap. This body is merely skin on fat on muscle on bone. It was only here to get you through this world, the business of walking and speech. You never loved it, and you won't need it. You have nothing to fear. This is a relief. This is your reward."

The abbot had closed his eyes, but his brow wasn't smooth; his lips opened dryly, but he made no sound. Felix felt something spoiled roll off his heart and waddle away, perhaps to find a home under the bed with the other purloined bits of flesh.

"I thought they'd cure me," the abbot said.

Felix pressed into the bones of the dying man's palm, felt them shift among the veins and tendons. What person's remains first birthed a miracle? Was it the Jew Elisha, into whose tomb someone tossed a body and the body then came to life? [Or was proximity to the dead always just a game of chicken, coming that close to one's ultimate fear a guarantee of adrenaline, that sweet chemical that makes earth's certainty bearable? You and I have more in common than I thought. Let me set your own timer now. I'll turn your mutating cells to the five-minute mark—there's the telltale tick.]

But the stolen heaped relics hadn't cured him. He'd snuck through the nave at night with a robber's sack to no avail. He'd hoodwinked his own brotherhood, robbed the catacombs, sacrificed a novitiate, and cheated a congregation, and here he lay in that inevitable watery in-between, a single fish, alone.

The doctor touched his shoulder and indicated that his audience was complete, and Felix left the room without hearing the abbot speak again, and a senior monk replaced him to perform the last rites, and it was all real—the Father was really dying, and this drama was for nothing, and even as it concluded it had no conclusion. His only job now was to shift the corpses below to make room. He understood mortality but had no answer for the living.

"DO YOU know who else has died?" Sixtus asked while the abbot was still in the long act of perishing. "The pope."

"Another pope?"

Sixtus leaned against the door to the crypt, his sketching paper beneath his arm. After months of study, he was finally drawing animals that appeared to be vertebrate. Felix was calculating how he'd make the shift in bodies, whether the abbot's presence in the putridarium would make the other bodies clam up, quit their dead-person gossip. Bernardo was just entering that magic state between human and skeleton when the recognizable becomes otherworldly.

"Does it make you question your pledges to the church?" Sixtus asked.

"Wasn't Stephen already in jail? Poisoned?"

"Strangled," Sixtus said. "A twist."

"The pope isn't my god."

"Shouldn't he be a translator?"

Felix took a comb to Benedictus's hair—Benedictus, who was feeling left out. "God knows what's afoot. I like to think he's reminding us of the challenge he set."

"We're soldiers in the wilderness, is that it?"

"We're wilderness in the middle of war."

Sixtus scratched his chin with his stylus. Two weeks before, it had been Mino in this room, carving into the mysteries of the world with a poor-repaid innocence, asking all the questions. At least the tears wouldn't have lasted long. He didn't have a monk's patience for misery, that lost son, and was all the more blessed for it.

"What sorts of things did he ask?"

"I don't seem to know when my mouth is closed. Was I speaking of Mino?"

Sixtus stuck the pen behind his ear. "I only stand the stench down here because you get so lonely."

"I've never been lonely!" He smiled when he said it. Felix had nearly mastered the art of self-containment; only a friend without ego could have spotted the cracks.

"He'd ask why they keep farting."

"Of course," Felix said. "But also whether they'd still look so ugly in heaven, where all things should be perfect."

"And will they?"

"Augustine says no—we'll all be smoothed over, our blemishes unblemished, our hair and nails trimmed. Only the martyrs will keep their scars, which are holy prizes. But the fat will be thin, and the skinny will be given lovely curves. Infants will age to the height of their potential, and the elderly will lose their years. Everyone will be thirty. Everyone will look like Jesus."

"Sounds nice. This is what you told the boy?"

Felix set the comb down and took in the grotesque lineup of his charges: heads askew, hands flopped, lips pulling back over empty gums, a few tongues lolling, everyone's bottom bare. "No. I told him my little sacrilege."

"You think we rise up to the Lord like this."

He looked over at his friend, the man who without show or emotion had been steadfast far beyond Felix's own family or first love. There were dark nights when even his happiest self thought he had nothing. What folly. So he would never have a wife or a child, never have a kiss or a fumble, so he had been banished from them who'd raised him, so he'd taken on his own heavy sins. Still God provides.

"I think we rise up to the Lord with every mark of life blazoned on us," he said. "It'd be an insult to give up anything he gave."

"Rolls of fat included."

"And a knocked nose, and all our teeth gone lost, and the hair on our scalp half-missing and frizzed, and our toenails yellow and thick."

"Our pimples full of pus, one failed hip, ears that droop to our chins, an arse still stocked with shit."

Felix smiled. "What a glory."

THE PARADISE

[165]

THE BEARDED MAN did not survive. Hierax, and Justin, and Chariton, and whoever else the prefect dragged in made their confessions. They said yes to *are you a Christian*, and when it was asked *who taught you*, Paeon said his parents, and Euelpistus said his parents, and Hierax the bearded man said his parents, and to the follow-up *where are your parents*, Hierax said what all the others wished they'd been smart enough to say: "Christ is our true father, and faith in Him is our mother." Earthly parents were a disappointment, again and again. Christ was her father. Faith was her mother. The prefect asked the men to sacrifice to the idols, and they refused. Were their teeth chattering? Did they glance sideways at one another? Did they think of all the tangible treasures of this world, which are not guaranteed to exist in heaven? [I slipped into their skulls and squeezed out their tears. In a few months, they'll arrest Felicitas and her seven sons, killing each of the boys before their mother's dry gaze—there Januarius is broken beneath the strap with nails, there buckles Philip's head under the club, there goes Silvanus's body off the Tarpeian Rock; after each, she merely adds a prayer to her litany. Her models will not be these bearded men.] A burly man with a thick leather whip beat them until their skin split open and then—

"Prisca, the eggs for dinner," her mother said. The men in the room turned with surprise; she'd been hiding under the table by the door. Their beards hid how pale they'd become.

The hens were not laying as much in the drought, but she found four speckled eggs and one the size of a fat marble, still rubbery in her hand. The coop was warm and dusty, and her head ached. How much easier to be an animal. To pee in the straw, and sleep in the field, and have no thought but for hay or milk or sex. (Yes, Prisca knew.)

After dinner, her mother finished the story. "Beheaded," she said.

She wanted to think entirely of them, of their last moments, as she lay in her bed staring out at the cooling night and the smatter of stars, but Crispus kept rising in her like bubbles. Her body, her mother told her, now had a purpose. The blood was a gift from Ceres. She was being welcomed by an army of women into this wombiness, and even her sober mother got wet in the eye when describing how the inside of her was ready to play hostess.

"But to get that baby I'd have to lie down with someone," Prisca had said.

"No," her mother had said, biting a thumbnail. "You have some years yet. That's not to be thought of." And she quickly switched to talking about the mare in the stables that was full with foal, and how Prisca should watch when the time came, making birth seem like a lovely secret pact between a girl-thing and a child-thing.

Oh, but the lying down *was* to be thought of. She had two small wooden cows that she used to bang together, bottom to bottom, to produce a calf; there was nothing romantic in it. Nor was she impressed when she and Servius stumbled upon a pair of male slaves crouched behind a mausoleum on the road to town, tunics hoisted up and pale thighs quivering. Her brother had stuttered back and turned red and laughed and walked ahead very quickly. The body was a source of smells that needed masking, a place for grime to collect. Why would people want to put them so close together? [Because humans are cold, cold, and cannot feel their own heat. And oh, the silk of the underside of an upper arm . . . Sometimes I think God made bodies for me— Am I dwelling? Would you tell me, mini-saint, if I needed to move on?]

But in the past few months, her curiosity had outpaced her disgust. Even her unclothed mother rising from the baths made her twitch, made her want a body that someone would find desirable, made her desire. Idiocy. Her own breasts like toy pyramids. Her interest in the lying down, the things people did to make the twitch stop (or to make the twitch worse?), this had the same gruesome fascination as the disemboweling of a goat—it was a dark horror, a secret she couldn't touch. The thought of her body having a purpose was natural and pleasurable, but the purpose that was proposed—spitting out another human, and having a foreign object stuck into it along the way—seemed inadequate. To be poked into and pushed out of, like something static, something without legs, without a brain.

Yes, she replayed the kiss like it was a single hieroglyph painted again and again, with small variations: this one had his tongue against her lip, this one had his hand on her arm—no, her waist; in this one there was no watery space between their hips, but his bones were against her bones, and it got to where she couldn't remember what had actually happened, maybe it was a hallucination. And she didn't *want* to be thinking of him, pagan, but of the better men whose souls were now floating up like holy smoke to heaven. Did the white-sharp cut of the blade on the neck bring any perverse pleasure of its own? Did it jangle the nerves, sear the deep unscratchable twitch in the groin, make the eyes pop with a *yes*? [Oh, chickie, there is no line between pain and want.] *That* was purpose. That's what she wanted to believe in.

She didn't believe in a nameless girl-child on a nameless farm following her curiosity to a brushy grove where she and a nameless boy-child shed their tunics and figured out how to place their skin against each other to stir pleasure, and after the pleasure burst and the warmth subsided and the boy-child snuck away, the girl-child being left with seeds inside her to sprout into more nameless children, who would grow up to find other bodies to be terrified of, to be hungry for, so that in a few generations, when all the nameless souls were underground, no one would remember anyone.

Halfway through the night, she woke up sweating: a bony hand had reached all the way down her throat and played her insides like a lute. She could not tell if it was Crispus or Christ.

SERVIUS ASKED her to run sprints with him in the new-mown wheat fields—cut early for hay, in hopes of saving the cattle—only because Quintus had lessons and Marcus was sneezing and the tutor was visiting his mother in Greece. They stretched their legs like Olympic runners, his exaggerated knee bends making Prisca laugh. It was easier to pretend they were part of the same organism when they were younger.

They shouted *start* together, and her body fell forward into a great thrust of energy, her thin legs digging at the soil, paddling it back, her elbows punching behind her as if the air back there was the enemy to speed. No thought at all, just legs and arms hoisting, first feeling gloriously unhinged and wild—matching Servius stride for stride, she felt like a wind nymph, melting the atmosphere, all resistance—but then she saw her brother inch ahead, and the ground came back up to fight her feet, and the air became glue, and her lungs shrank, and her thighs turned leaden and shrieking, and though she pushed and pushed, she couldn't grab that freedom back. Servius won, as he always did.

"It's your flubbies weighing you down," he said, thumping his chest with a smile.

She spat at him.

When he timed her sprints, she tore at the air, her teeth bared. In her slowed-down mind, she dreamed of pushing her body so hard it broke. Servius would rush to the cart path and find her collapsed, or better yet, on fire—all that friction between flesh and sky having lit the spark.

ANNA STARTED the morning with a wool shawl, and by the time she went to cut herbs for lunch, she was wiping the sweat from the crannies in her neck and saying blasphemous things about Jupiter. The day was too hot for the season. The wind had stopped, and the sparrows came closer to the house, boldly begging. Inside, everyone complained of headache.

Prisca lingered in her father's study. He wasn't speaking to her, but he wasn't busy at his papers either, so she waited. She picked up his old shirt of scale armor, the bronze plates of which had begun to turn green, and looped her arms into it. She liked to run her fingers up and down the fishy flaps. It was hard to imagine him wearing this heavy thing, homesick.

"You look absurd," he said.

She knew very well how she looked. "What're you going to do next?" she asked. "Go back to secret prayer?" She raised an arm high to hear how her sleeve flapped, rung.

"Jesus didn't seek death; he accepted it." He gave his head a quick shake, seemed surprised that it was her standing before him and not the bearded man. "Prisca, I don't want you to worry about any of this. We're safe, everyone's safe. I'm grateful—" He had to think carefully about what exactly he was grateful for. "It's a blessing that you're interested in the Word, that you say you believe. That's enough for now. Your mother and I agree, you're just a child."

Prisca tucked both arms inside the mail shirt and punched a fist out—*boom, boom*—like her heart was beating through the bronze. As if her parents really sat down after she'd gone to bed and asked each other, "Do you think Prisca is a child?" and weighed the evidence ("On the one hand, she's four and a half feet tall; on the other, she can seem very somber sometimes") and finally came to the conclusion that, yes, she was not yet an adult. She lifted the mail off with a grunt, felt her little pyramid breasts spring back. She had a quick fantasy of smearing her father's library with her monthly blood, dipping into her warm supply and dragging her red fingers across his rows of scrolls.

"Faith is not for cowards," she said, then dropped her voice to what she hoped was a menacing whisper. "*Jesus loves children.*"

In and around the outbuildings she dragged her feet through the thirsty dirt, creating clouds of dust, hoping that Crispus would come, that Crispus would not come, that God would somehow send her the strength she lacked, that he, God, would look at her weak girl's body and want it for his own.

"Call me," she said quietly. The air fell on her shoulders like a blanket. The slaves in the far fields had gathered under a tree with a bucket of water. The grasshoppers were silent. The twitch inside her had grown; she felt desperate in her stomach and her throat and her ankles. "Call me," she said. "Use this body."

Men would come for her; she would turn cold, unkind; she would succumb to that desire for warm skin; she would learn how to dissemble without guilt, because that was how grown-ups built the shaky houses of their lives, on lies, on closing their eyes to so many big, hard, real things. Like: *There are a thousand moments to be afraid of, but death isn't one of them.*

"I'm the one you should want," she said to the sky, to the one vulture floating on some unfelt high wind. "Want me."

THEY WEREN'T supposed to go to Rome—or was it that they were supposed to wear shawls to mask themselves—but their father had a manuscript that must be delivered, and of course he couldn't show his face, and Anna needed new sponges for cleaning, fresh from the sea and rough, but her bunions kept her at home. Servius brought a sack of cherries just so he could spit the pits at her.

When they were younger, the Via Appia was an unfurling obstacle course, with imaginary games built into the journey—hide-and-go-seek among the tombs, find-the-nut in the carriage ruts, dare-you-to-fart when a soldier passed. But the older she got, the less interesting her brother found her. It felt as if she was walking into the empty horizon of young womanhood, where no one else would come.

Behind the apartments growing taller and the wall that separated the sophisticated from the farmers—or maybe the city-poor from the country-poor, or maybe just the riotous world from the lonely girl—the Aqua Claudia rose up like a honeycomb. A half-dozen boys were throwing rocks through the arches.

"I'll meet you back here," Servius said, looking not at her but at a buxom woman walking past with a monkey on a leash.

"She's fifty years old," Prisca said. "Where are you going?"

He handed over the scroll he'd kept in his belt. "This goes to the lawyer's, and Anna wants three sponges. If you get them from Maxentius, he'll sell them on credit."

"What, was *I* supposed to pay for them? You didn't get any money?"

They could've been urchins; no one would've cared.

"Two hours," he said.

"But you don't know anyone!"

"Crispus is at the baths. Be good."

By the time she came up with a retort, he'd swum into the strangers. She began trotting after him. She didn't want him—she didn't want to spend time with him—but she wasn't certain enough of anything to spend time with herself. And Crispus. Crispus's lips were in those baths. What if her brother left and never returned? [The list of worse things is so long I'm already bored. Stop sitting on your ass. Fossilize your impact so well that Latin Prisca will become Prisca Latinized, the Priscasaurus whose ancient diet consisted of mollusks and swoons. Breeze through phantom tourists at the foot of the Colossus, the referent in Bede's prophesy, "As long as the Colossus stands, so shall Rome"—that bronze, hundred-foot man that, contrary to Byron's comforting mistranslation ("When falls the Coliseum, Rome shall fall"), is in fact no more. Once you've swallowed enough future ghosts, go back to your sorry brother and his weak-veined friend and tell me they still bother you.]

Everything was hotter in the city; she felt the grit on her ankles rubbing up her calves, and though water was right there, sliding into the capital from the empty hills, a hundred feet above her head, she could not touch it. A sheep pushed into her. Past the expanse of the Circus Maximus, temples rose like mushrooms. Across this city, people were buying, arguing, every now and then maybe fornicating, and then walking hushed into the temples and asking the gods to grant them luck. Prisca got a sour taste in her mouth.

Inside the Baths of Trajan, she saw Servius stop at an oasis in the grass courtyard, where a palm sagged over a fountain and a boy and a girl were sitting, their hands draped in the water. Prisca was desperate for a drink. Men leaving their afternoon baths brushed past her, and a woman with her hair still wet asked if she'd lost someone. Prisca pretended not to speak the language. She recognized the back of his neck, those two ropes leading down his head to his spine, that shallow gully between them where a hand ought to rest. She did *not* recognize the tickling fingers that reached up to that sacred skin and pulled a hank of his hair.

She was too far to hear, half-hidden behind an oleander, but Servius knew the girl, nodded amiably at her, and the three began their game of laughing, of stupid jokes, of lounging around admiring their own nearly grown-up bodies. Crispus's hand found the girl's waist; he squeezed. Servius gestured toward the tepidarium, but Crispus shook him off, his body twisted toward the girl's. Servius dropped his shoulders into a slouch, cocked a knee. Studiously not caring. The sun was cutting in the side of Prisca's eyes—that's what caused the tearing, and that's what conjured a halo around the fountain and made it look like something unworldly and preordained when Crispus's long lean limbs folded over finally and wrapped up the strange girl in a mouth-on-mouth embrace. If it weren't so bright, Prisca wouldn't have been crying.

Two hours later, sponges in hand, she stood at the base of the aqueduct—unflinching—as Servius and Crispus and his girl approached, freshly cleansed and sweat-glowing from the baths, which were filled whether or not there was drought, because the emperor was a minor god.

"Livia," Crispus said, and the stranger nodded.

No one said Prisca's name.

She offered the girl a sponge.

JESUS, SON *of a king, and nobody's daughter, what are men thinking? Did you, God, make their hearts in a different shape? Did you put rocks in their chests and plums in ours? Is human love a game, a long distraction, a swamp where you catch the sinners? If so, will you show me how to climb out? I don't know if you knew this—we were nearly underwater— but he kissed me. The son of a whore. He's your son too, God, what's your responsibility? My outside says, "I am twelve years old and grown and I do not mind," but my inside is a plum underfoot, an old rotten plum*

that jumped off its tree in chase of a lamb—my only hope left being that
maybe Crispus caught my pit in his hoof and will be forever a little bit
lame. Jesus, you who are better than a man, cure me of my sinful heart
and let me not mind how I am used.

THEY DROPPED Livia at her family's apartment just outside the
wall—half a mile of walking and her robe still white as blank marble.
Prisca's eyes, aimed hard at the ground, still caught Crispus grasping
the girl's hand, twiddling his fingers across hers in a tumbly water-
fall. The nerves across her collarbone all seemed to snap at once.

Heading home, the boys talked about fishing. Crispus wanted to
scout the far stream, but he'd run out of hooks.

"I've got one," she said. "A pretty good one."

"You look green."

"Only Father won't take me out anymore."

"She beaned a fish so good only half was left to eat," Servius elab-
orated. "What a waste."

"You didn't mind Livia, did you?"

"Me?" Prisca's palms held balls of snow, and worms came out of
the ice and crawled to each of her fingertips; she beat them against
her hips to stop their tingling.

"She's rich as a devil," Servius said.

"What makes you think devils have any coin?"

"You wouldn't be chasing her around if she didn't come with
an estate. You could hunt quail through winter." Servius raised
his imaginary bow, squinted one eye, let an arrow go winging out
through the spindly pines.

"Why do you care?" Prisca said. "What I think?" She was trying
to remember where she'd put the hook so she could give it to him as
soon as they got home, so he wouldn't have time to forget, so nothing would waver.

"I just wanted to make sure you weren't—you know."

Servius lunged for his friend's armpits, and the boys scampered across the stones. From beneath a headlock, Crispus looked back at her with eyebrows raised, as if to say *Will you pardon me or not?*

Was this a scene from the Bible? Was she a Samaritan or was she Judas? Should she be Christian and honest (*I am brokenhearted, I am gutted, I'm forced to wonder: Am I so ugly? Am I so dull? Am I just a gathering of flesh, like an apple is a gathering of fruit, to be consumed?*)—or should she be Christian and kind (*No, I do not mind*)? [I'd guess you can only be honest about the kind things. He doesn't want to hear the rest. I've fattened myself on his id's prayers. This is my girlish consolation, my arm tentative around your shoulder, one ruptured heart to another. I don't know how many times this earth has to spin for our wounds to scab.]

The boys were now far enough down the road that she could say, "I think your girlfriend looks like a skinned mink." A cloud didn't pass over the sun; a bush didn't burst into flame. "I hope she falls into a well where the sides are so slippery she can't climb out, and after she's just a skeleton, you'll fall in too and I'll walk by and you'll say, 'Prisca, throw me a ladder,' and I'll say, 'Make a ladder out of your girlfriend's bones, you rat.'"

JESUS, BLESSED boy-king, forgive me. I have been willfully bad. I have thought unkindly about someone I love. I have said cruel things, though out of earshot. I have taken the life of an animal with clumsiness. I have recognized an injustice and done nothing about it. I have not tangibly helped anyone, not even Anna when she was folding napkins. But will you allow that I am learning?

The latest broken butterfly she'd rescued and put on her window-sill with a dish of dampened bread crumbs was now tossing slightly in the breeze—the wing and a half levering back and forth, its furry abdomen the only weight keeping it from blowing off the sill. It was easy to mistake this movement for life.

There was no shame in Jesus. He did not make you feel dirty, he did not invade you, he did not bring you questionable joy, he was not secretly keeping a girl on the side, he did not have obscure motives, his affection for your soul was unconditional, he forgave you your awkward shape, your freckles, no one said it was wrong to seek him out, to want him every hour, to be alone with him, to linger on the wounds of his body. He could not hurt you. To give your love to anyone else was masochistic.

She and Christ would be latched together like the eel and the hook, except the pain would be pleasure.

THE AFTERNOON finally felt like October. The dust had fallen from the white temples and the brick apartments so the city briefly gave the impression of newness. A drizzle in the night had wet the tongues of prayer.

"Don't poke along like a snail," her father said.

She'd walked into his study that morning—spine straight, chin down, her fidgeting hands wrapped behind her back—and asked if she could come to town with him that afternoon. He'd been given the all clear from his comrades in the city.

"I'm just delivering papers," he'd said. "Your mother says you've been in the sun too much as it is. Might be time to—you know. Have you seen where I put the long map of the fields? Anyway, what's there for little girls in the city?" He'd hardly spoken of religion since he lost Hierax. He was cooling just as all the little fires in Prisca were being set.

"I'm twelve."

"Well," he said, shuffling his papers together and scrolling them round, tying them off with cords he kept in an old boot on his desk. "It's time you were thinking about other things, perhaps."

She knew what he meant. She put her hand on the delta between her legs. "This?"

She shouldn't have done it, but there was something so provoking in the way he looked over her head. His mouth went small and stern, and he came from behind his desk and without saying anything slapped her arm hard and walked out, the scrolls drawn tight against him.

What a powerful little space, this secret part of hers. How sad to think that God had none.

They didn't speak all along the wide stone road to town, the crooked pines above them unmoving in the wind, like wooden models of trees. By the time the meadows turned to buildings, he softened and began to remark on the red squirrels dashing around trunks in dizzy circles, the hawks leering at them from high branches, the mausoleum that reminded him of what he wanted on his own one day: a frieze of men bearing baskets of wheat. A beggar sat on the side of the road with no legs below his knees, and Prisca asked her father how he would stand at the end of the day and find his home.

"The Lord provides," he said.

She left her father in the forum and fetched the bread from the only baker her mother said didn't cut his flour with dust, an old man who'd reached that point when he could never look older than he already was. He winked as he pulled the loaves from the barrels, though he surely didn't know her. She was still leaned into a corner with three coins rolling in her palm when the street outside turned violent: a loud burst of flesh against flesh, the autumn-settled dust kicking up again in an orange wave around the figures. Hunger worked its way from the stomach to the brain. The red flash of a soldier stepped into view, and soon the street quieted.

When he walked into the store to wash his hands—his helmet askew, his armor grimed—the baker averted his eyes and fetched the bucket of water without saying anything. Prisca clinked her coins.

"What happened?" she asked.

The soldier looked around with raised eyebrows. "Nosy girls," he said to no one.

She repeated herself, this time more slowly, to convey her assessment of his intelligence. "What hap-pened?"

He had his hands in the water now, and maybe there was blood along with the dust, but maybe there wasn't.

"Did someone get hurt?"

"Slaves," he said. He directed his answer at the baker. "Spend their last coin on flowers for their girl, and turns out she's seeing some other fellow too, right? Can't get them to care about their work, too busy breeding. That one was liable to take off the other's ear in his teeth. Don't see that on the northern front."

"It's hard to teach them culture," the baker said.

"Perhaps religion would do them good," Prisca said. "Kindness." She could have said *freedom*, but this seemed juvenile. *Kindness* was also a pretty stupid thing to say. She thought of her father and how deeply, conscientiously silent he would be.

"It's not my business to go around breaking up street fights. Someone should suit them up and send them to the arena. I was on my way to arrest a woman for stabbing her husband's business partner. That's more my line."

"And paid well for it, I imagine," the baker said. He emptied the dirty water out the window to the alley.

"You'd be surprised at how a woman'll throw herself on your mercy. Throw themselves skirts first, is what I'm saying. Maybe I make the arrest, maybe I stay for a taste instead. Who's to know the difference?"

"God," Prisca said. She imagined Crispus in a red soldier's tunic, laughing.

The baker wrapped her loaves in a straw basket and held his hand out for her money.

"Do you not believe in God?" Prisca stepped up to the soldier, her head at his armpit, her growing feet close to his.

"You better get back to your father now," the baker said.

"No, let her preach. What god are you campaigning for, girl? I believe in the ones that see to my needs, and I don't skip the sacrifices. Bad luck's a curse."

"I mean the one God, the God of Christ who was hung on the cross and rose from the dead." The light fell in the shop—what a sign rain would be right now—and she felt a twinge in her bones, as if she'd placed one foot into Hades and the three-headed dog had licked her toes. There was always time to make different decisions, or else there was never time; once she spoke, it was impossible in the tightly woven fabric of the world that she had ever not spoken. "If you don't believe in Him, and in Christ, and in the Holy Ghost"— though she wasn't entirely clear on the Ghost's physiology or relation to the trinity—"then you cannot come to heaven. Nor do you have any native goodness to lift you. You're nothing but a weak man who pretends to be strong, and when the world ends, I daresay you'll burn in flames."

The soldier flushed and looked with outrage at the baker, as if he were responsible, but the baker had his hands on Prisca's back now and was urging her outside, and through the doorway she got a better glimpse of the afternoon disturbance: only one slave was left, but he squatted against the building across the street, his hand covering a raw red ear, the dirt on his open face run through with tears. A man who an hour before had been in love, now vacant. Prisca would've liked to kneel down with him and speak of the heart's tyranny, to tell him that human love is a very bad joke, and the only being who could love him without betrayal, without diminishment, was a great swallowing spirit above. Wouldn't it be a balm to hear it? [Don't spread lies. No one has loved me with more betrayal, more diminishment, than He. On days I don't despise Him, I tell myself He is good, only to stop my writhing. But here I am in grudging love with his creations, and heaven help me, I begin to think if He does right by you, pet, even He could be redeemed.] It was madness that her father kept this secret. Everything seemed very clear, that doses of Jesus, like opium, would turn all this sordid degradation into beams of light. Here, slave: a dose for you, to salve your heart wound. Here, baker: a dose for you, to give you conviction. Here, soldier: a dose for you, so you'll throw yourself at the feet of the women you've wronged and beg them to forgive your cowardice. Underneath all that dirt was somewhere a pure city.

Her hands were still scrabbling at the doorjamb when the soldier pushed the shopkeeper away and scooped her under one arm like a writhing sack of chickens.

"Little bastard," he whispered. He took her out into the street and the baker began shouting, and everything she saw became sharper now; the patterned swirls of red dirt in the road and the melody the weeping slave sang under his breath were portents to be read— surely the rain was coming—and the whole tight world of Rome was laid out in two dimensions.

He pushed through the bustle of the street and the baker's shouts grew fainter, and Prisca bounced against his hip until the soldier's arm failed, and then he threw her over his shoulder, her bottom now skyward, her head bouncing against his back, all rushed and ringing with blood, and though she could've used her hands to pummel him, she let them hang, watched them swaying above the footprints the soldier left, above the street litter: a broken cup, spilled oats, another bunch of sunflowers rejected by a woman, the stems split and scattered. Sandaled feet, dusty hems, pale ankles, brown ankles. A beggar on the corner, his face covered in boils, one eye lost to disease or gouging: he too a testament to God's mercy. Why, again, was there suffering? [Because God in His omnipotence could not curb me, and cast me out, and with only the weapon of suggestion I writhed into the human sphere and ushered you out of the garden into the drought. Or: *I* am the one listening, a fellow imperfect, and God is testing your free will in His after-dinner game of chance. This city holds adherents of both camps, and all other camps besides, and do you think rain is falling unevenly on this expanse? Do clouds hover over the orchards of only the faithful? In 250 years, the Visigoths will lay ruin to a Christian emperor, and his sister will order the strangling of his general's wife, and Rome will crumple like a tissue in a pagan's hand. Was that my doing, or your Lord's? The street you're bouncing down will run with the blood of Cola di Rienzo, who visioned a single Italy five hundred years too soon, and who was mob-slaughtered on this very hill (where now the public augurs sit) that will sprout the church of Santa Maria in Aracoeli, which to most tourists in fanny packs will seem too high to climb. Do you smell his gore on this stone? Suffering is a brief wipe across time's face. It's not there for any reason; I didn't create it, nor He. It comes from the dirt, and from your deeds—no monk, or Medici, or man is spared.]

They were in the forum now—the apartments and shops had become temples and open markets—and she wondered where her father was, and if he would be surprised when she didn't show up to meet him and if below the worry would be a small spark of relief. As soon as they began to climb the Palatine, the soldier put her down and took her by the wrist. The pines curved above her defensively.

He took her through a side entrance into a tall brick building with so many arches it looked like it might fly away. The floor was tiled with reds and blues and blacks and greens; she nearly ran into a column. The soldier dragged her to a halt before a cluster of guards. He told her not to move and conferred with an older guard with a man-sized lance. The other men looked at her like she was a mouse. She'd spent enough time in Rome to know which hill was which. She was in the palace of the emperor, Marcus Aurelius, hail Caesar.

PRISCA HAD not been afraid when the soldier pulled her to a smaller room, or when a man in purple robes asked her questions about her family, or when another man in heavier purple robes asked her to spout sacrilegious swears. Imagine the bearded man looking down from heaven, or what her father would say. Think of the story this would make for Crispus, if Crispus had ever listened to her. Remembering his mouth made her wince.

The cell they put her in wasn't the damp hole she'd hoped for, but a small bright room with a ceiling that stretched up almost three times her own height. It wasn't clear what the emperor used it for when he wasn't storing little girls. The window was too high to see anything except the darkening sky and the brushy corner of a tree, where a jackdaw spied on her. It was past dinnertime. Her mother would know by now. Her bladder was full, and it pressed in a tingly way; she crossed her legs twice (right thigh over left thigh, right ankle under left ankle), but this wouldn't last long. She wondered if all arrested girls got sunny rooms without pots to piss in, and whether the emperor thought women were parakeets.

When night came and she realized she'd have to sleep, she felt the first small prick of fear. Her mother wasn't coming. This was not pretend. She went to one corner of the room and lifted her robe and peed, hating the sound of the liquid on tile, then crossed to the other corner and knelt with her face to the wall, her hands clasped against her chest. Her shoes had been lost, and the soles of her bare feet cupped her bottom. She'd often wondered what bodies were for—we fill them with food and then evacuate the food; we walk from place to place; we get sick; grown-ups do grown-up things with their secret parts; bodies get burned or broken or invaded, grabbed without permission, manipulated into shapes. It made no sense that Jesus would want one. Her stomach stopped growling and began to chew on itself. Her fingers, interwoven, shook a little. Her blood would come again soon, and she didn't want to be humiliated in front of these men.

THE TEMPLE was bright with gold and colored marble and sunlight piercing through the yellow columns, but they wouldn't let her inside. The guards lined up by the ivory doors with spears all angled the same way. Next to the crisp-robed priest, Prisca felt small and soiled, her eyes wide, her hair in a knot. No one could've slept on such a hard floor. He put the incense in her hand and gently pushed her toward the outdoor altar, and she wondered why on earth they were going to so much trouble, and weren't there louder and more dangerous Christians than she.

"I will not," she said, clenching her fist so tight against her chest that the incense crumbled. A low fire skittered across the altar, and around it the four big oxen seemed to snort at her through their bronze nostrils. Men walking in the distance stopped to look.

"Think of everything Apollo has given you," the priest murmured. His statue loomed over them, one arm cradling a lyre, his mouth open, saying she knew not what. "You come from farmers, yes? Think of the crops that reach up toward the sun, the grain and olives that fill your belly. Think of how beautiful this day is!"

But sun was the opposite of what they wanted. He was a kind man, really. She could see in his pattern of wrinkles that he liked smiling. But no one had ever told him he had no consequence.

"God gives us sunny days," she said.

"Yes, this god. Just thank him, that's all. You don't want to be ungrateful, do you?"

She was grateful for her fists that were doing the crushing, and her stretchy strong mind that had led her away from falsehood and make-believe. She'd once offered her small-girl treasures to Apollo at the family shrine, but he'd offered nothing back. He'd never walked the earth on man-feet, put the back of his hand on the foreheads of the weak.

"I cannot," she answered him.

"What will your parents say when they hear you've been disobedient?"

"My mother will weep," she said, "and my father will look into his own soul and wonder why he's such a coward that he went silent when the Word needed trumpeting."

"You are a very bad girl," the priest said. "You'll be hurt if you don't obey, do you understand? This is just a brief moment in your life when you think one thing might be true, but someone has led you astray, and you're too young to know better. You're made to be sweet—just look at your face." And he reached out a hand to stroke her cheek. "Put the incense in the fire and go home. Look at your sweet round face. Go ahead, throw the incense. You're a good girl."

She dropped the incense and ground it beneath her heel and said in her most proper voice, "I'm very sorry, sir. I know you're a good boy, and I don't like to make you mad."

He straightened up, and his mouth crunched like a caterpillar. He turned to the guards. None of them looked happy when they came to surround her, but the one with the whip looked least pleased. They pulled her robe down so her back was bare, though she was only conscious of her front, the almost-breasts being exposed in this lovely open place, and her face turned red with shame, so that when the blows came, the pain was almost a relief.

The first time her father beat her, she'd stolen a scroll from his library and used it to wrap a handful of apricots. She'd wanted to give them to a friend—a neighbor girl who'd since moved away, ruining her chances at female friendship. It was from a book of her father's favorite poetry, and as he lashed her bottom with an olive branch he made it clear he wasn't just angry at the loss of words but disappointed in his daughter's intellect. "The next time you steal a book from me," he said, "read it." She'd had red welts that took a week to subside, but she hadn't bled.

Now the pain was higher, shriekier. When the blood came, her skin felt like it was raining. Her arms still crossed against her chest, pressing in the tender spots, covering her growing self. She prayed God wasn't watching. She had planned to be brave, but she hadn't considered humiliation. Is it true that you cannot be hurt unless you allow yourself to feel hurt? [No.]

Someone wrapped her tunic around her delicately, and she walked back with them, head down, past the other buildings in the emperor's compound, past the palace where she'd spent the night, and down the hill, where the scattered pine needles made the path slippery. Most of the guards had peeled away, and only one was left. He held her upper arm like it was a horse's rein. Her back was drying; she could feel the cloth beginning to stick. If they thought she wouldn't run, they were right. Refusing to surrender the soul meant sacrificing the body. They could do what they liked—she would only confess to the roaches how hungry she was.

IN HER new cell, as crawly and dank as she'd fantasized, another woman sat cross-legged in the center of the room, weaving her fingers through silver hair. Prisca stood politely by the door and waited for a hello. The woman had northern features, so must be a slave. After five heartbeats of silence, Prisca remembered that Christians knew nothing of class, and she fell to her knees and reached out a hand.

"Forgive me," she said and introduced herself.

The woman smiled. She seemed to have more teeth than most people. "Where's your mother?"

"My mother is the church," she said, "and my father is God."

"A Jew!" the woman said with delight.

"No, a Christian."

"A Christian Jew! Welcome, fool. Are you hungry?"

Prisca nodded.

"I saved you some." And she got stiffly to her hands and knees and scuttled to the corner of the dirt-floored room, where she turned a cedar bucket right side up. Beneath it were a hunk of bread and a seashell. "Oyster?" she said.

"Thank you," Prisca said, bewildered.

"Faith alone not enough?" she asked.

Prisca acknowledged the joke with a smile.

"How old are you?"

"How old are *you*, madam?"

"Ah! A playful one! Here, go stand behind the door. That's right. Very quiet. The guard'll stop by soon with your dinner, which you'll like, but don't make a cluck and we'll have our little fun."

When the old woman stood, Prisca saw her robes were hemmed with a purple band. "Soldier, soldier! Help!" Silence in the hallway. "Soldier, it's the girl!"

Someone clanked down the hall and opened the pass-through at the top of the door.

"A miracle," she said breathlessly. "The Jewish girl—her god must have come for her. One second here, next second gone in smoke." She clapped her hands. "Poof! Do you smell it?"

The guard was hurrying at the locks as she continued to prattle.

"Enough to make me believe," she said. "All praise to Mithras."

He was in now, Prisca hidden behind the swung door, and was looking frantically in the corners.

"I don't know why you bother locking the Jews up; their god always comes to get them. And I was so happy to have another lady in here, someone to share the gossip with—you know, which guard is heavy-handed with the ladle, which has a little humor."

The guard stopped. Prisca let out the tiniest snicker, and he swung the door back slowly, saw her pinched in there, her hands over her mouth. He neither smiled nor sighed, but walked heavily out again, closing the door behind him and shutting the pass-through.

She didn't care if the woman was a murderer, she was glad to know her.

SOMETIME IN the night, the old woman unclothed herself and draped her robe over Prisca's sleeping body. In the morning, she braided the girl's hair in loops tighter than her mother ever had. In the afternoon, a speck of sun got through the high window, and the old woman pretended to chase it with a net. Prisca lay down on her side and rubbed her feet.

"Are you a slave?" she asked. "Did you steal from your master?"

"My husband?" She sat down, spreading out the purple band of cloth. "Minister to Caesar, hail to all that. What could I have stolen? Nothing but his good humor. After all those years, from gangly boy to proclaiming on the rostrum, and he lost his ability to see the joke."

"You made fun of him." Prisca scratched her shins, where the hazy hair was growing thicker.

"Women are good at cutting themselves down. Men are good at

pretending they never shit." She inched closer; Prisca could feel her salty breath on her face. She had such puzzling, hawkish eyes. "What does your messiah say about little girls? Does he call you special?"

Prisca squeezed her eyes shut and tried to summon him. Sometimes Crispus strode across the backs of her lids; sometimes she herself appeared there, hands on hips, as if to say, *What else do you want?*

"A martyr without a voice in her head?"

"I'm not a martyr," Prisca said, sitting up quickly.

"What do you think they're going to do to you?"

Beat her, beat her, they were going to beat her.

When Prisca showed her how to pray, the woman knelt facing the corner and whispered, "Jesus, show mercy to us all. Bless my husband, may he rot from the inside out, and bless my children, may they be told lies about their mother. Jesus, most of all, be a real thing. If you disappoint my small friend, I'll come find you in the depths of the underworld and kick your balls until your human half collapses in agony and begs for a woman's pity. We'll see who has pity then. I'd also like you to explain why when you came down to earth you wore a man's shape and took only men as your disciples; it's enough to make me spew, imagining you all sitting around pretending you don't shit. Praise be to Ceres. Amen."

Prisca couldn't help smiling. "That was *terrible*."

THE SECOND time they asked her to deny her faith, they took her to a larger room, with more people, more purple. She wondered if her cellmate's husband was here, and whether he was lonely, and whether her mother was lonely or if it was a reprieve to lose her daughter's growing body as the crops shrank. They asked the questions she'd dreamed about, and though Jesus didn't appear like a holy tutor to help her, she knew most of the answers. *No; no; no; I will not*; and *I cannot tell you where the meetings are held or how many are present.* They spoke of her youth—that's a passing thing, she said, like beauty, or appetite, and shouldn't matter. They spoke of her ignorance—I know enough to know right from wrong, she said, and I needn't see the whole world to guess at the contents of heaven. They spoke of her family—she was about to repeat Hierax's dodge but remembered Jesus was someone's child too, and he forsook no one.

She looked to see if there was a scribe writing down her statement, but everyone just sat there glumly, staring at the ceiling or picking at their fingernails. How many halfhearted men did it take to persecute a single girl? [For me, it only took one. I'm starting to see Him now through your eyes; I spy the crocus of forgiveness nuzzling from the bulb in your heart, still in the dark soil, and there's an echoing uncomfortable murmur in mine.]

They announced the sentence. She was beginning to understand that each time it would be worse, and one of those times, if they did not wake up to their own meanness, she would very probably die. She was twelve years old. She had been on the earth for no more than twelve years.

They took her to an open square far enough from the forum to avoid disrupting business. There were orange trees nearby; she could smell them. A middle-aged woman with an armful of wrapped meat and a small child stopped to watch as the guards tied Prisca's feet to an iron ring in the center of the piazza. She could see the sweat on the woman's neck like a web of jewels. Her braids with kinks in them, messily done. The child pointed at Prisca and whispered something to its mother. From a nearby blacksmith they brought the iron pot sloshing with melted wax.

She felt the sun first, its melty golden ball, its dripping hazy edges, how it yellowed the piazza and the woman and her child and how even the workers pausing on their lunchtime stroll caught some of that rich edge, so when the wax first hit her skin—the leading drop, sizzle and fat—it only seemed like the sun had finally leaned in far enough for a kiss, and her back writhed in a kind of pleasure. It was the woman's face that first frightened her—not the child's, which was vacant and openmouthed, but the woman's, her lips peeled back in reflected pain. Only then did Prisca understand the drop had become a pour and her whole back was seething, her upper arms and legs carrying the drippings, her skin already exploding in a single fluid blister. She didn't want to cry; the woman was crying. She closed her eyes tight to imagine the tallow as sunshine—it was just sunshine, hot and wet and now hard—and when she opened them the woman was walking quickly away, pulling at the child, who still looked back at Prisca blankly. The sear became a shock, and her back collapsed. She pressed against the stones, the wax an endless bubbling weight, and she was under an ocean on fire. She couldn't form prayer, but just repeated his name. *Jesus, Jesus, Jesus.* She would have to live inside time like a patient spore. Waiting. Breathing.

HER CELL was empty. The old woman with hair like white water was gone. Prisca lay on her stomach in the dirt and straw, the air alone on her blistered back as sharp as any knife. In the quiet and the dark, she crawled out of her turtle shell, and her pink, raw self shuddered into tears. She wished she had something of her own here, so she wouldn't feel so entirely scrubbed away—the little wooden cow, or the lock she'd saved from Crispus's haircut, or the hook she'd caught the eel on. The eel she'd stoned to death. She was a half-wit to think she could go to heaven.

Somewhere her parents were fighting again: *You've abandoned the gods, and now look. No,* you've *closed your ears to Christ, and now look.* She wanted to tell them there was no way to know, you just had to trust. *Trust what?* She didn't know. Faith was a tiny shard of mirror in the chest that sometimes cut and sometimes flashed light.

When she was done with sobs, she crawled to the plate of bread by the door and pulled it into strips and rolled the strips into balls and had a game of marbles until the guard brought her water and a sponge to wash her wounds and told her she'd better eat that because she didn't know when it'd be her last. Famine wasn't her family being reduced to eating pigeons; it was fearing to eat the bread because as long as the bread was there, there'd be bread.

"I can help with washing if you need it."

She looked down at the sponge, tired. "Yes, please."

The guard's hands didn't know how to be soft, but he did his best, and she tried to smile through the tears so he wouldn't worry.

"I don't know why you do it," he said. "Stubborn."

"I don't know why," she said.

"I always tell folks better to confess, or whatever they're asking. Silly making a fuss over it, especially when they're like to be inventive. Tallow today, who knows what tomorrow. Only a fool'd stick around to find out."

"Do you have a wife?"

"Course I do, and never raised a fist."

"Didn't you ever make a fool of yourself trying to win her over?"

He paused, sponge in hand. Gave a chuckle. "Well, now."

His kindness, and hers, made her feel good. She didn't know whether she was supposed to feel good. But when she curled up for sleep, a crinkling spider noise across the ceiling made her turn onto her back to see, and the straw scoring her blisters reminded her how much more bad she felt than good; but then, was it wrong to feel so bad? [I will make them build you a monument. I'll snake my slender fingers in their hands and lift the yellow bricks myself, I'll keep stacking them higher than last year's rubble so your name

is inerasable, I'll mount you on a hill, I'll send you monks, pilgrims, tourists, I'll wet future tongues with your twin syllables. I
am who makes history.]

THIS TIME they quizzed her in a wooden stall below the arena. The
tigers' moans made the horses kick against the boards. She got sand
in her toenails. She'd always wanted to see the subterranean labyrinth; it was messier than she'd pictured. They needed a few good
stable boys to keep the animals mucked and to make sure the fighters
were polite. She was hearing the most terrible words down here.

One of the soldiers leaned into another and whispered, "Is this
all right?"

Look at all those tall men surrounding that one little girl. The
nearest woman was probably two stories up somewhere in the stands,
with a fan and a sack of lupin beans, sucking away at the brine, waiting for the spectacles and wondering whether her husband would be
able to smell the circus on her. But no—a gladiator stopped by the
open door of the stall and gave Prisca a glance before striding on,
revealing a tumble of long hair falling against the leather shine of
armor. A gladiatrix.

It was hard to hear their questions this time, the tumult of the
arena rocking around them like a musty underground sea, but she
knew them well enough by now. *No*, she said, and *no*, and *I will not*,
and *Faith is my father*. They looked worn down, worse than her.

"You want to take her up?" the man with the most feathers in his
helmet said to the man with the least.

He looked her brother's age and was ghoulishly pale when he
nodded and reached out for her arm. She politely lifted her wrist and
placed it in his hand—that movement alone setting off a chain of
shocks across her scathed back—and she didn't look too closely at
the pimples crowding on his chin, as if he had nodded so much that

they'd all fallen to the bottom of his face. He led her past the other stalls, a racket of fangs and pacing muscles, and the other guards fell in line behind them. Down below, their feet sounded like delicate deer feet.

Up the stairs they went, and the animal noises thundered into human noises, hooves into sandals, and the sun washed it all white, so Prisca had to raise an arm to her eyes to keep from stumbling. She should've eaten the bread. Her guard still clung to her. There was a chance that if she kept calmly walking, she could guide him right out of the stadium. But she stopped at the fence around the arena and was awestruck in spite of herself. In the sand had been planted dozens of palms and cyclads, mini-oases between the piled dunes, and camels were being circled through the scene by men with bells on their shoes; surely this was like Jerusalem. The audience booed. They were used to the wonders of the world. When the camels dispersed, the lions came in: two, with ribs as clear as sticks. Their mouths hung open, and their heads swayed side to side. Still eyes, empty eyes. Paws as big as bowls.

"Nothing but house cats," the guard said, possibly to himself.

The one with the scraggled mane stopped at a palm trunk, catching a smell, and began rubbing its cheek against the bark, back and forth, so hard it must have gotten splinters. The maneless one climbed to the top of a dune and stood perfectly still, not even scanning the crowd, its jaw gaping dully, the only thing moving its *switch-switch* of a black-tipped tail. Maybe they were so skinny because they were bad at their jobs.

On the opposite side of the arena, another gate opened and three moon-pale men with chained wrists were pushed out onto the sand. Two of them clung to the wall, sliding their bodies around the edge, feeling around for another exit. The third, whose hair sprang from his head in curly clumps, started running. With his wrists held high above his head, he had an expression almost of ecstasy. Running, stumbling, full tilt across the sand, with the only knowledge that mattered: they were all going to die today, but at least it would happen in the sun. His atrophied legs carried him along with pride. The maneless one went for him first; the bigger lion strolled along the perimeter, being patient with the cowards. Prisca kept her attention on the wild man's face, how it never slackened as his hunter loped up behind. The lion never had to leap—it was more like a lunge, fluid and all of a piece—and the man toppled, his hands still in the air, the chains the last part of him to hit the ground.

Prisca turned around and squinched her eyes shut and listened to the crowd as it applauded and cringed and rose to its feet and booed and urged the murder on with a noisy thirst, so that she knew exactly when the last man had been killed. Men in armor with long poles came out to drag the bodies away before the lions could eat their fill.

The guard opened her gate. It gave a shy *clank* behind her, and she knew he wouldn't watch. She looked around for other Christians or criminals to be propelled from other openings, but no one followed her. At first she didn't spot the lions. As she walked toward the oases with as much slow and sane grace as she could muster—remembering how Crispus's Livia looked under similar palms, how womanly; damn her for existing in this moment!—she saw one lying down in the shade, its mouth still open, its empty stomach going in and out like a robe on the clothesline. Her legs went light-headed, but no one in the stands could see anything but her slow, sane walk, one foot and then another foot. The one without a mane, the hungrier one, had been making a loop around the edges, sniffing out the blood left there, and when it spotted Prisca it stopped. The crowd was chanting something that rhymed. She forgot why she was there. What on earth. Little Prisca, a recent Christian, fresh from the farm, here before several thousand eyes like an acrobat or an emperor. But it was her death they were eager to see, the death of little Prisca, a recent Christian.

Then let them watch! The lion moved so slowly toward her, maybe because she'd locked her eyes on it; it was pretending it wasn't moving at all. She pressed her hands together, not because that was how she best liked to pray, but so the pagans in the stands could see. Of all the ways they'd devised to kill off the faithful, she rather thought this was the nicest.

"Come here, old cat," she whispered, her hands still clasped in front of her chest. "*Tch, tch, tch.*"

The lion stopped again, one paw raised midair, but Prisca kept strolling. She glanced to the bundle of palms off to her left, but the boy lion was on his side now, his eyes winking closed in some pleasant memory. Both of them had rusty muzzles. She wasn't trying to think of a way to save herself, but of how to stage a scene of sacrifice so lovely that the women would go home and tell their children how good the Christian girl was and how maybe Jesus could train them too, before they'd broken every pot in the kitchen with their clowning. She was glad the guards had allowed her a clean tunic this morning; she hoped she gleamed.

"Come here, cat. Let me tell you a story."

What funny moves we make for the ones we love. And if there was no such thing as a singular God or Christ his son, how the pagan pantheon must be laughing. Maybe it was a luxury to claim goodness. Maybe you relied on the stronger people to carry on the business of life while you swanned around denying yourself pleasure. The Bible was unclear on this point, but it was very possible that her presence here in this stadium—alone, egged on by the prurient hordes—was the worst kind of egotism.

She began to cry. She stopped where she was and fell down to her bruised knees and had a good, all-out sob. The crowd quieted. The lion paused again, three strides closer. Prisca suddenly was very conscious of all the mistakes she'd ever made in her life, including the fact that this, her showy attempt at penance, might be one of them. To be turned to a hot ball of need at the very last instant—*oh, everyone close your eyes*. She was all the way down now, her limbs on the ground, her tears making puddles in the sand. When she opened her eyes there was a paw in front of her, and with nothing but a tumbling train of apologies to God in her head, she reached out and brushed the top of the paw with her fingers.

"Hello, cat," she said. "We're both hungry."

She felt it snuffling around at the top of her hair, snorting in her smell. A stiff whisker poked her ear. She raised her head and saw first the bloody jaw and clotted fur and then the wet black leather of the nose, the nostrils still exploring. She sat up as slowly as a sprouting seed and scratched the top of the lion's paw with the hand she'd left there. Its breath came out in short huffs. Her hand climbed up to its knee—or was it ankle? [elbow]—and then to its broad haunch, scratching all the way. The fluff behind its shoulder was like white silk, and she dug at the knots there, pulling out a burr that must have traveled with it from Africa.

As she rubbed up into the roll of skin behind its neck, the lion's chest began emitting a guttural noise, like the hard sputtering of the plow through rocky soil, and its eyes—which she glanced at for the first time now—narrowed. Her hand found the short fur at the base of the ear and pulled at the skin there, first tenderly, then digging in with her fingernails. The lion twisted its head against her hand, pushing into it, eyes fully closed, jaw wide. Half its teeth were stained brown or missing altogether, and the remaining canines were dull. How terrible for those men, to be gnawed into with dull spokes. How terrible for *her*. She dragged her fingers along its chin, unclotting the rough stains of blood, and it leaned its great head back and pushed so hard against the pleasure that it collapsed onto its side, trapping Prisca's hand beneath its head, where it continued to rub and roll and send its rocky rattling purr through its broken cage of teeth.

She became aware of the crowd chanting again, loud boos, and she instinctively pulled her hand back. The lion took her shinbone in his jaws, so gentle, and licked the top of her foot with a great rasping tongue. *Don't stop*, it said. She held its giant head in both hands and rubbed her thumbs against its cheekbones, in the hollows below its eyes. She picked out a gnarled strand of mucus from the corner of its eye, and it half shook its head in frustration. She stood up. She didn't know what was happening. The maned lion under the distant palm was sitting up now, intrigued. Prisca took two steps backward.

Pieces of bread and clay cups were being thrown onto the open sand, and a cluster of guards gathered at a nearby gate with lances, prepared to agitate the beasts.

"This wasn't the time, cat," she said, and the lion stood again, circling its long blond body around her hips. "I wasn't ready. I wasn't good enough yet." She had a strong childish desire to leap onto its back, just to see if it would hold her. Let her take this bizarre victory as a rebuke from the Lord. And let the thousands watching tremble at his power. Were they not cowed? [Did He scorn me too to save me? I'd claw the love out of my heart if I thought I could survive its absence. Hold it gentle, girl; don't let it drop.]

A messenger from the emperor's box scurried over to the waiting guards and gesticulated. They nodded and brought their lances up straight, a sign that active engagement had been deferred. The messenger turned toward the desert scene and made another broad hand motion at Prisca.

"They've had enough of this show, old cat."

She walked toward the gate as slowly as she'd walked into this nightmare, listening for the footfalls of the cat in sand. Maybe there was a town somewhere beyond the far reaches of the empire where people grew food and ate food and in the evenings smiled and listened and put their hands on one another's skin. That's the town that would have no need for religion.

When they opened the gate for her, their faces were angry and scared, and the messenger seized her arm and pulled her through the pelting crowd into the tunnel that led to the stairs that took her back down to where the day's offerings, human and animal, waited to be sacrificed. "Filthy," the messenger said, pushing her into an empty stall. Somewhere a horse bellowed and kicked its door with an echoing hoof. Prisca knelt down again in the dirt and hay and touched the small indentations on her calf where the lion had placed its jaws, and the bruise on her upper arm where the messenger had grabbed her, and the blisters on her back where the wax had boiled through, and beneath them the welts from her first lashing at the Temple of Apollo, back on that sunny afternoon when her father had gone to the forum to attend to business and she had visited the baker's to get loaves for dinner. She reached her hands inside her robe and touched her chest, where no one else had touched, but it too ached.

HER NEXT home was a slaves' prison. A dozen other women stared as she hoisted her tunic to pee in the corner bucket. None of them reached toward her with a sponge for wiping or, seeing her dry lips, a ladle of water. There wasn't any water. Their eyes were sunk deep, and their wrists and ankles were red. As she squatted over the bucket, she felt the clumps of her menses come glooping out in the steady stream of her urine. What a small thing to make the heart sink. She tore a strip from the bottom of her new robe and wadded it up and buried it in her underthings.

The next-youngest prisoner looked eighteen or nineteen, and Prisca sat beside her. The girl didn't speak. Her hair was unbraided and black, and she had a hawk nose and a small rabbit mouth. She was digging beneath her fingernails to clean them.

Politeness didn't make friends; secrets did. Prisca leaned over so her mouth was close to the other girl's ear. "I got my period today," she whispered. "It's a mess."

A brown-skinned woman in the corner yelled, "Stank so much the lions wouldn't have her!" and threw a cup at Prisca.

The girl with the pointy nose got up and walked away. "Fecking martyr," she said.

NIGHT CAME and sent most of the women to fitful sleep, and Prisca lay carefully so she wasn't touching anyone. Every few minutes she'd feel another warmth of blood slip through onto the wadded cloth. When she dozed, she had nightmares that the cloth was soaked, flooded, and she'd wake up in a panic to check, and no, it was a regular trickling; she wasn't dying. A dark flutter flew from one corner of the ceiling to the other. It must have been a bat, but she couldn't think how it got in, there being no windows. Maybe it emerged like an omen from her womb.

Her body, which had been singular, was now splitting into multiple futures: the one in which she stayed a sole person, Prisca, for as long as she so desired, no one ever quite understanding her feelings but no one trying to change them either; the one in which she used her budding blood for its most direct purpose and found a man to tie herself to, using his seed to make a child, and then another, and then another until the blood dried up or he proved to be a lying liar with a stone heart and a secret girlfriend in the city, who didn't deserve all the purpose she'd saved up to give him; or the one in which she finally became a woman, like Mary, and offered all the complexities of her sex to the idea of a life everlasting, in which goodness fell like a warm blanket over the sordid, over manipulations and betrayals and deceptions, and smothered them. She wanted her blood to be a seal on the promise she made to Christ—that she would be good, she would be good, she would be good—and in return, he would give her love without pain.

A BLOND pebble in the corner of the cell shone like a crumb. She crawled toward it, grabbed it, but it was a stone after all, hard and inedible. She hadn't eaten in three days. The other women, none of whom would share their rations, had been taken away, one by one, to fates uncertain. Only one was left, an African who was nothing but rib and elbow and knee. They were both stacks of bones, she and Prisca, and the guard stopped coming altogether. The dark-skinned woman no longer used the pot in the corner. Her arms folded against what was left of her stomach like broken poles; she listed to one side. Prisca had tried talking—asked after her family, stroked her skin— but the woman never raised her eyes. In her state, being thrown to the animals would make poor sport; what was their plan? Was she part of Prisca's punishment, left so the girl might watch what happens to the body of a disobedient woman: collapse, desiccation, and then rot? [You can shut your eyes. Suffering won't cease because you see it. I only pause my plot to judge if He has some little bean of empathy left—to see if He'll save you, child of belief, my fallible girl. I want my love for Him, at least, to be worthy. I tried to sway you all, trumpet my appeal so it'd prick His judging heart, but earth is unwinnable; you lust and fight and fix and forgo with no mystic impetus at all.] The only hint that death was still waiting was the butterfly rise of the woman's chest, the short contractions of skin across the dunes of the rib cage.

Prisca's stomach had stopped crooning and had begun curling

over on itself—all her organs seemed to crawl and climb around her torso—and her limbs went trembly, her head as light as a balloon. Her eyes balloons within the balloon, feeling so bulbous they threatened to detach and float away all on their own. She chewed on the sling of skin between her thumb and fingers, for there was always salt to be found there. When she ran her fingers through her hair, the knots came out like many-legged spiders. Once she woke in the middle of the night, or what she assumed was night, and had lost the sense of whose body was whose, and found herself licking the cheek of the African woman until she was awakened fully by the richness of a new kind of salt. *That's not my skin*, she thought.

THEY BROUGHT her to another grand room for her last chance. She didn't know why she was being given so many chances. The gold was blinding, all the luxury of sofas and thrones, marble and tile, several dozen purpled men, bowls of overflowing fruit. The fruit wasn't there to be eaten; it was there as a lure. She saw a woman in the corner, some rich wife, turn away at the sight of her.

Someone flicked a hand, and a man brought her a stool. What an unfamiliar comfort. Her knees popped when she sat down. She twisted her tunic so the torn edges would be less noticeable, but this pulled a swath of bubbled skin off her back. Her teeth were sore from clenching. The wad between her legs was drying out; it was coming to an end. Two men whispered by a gray-veined column, one with a gold wreath around his head. Both were bearded and handsome and reminded her of Hierax, and for an instant it occurred to her that she might already have died and this was heaven, though it was a disappointment for heaven to look so much like Rome.

The one with the wreath and curls nodded, looked at her with an inquisitive sympathy, and left the room.

"The emperor has heard much about this little philosopher," the other man said, approaching.

"Was that him?" She turned around. "Where did he go?"

"He would've liked to question you himself, but he's afforded me that privilege."

"Was he afraid?"

Some of the other men in the room were listening, but they stood at an angle to her so she wouldn't have a clear audience. Others mumbled to one another, or to the handful of wives, most of whom looked at the floor and seemed somewhat emotional.

"He's a great man, Marcus Aurelius. A king of reason and thought."

Being a king of thought seemed silly, given that the only territory you could govern was your own.

"We're all curious about your devotion, and sorrowful for it. The emperor believes in kindness and justice, but peace comes not from fervor but from self-control."

She considered herself extremely self-controlled, having not eaten her cellmate.

"And being a man of forgiveness, he would like to extend to you a final opportunity to renounce your allegiance to the Christian god."

The man had strolled around her stool during these speeches and now stood before her with his hands together in a pose reminiscent of prayer.

"Your family is waiting outside to take you home. They are greatly aggrieved."

But her father was a Christian—unless, of course, he wasn't. It seemed hard to believe they were all out there. Her weeping mother and Servius too, kicking his sandals against whatever hard surface he could find, and—now her vision was really turning golden—even Crispus, come along to add his powers of persuasion, to fall to the floor with apologies, to clutch at her calves in supplication, to speak of regret and even, could it be, of delayed affection? [Yes, yes, *imagine* it. Stay on this earth for it. Surely your boy isn't like mine, who once He shuts his heart to you— Once He chooses not to love you—] It came back to her like a shock: the kiss, the pond, the warmth in cold places, the rupture, that moment when her lips were no longer touching anything but air, like the first break between an infant and its mother. This was goodness, but it was human, so it was flawed; it wasn't religion.

The emperor's surrogate was droning on about rationalism and stoicism and the alleviation of pain through the management of emotion, and she believed all this and it was true, just as her brief fire of want was true, her desperate reaching for touch, for closeness, for profane understanding, and it was very possible that in this moment she was making a mistake—was mistaking Jesus for her own thwarted potential—and that human love as moderated by patience and reason was really the highest attainable paradise and she should return to the nest of her home with humility and spend the remainder of her earthly life cultivating empathy, but she was *twelve*. Settling for an imperfect existence was *not enough*. This war could not be won through reason, not if you were a little girl in this world.

She stood up. "I believe in my own sorry power," she said. "And so does the Lord. I love every one of you here, but not one of you loves me back, and you won't love me any more for turning tail and going home. I'm ready for the pyre because it's possible that maybe just one person who watches me burn will be stricken with the same belief."

Her blood thumped in her ears, behind her eyes, in the red rag between her legs. Everyone was staring at her now, except the women, who already knew everything. She felt a great wildness. Her little hands were clenched in fists. Just try to dispossess her!

The man in front of her coughed. He went through the remainder of the questions by rote—where are the meetings held, what are the names of others—and then he summoned two guards, but she knew by now how to walk without being dragged. Half the population of Rome must be guards. Outside the room was a hallway, and a steep set of stairs, and down the stairs was a large foyer, and across the foyer were two tall doors, and through them was another sun-beaten square—she hadn't stopped waiting for the rain—and as the guards ushered her toward a chariot she saw, though she was half-blinded, a group of mourners: she thought it was her family. Her father, a grand chief of cowards, eyes shot through with lava; her mother crying with gusto; Servius looking like a lost boy, not a man at all. Their fields still as dry as when she'd learned Christ's name. She was breaking her family. But then the sun splintered, and it was some other family, some bunch of weeping strangers. Crispus, Crispus, where was his mouth.

She kept marching. The sun was a hot seal on her neck. God's lips on her skin. She ran through the commandments, the miracles of the Old Testament, the passion of Christ. She had already seen her mother; there was no one to wipe her face. They bustled her into the chariot, and someone snapped a whip at the horses—two horses, black and white—and they were leaving the Palatine Hill, crossing the templed plain, when she overcame the house-collapsing sound of her heart and asked where they were going and one of the men said, "Ostia."

The sea!

They wouldn't burn her at all but drown her, and this was a comfort because she'd wanted to visit the shore again and her father, full of promises, wouldn't take her, and she thought of all the ways Jesus had touched water and decided this was a good way to die, and she was ready. Imagine the pebbly sand and her ankles in the water, and then all the way up to her hips, the salt burrowing in her wounds, lighting them up, reminding her one last time of life and its necessary anguish. The sea would wash the blood out of her. There'd be gulls and shearwaters and terns, and while her lungs filled with heavy water to carry her starved body down, they'd form a great feathered net to carry her soul up to wherever it belonged.

The chariot rumbled past the fine houses and then the poorer houses, through the piazzas and between teetering tenements, and when they came to the great stone arch of the Servian gate, the horses slowed to walk with gravity underneath and down the Ostian Road, where they picked up their pace again on the broad stones. They passed a great white pyramid Prisca had heard of but never seen, and beyond it a hill where men were stacking the shards of oil jars. The city gave way to the country, the road punctuated again with mausoleums, the country being the same everywhere. They passed a spring bubbling up from a stone basin, and Prisca remembered that somewhere along this road, this very road to the ocean, the Apostle Paul had been killed. His head, released from his body, had bounced three times, and where his saintliness struck earth, water began to flow. Had he thought he was going to the ocean? [Stop. Turn around. Goddamn God, goddamn it, who gave us hearts to break and bodies to bury and told us instead to think of souls, what sleight of hand was that? It wasn't Him I loved at all, but what He made, and now He's taking it back, and though nothing ever ends in time's long loop, I somehow never know what's left. What sacrifice is great enough?]

At the ninth milestone, Prisca became aware of strange trees along the side of the road, abnormally straight with few branches. As the horses slowed again, the branches became clearer: white and rickety. The trees weren't trees at all but poles, and the branches weren't made of wood but bones.

The chariot stopped at the tenth milestone.

———

THE MEN pulled a wooden block from beneath the wheels and a sword, and it became clear, her short life and its conclusion, all at once, like a string of yarn become a ball. She didn't cry, except she was, she was in fact crying, and the man hauling the block to the side of the road stopped, abashed. The second one had Prisca's arm in his hand, and his grip loosened and he began to stroke her skin unconsciously.

The man on the side of the road wiped his forehead clean of sweat and looked down at his shoes. These were to be her last friends, and she didn't know them.

"They make us take you out of the city," the one next to her said. "You not being a citizen anymore. Look, it's very pretty."

And it was pretty, the rustling poplars like women in dresses, the willows leaning like they were looking for something they'd dropped, the hush of the Tiber to the north—or was that the wind, or was that the burst of birds' wings as a family of swans took flight.

The man beside her dug through his bag and brought out a quartered pomegranate wrapped lazily in cloth, the stains like monthly blood. He offered a slice to her and she took it without pause, digging her dirty fingernails into the pith, picking out the bursting seeds, sucking on her fingers with nothing like grace. Her mouth became thick and sweet and bitter and dry, and she chewed through the wood of the seeds and let the sharp juice rest in the pockets of her cheeks, and this food, which would never fill her, was like a miracle. She was Proserpine, but she was eating the food of the living, may it not keep her from the land of the dead.

The guard helped her down from the chariot and she stood in the grass with the afternoon sun like a warm cloth on her face. Behind her, she heard him sharpening the sword. *Jesus, Jesus, Crispus, home, afraid, I want, not afraid, I want.* She put her hands on her hair to smooth it out, no reason why. She touched her chin, just to feel it a final time. *Be a strong girl, be a better girl, love, love these men.* She put her arms around her chest, her waist, hugged herself. *Going home, God will come, God is watching, watch my strength.* Now touch felt urgent, insistent; she ran her hands down her hips and thighs and over the bony humps of her knees and crouched into a ball there in the grass so she could wrap her arms around her whole body, so she could take in all of herself at once. This body! Sweet child limbs, sweet stinky toes, flat bottom that hadn't yet grown round, wrists too thin for bracelets, nipples the color of dawn, all the places that ached, all the places that yearned, her proud ears, her blazing eyes, the open melted wound of her loyal back.

The guards looked nervous, so she stood and smoothed her robes and saw they were her last responsibility.

"I'm all right," she said.

And when she knelt down in the tickly grass, she didn't think of her sins or her frailties, not of desire or jealousy or pride, not even of Jesus who had saved her from a faulty world, but of the eel she once caught with her father's fishhook, its slippery small body under her human hand. She had knelt in the grass then too, looming above it with a rock, trembling, reading the terror in its eye. She hoped what she mistook for fear had been faith.

ACKNOWLEDGMENTS

FOR READING CHAOS and nudging it toward order: Anya Groner and Jonathan Lee.

For offering maps: Deborah Johnson, Odie Lindsey, Katie Parla, and Nathaniel Rich.

For peeling back the layers: Paola Fornasier, Viola di Grado, Ilaria Mazzini, Stefano Sarcinelli, Francesco Sorce, and Martina Testa.

For unexpected faith: Bill Clegg, Terry Karten, Jonathan Burnham, and Millsaps College.

For my family, which grows and subsides, like a city changing in everything but its immortality.

ABOUT THE AUTHOR

KATY SIMPSON SMITH was born and raised in Jackson, Mississippi. She received a PhD in history from the University of North Carolina at Chapel Hill and an MFA from the Bennington Writing Seminars. She is the author of *We Have Raised All of You: Motherhood in the South, 1750–1835*, and the novels *The Story of Land and Sea* and *Free Men*. Her writing has also appeared in the *New York Times Book Review*, the *Oxford American*, *Granta*, *Literary Hub*, *Garden & Gun*, *Catapult*, and *Lenny*. She lives in New Orleans and serves as the Eudora Welty Chair for Southern Literature at Millsaps College.

ALSO BY **KATY SIMPSON SMITH**

FREE MEN
A NOVEL

"A brilliant, wild ride.... Smith has succeeded in writing a novel of American masculinity that deserves comparison with Cormac McCarthy, Jim Harrison and Herman Melville."

—Jackson Clarion-Ledger

A captivating novel, set in the late eighteenth-century American South, that follows a singular group of companions—an escaped slave, a white orphan, and a Creek Indian—who are being tracked down for murder.

THE STORY OF LAND AND SEA
A NOVEL

"A luminous debut."

—*O, the Oprah Magazine*

Set in a small coastal town in North Carolina during the waning years of the American Revolution, this incandescent novel follows three generations of family—fathers and daughters, mother and son, master and slave, characters who yearn for redemption amidst a heady brew of war, kidnapping, slavery, and love.